❋ ❋ THE DEADLIEST DREAM ❋ ❋

It was when Tam-Sin, she who had been Tamisan in another reality, stood over the Sea Lord's unconscious body that she realized the power this terrifying trap was rousing. For that was the sensation she caught, something horribly sated stirred from a gluttoned sleep. She would be caught in turn . . . only the fact that it had feasted well had so far served her.

The light was growing stronger. She glanced to the globe, saw a swirling deep inside. Something closed upon her, wrapped her around as if to smother, driving air from her lungs. It would . . . take . . . her!

The globe pulsated with light. A vast, arrogant confidence spread from it to her. This thing had never known defeat, it had gathered its victims as *It* chose and none could stand against it.

She drew upon that part of her which was dreamer, Tide-Singer.

The globe . . . That which lived within it was growing stronger—ready to overpower her. She reversed the sword she still held. Though the sharp-toothed edges cut painfully into her flesh, she raised it high, and brought the pommel down on the globe.

It did not shatter as she had hoped, though under her blow the light swirled malignantly and she swayed under the return blow of willed force. A second time she struck at the bubble, blood from her scored hands making the blade slippery in her grip.

It would not break. And in another breath, perhaps two, she would be overtaken by its power . . .

Baen Books
by
Andre Norton

❖ ❖ ❖ ❖

Time Traders
Time Traders II
Star Soldiers
Warlock
Janus
Darkness & Dawn
Gods & Androids
Dark Companion
Masks of the Outcasts
Moonsinger
Crosstime
From the Sea to the Stars
Star Flight
Search for the Star Stones
The Game of Stars and Comets
Deadly Dreams

DEADLY DREAMS

ANDRE NORTON

DEADLY DREAMS

Perilous Dreams copyright © 1976 by Andre Norton.
The first part of *Perilous Dreams*, "Toys of Tamisan," appeared in *If* magazine and is copyright © 1969 by Galaxy Publishing Corp.
Knave of Dreams copyright © 1975 by Andre Norton.

A Baen Books Original

Baen Publishing Enterprises
P.O. Box 1403
Riverdale, NY 10471
www.baen.com

ISBN: 978-1-4391-3444-3

Cover art by Darrell K. Sweet

First Baen paperback printing, June 2011

Distributed by Simon & Schuster
1230 Avenue of the Americas
New York, NY 10020

Printed in the United States of America

10 9 8 7 6 5 4 3 2 1

Contents

Perilous Dreams

PART ONE
Toys of Tamisan

Toys of Tamisan

I

"SHE IS CERTIFIED by the Foostmam, Lord Starrex, a true action dreamer to the tenth power!"

Jabis was being too eager, or almost so; he was pushing too much. Tamisan sneered mentally, keeping her face carefully blank, though she took quick glances about from beneath half-closed eyelids. This sale very much concerned herself, since she was the product being discussed, but she had nothing to say in the matter.

She supposed this was a typical sky tower. It seemed to float, since its supports were so slender and well concealed, lifting it high above Ty-Kry. However, none of the windows gave on real sky. Each framed a very different landscape, illustrating, she guessed, other planet scenes; perhaps some were dream remembered or inspired.

There was a living lambil-grass carpet around the easirest on which the owner half lay and half sat, but

Jabis had not even been offered a pull-down wall seat, and the two other men in attendance on Lord Starrex stood also. They were real men and not androids, which placed the owner in the multi-credit class. One, Tamisan thought, was a bodyguard, and the other, who was younger and thinner, with a dissatisfied mouth, had on clothing nearly equal to that of the man on the easirest, but with a shade of difference which meant a lesser place in the household.

Tamisan catalogued what she could see and filed it away for future reference. Most dreamers did not observe much of the world about them, they were too enmeshed in their own creations to care for reality. Tamisan frowned. She *was* a dreamer. Jabis, and the Foostmam could prove that. The lounger on the easirest could prove it if he paid Jabis's price. But she was also something more; Tamisan herself was not quite sure what. That there was a difference in her, she had had mother wit enough to conceal since she had first been aware that the others in the Foostmam's Hive were not able to come cleanly out of their dreams into the here and now. Why, some of them had to be fed, clothed, cared for as if they were not aware they had any bodies!

"Action dreamer." Lord Starrex shifted his shoulders against the padding which immediately accommodated itself to his stirring to give him maximum comfort. "Action dreaming is a little childish."

Tamisan's control held. She felt inside her a small flare of anger. Childish was it? She would like to show him just how childish a dream she could spin to enmesh a client. But Jabis was not in the least moved by that derogatory remark from a possible purchaser, it was in his eyes only a logical bargaining move.

"If you wish an E dreamer . . ." He shrugged. "But your demand to the Hive specified an A."

He was daring to be a trifle abrupt. Was he so sure of this lord as all that, Tamisan wondered. He must have some inside information which allowed him to be so confident, for Jabis could cringe and belly-down in awe as the lowest beggar if he thought such a gesture needful to gain a credit or two.

"Kas, this is your idea; what is she worth?" Starrex asked indifferently.

The younger of his companions moved forward a step or two; he was the reason for her being here. He was Lord Kas, cousin to the owner of all this magnificence, though certainly not, Tamisan had already deduced, with any authority in the household. But the fact that Starrex lay in the easirest was not dictated by indolence, but rather by what was hidden by the fas-silk lap robe concealing half his body. A man who might not walk straight again could find pleasure in the abilities of an action dreamer.

"She has a ten-point rating," Kas reminded the other.

The black brows which gave a stem set to Starrex's features arose a trifle. "Is that so?"

Jabis was quick to take advantage. "It is so, Lord Starrex. Of all this year's swarm, she rated the highest. It was . . . is . . . the reason why we make this offer to your lordship."

"I do not pay for reports only," returned Starrex.

Jabis was not to be ruffled. "A point ten, my lord, does not give demonstrations. As you know, the Hive accrediting cannot be forged. It is only that I have urgent business in

Brok and must leave for there that I am selling her at all. I have had an offer from the Foostmam herself to retain this one for lease outs."

Tamisan, had she had anything to wager, or someone with whom to wager it, would have set this winning of this bout with her uncle. Uncle? To Tamisan's thinking she had no blood tie with this small insect of a man, with his wrinkled face, his never-still eyes and his thin hands with their half-crooked fingers always reminding her of claws outstretched to grab. Surely her mother must have been very unlike Uncle Jabis, or else how could her father ever have seen aught worth bedding (not for just one night but for half a year) in her.

Not for the first time her thoughts were on the riddle of her parents. Her mother had not been a dreamer, though she had had a sister who had regrettably (for the sake of the family fortune) died in the Hive during adolescent stimulation as an E dreamer. Her father had been from off world—an alien, though humanoid enough to crossbreed. He had disappeared again off world when his desire for star roving had become too strong to master. Had it not been that she had early shown dreamer talent, Uncle Jabis and the rest of the greedy Yeska clan would never have taken any thought of her after her mother had died of the blue plague.

She was crossbred and had intelligence enough to guess early that that had given her the difference between her powers and those of others in the Hive. The ability to dream was an inborn talent. For those of low power it was a withdrawal from the world, and those dreamers were largely useless. But the others, who could project dreams to include others through linkage, brought high prices, according to the strength and stability of their creations. E dreamers, who created erotic and lascivious otherworlds, once were rated more highly than action dreamers. But of late years the swing had been in the opposite direction, though how long that might hold no one could guess. Those lucky enough to have an A dreamer to sell were pushing their wares speedily lest the market decline.

Tamisan's hidden talent was that she herself was never as completely lost in the dream world as those she conveyed to it. Also, (and this she had discovered very recently and hugged that discovery to her) she could in a measure control the linkage so she was not a powerless prisoner forced to dream at another's desire.

She considered what she knew concerning Lord Starrex. That Jabis would sell her to the owner of one of the sky towers had been clear from the first, and naturally he would select what he thought would be the best bargain. But, though rumors wafted through the Hive, Tamisan believed that much of their news of the outer worlds was inaccurate and garbled. Dreamers were roofed and walled from any real meeting with everyday life, their talents feverishly fed and fostered by long sessions with tri-dee projectors and information tapes.

Starrex, unlike most of his class, had been a doer. He had broken the pattern of caste by going off world on lengthy trips. It was only after some mysterious accident had crippled him that he became a recluse, supposedly hiding a maimed body. He did not seem like the others who had come to the Hive seeking wares. Of course, it had been Lord Kas who had summoned them here.

Stretched out on the easirest with that cover of fabulous silk across most of his body, he was hard to judge. She thought that standing he would top Jabis, and he seemed to be well muscled, more like his guard than his cousin.

He had a face unusual in its planes, broad across the forehead and cheek bones, then slimming to a strong chin which narrowed to give his head a vaguely wedge-shaped line. He was dark skinned, almost as dark as a space crewman. His black hair was cut very short so that it was a tight velvet cap, in contrast to the longer strands of his cousin.

His lutrax tunic of a coppery rust shade was of rich material but less ornamented than that of the younger man. Its sleeves were wide and loose, and now and then he ran his hands up his arms, pushing the fabric away from his skin. He wore only a single jewel, a koros stone set in an earring as a drop which dangled forward against his jawline.

Tamisan did not consider him handsome, but there was something arresting about him. Perhaps it was his air of arrogant assurance, as if in all his life he had never had his wishes crossed. But he had not met Jabis before, and perhaps now even Lord Starrex would have something to learn.

Twisting and turning, indignant and persuasive, using every trick in a very considerable training for dealing and under-dealing, Jabis bargained. He appealed to gods and demons to witness his disinterested desire to please, his despair at being misunderstood. It was quite a notable act and Tamisan stored up some of the choicer bits in her mental reservoir for the making of dreams. It was far more stimulating to watch than a tri-dee, and she wondered why this living drama material was not made available to the Hive. Perhaps, the Foostmam and her assistants feared it, along with any other shred of reality, which might awaken the dreamers from their conditioned absorption in their own creations.

For an instant or two she wondered if Lord Starrex was not enjoying it, too. There was a kind of weariness in his face which suggested boredom, though that was normal for anyone wanting a personal dreamer. Then, suddenly, as if he were tired of it all, he interrupted one of Jabis's more impassioned pleas for celestial understanding of his need for receiving just dues with a single sentence.

"I tire, fellow; take your price and go." He closed his eyes in dismissal.

It was the guard who drew a credit plaque from his belt, swung a long arm over the back of the easirest for Lord Starrex to plant a thumb on its surface to certify payment, and then tossed it to Jabis. It fell to the floor, so the small man had to scrabble for it with his fingers. Tamisan saw the look in his darting eyes. Jabis had little liking for Lord Starrex, which did not mean, of course, that he disdained the credit plaque he had to stoop to catch up.

He did not give a glance to Tamisan as he bowed himself out. She was left standing as if she were an android. It was Lord Kas who stepped forward and touched her lightly on the arm as if he thought she needed guidance.

"Come," he said, and his fingers about her wrist drew her after him. The Lord Starrex took no notice of his new possession.

"What is your name?" Lord Kas spoke slowly, emphasizing each word, as if he needed to do so to pierce some veil between them. Tamisan guessed that he had had contact with a lower-rated dreamer, one who was always bemused in the real world. Caution suggested that she allow him to believe she was in a similar daze. So she raised her head slowly and looked at him, trying to give the appearance of one finding it difficult to focus.

"Tamisan," she answered after a lengthy pause. "I be Tamisan."

"Tamisan, that is a pretty name," he said as one would address a dull-minded child. "I am Lord Kas. I am your friend."

But Tamisan, sensitive to shades of voice, thought she had done well in playing bemused. Whatever Kas might be, he was not her friend, at least not unless it served his purpose.

"These rooms are yours." He had escorted her down a hall to a far door where he passed his hand over the surface in a pattern to break a light lock. Then his grip on her wrist brought her into a high-ceilinged room. There were no windows to interrupt its curve of wall; the place was oval in shape. The center descended in a series of wide, shallow steps to a pool where a small fountain raised a perfumed mist to patter back into a bone-white basin. On the steps were a number of cushions and soft lie-ons, of many delicate shades of blue and green. The oval walls were draped with a shimmer of zidex webbing of pale gray covered with whirls and lines of the palest green.

A great deal of care had gone into the making and furnishing of the room. Perhaps Tamisan was only the latest in a series of dreamers, for this was truly a rest place, raised to a point of luxury unknown even in the Hive, for a dreamer.

A strip of the web tapestry along the wall was raised and a personal-care android entered. The head was only an oval ball with faceted eye-plates and hearing sensors to break its surface; its unclothed, humanoid form was ivory-white. "This is Porpae," Kas told her. "She will watch over you."

My guard, Tamisan thought. That the care the andriod would give her would be unceasing and of the best, she did not doubt, any more than that ivory being would stand between her and any hope of freedom.

"If you have any wish, tell it to Porpae." Kas dropped his hold on her arm and turned to the door. "When Lord Starrex wishes to dream, he will send for you."

"I am at his command," she mumbled; it was the proper response.

She watched Kas leave and then looked to Porpae. Tamisan had cause to believe that the android was programmed to record her every move. But would anyone here believe that a dreamer had any desire to be free? A dreamer wished only to dream; it was her life, her entire life. To leave a place which did all to foster such a life, that would be akin to self-killing, something a certified dreamer could not think on.

"I hunger," she told the android. "I would eat."

"Food comes." Porpae went to the wall, swept aside the web once more, to display a series of buttons she pressed in a complicated manner.

When the food did arrive in a closed tray with the

viands each in their own hot or cold compartment, Tamisan ate. She recognized the usual dishes of a dreamer's diet, but they were better cooked and more tastily served than in the Hive. She ate, she made use of the bathing place Porpae guided her to behind another wall web, and she slept easily and without stirring on the cushions beside the pool where the faint play of the water lulled her.

Time had very little meaning in the oval room. She ate, slept, bathed, and looked at the tri-dees she asked Porpae to supply. Had she been as the others from the Hive, this existence would have been ideal. But instead, when there was no call to display her art, she grew restless. She was a prisoner here and none of the other inhabitants of the sky tower seemed aware of her.

There was one thing she could do, Tamisan decided upon her second waking. A dreamer was allowed, no, required, to study the personality of the master she must serve, if she was a private dreamer and not a lessee of the Hive. She had a right now to ask for tapes concerning Starrex. In fact, it might be considered odd if she did not, and accordingly she called for those. Thus she learned something of Starrex and his household.

Kas had had his personal fortune wiped out by some catastrophe when he was a child. He had been in a manner adopted by Starrex's father, the head of their clan, and, since Starrex's injuries, had acted in some fashion as his deputy.

The guard was Ulfilas, an off-world mercenary Starrex had brought back from one of his star voyages.

But Starrex, save for a handful of bare facts, remained an enigma. That he had any human responses to others,

Tamisan began to doubt. He had gone seeking change off world, but what he might have found there had not cured his eternal weariness of life. His personal recordings were meager. She now believed that to him anyone of his household was only a tool to be used, or swept from his path and ignored. He was unmarried and such feminine companionship as he had languidly attached to his household (more by the effort of the woman involved than through any direct action on his part) did not last long. In fact, he was so encased in a shell of indifference that Tamisan wondered if there was any longer a real man within that outer covering.

She began to speculate as to why he had allowed Kas to bring her as an addition to his belongings. To make the best use of a dreamer the owner must be ready to partake, and what she read in these tapes suggested that Starrex's indifference would raise a barrier to any real dreaming.

The more Tamisan learned in this negative fashion, the more it seemed a challenge. She lay beside the pool in deep thought, though that thought strayed even more than she herself guessed from the rigid mental exercises used by a point-ten dreamer. To deliver a dream which would captivate Starrex was indeed a challenge. He wanted action, but her training, acute as it had been, was not enough to entice him. Therefore, *her* action must be able to take a novel turn.

This was an age of oversophistication, when star travel was a fact; and by the tapes, though they were not detailed as to what Starrex had done off world, the lord had experienced much of the reality of his time.

So he must be served the unknown. She had read

nothing in the tapes to suggest that Starrex had sadistic or perverted tendencies, and she knew that if he were to be reached in such a fashion she was not the one to do it. Also, Kas would have stated such a requirement at the Hive.

There were many rolls of history on which one could draw, but those had also been mined and remined. The future had been overused, frayed. Tamisan's dark brows drew together above her closed eyes. It was trite; everything she thought of was trite! Why did she care anyway? She did not even know why it had become so strong a drive to build a dream that, when she was called upon to deliver it, would shake Starrex out of his shell, to prove to him that she was worth her rating. Maybe it was partly because he had made no move to send for her and try to prove her powers; his indifference suggesting that he thought she had nothing to offer.

She had the right to call upon the full library of tapes from the Hive, and it was the most complete in the star lanes. Why, ships were sent out for no other reason than to bring back new knowledge to feed the imaginations of the dreamers!

History . . . her mind kept returning to the past though it was too threadbare for her purposes. History, what was history? It was a series of events, actions by individuals or nations. Actions had results. Tamisan sat up among her cushions. *Results of action!* Sometimes there were far-reaching results from a single action: the death of a ruler, the outcome of one battle, the landing of a star ship or its failure to land.

So . . .

Her flicker of an idea became solid. History could have

had many roads to travel beside the one already known. Now, could she make use of that? Why, it had innumerable possibilities. Tamisan's hands clenched the robe lying across her lap. Her mind began to see the problem. She needed more time . . . She no longer resented his indifference. She would need every minute it was prolonged.

"Porpae!"

The android materialized from behind the web.

"I must have certain tapes from the Hive." Tamisan hesitated. In spite of the spur of impatience, she must build smoothly and surely. "A message to the Foostmam: send to Tamisan an' Starrex the rolls of the history of Ty-Kry for the past five hundred years."

It was the history of the single city which based this sky tower. She would begin small, but she could test and retest her idea. Today it would be a single city, tomorrow a world, and then, who knows? Perhaps a solar system. She reined in her excitement. There was much to do; she needed a note recorder, and time. But by The Four Breasts of Vlasta . . . *if* she could do it!

It would seem she would have time, though always at the back of Tamisan's mind was the small spark of fear that at any moment the summons to Starrex might come. But the tapes arrived from the Hive and the recorder, so that she swung from one to the other, taking notes from what she learned. After the tapes had been returned, she studied those notes feverishly. Now her idea meant more to her than just a device to amuse a difficult master, it absorbed her utterly, as if she were a low-grade dreamer caught in one of her own creations.

When Tamisan realized the danger of this, she broke

with her studies and turned back to the household tapes
to learn again what she could of Starrex.

But she was again running through her notes when at
last the summons came. How long she had been in Starrex's
tower she did not know, for the days and nights in the oval
room were all alike. Only Porpae's watchfulness had kept
her to a routine of eating and rest.

It was the Lord Kas who came for her, and she had
just time to remember her role of bemused dreamer as he
entered.

"You are well, happy?" he used the conventional
greeting.

"I enjoy the good life."

"It is the Lord Starrex's wish that he enter a dream."
Kas reached for her hand and she allowed his touch. "The
Lord Starrex demands much; offer him your best,
dreamer." He might have been warning her.

"A dreamer dreams," she answered him vaguely.
"What is dreamed can be shared."

"True, but the Lord Starrex is hard to please. Do your
best for him, dreamer."

She did not answer, and he drew her on, out of the
room to a gray shaft and down that to a lower level. The
room into which they finally went had the apparatus very
familiar to her; a couch for the dreamer, the second for
the sharer with the linkage machine between. But here
there was a third couch; Tamisan looked at it in surprise.
"Two dream, not three."

Kas shook his head. "It is the Lord Starrex's will that
another share also. The linkage is of a new model, very
powerful. It has been well tested."

Who would be that third? Ulfilas? Was it that Lord Starrex thought he must take his personal guard into a dream with him?

The door swung open again and Lord Starrex entered. He walked stiffly, one leg swinging wide as if he could not bend the knee nor control the muscles, and he leaned heavily on an android. As the servant lowered him onto the couch he did not look at Tamisan but nodded curtly to Kas.

"Take your place also," he ordered.

Did Starrex fear the dream state and want his cousin as a check because Kas had plainly dreamed before?

Then Starrex did turn to her as he reached for the dream crown, copying the motion by which she settled her own circlet on her head.

"Let us see what you can offer." There was a shadow of hostility in his voice, a challenge to produce something which he did not believe she could.

SHE MUST NOT allow herself to think of Starrex now, but only of her dream. She must create and have no doubt that her creation would be as perfect as her hopes. Tamisan closed her eyes, firmed her will, drew into her imagination all the threads of the studies' spinning and began the weaving of a dream.

For a moment, perhaps two fingers' count of moments, this was like the beginning of any dream and then. . . .

She was not looking on, watching intently and critically, as she spun with dexterity. No, it was rather as if that web suddenly became real and she was caught tightly in it, even as a blue-winged drotail might be enmeshed in a fess-spider's deadly curtain.

This was no dreaming such as Tamisan had ever known before, and panic gripped so harshly in her throat and chest that she might have screamed, save that she had no voice left. She fell down and down from a point above, to strike among bushes which took some of her weight, but with an impact that left her bruised and half senseless. She lay unmoving, gasping, her eyes closed, fearing to open them to see that she was indeed caught in a wild nightmare and not properly dreaming.

As she lay there, she came slowly out of her dazed bewilderment and tried for control, not only over her fears, but also over her dreaming powers. Then she opened her eyes cautiously.

An arch of sky was overhead, pallidly green, with traces of thin, gray cloud like long, clutching fingers. It would have been as real as any sky might be, did she walk under it in her own time and world. *My own time and world!*

She thought of the idea she had built upon to astound Starrex; her wits quickened. Had the fact that she had worked with a new theory, trying to bring a twist to dreaming which might pierce the indifference of a bored man, precipitated *this?*

Tamisan sat up, wincing at the protest of her bruises, to look about her. Her vantage point was the crest of a small knob of earth. The land about her was no wilderness. The turf was smooth and cropped, and here and there were outcrops of rock cleverly carved and clothed with flowering vines. Other rocks were starkly bare, brooding. All faced downslope to a wall.

These forms varied from vaguely acceptable humaaoid shapes to grotesque monsters. Tamisan decided that she liked the aspect of none when she studied them more closely. These were *not* of her imagining.

Beyond the wall began a cluster of buildings. Since

she was used to seeing the sky towers and the lesser, if more substantial structures, beneath those, these looked unusually squat and heavy. The tallest she could see was no more than three stories high. Men did not build to the stars here; they hugged the earth closely.

But where was *here?* It was not her dream. Tamisan closed her eyes and concentrated on the beginnings of her planned dream. They had been about to go into another world, born of her imagining, but not this. Her basic idea had been simple enough, if not one which had been used, to her knowledge, by any dreamer before her. It all hinged on the idea that the past history of her world had been altered many times during its flow. She had taken three key points of alteration and studied what might have resulted had those been given the opposite decision by fate. Now, keeping her eyes firmly closed against this seeming reality into which she had fallen, Tamisan concentrated with fierce intentness upon her chosen points.

"The Welcome of the Over-queen Ahta." She recited the first.

What would have happened if the first starship on its landing had not been accepted as a supernatural event, and the small kingdom in which it had touched earth had not accepted its crew as godlings, but had greeted them instead with those poisoned darts the spacemen had later seen used? That was her first decision.

"The loss of the *Wanderer.*" That was the second.

It had been a colony ship driven far from its assigned course by computer failure, so that it had to make a landing here or its passengers would die. If that failure had not occurred and the *Wanderer* landed to start an unplanned colony, what would have come to pass?

"The death of Sylt the Sweet-Tongued before he reached the Altar of Ictio."

That prophet might never have arisen to ruthless power, leading to a blood-crazed insurrection from temple to temple, setting darkness on three quarters of this world.

She had chosen those points, but she had not even been sure that one might not have canceled out another. Sylt had led the rebellion against the colonists from the *Wanderer.* If the welcome had not occurred . . . Tamisan could not be sure, she had only tried to find a pattern of events and then envision a modern world stemming from those changes.

She opened her eyes again. This was not her imagined world. Nor did one in a dream rub bruises, sit on damp sod, feel wind pull at them, and allow the first patter of rain to wet hair and robe. She put both hands to her head. *What of the dream crown?*

Her fingers found a weaving of metal, but there were no cords from it. For the first time she remembered that she had been linked with Starrex and Kas when this happened.

Tamisan got to her feet to look around, half expecting to see the other two somewhere near; but she was alone and the rain was falling heavier. There was a roofed space near the wall and Tamisan hurried for it.

Three twisted pillars supported a small dome of roof. There were no walls and she huddled in the very center, trying to escape the wind-borne moisture. She could not keep pushing away the feeling that this was no dream but true reality.

If . . . if one could dream *true*. Tamisan fought panic and tried to examine the possibilities. *Had* she somehow landed in a Ty-Kry which might have existed had her three checkpoints actually been the decisions she envisioned? If so, could one get back by simply visioning them in reverse? She shut her eyes and concentrated. There was a sensation of stomach-turning giddiness. She swung out, to be jerked back, swung out, to return once more. Shaking with nausea, Tamisan stopped trying. She shuddered, opening her eyes to the rain. Then again she strove to understand what had happened. That swing had in it some of the sensation of dream breaking, which meant that she was in a dream. But it was just as apparent that she had been held prisoner here. *How? And why?* Her eyes narrowed a little, though she was looking inward, not at the rain-misted garden before her. *By whom?*

Suppose . . . suppose one or both of those who had prepared to share my dream had also come into this place, though not right here . . . then I must find them. We must return together or the missing one will anchor the others. Find them, and now!

For the first time she looked down at the garment clinging damply to her slender body. It was not the gray slip of a dreamer, for it was long, brushing her ankles. And in color it was a dusky violet, a shade she found strangely pleasing and right.

From its hem to her knees there was a border of intricate embroidery so entwined and ornate that she found it hard to define in any detail. Though, oddly enough, it seemed the longer she studied it, the more it appeared to be not threads on cloth, but words on a page of manuscript, such as she had viewed in the ancient history video tapes. The threads were a metallic green and silver, with only a few minor touches of a lighter shade of violet.

Around her waist was a belt of silver links, clasped by a broad buckle of the same metal set with purple stones. This supported a pouch with a clasped top. The dress or robe was laced from the belt to her throat with silver cords running through metal eyelets in the material. Her sleeves were long and full, though from the elbow down they were slit into four parts, those fluttering away from her arms when she raised them to loosen the crown.

What she brought away from her head was not the familiar skullcap made to fit over her cropped hair, rather it was a circlet of silver with inner wires or strips rising to close in a conical point to add a foot or more on her height. On that point was a beautifully fashioned flying thing, its wings a little lifted as if to take off, the glitter of tiny jewels marking its eyes.

So was it made that, as she turned the crown around, its long neck changed position and the wings moved a fraction. Thus, at first, she was almost startled enough to drop the circlet, thinking it might be alive.

But the whole she recognized from one of the history tapes. The bird was the flacar of Olava. Wearing it so meant that she was a Mouth, a Mouth of Olava, part priestess, part sorceress and, oddly enough, part entertainer. But fortune had favored her in this; a Mouth of Olava might wander anywhere without question, search, and seem merely to be about her normal business.

Tamisan ran her hand over her head before she replaced the crown. Her fingers did not find the bristly stubble of a dreamer, but rather soft, mist-dampened strands which curled down long enough to brush her forehead and tuft at the nape of her neck.

She had imagined garments for herself in dreams, of course. But this time she had not provided herself with such, and so the fact that she stood as a Mouth of Olava was not of her willing. But Olava was part of the time of the Over-queen's rule. Had she somehow swept herself back in time? The sooner she found knowledge of where and when she was, the better.

The rain was slackening and Tamisan moved out from under the dome. She bunched up her robe in both hands to climb back up the slope. At its top, she turned slowly, trying to find some proof that she had not been tossed alone into this strange world.

Save for the figures of stone and beds of rank-looking growth there was nothing to be seen. The wall and the dome lay below. But behind her when she faced the dome was a second slope leading to a still higher point, which was crowned by a roof to be seen only in bits and patches through a screen of oarn trees. The roof had a ridge which terminated at either side in a sharp upcurve, giving the building the odd appearance of having an ear on either end. It was green with a glittering surface, almost brilliantly so in spite of the clouds overhead.

To her right and left Tamisan caught glimpses of the wall curving and of more stone figures and flower or shrub plantings. Gathering up her skirts more firmly, she began to walk up the curve of the higher slope in search of some road or path leading to the roof.

She came across what she sought as she detoured to avoid a thicket of heavy brush in which were impaled huge scarlet flowers. It was a wide roadway paved with small colored pebbles embedded in a solid surface, and it led from an open gateway up the swell of the slope to the front of the structure. In shape, the building was vaguely familiar, though Tamisan could not identify it. Perhaps it resembled something she had seen in the tri-dees. The door was of the same brilliant green as the roof, but the walls were a pale yellow, cut sharply at regular intervals by very narrow windows, so tall that they ran from floor to roof level.

Even as she stood there wondering where she had seen such a house before, a woman came out. As did Tamisan, she wore a long-skirted robe with laced bodice and slit sleeves. But hers was the same green as that of the door so that, standing against it, only her head and arms were clearly visible. She gestured with vigor, and Tamisan suddenly realized that it must be she who was being summoned as if she were expected.

Again she fought down unease. In dreams, she was well used to meetings and partings, but always those were of her own devising and did not happen for a purpose which was not of her wish. Her dream people were toys, game pieces, to be moved hither and thither at her will, she being always in command of them.

"Tamisan, they wait; come quickly!" the woman called. Tamisan was minded in that instant to run in the other direction, but the need to learn what had happened made her take what might be the dangerous course of joining the woman.

"Fha, you are wet! This is no hour for walking in the garden. The First Standing asks for a reading from the Mouth. If you would have lavishly from her purse, hurry, lest she grows too impatient to wait!"

The door gave upon a narrow entry and the woman in green propelled Tamisan toward a second opening directly facing her. She came into the large room where a circle of couches was centered. By each stood a small table now burdened with dishes which serving maids were bearing away as if a meal had just been concluded. Tall candle-sticks, matching Tamisan's own height, stood also between the divans; the candles in each, as thick as her forearm, were alight, to give forth not only radiance but also a sweet odor as they burned.

Midpoint in the divan circle was a tall-backed chair over which arched a canopy. In it sat a woman, a goblet in her hand. She had a fur cloak pulled about her shoulders hiding almost all of her robe, save that here and there a shimmer of gold caught fire from the candlelight. Only her face was visible in a hood of the same metal-like fabric and it was that of a very old woman, seamed with deep wrinkles, sunken of eye.

The divans, Tamisan marked, were occupied by both men and women, the women flanking the chair and the men farthest away from the ancient noblewoman. Directly facing her was a second impressive chair, lacking only the canopy; before it was a table on which stood, at each of its four corners, small basins: one cream, one pale rose, one faintly blue, and the fourth sea-foam green.

Tamisan's store of knowledge gave her some preparation. This was the setting for the magic of a Mouth and it was apparent that her services as a foreseer were about to be demanded. What had she done in allowing herself to be drawn here? Could she make pretense her savant well enough to deceive this company?

"I hunger, Mouth of Olava; I hunger not for that which will feed the body, but for that which satisfies the mind." The old woman leaned forward a little. Her voice might be the thin one of age, but it carried with it the force of authority, of one who has not had her word or desire questioned for a long time.

She must improvise, Tamisan knew. She was a dreamer and she had wrought in dreams many strange things, let her but remember that. Her damp skirts clung clammily to her legs and thighs as she came forward, saying nothing to the woman in return, but seating herself in a chair facing her client. She was drawing on faint stirrings of a memory which seemed not truly her own for guidance, though she had not yet realized that fully.

"What would you know, First Standing?" Tamisan raised her hands to her forehead in an instinctive gesture, touching forefingers to her temples, right and left.

"What comes to me . . . and mine." The last two words had come almost as an afterthought.

Tamisan's hands went out without her conscious ordering. She stifled her amazement. It was as if she were repeating an act as well learned as her dreamer's technique had been. With her left hand, she gathered up a palmful of the sand from the cream bowl. It was a shade or two darker than the container. She tossed this with a sharp movement of her wrist and it settled smoothly as a film on the tabletop.

What she was doing was not of her conscious mind, as if another had taken charge of her actions. By the way the woman in the chair leaned forward, and by the hush which had fallen on her companion, this was right and proper.

Without any order from her mind, Tamisan's right hand went now to the blue bowl with its dark blue sand. But this was not tossed. Instead, she held the fine grains in her upright fist, passing it slowly over the tabletop so that a very tiny trickle of grit fed down to make a pattern on the first film.

It was a pattern, not a random scattering. What she had so drawn was a recognizable sword with a basket-shaped hilt and a slightly curved blade tapering to a narrow point.

Now her hand moved to the pink bowl. The sand she gathered there was a dark red, more vivid than the other colors, as if she dealt now with flecks of newly shed blood. Once more, she used her upheld fist and the shifting stream fed from her palm became a spaceship! It was slightly different in outline from those she had seen all her life, but it was unmistakably a ship, and it was drawn on the tabletop as if it threatened to descend upon the pointed sword. *Or is it that the sword threatens it?*

She heard a gasp of surprise, or was it fear? But that sound had not come from the woman who had bade her foretell. It must have broken from some other member of the company intent upon Tamisan's painting with the flowing sand.

It was to the fourth bowl now that her right hand

moved. But she did not take up a full fistful, rather a generous pinch between thumb and forefinger. She held the sand high above the picture and released it. The green specks floated down . . . to gather in a sign like a circle with one portion missing.

She stared at that and it seemed to alter a little under the intensity of her gaze. What it had changed to was a symbol she knew well, one which brought a small gasp from her. It was the seal, simplified it was true, but still readable, of the House of Starrex, and it overlaid both the edge of the ship and the tip of the sword.

"Read you this!" the noblewoman demanded sharply.

From somewhere the words came readily to Tamisan. "The sword is the sword of Ty-Kry raised in defense."

"Assured, assured." A murmur ran along the divans.

"The ship comes as a danger."

"That thing, a ship? But it is no ship."

"It is a ship from the stars."

"And woe, woe, and woe." That was no murmur, but a full-throated cry of fright. "As in the days of our fathers when we had to deal with the false ones. Ahta, let the spirit of Ahta be a shield to our arms, a sword in our hands!"

The noblewoman made a silencing gesture with one hand. "Enough! Crying to the revered spirits may bring sustenance, but they are not noted for helping those not standing to arms on their own behalf. There have been other sky ships since Ahta's days, and with them we have dealt— to *our* purpose. If another comes, we are forewarned, which is also forearmed. But what lies there in green, oh, Mouth of Olava, which surprised even you?"

Tamisan had had precious moments in which to think. If it were true, as she had deduced, that she was tied to this world by those she had brought with her, then she must find them; and it was clear that they were not of this company. Therefore, this last must be made to work for her.

"The green sign is that of a champion, one meant to be mighty in the coming battle. But he shall not be known save when the sign points to him, and it may be that this can only be seen by one with the gift."

She looked to the noblewoman and, meeting those old eyes, Tamisan felt a small chill rise in her, one which had not been born from the still damp clothing she wore. There was that in those two shadowed eyes which questioned coldly and did not accept without proof.

"So should the one with the gift you speak of go sniffling all through Ty-Kry and the land beyond the city, even to the boundaries of the world?"

"If need be." Tamisan stood firm.

"A long journey mayhap, and many strides into danger. And if the ship comes before this champion is found? A thin cord I think, oh, Mouth, on which to hang the future of a city, a kingdom, or a people. Look if you will, but I say we have more tested ways of dealing with these interlopers from the skies. But, Mouth, since you have given warning, let it so be remembered."

She put her hands on the arms of her chair and arose, using them to lever her. So did all her company come to their feet, two of the women hurrying to her so that she could lay her hands upon their shoulders for support. Without another look at Tamisan she went, nor did the dreamer rise to see her go. For suddenly, she was spent, tired as she had been in the past when a dream broke and left her supine and drained. But this dream did not break; it kept her sitting before the table and its sand pictures, looking at that green symbol, still caught fast in the web of another world.

The woman in green returned, bearing a goblet in her two hands and offering it to Tamisan.

"The First Standing will go to the High Castle and the Over-queen. She turned into that road. Drink, Tamisan, and mayhap the Over-queen herself will ask you for a seeing."

Tamisan? That was her true name; twice this woman had called her by it. *How is it known in a dream?* Yet she dared not ask that question or any of the others she needed answers to. Instead, she drank from the goblet, finding the hot, spicy liquid driving the chill from her body.

There was so much she must learn and must know; but could not discover it, save indirectly, lest she reveal what she was and was not.

"I am tired."

"There is a resting place prepared," the woman returned. "You have only to come."

Tamisan had almost to lever herself up as the noble-woman had done. She was giddy and had to catch at the back of the chair. Then she moved after her hostess, hoping desperately to know.

III

DID ONE SLEEP IN A DREAM, *dream upon dream, perhaps?* Tamisan wondered as she stretched out upon the couch her hostess showed her. Yet, when she set aside her crown, laid her head upon the roll which served as a pillow, she was once more alert, her thoughts racing, or entangled in such wild confusion that she felt as giddy as she had upon rising from her seer's chair.

The Starrex symbol overlying both that of the sword and the spaceship in the sand picture, could it mean that she would only find what she sought when the might of this world met that of the starmen? Had she indeed in some manner fallen into the past where she would relive the first coming of the space voyagers to Ty-Kry? But the noblewoman had mentioned past encounters with them which had ended in favor of Ty-Kry.

Tamisan had tried to envision a world of her own time, but one in which history had taken a different road. Yet much of that around her was of the past. Did that mean that, without the decisions of her own time, the world of Ty-Kry remained largely unchanged from century to century?

Real, unreal, old, new. She had lost all a dreamer's command of action. Tamisan did not play now with toys which she could move about at will, but rather was caught up in a series of events she could not foresee and over which she had no control. Yet, twice, the woman had called her by her rightful name and, without willing it, she had used the devices of a Mouth of Olava to foretell, as if she had done so many times before.

Could it be? Tamisan closed her teeth upon her lower lip and felt the pain of that, just as she felt the pain of the bruises left by her abrupt entrance into the mysterious here. *Could it be that some dreams are so deep, so well woven, that they are to the dreamer real? Is this indeed the fate of those "closed" dreamers who were worthless for the Hive? Do they in their trances live a countless number of lives?* But she was not a closed dreamer.

Awake! Once more, stretched as she was upon the couch, she used the proper technique to throw herself out of a dream and, once more, she experienced that weird nothingness in which she spun sickeningly as if held helplessly it some void, tied to an anchor which held her back from the full leap to sane safety. There was only one explanation: that somewhere in this strange Ty-Kry, one or both of those who had prepared to share her dream was now to be found and must be sought out before she could return.

So, the sooner that is accomplished, the better! But when should I start seeking? Though a feeling of weakness

clung to her limbs, making her move slowly as if she strove
to wall against the pull of a strong current, Tamisan arose
from the couch. She turned to pick up her Mouth's crown
and so looked into the oval of a mirror, startled thus into
immobility. For the figure she looked upon as her own
reflection was not one that she had seen before.

It was not the robe and the crown that had changed
her; she was not the same person. For a long time, ever
since she could remember, she had had the pallid skin, the
close cropped hair of a dreamer very seldom in the sunlight.
But the face of the woman in the mirror was a soft, even
brown. The cheekbones were wide, the eyes large and the
lips very red. Her brows . . . she leaned closer to the
mirror to see what gave them that odd upward slant and
decided that they had been plucked or shaven to produce
the effect. Her hair was perhaps three fingers long and
not the well-known fair coloring, but dark and curling.
She was not the Tamisan she knew, nor was this stranger
the product of her own will.

It would follow logically that if she did not look like
her normal self, then perhaps the two she sought were no
longer as she remembered either. Thus her search would
be twice as difficult. Could she ever recognize them?

Frightened, she sat down on the couch facing the
mirror. She dared not give way to fear, for if she once let
it break her control, she might be utterly lost. Logic, even
in such world of unlogic, must make her think lucidly.
Just how true was her soothsaying? At least she had not
influenced that fall of the sand. Perhaps the Mouth of
Olava did have supernatural powers. She had played with
the idea of magic in the past to embroider dreams, but that

had been her own creation. Could she use it by will now? It would seem this unknown self of hers did manage to draw upon some unknown source of power.

She must fasten her thoughts upon one of the men and hold him in her mind. Could the dream tie pull her to Kas or Starrex? All she knew of her master she had learned from tapes, and tapes gave one only superficial knowledge. One could not well study a person going through only half-understood actions behind a veil which concealed more than it displayed. Kas had spoken directly to her, his flesh had touched hers. If she must choose one to draw her, then it had better be Kas.

In her mind, Tamisan built a memory picture of him as she would build a preliminary picture for a dream. Then, suddenly, the Kas in her mind flickered, changed; she saw another man. He was taller than the Kas she knew, and he wore a uniform tunic and space boots; his features were hard to distinguish. That vision lasted only a fraction of time.

The ship! The symbol had lain touching both ship and sword in the sand seeing. It would be easier to seek a man on a ship than wandering through the streets of a strange city with no better clue than that Starrex's counterpart might be there.

It was so little on which to pin a quest: a ship which might or might not be now approaching Ty-Kry, and which would meet a drastic reception when it landed. *Suppose Kas, or his double, is killed? Would that anchor me here for all time?* Resolutely, Tamisan pushed such negative speculation to the back of her mind. *First things first: the ship has not yet planeted.* But when it came, she must make sure that she was among those preparing for its welcome.

It seemed that having made that decision, she was at last able to sleep, for the fatigue which had struck at her in the hall returned a hundredfold and she fell back on the couch as one drugged, remembering nothing more until she awakened. She found the woman in green standing above her, one hand on her shoulder shaking her gently back to awareness.

"Awake, there is a summons."

A summons to dream, Tamisan thought dazedly, and then the unfamiliar room and the immediate past came completely back to her.

"The First Standing Tassa has summoned." The woman sounded excited. "It is said by her messenger, he has brought a chair cart for you, that you are to go to the High Castle! Perhaps you will see for the Over-queen herself! But there is time, I have won it for you, to bathe, to eat, to change your robe. See, I have plundered my own bride chest." She pointed to a chair over which was spread a robe, not of the deep violet Tamisan now wore, but of a purple-wine. "It is the only one of the proper color, or near it." She ran her hand lovingly over the rich folds.

"But haste," she added briskly. "As a Mouth, you can claim the need for making ready to appear before high company, but to linger too long will raise the anger of the First Standing."

There was a basin large enough to serve as a bath in the room beyond, and, as well as the robe, the woman had brought fresh body linen. When Tamisan stood once more before the mirror to clasp her silver belt and assume the

Mouth crown, she felt renewed and refreshed and her thanks were warm.

But the woman made a gesture of brushing them aside. "Are we not of the same clan, cousin? Shall one say that Nahra is not open-handed with her own? That you are a Mouth is our clan pride, let us enjoy it through you!"

She brought a covered bowl and a goblet and Tamisan ate a dish of meal into which had been baked dried fruit and bits of what she thought well-chopped meat. It was tasty and she finished it to the last crumb, just as she emptied the cup of a tart-sweet drink.

"Wellaway, Tamisan, this is a great day for the clan of Fremont, when you go to the High Castle and perhaps stand before the Over-queen. May it be that the seeing is not for ill, but for good. Though you are but the Mouth of Olava and not the One dealing fortune to us who live and die."

"For your aid and your good wishing, receive my thanks," Tamisan said. "I, too, hope that fortune comes before misfortune on this day." And that is stark truth, she thought, for I must gather fortune to me with both hands and hold it tight, lest the game I play be lost.

First Standing Jassa's messenger was an officer, his hair clubbed up under a ridged helm to give additional protection to his head in battle, his breastplate enameled blue with the double crown of the Over-queen, and his sword very much to the fore. It was as if he already strode the street of a city at war. There was a small griffin between the shafts of the chair cart and two men-at-arms ready, one at the griffin's head, the other holding aside the curtains as their officer handed Tamisan into the chair. He briskly jerked the curtains shut without asking her pleasure, and she decided that perhaps her visit to the High Castle was to be a secret matter.

Between the curtain edges, she caught sight of this Ty-Kry and, though, in parts it was very strange to her, there were enough similarities to provide her with an anchor to the real. The sky towers and other off-world forms of architecture which had been introduced by space travelers were missing. But the streets themselves and the many beds of foliage and flowers were those she had known all her life.

The High Castle, she drew a deep breath as they wound out of town and along the river, had been part of her world, too, though then as a ruined and very ancient landmark. Part of it had been consumed in the war of Sylt's rebellion, and it had been considered a place of misfortune, largely shunned, save for off-world tourists seeking the unusual.

Here it was in its pride, larger and more widely spread than in her Ty-Kry, as if the generations who had deserted it in her world had clung to it here, adding ever to its bulk. It was not a single structure, but a city in itself. However, it had no merchants or public buildings. It provided homes to shelter the nobles who must spend part of the year at court, all their servants and the many officials of the kingdom.

In its heart was the building which gave it its name, a collection of towers, rising far above the lesser structures at the foot. The buildings' walls were gray at their bases and changed subtly as they arose until their tops were a deep, rich blue. The other buildings in the great pile were wholly gray as to wall, a darker blue as to roof.

The chair creaked forward on its two wheels, the griffin being kept to a steady pace by the man at its head, and passed under the thick arch in the outer wall, then up a street between buildings which, though dwarfed by the towers, were in turn dwarfing to those who walked or rode by them.

There was a second gate, more buildings, a third gate and then the open space about the central towers. They passed people in plenty since they had entered the first gate. Many were soldiers of the guard, but some of the armed men had worn other colors and insignia being, Tamisan guessed, the retainers of court lords. Now and then, some lord came proudly, his retinue strung along behind him by threes to make a show which amused Tamisan. *As if the number of followers to tread on one's heels enhanced one's importance in the world.*

She was handed down with a little more ceremony than she had been ushered into the chair, and the officer offered her his wrist, his men falling in behind as a groom hurried forward to lead off the equipage, thus affording her a tail of honor, too.

But the towers of the High Castle were so awe-inspiring, so huge a pile, that she was glad she had an escort into their heart. The farther they advanced through the halls, the more uneasy she became. It was as if once she were within this maze, there might be no retreat and she would be lost forever.

Twice they climbed staircases until her legs ached with the effort and they took on the aspect of mountains.

Then her party passed into a long hall which was lighted not only by the candle trees, but some thin rays filtering through windows placed so high above their heads that nothing could be seen through them. Tamisan, in that part of her which seemed familiar with this world, knew this to be the Walk of the Nobles, and the company now gathered here were the Third Standing, nearest, then the Second, and, at the far end of that road of blue carpet onto which her guide led her, First Standing. They were sitting; there were two arcs of hooded and canopied chairs, with above them a throne on a three-step dais. The hood over that was upheld by a double crown which glittered with gems. On the steps were grouped men in the armor of the guard and others wearing bright tunics, their hair loose upon their shoulders.

It was toward that throne that the officer led her and they passed through the ranks of the Third Standing, hearing a low murmur of voices. Tamisan looked neither to right nor left; she wished to see the Over-queen, for it was plain she was being granted full audience. Something stirred deep within her as if a small pin pricked. The reason for this she did not know, save that ahead was something of vast importance to her.

Now they were equal with the first of the chairs and she saw that the greater number of those who so sat were women, but not all. Mainly, they were at least in middle life. So Tamisan came to the foot of the dais and, in that moment, she did not go to one knee as did the officer, but rather raised her fingertips to touch the rim of the crown on her head; for, with another of those flashes of half recognition, she knew that in this place that which she represented did not bow as did others, but acknowledged only that the Over-queen was one to whom human allegiance was granted after another and greater loyalty was paid elsewhere.

The Over-queen looked down with a deeply searching stare as Tamisan looked up. What Tamisan saw was a woman to whom she could not set an age; she might be either old or young, for the years had not seemed to mark her. The robe on her full figure was not ornate, but a soft pearl color without ornamentation, save that she wore a girdle of silvery chains braided and woven together, and a collarlike necklace of the same metal from which fringed milky gems cut into drops. Her hair was a flame of brightly glowing red, in which a diadem of the same creamy stones was almost hidden. Was she beautiful? Tamisan could not have said; but that she was vitally alive there was no doubt. Even though she sat quietly, there was an aura of energy about her suggesting that this was only a pause between the doing of great and necessary deeds. She was the most assertive personality Tamisan had ever seen and, instantly, the guards of a dreamer went into action. To serve such a mistress, Tamisan thought, would sap all the personality from one, so that the servant would become but a mirror to reflect from that moment of surrender onward.

"Welcome, Mouth of Olava who has been uttering strange things." The Over-queen's voice was mocking, challenging.

"A Mouth says naught, Great One, save what is given it to speak." Tamisan found her answer ready, though she had not consciously formed it in her mind.

"So we were told, though gods may grow old and

tired. Or is that only the fate of men? But now, it is our will that Olava speak again if that is fortune for this hour. So be it!"

As if that last phrase were an order, there was a stir among those standing on the steps of the throne. Two of the guards brought out a table, a third a stool, the fourth a tray on which rested four bowls of sand. These they set up before the throne.

Tamisan took her place on the stool, again put her finger to her temples. Would this work again, or must she try to force a picture in the sand? She felt a small shiver of nerves she fought to control.

"What desires the Great One?" She was glad to hear her voice steady, no hint of her uneasiness in it.

"What chances in, say, four passages of the sun?"

Tamisan waited. Would that other personality, or power, or whatever it might be, take over? Her hand did not move. Instead, that odd, disturbing prick grew the stronger; she was drawn, even as a noose might be laid about her forehead to pull her head around. So she turned to follow the dictates of that pull and looked where something willed her eyes to look. All she saw was the line of officers on the steps of the throne and they stared at and through her, none with any sign of recognition. *Starrex!* She grasped at that hope, but none of them resembled the man she sought.

"Does Olava sleep? Or had his Mouth been forgotten for a space?"

The Over-queen's voice was sharper and Tamisan broke that hold on her attention, looking back to the throne and the woman on it.

"It is not meet for the Mouth to speak unless Olava wishes." Tamisan began, feeling increasingly nervous. That sensation gripped her left hand, as if it were not under her control but possessed by another will. She fell silent as it gathered up the brownish sand and tossed it to form a picture's background.

This time she did not seek next the blue grains; rather, her fist dug into the red and moved to paint the outline of the spaceship, above it a single red circle.

Then, there was a moment of hesitation before her fingers strayed to the green, took up a generous pinch and again made Starrex's symbol below the ship.

"A single sun," the Over-queen read out. "One day until the enemy comes. But what is the remaining word of Olava, Mouth?"

"That there be one among you who is a key to victory. He shall stand against the enemy and under him fortune comes."

"So? Who is this hero?"

Tamisan looked again to the line of officers. Dared she trust to instinct? Something within her urged her on.

"Let each of these protectors of Ty-Kry," she raised a finger to indicate the officers, "come forward and take up the sand of seeing. Let the Mouth touch that hand and may it then strew the answer. Perhaps Olava will make it clear in this manner."

To Tamisan's surprise the Over-queen laughed. "As good a way as any perhaps for picking a champion. To abide by Olava's choice, that is another matter." Her smile faded as she glanced at the men, as if there was a thought in her mind which disturbed her.

At her nod, they came one by one. Under the shadows of their helmets, their faces, being of one race, were very similar and Tamisan, studying each, could see no chance of telling which Starrex might be.

Each took up a pinch of green sand, held out his hand, palm down, and let the grains fall while she set fingertip to his knuckles. The sand drifted but in no shape and to no purpose.

It was not until the last man came that there was a difference, for then the sand did not drift, but fell to form again the symbol which was twin to the one already on the table. Tamisan looked up. The officer was staring at the sand rather than meeting her eyes and there was a line of strain about his mouth, a look about him as might shadow the face of a man who stood with his back to a wall and a ring of sword points at his throat.

"This is your man," Tamisan said. Starrex? She must be sure; if she could only demand the truth in this instant!

But her preoccupation was swept aside.

"Olava deals falsely!" That cry came from the officer behind her, the one who had brought her here.

"Perhaps we must not think ill of Olava's advice." The Over-queen's voice had a guttural, feline purr. "It may be his Mouth is not wholly wedded to his service, but speaks for others than Olava at times. Hawarel, so you are to be our champion?"

The officer went to one knee, his hands clasped loosely before him as if he wished all to see he did not reach for any weapon.

"I am no choice, save the Great One's." In spite of

the strain visible in his tense body, he spoke levelly and without a tremor.

"Great One, this traitor . . ." Two of the officers moved as if to lay hands upon him and drag him away.

"No. Has not Olava spoken?" The mockery was very plain in the Over-queen's tone now. "But to make sure that Olava's will be carried out, take good care of our champion-to-be. Since Hawarel is to fight our battle with the cursed starmen, he must be saved to do it." And now she looked to Tamisan, startled by the quick turn of events and their hostility to Olava's choice. "Let the Mouth of Olava share with Hawarel this waiting that she may, perhaps, instill in Olava's choice the vigor and strength such a battle will demand of our chosen champion," Each time the Over-queen spoke the word "champion" she made of it a thing of derision and subtle menace.

"The audience is finished." The Over-queen arose and stepped behind the throne as those about Tamisan fell to their knees; then she was gone. But the officer who had guided Tamisan was by her side. Hawarel, once more on his feet, was closely flanked by two of the other guards, one of whom pulled their prisoner's sword from his sheath before he could move. Then, with Hawarel before her, Tamisan was urged from the hall, though none laid a hand on her.

At the moment, she was pleased enough to go, hoping for a chance to prove the rightness of her guess, that Hawarel and Starrex were the same and she had found the first of her fellow dreamers.

They transversed more halls until they came to a door which one of Hawarel's guards opened. The prisoner walked through and Tamisan's escort waved her after him. Then the door slammed shut, and at that sound Hawarel whirled around.

Under the beaking foreplate of his helmet, his eyes were cold fire and he seemed a man about to leap for his enemy's throat.

His voice was only a harsh whisper. "Who . . . who set you to my death wishing, witch?"

✻ ✻ IV ✻ ✻

HIS HANDS reached for her throat. Tamisan flung up her arm in an attempt to guard and stumbled back.

"Lord Starrex!" *If I have been wrong, if . . .*

Though his fingertips brushed her shoulders, he did not grasp her. Instead it was his turn to retreat a step or two, his mouth half-open in a gasp.

"Witch! Witch!" The very force of the words he hurled at her made them darts dispatched from one of the crossbows of the history tapes.

"Lord Starrex," Tamisan repeated, feeling on more secure ground at his stricken amazement and no longer fearing he would attack her out of hand. His reaction to that name was enough to assure her she was right, though he did not seem prepared to acknowledge it.

"I am Hawarel of the Vanora." He brought out those words as harsh croaking.

Tamisan glanced around. This was a bare-walled room, with no hiding place for a listener. In her own time and place she could have feared many scanning devices, but she thought those unknown to this Ty-Kry. To win Hawarel-Starrex into cooperation was very necessary.

"You are Lord Starrex," she returned with bold confidence, or at least what she hoped was a convincing show of it. "Just as I am Tamisan, the dreamer. And this, wherein we are caught, is the dream you ordered of me."

He raised his hand to his forehead, his fingers encountered his helmet and he swept it off unheedingly, so that it clanked and slid across the polished floor. His hair, netted into a kind of protecting cushion was piled about his head, giving him an odd appearance to Tamisan. It was black and thick, just as his skin was as brown-hued as that of her new body. Without the shadow of the helmet, she could see his face more clearly, finding in it no resemblance to the aloof master of the sky towers. In a way, it was that of a younger man, one less certain of himself.

"I am Hawarel," he repeated doggedly. "You try to trap me, or perhaps the trap has already closed and you seek now to make me condemn myself with my own mouth. I tell you, I am no traitor. I am Hawarel and my blood oath to the Great One has been faithfully kept."

Tamisan experienced a rise of impatience. She had not thought Lord Starrex to be a stupid man. But it would seem his counterpart here lacked more than just the face of his other self.

"You are Starrex, and this is a dream!" If it was not, she did not care to raise that issue now. "Remember the sky tower? You bought me from Tabis for dreaming. Then you summoned me and Lord Kas and ordered me to prove my worth."

His brows drew together in a black frown as he stared at her.

"What have they given you, or promised, that you do this to me?" came his counterdemand. "I am no sworn enemy to you or yours, not that I know."

Tamisan sighed. "Do you deny you know the name Starrex?" she asked.

For a long moment he was silent. Then he turned from her, took a stride or two; his toe thumped against his helmet, sending it rolling ahead of him. She waited. He turned again to face her.

"You are a Mouth of Olava. . . ."

She shook her head, interrupting him. "We have little time for such fencing, Lord Starrex. You do know that name, and it is in my mind that you also remember the rest, at least in some measure. I am Tamisan the dreamer."

It was his turn to sigh. "So you say."

"So I shall continue to say, and, mayhap as I do, others than you will listen."

"As I thought!" he flashed. "You would have me betray myself."

"If you are truly Hawarel as you state, then what have you to betray?"

"Very well. I am . . . am two! I am Hawarel and I am someone else who has queer memories and who may well be a night demon come to dispute ownership of this body. There, you have it. Go and tell those who sent you and have me out to the arrow range for a quick ending there. Perhaps that will be better than to continue as a battle-field between two different selves."

Perhaps he was not just being obstinate, Tamisan

thought. It might be that the dream had a greater hold on him than it did on her. After all, she was a trained dreamer, one used to venturing into illusions wrought from imagination.

"If you can remember a little, then listen." She drew closer to him and began to speak in a lower voice, not that she believed they could be overheard, but it was well to take no chance. Swiftly she gave her account of the whole tangle, or what had been her part in it.

When she was done, she was surprised to see that a certain hardening had overtaken his features, so that now he looked more resolute, less like one trapped in a maze which had no guide.

"And this is the truth?"

"By what god or power do you wish me to swear to it?" She was exasperated now, frustrated by his lingering doubts.

"None, because it explains what was heretofore unexplainable, what has made my life a hell of doubt these past hours, and brought more suspicion upon me. I have been two persons. But if this is all a dream, why is that so?"

"I do not know." Tamisan chose frankness as best befitting her needs. "This is unlike any dream I have created before."

"In what manner?" he asked crisply.

"It is a part of a dreamer's duty to study her master's personality, to suit his desires, even if those be unexpressed and hidden. From what I had learned of you, of Lord Starrex, I thought that too much had been already seen, experienced and known to you, that it must be a new approach I tried, or else you would find that dreaming held no profit.

"Therefore, it came to me suddenly that I would not dream of the past, nor of the future, which are the common approaches for an action dreamer, but refine upon the subject. In the past there were times in history when the future rested upon a single decision. And it was in my mind to select certain of these decisions and then envision a world in which those decisions had gone in the opposite direction, trying to see what would be the present result of actions in the past."

"So this is what you tried? And what decisions did you select for your experiment at the rewriting of history?" He was giving her his full attention.

"I took three. First, the welcome of the Over-queen, Ahta; second, the drift of the colony ship, *Wanderer;* third, the rebellion of Sylt. Should the welcome have been a rejection, should the colony ship never reach here, should Sylt have failed, these would produce a world I thought might be interesting to visit in a dream. So I read what history tapes I could call upon. Thus, when you summoned me to dream I had my ideas ready. But it did not work as it should have. Instead of spinning the proper dream, creating incidents in good order, I found myself fast caught in a world I did not know or build."

As she spoke, she could watch the change in him. He had lost all the fervent antagonism of his first attack on her. More and more, she could see what she had associated with the personality of Lord Starrex coming through the unfamiliar envelope of this man's body.

"So it did not work properly."

"No. As I have said, I found myself in the dream, with no control of action and no recognizable creation factors. I do not understand."

"No? There could be an explanation." The frown line was back between his brows, but it was not a scowl aimed at her. It was as if he were trying hard to remember something of importance which eluded his efforts. "There is a theory, a very old one. Yes, that of parallel worlds."

In her wide use of the tapes, she had not come across that and now she demanded the knowledge of him almost fiercely. "What are those?"

"You are not the first, how could you be, to be struck by the notion that sometimes history and the future hang upon a very thin cord which can be twisted this way and that by a small chance. A theory was once advanced that when that chanced, it created a second world, one in which the decision was made to the right, when that of the world we know went to the left."

"But alternate worlds, where, how did they exist?"

"Thus, perhaps," he held out his two hands horizontally, one above the other, "in layers. There were even old tales created for amusement, of men traveling not back in time, nor forward, but across it from one such world to another."

"But here we are. I am a Mouth of Olava and I don't look like myself, just as to the eye you are not Lord Starrex."

"Perhaps we are the people we would be if our world had taken the other side of your three decisions. It is a clever device for a dreamer to create, Tamisan."

She told him now the last truth. "Only, I do not think I have created it. Certainly I cannot control it."

"You have tried to break this dream?"

"Of course, but I am tied here. Perhaps it is by you and Lord Kas. Until we three try together, maybe we cannot any of us return."

"Now you must go searching for him with that board and sand trick of yours?"

· She shook her head. "Kas, I think, is one of the crew on the spacer about to set down. I believe I saw him, though not his face." She smiled a little shakily. "It seems that though I am mainly the Tamisan I have always been, yet also do I have some of the powers of a Mouth; likewise, you are Hawarel as well as Starrex."

"The longer I listen to you," he announced, "the more I become Starrex. So we must find Kas on the spacer before we wriggle free from this tangle? But that is going to be rather a problem. I am enough of Hawarel to know that the spacer is going to receive the usual welcome dealt off-world ships here: trickery and extinction. Your three points have been as you envisioned them. There was no welcome, but rather a massacre; no colony ship ever reached here; and Sylt was speared by a contemptuous man-at-arms the first time he lifted his voice to draw a crowd. Hawarel knows this as truth; as Starrex, I am aware there is another truth which did radically change life on this planet. Now, did you seek me out on purpose, your champion tale intended to be our bridge to Kas?"

"No, at least I did not consciously arrange it so. I tell you, I have some of the powers of a Mouth; they take over."

He gave a sharp bark of sound which was not laughter but somewhat akin to it. "By the fist of Jimsam Taragon, we have it complicated by magic, too! And I suppose you cannot tell me just how much a Mouth can do in the way of foreseeing, forearming or freeing us from this trap?"

Tamisan shook her head. "The Mouths were mentioned in the history tapes; they were very important once. But after Sylt's rebellion, they were either killed or disappeared. They were hunted by both sides and the most we know about them is only legend. I cannot tell you what I can do. Sometimes something, perhaps the memory and knowledge of this body, takes over and then I do strange things. I neither will nor understand them."

He crossed the room and pulled two stools from a far corner. "We might as well sit at ease and explore what we can of this world's memories. It just might be that united, we can learn more than when trying alone. The trouble is . . ." He reached out a hand and, mechanically, she touched fingertips to the back of it in an oddly formal ceremony which was not part of her own knowledge. He guided her to one of the stools and she was glad to sit down.

"The trouble is," he repeated as he dropped on the other stool, stretching out his long legs and tugging at his sword belt with that dangerously empty sheath, "that I was more than a little mixed up when I awoke, if you might call it that, in this body. My first reactions must have suggested mental imbalance to those I encountered. Luckily, the Hawarel part was in control soon enough to save me. But there is a second drawback to this identity: I am suspect as coming from a province where there has been a rebellion. In fact, I am here in Ty-Kry as a hostage, rather than a member of the guard in good standing. I have not been able to ask questions, and all I have learned is in bits and pieces. The real Hawarel is a quite uncomplicated, simple soldier who is hurt by the suspicion against him and quite fervently loyal to the crown. I wonder how Kas took his waking. If he preserves any remnant of his real self, he ought to be well established by now."

Surprised, Tamisan asked a question to which she hoped he would give a true and open answer. "You do not like . . . you have reason to fear Lord Kas?"

"Like? Fear?" She could see that thin shadow of Starrex overlaying Hawarel become more distinct. "Those are emotions. I have had little to do with emotions for some time."

"But you wanted him to share the dream," she persisted.

"True. I may not be emotional about my esteemed cousin, but I am a prudent man. Since it was by his urging, in fact his arrangement, that you were added to my household, I thought it only fair he share in his plan for my entertainment. I know that Kas is very solicitous of his crippled cousin, ready handed to serve in any way, so generous of his time and his energy."

"You suspect him of something?" She thought she had sensed what lay behind his words.

"Suspect? Of what? He has been, as all would assure you freely, my good friend, as far as I would allow." There was a closed look about him warning her off any further exploration of that.

"His crippled cousin." This time Hawarel repeated those words as if he spoke to himself and not to her. "At least you have done me a small service on the credit side of the scale." Now he did look to Tamisan as he thumped his right leg with a satisfaction which was not of the Starrex she knew. "You have provided me with a body in good working order, which I may well need since, so far, bad has outweighed the good in this world."

"Hawarel, Lord Starrex . . ." She was beginning when he interrupted her.

"Give me always Hawarel, remember. There is no need to add to the already heavy load of suspicion surrounding me in these halls."

"Hawarel, then, I did not choose you for the champion; that was done by a power I do not understand, working through me. If they agree, you have a good chance to find Kas. You may even demand that he be the one you battle."

"Find him how?"

"They may allow me to select the proper one from the off-world force," she suggested. It was a very thin thread on which to hang any plan of escape, but she could not see a better one.

"And you think that this sand painting will pick him out, as it did me?"

"It did you, did it not?"

"That I cannot deny."

"And the first time I foresaw, for one of the First Standing, it made such an impression on her that she had me summoned here to foresee for the Over-queen."

"Magic!" Again he uttered that half laugh.

"To another world, much that the space travelers can do might be termed magic."

"Well said. I have seen strange things; yes, I have seen

things myself, and not while dreaming either. Very well, I am to volunteer to meet an enemy champion from the ship and then you sand paint out the proper one. If you are successful and do find Kas, then what?"

"It is simple; we wake."

"You take us with you, of course?"

"If we are so linked that we cannot leave here without one another, then a single waking will take us all."

"Are you sure you need Kas? After all, I was the one you were planning this dream for."

"We go, leave Lord Kas here?"

"A cowardly withdrawal you think, my dreamer. But one, I assure you, which would solve many things. However, can you send me through and return for Kas? It is in my mind I would like to know what is happening now for myself in our own world. Is it not by the dreamer's oath that he for whom the dream is wrought has first call upon the dreamer?"

He did have some lurking uneasiness tied to Kas, but in a manner he was right. She reached out before he was aware of what she would do and seized his hand, at the same time using the formula for waking. Once more, that mist which was nowhere enveloped her. But it was no use, her first guess had been right; they were still tied. She blinked her eyes open upon the same room. Hawarel had slumped and was falling from his stool so that she had to go to one knee to support his body with her shoulder or he would have slid full length to the floor. Then his muscles tightened and he jerked erect, his eyes opened and blazed into hers with the same cold anger with which he had first greeted her upon entering this room.

"Why?"

"You asked," she countered.

His lids drooped so she could no longer see that icy anger. "So I did. But I did not quite expect to be so quickly served. Now, you have effectively proven your point; three go or none. And it remains to be seen how soon we can find our missing third."

He asked her no more questions and she was glad, since that whirl into nowhere in the abortive attempt at waking had tired her greatly. She moved the stool a little so her back could rest against the wall and she was farther from him. In a little while, he got to his feet and paced back and forth as if some driving desire for wider action worked in him to the point where he could not sit still.

Once the door opened, but they were not summoned forth. Instead, food and drink were brought to them by one of the guards; the other stood ready with a crossbow at thigh, his eyes ever upon them.

"We are well served." Hawarel opened the lids of the bowls and inspected their contents. "It would seem we are of importance. Hail, Rugaard, when do we go forth from this room, of which I am growing very tired?"

"Be at peace; you shall have action enough, when the Great One desires it," the officer with the crossbow answered. "The ship from the stars has been sighted; the mountain beacons have blazed twice. They seem to be aiming for the plain beyond Ty-Kry. It is odd that they are so single-minded and come to the same pen to be taken each time. Perhaps Dalskol was right when he said that they do not think for themselves at all, but carry out the orders of an off-world power which does not allow them independent judgment. Your service time will come; and, Mouth of Olava," he took a step forward to see Tamisan the better, "the Great One says that it might be well to read the sand on your own behalf. False seers are given to those they have belittled in such seeing, to be done with as those they have so shamed may decide."

"As is well known," she answered him. "I have not dealt falsely, as shall be seen at the proper time and in the proper place."

When they were gone, she was hungry and so it seemed was Hawarel, for they divided the food fairly and left nothing in the bowls.

When they were done he said, "Since you are a reader of history and know old customs, perhaps you remember one which it is not too pleasant to recall now, that among some races it was the proper thing to dine well as a prisoner about to die."

"You choose a heartening thing to think on."

"No, you chose it, for this is your world; remember that, my dreamer."

Tamisan closed her eyes and leaned her head and shoulders back against the wall. There was a clang of sudden noise, and she gasped out of a doze. The room had grown dark, but at the door was a blaze of light; in that stood the officer, with a guard of spearmen behind.

"The time has come."

"The wait has been long." Hawarel stood up, stretched wide his arms as one who has been ready for too long. Then he turned to her and, once more, offered his wrist. She would have liked to have done without his aid, but she found herself stiff and cramped enough to be glad of it.

They went on a complicated way through halls, down stairs, until at last they issued out into the night. Waiting for them was a covered cart, much larger than the chair on wheels which had brought her to the castle, with two griffins between its shafts.

Into this their guard urged them, drawing the curtains and pegging those down tightly outside so that even, had they wished, they could not have looked out. As the cart creaked out, Tamisan tried to guess by sound where they might be going.

There was little noise to guide her. It was as if they now passed through a town deep in slumber. But in the gloom of the cart, she felt rather than saw movement, and then a shoulder brushed hers and a whisper so faint she had to strain to hear it was at her ear.

"Out of the castle."

"Where?"

"My guess is the field, the forbidden place." The memory of the this-world Tamisan supplied explanation. That was where two other spacers had planeted, not to rise again. In fact, the one which had come fifty years ago had never been dismantled; it stood, a corroded mass of metal, to be a double warning: to the stars not to invade and to Ty-Kry to be alert against such invasion.

It seemed to Tamisan that that ride would never come to an end. Then there was an abrupt halt which bumped her soundly against the side of the cart and lights bedazzled her eyes as the curtains were pulled aside. "Come, Champion and Champion-maker!" Hawarel obeyed first and turned to give her assistance once more, but was elbowed aside as the officer pulled rather than led her into the open. Torches in the hands of spearmen ringed them. Beyond was a colorful mass of people, with a double rank of guards drawn up as a barrier between those and the dark of the land beyond.

"Up there." Hawarel was beside her again. Tamisan raised eyes. She was almost blinded by the glare as a sudden pillar of fire burst across the night sky. A spacer was riding down on tail rockets to make a fine landing.

❈ ❈ V ❈ ❈

BY THE LIGHT of those flames, the whole plain was illumined. Beyond, stood the hulk of the unfortunate spacer which had last planeted. There, drawn up in lines, was a large force of spearmen, crossbowmen, officers with the basket-hilted weapons at their sides. However, as they waited, they appeared a guard of honor for the Over-queen, who sat raised above the rest on a very tall chair cart, certainly not an army in battle array.

Those in the ship might well look contemptuously on such archaic weapons as useless. How *had* those of Ty-Kry taken the other ship and her crew? Was it by wiles and treachery, as the victims might declare, or by clever tricks, as suggested that part of Tamisan who was the Mouth of Olava.

The surface of the ground boiled away under the descent rockets. Then the bright fires vanished, leaving the plain in semidarkness until their eyes adjusted to the lesser light of the torches.

There was no expression of awe by the waiting crowd. Though they might be, by their trappings, dress and arms, accounted centuries behind the technical knowledge of the newcomers, they were braced by their history to know that they were not to face gods of unknown powers, but mortals with whom they had successfully fought before. *What gives them this attitude toward the star rovers,* Tamisan wondered, *and why are they so adverse to any contact with star civilization? Apparently they are content to stagnate at a level of civilization perhaps five hundred years behind my world. Do they not produce any inquiring minds, any who desire to do things differently?*

The ship was down; it gave no outward sign of life, though Tamisan knew its scanners must be busy feeding back what information they gathered to appear on video screens. If those had picked up the derelict ship, the newcomers would have so much of a warning. She glanced from the silent bulk of the newly landed spacer to the Over-queen just in time to see the ruler raise her hand in a gesture. Four men came forward from the ranks of nobles and guards. Unlike the latter, they wore no body armor or helmets, but only short tunics of an unrelieved black. In the hands of each was a bow, not the crossbow of the troops, but the yet older bow of expert archers.

That part of Tamisan which was of this world drew a catch of breath, for those bows were unlike any other in the land and those who held them unlike any other archers. It was no wonder ordinary men and women gave them wide room, for they were a monstrous lot. Over the head of each was fitted so skillfully fashioned a mask that it seemed no mask at all, but his natural features, save that the features were not human; the masks were copies of the great heads, one for each point of the compass, which surmounted the defensive walls of Ty-Kry. Neither human nor animal, they were something of both and something beyond both.

The bows they raised were fashioned of human bone and strung with cords woven of human hair. They were the bones and hair of ancient enemies and ancient heroes; the intermingled strength of both were ready to serve the living.

From closed quivers, each took a single arrow and in the torchlight those arrows glittered, seeming to draw and condense radiance until they were shafts of solid light. Fitted to the cords they had a hypnotic effect, holding one's attention to the exclusion of all else. Tamisan was suddenly aware of that and tried to break the attraction, but at that moment the arrows were fired. And her head turned with all the rest in that company to watch the flight of what seemed to be lines of fire across the dark sky, rising up and up until they were well above the dark ship, then following a curve, to plunge out of sight behind it.

Oddly enough, in their passing they had left great arcs of light behind, which did not fade at once, but cast faint gleams on the skin of the ship. It was ingathering, one part of Tamisan's mind knew. A laying on of ancient power to influence those in the spacer. That of her which was a dreamer could not readily believe in the efficacy of any such ceremony.

There had been sound with those arrows' passing, a shrill, high whistling which hurt the ears so that those in the throng put hands to the sides of their heads to shut out the screech. A wind arose out of nowhere, with it a loud crackling. Tamisan looked up to see above the Over-queen's head a large bird flapping wings of gold and blue. A closer look revealed it was no giant bird, but rather a banner so fashioned that the wind set it flying to counterfeit live action.

The black-clad archers still stood in a line a little out from the ranks of the guards. Now, though the Over-queen made no visible sign, those about Hawarel and Tamisan urged them forward until they came to front both the archers and the Over-queen's tall throne-cart.

"Well, Champion, is it in your mind to carry out the duties this busy Mouth has assigned you?" There was jeering in the Over-queen's question, as if she did not honestly believe in Tamisan's prophecy but was willing to allow a dupe to march to destruction in his own way.

Hawarel went to one knee, but as he did so he swung his empty sword sheath across his knee, making very visible the fact that he lacked a weapon.

"At your desire, Great One, I stand ready. But is it your will that my battle be without even steel between me and the enemy?"

Tamisan saw a smile on the lips of the Over-queen and at that moment glimpsed a little into this ruler, that it might just please her to will such a fate on Hawarel. But if the Over-queen played with that thought for an instant or two, she put it aside. Now she gestured.

"Give him steel, and let him use it. The Mouth has said he is the answer to our defense this time. Is that not so, Mouth?"

The look she gave to Tamisan had a cruel core.

"He has been chosen in the farseeing, and twice has it read so." Tamisan found the words to answer in a firm voice, as if what she said was a decree.

The Over-queen laughed. "Be firm, Mouth; put your will behind this choice of yours. In fact, do you go with him, to give him the support of Olava!"

Hawarel had accepted a sword from the officer on his left. He rose to his feet and, swinging the blade, he saluted with a flourish which suggested that, if he knew he were going to extinction, he intended to march there as one who moved to trumpet and drums.

"The right be strength to your arm, a shield to your body," intoned the Over-queen. There was that in her voice which one might detect to mean that the words she spoke were only ritual, not intended to encourage this champion.

Hawarel turned to face the silent ship. From the burned and blasted ground about its landing fins arose trails of steam and smoke. The faint arcs left in the air from the arrow flights were gone.

As Hawarel moved forward, Tamisan followed a pace or two behind. If the ship remained closed to them, if no hatch opened, no ramp ran forth, she did not see how they could carry out their plans. If that were so, would the Over-queen expect them to wait hour after hour for some decision from the spacer's commander as to whether or not he would contact them?

Fortunately, the space crew were more enterprising. Perhaps the sight of that hulk on the edge of the field had given them the need to learn more. The hatch which opened was not the large entrance hatch, but a smaller door above one of the fins. From it shot a stunner beam.

Luckily it caught its prey, both Hawarel and Tamisan, before they had reached the edge of the sullenly burning turf so that their suddenly helpless bodies did not fall into the fire. They did not lose consciousness, but only the ability to control slack muscles.

Tamisan had crumpled face down, and only the fact that one cheek pressed the earth gave her room to breathe. Her sight was sharply curtailed at the edge of burning grass which crept inexorably toward her. Seeing that she forgot all else.

These moments were the worse she had ever spent. She had conjured up narrow escapes in dreams, but always there had been the knowledge that at the last moment escape was possible. Now there was no escape, only her helpless body and the line of advancing fire.

With the suddenness of a blow, delivering shock through her still painful bruises, she was caught, right side and left, in what felt like giant pincers. As those closed about her body, she was drawn aloft, still face down, the fumes and heat of the burning vegetation choking her. She coughed until the spasms made her sick, spinning in that brutal clutch, being drawn to the spacer.

She came into a burst of dazzling light. Then hands seized her, pulling her down, but holding her upright. The force of the stunner was wearing off; they must have set the beam on lowest power. There was a prickle of feeling returning in her legs and her heavy arms. She was able to lift her head a fraction to see men in space uniforms about her. They wore helmets as if expecting to issue out on a hostile world, and some of them had the visors closed. Two picked her up easily and carried her along, down a corridor, before dropping her without any gentleness in a small cabin with a suspicious likeness to a cell.

Tamisan lay on the floor recovering command of her own body and trying to think ahead. Had they taken Hawarel, too? There was no reason to believe they had not, but he had not been put in this cell. She was able to sit up now, her back supported by the wall, and she smiled shakily at her thought that their brave boast of a championship battle had certainly been brought quickly to naught. It was not that what the Over-queen desired might have run far counter to what happened, but she and Starrex had gained this much of their own objective: they were in the ship she believed also held Kas. Only let the three of them make contact, and they could leave the dream. *And, would our leaving shatter this dream world? How real is it?* She was sure of nothing, and there was no reason to worry over side issues. The time had come to concentrate upon one thing only: Kas.

What should I do? Pound on the door of this cell to demand attention, to speak with the commander of this ship? Would she ask to see all the crew so she could pick out Kas in his this-world masquerade? She had a suspicion that while Hawarel-Starrex had accepted her story, no one else might.

The important thing was some kind of action to get her free and let her search.

The door was opening. Tamisan was startled by what seemed a quick answer to her need.

There was no helmet on the man who stood there, though he wore a tunic bearing the insignia of a higher officer, slightly different from that Tamisan knew from her own Ty-Kry. He also had a stunner aimed at her; at his throat was the box of a vocal interpreter.

"I come in peace."

"With a weapon in hand?" she countered.

He looked surprised; he must have expected a foreign tongue in answer, but she had replied in the Basic which was the second language of all Confederacy planets.

"We have reason to believe that weapons are necessary with your people. I am Glandon Tork of Survey."

"I am Tamisan and a Mouth of Olava." Her hand went to her head and discovered that somehow, in spite of her passage through the air and her entrance into the ship, her crown was still there. Then she pressed the important question:

"Where is the champion?"

"Your companion?" The stunner was no longer centered on her and his tone had lost some of its belligerency. "He is in safe keeping. But why do you name him champion?"

"Because that is what he is—come to engage *your* selected champion in right battle."

"I see. And we select a champion in return, is that it? What is right battle?"

She answered his last question first. "If you claim land, you meet the champion of the lordship of that land in right battle."

"But we claim no land," he protested.

"You made claim when you set your fiery ship down on the fields of Ty-Kry."

"Your people then consider our landing a form of invasion? But this can be decided by a single combat between champions? And we pick our man . . ."

Tamisan interrupted him. "Not so. The Mouth of Olava selects; or rather the sand selects, the seeing selects. That is why I have come, though you did not greet me in honor."

"You select the champion how?"

"As I have said, by the seeing."

"I do not see, but doubtless it will be made plain in the proper time. And where then is this combat fought?"

She waved to what she thought were the ship walls. "Out there, on the land being claimed."

"Logical," he conceded. Then he spoke as if to the air around them. "All that recorded?" Since the air did not answer him, he was apparently satisfied by silence.

"This is your custom, Lady, Mouth of Olava. But since it is not ours, we must discuss it. By your leave, we shall do so."

"As you wish." She had this much on her side, he had introduced himself as a member of Survey, which meant that he had been trained in the necessity of understanding alien folkways. The simple underlying principle of such training was, wherever possible, to follow planet customs. If the crew did accept this idea of championship, then they might also be willing to follow it completely. She could demand to see every member of the crew and thus find Kas. Once that was done, she could break dream.

But, Tamisan told herself, *do not count on too easy an end to this venture.* There was a nagging little doubt lurking in the back of her mind, and it had something to do with those death arrows, and the hulk of the derelict. The people of Ty-Kry, seemingly so weakly defended, had managed through centuries to keep their world free of spacers. When she tried to plumb the Tamisan-of-this-world's memories as to how that was accomplished she had no answer but what corresponded to magic forces only partly understood. That the shooting of the arrows was the first step in bringing such forces into being she was aware. Beyond that seemed only to lie a belief akin to her Mouth power, and that she did not understand even when she employed it.

She was accepting all of this, Tamisan realized suddenly, as if this world did exist, as if it was not a dream out of her control. Could Starrex's suggestion be the truth, that they had by some means traveled into an alternate world?

Her patience was growing short; she wanted action. Waiting was very difficult. She was sure that scanners of more than one kind were trained on her and she must play the part of a Mouth of Olava, displaying no impatience, only calm confidence in herself and her mission. That she held to as best she could.

Perhaps the time she waited seemed longer than it really was, but Tork returned to usher her out of the cell and escort her up a ladder from level to level. She found the long skirts of her robe difficult to manage. The cabin they came into was large and well furnished, and there were several men seated there. Tamisan looked from one to another searchingly. She could not tell; she felt none of the uneasiness she had known in the throne room when Hawarel had been there. Of course, that could mean Kas was not one of this group, though a Survey ship did not carry a large crew, mainly specialists of several different callings. There were probably ten, perhaps twenty more than the six before her.

Tork led her to a chair which had some of the attributes of an easirest, molding to her comfort as she settled into it.

"This is Captain Lowald, Medico Thrum, Psycho-Tech Sims and Hist-Techneer El Hamdi." Tork named names and each man acknowledged with a half bow. "I have outlined your proposal to them and they have discussed the matter. By what means will you select a champion from among us?"

She had no sand; for the first time Tamisan realized the handicap. She would have to depend upon touch alone, but somehow she was sure that would reveal Kas to her.

"Let your men come to me, touching hand to mine." She raised hers to lay it, palm up, on the table. "When I clasp that of he whom Olava selects, I shall know it."

"It seems simple enough," the Captain returned. "Let us do as the lady suggests." And he leaned forward to rest his own for a minute on hers. There was no response, nor was there any in the others. The Captain called an order on the intercom and one by one, the other members of the crew came to her, touching palm to palm. Tamisan, with mounting uneasiness, began to believe she had erred; perhaps only by the sand could she detect Kas. Though she searched the face of each as he took his seat opposite her and laid his hand on hers, she could see no resemblance to Starrex's cousin, nor was there any inner warning her man was here.

"That was the last," the Captain said as the final man arose. "Which is our champion?"

"He is not here." She blurted out the truth, her distress breaking through her caution.

"But you have touched hands with every man on board this ship," the Captain answered her. "Or is this some trick?" He was interrupted by a sound sharp enough to startle. The numbers which spilled from the com by his elbow meant nothing to Tamisan, but brought the rest in that cabin into instant action. A stunner in Tork's hand caught her before she could rise, and once more she was conscious but unable to move. As the other officers pushed through the door on the run, Tork put out his hand, holding her limp body erect in the chair, while with the other he thumped some alarm button set into the table.

His summons was speedily answered by two crewmen who carried her along, to thrust her once more into a cabin. *This is getting to be far too regular a procedure,* Tamisan thought ruefully, as they tossed her negligently on a bunk, hardly pausing to see if she landed safely on its surface or not. Whatever that alert had meant, it had certainly once more brought her to the status of prisoner. Apparently sure of the stunner beam, her guard went out, leaving the door open a crack so that she could hear the pad of running feet and the clangs of what could be secondary alarms.

What possible attack could the forces of the Over-queen have launched against a well-armed and already alert spacer? Yet it was plain that those men believed themselves in danger and were on the defensive. *Starrex and Kas. Where is Kas?* The Captain said she had met all on board. Did that mean that the vision she had earlier seen was false, that the faceless man in spacer dress was a creature of her too-active imagination?

I must not lose confidence. Kas is here, he has to be! She lay now trying vainly to guess by the sounds what was happening. But the first flurry of noise and movement were stilled, there was only silence. *Hawarel, where is Hawarel?*

The stunner's power was wearing off. She had pulled herself up somewhat groggily when the door of the cabin shot into its wall crack and Tork and the Captain stood there.

"Mouth of Olava, or whatever you truly are," the Captain said, with a chill in his voice which reminded Tamisan of Hawarel's earlier rage, "the winning of time may not have been of your devising, this nonsense of champions and right battle, or perhaps it was. Your superiors perhaps deceived you, too. At any rate, now it does not matter. They have done their best to make us prisoners and will not reply now to our signals for a parley, so we must use you for our messenger. Tell your ruler that we hold her champion and we can readily use him as a key to open gates shut in our faces. We have weapons beyond swords and spears, even beyond those which might not have saved those in that other ship. She can tie us here for a measure of time, but we can sever such bonds. We have not come as invaders, no matter what you believe, nor are we alone. If our signal does not reach our sister ship in orbit above, there will be such an accounting as your race has not seen, nor can conceive of. We shall release you now and you shall tell your Queen this. If she does not send those to talk with us before the dawn, then it will be the worse for her. Do you understand?"

"And Hawarel?" Tamisan asked.

"Hawarel?"

"The champion. You will keep him here?"

"As I have said, we have the means to make him a key for your fortress doors. Tell her that, Mouth. From what we have read in your champion's mind, you have certain authority here which ought to impress your Queen."

Read from Starrex's mind? What do they mean? Tamisan was suddenly fearful. *Some kind of mind probe? But if they did that, then they must know the rest.* She was utterly confused now, and found it very hard to center her attention on the matter at hand, that she must relay this defiant message to the Over-queen. Since there seemed to be nothing she could do to protest that action, she would do so. *What reception might I have in Ty-Kry?* Tamisan shuddered as Tork pulled her from the bunk and half carried, half led her along.

❋ ❋ VI ❋ ❋

FOR THE THIRD TIME, Tamisan sat in prison but this time she looked not at the smooth walls of a spaceship cabin, but at the ancient stones of the High Castle ringing her in. Captain Lowald's estimation of her influence with the Over-queen had fallen far short, and her plea in favor of a parley with the spacemen had been overruled at once. The threat concerning their strange weapons and their mysterious use of Hawarel as a "key" was laughed at. The fact that those of Ty-Kry had successfully dealt with this menace in the past made them confident that their same devices would serve as well now. What those devices were Tamisan had no idea, save that something had happened to the ship before she had been unceremoniously bundled out of it.

Hawarel they had kept on board, Kas had disappeared, and until she had both to hand she was indeed a captive. Kas . . . her thoughts kept turning back to the fact that he had not been among those who had faced her. Lowald had assured her that she had seen all his crew.

Wait! She set herself to recall his every word. *What had he said?* *"You have touched hand with every man aboard this ship."* But he had not said all the crew. *Had there been one outside the ship?* All she knew of space travel she had learned from tapes, but those had been very detailed as they needed to be to supply the dreamers with factual background and inspiration from which to build fantasy worlds. This spacer claimed to be a Survey vessel and not operating alone. *Therefore, it might have a companion in orbit and there Kas could be.* But, if that were so, she had no chance of reaching him.

Now if this were only a true dream . . . Tamisan sighed, leaned her head back against the dank stone of the wall, and then jerked away from that support as its chill struck into her shoulders. *Dreams* . . .

She sat upright, alert and a little excited. *Suppose I could dream within a dream and find Kas that way? Is it possible? You cannot tell until you proved it one way or another.* She had no stabilizer, no booster, but those were only needed when a dream was shared. She might venture as well on her own. *But, if I dreamed within a dream, can I do aught to set matters right? Why ask questions I cannot answer until it is put to proof!*

She stretched out on the stones of the cell floor resolutely blocking off those portions of her mind which were aware of the present discomfort of her body. Instead, she began the deep, even breathing of a dreamer, fastened her thoughts on the pattern of self-hypnosis, which was the door to her dreams. All she had as a goal was Kas and he as he was in his real person. *So poor a guide* . . .

She was going under; she could still dream.

Walls built up around her, but these were of a translucent material through which flowed soft and pleasing colors. It could not be a spaceship. Then the scene wavered and swiftly Tamisan thrust aside that doubt which might puncture the dream fabric. The walls sharpened and fixed into a solid state; this was a corridor, facing her was a door.

She willed to see beyond and was straightway, after the manner of a proper dream, in that chamber. Here, the walls were hung with the same sparkling web of stuff which had lined her chamber in the sky tower. Seeking Kas, she had returned to her own world. But she held the dream, curious as to why her aim had brought her here. Had she been wrong and Kas had never come with her? If that were so, why had she and Starrex been marooned in the other dream?

There was no one in the chamber, but she felt a faint pull drawing her on. She sought Kas; there was that which promised he was here. There was a second room; entering, she was startled. This she knew well: it was the room of a dreamer. Kas stood by an empty couch, while the other was occupied.

The dreamer wore a sharing crown, but what rested on the other couch was not a second sleeper, but a squat box of metal to which her dream cords were attached and Tamisan was not the dreamer. She had expected to see herself. Instead, the entranced was one of the locked minds, the blankness of her countenance unmistakable. Dream force was being created here by an indreamer, and seemingly it was harnessed to the box.

Given such clues, Tamisan projected the rest. This

was not the same dreaming chamber where she had fallen asleep; it was a smaller room. Kas was very much awake, intent upon some dials on the top of the box. The indreamer and the box, locked so together, could be holding them in the other world. *But what of that faint vision of Kas in uniform? To mislead me? Or is this a misleading dream, dictated by the suspicions I detected in Starrex concerning his cousin?* This was the logical reasoning from such suspicions, that she had been sent with Starrex into a dream world and therein locked by an indreamer and machine. *Real, or dream . . . which?*

Am I now visible to Kas? If this were a dream, she should be; if she had come back to reality . . . Her head reeled under the listing of things which might be true, untrue, half true. To prove at least one small fraction, she moved forward and laid her hand on Kas's as he leaned over to make some small adjustment to the box.

He gave a startled exclamation, jerked his hand from under hers and glanced around. But, though he stared straight at her, it was plain he saw nothing; she was as disembodied as a spirit in one of the old tales. *Yet, if he has not seen me, still he has felt something . . .*

Again, he leaned over the box, eyeing it intently as if he thought he must have felt some shock or emanation from it. The dreamer never moved. Save for the slow rise and fall of her breathing, which told Tamisan she was indeed deep in her self-created world, she might have been dead. Her face was very wan and colorless. Seeing that, Tamisan was uneasy. This tool of Kas's had been far too long in an uninterrupted dream. She would have to be awakened if she made no move to break it for herself. One of the dangers of indreaming was this possible loss of the power to break a dream. That occurring, the guardian must break it. Most of the dreamers' caps provided the necessary stimuli to do so. But the cap on this dreamer's head had certain modifications Tamisan had never seen before, and these might prevent breaking.

What would happen if Tamisan could evoke waking? Would that also release her and Starrex, wherever he might be, from *their* dream and return them to the proper world? She was well drilled in the technique of dream breaking. Those she had used when she stood in reality beside a victim who had overstayed the proper dream time.

She reached out a hand, touched the pulse on the sleeper's throat and applied slight massage. But, though her hands seemed corporeal and solid to her, there was no response in the other. To prove a point, Tamisan aimed a finger, thrusting it deeply as she could into the pillow on which the dreamer's head rested. Her finger did not dent that soft roundness, but went into it as if her flesh and bone had no substance.

There was yet another way; it was harsh and used only in cases of extremity. But to Tamisan this could be no else. She put those unsubstantial fingers on the temples of the sleeper, just below the rim of the dream cap, and concentrated on a single command.

The sleeper stirred, her features convulsed and a low moan came from her. Kas uttered an exclamation and hung over his box, his fingers busy pushing buttons with a care which suggested he was about a very delicate task.

"Awake!" Tamisan commanded with such force as she could summon.

The sleeper's hands arose very slowly and unsteadily from her sides and they wavered toward the cap, though her eyelids did not rise. Her expression was now one of pain. Kas, breathing hard and fast, kept to his adjustments on the box.

So they fought their silent-battle for possession of the dreamer. Slowly, Tamisan was forced to concede that whatever force lay in that box overrode all the techniques she knew. But the longer Kas kept this poor wretch under, the weaker she would grow. Death would be the answer, though perhaps that did not trouble him.

If she could not wake the dreamer and break the bonds which she was certain now were what tied her and Starrex to that other world, then she must somehow get at Kas himself. He had responded to her touch before.

Tamisan slipped away from the head of the couch and came to stand behind Kas. He straightened up, a faint relief mirrored on his face as apparently his box reported that there was no longer any disturbance.

Now Tamisan raised her hands to either side of his head, spreading wide her fingers so they might resemble the covering of a dreamer's cap, and then brought them swiftly down to cover his head, putting firm touch on his temples though she could not exert real pressure there.

He gave a muffled cry, tossed his head from side to side as if to free himself from a cloud. But Tamisan, with all the determination of which she was capable, held fast. She had seen this done once in the Hive; however, then it had been used on a docile subject and both the controlled and the dreamer had been on the same plane of existence. Now, she could only hope that she could disrupt Kas's train of thought long enough to make him release the dreamer himself. So she brought to bear all her will to that purpose. He was not only shaking his head from side to side now, making it very hard to keep her hands in the proper position, but he was swaying back and forth, his hands up, clawing as if to tear her hold away. It appeared he could not touch her any more than she could lay firm grip on him.

That fund of energy which had enabled her to create strange worlds and hold them for a fellow dreamer was bent to the task of influencing Kas. But, to her dismay, though he ceased his frenzied movements, his clawing for the hands he could not clutch growing feebler, his eyes closed and his face screwed into an expression of horror and rejection of a lightened child. He did not move to the box.

Instead, he slumped forward so suddenly that Tamisan was taken wholly unaware, falling half across the divan. In that fall, he flailed out with an arm to send the box smashing to the floor, its weight dragging the cap from the dreamer.

She drew several deep breaths, her haggard face now displaying a small trace of returning color. Tamisan, still startled at the results of her efforts to influence Kas, began to wonder if she might have made matters worse. She did not know how much the box had to do with their transportation to the alternate world and whether, if it was broken, they could ever return.

There was one precaution, if she could take it. *If I*

return to that prison cell in the High Castle, I must, or leave Starrex-Hawarel lost forever, then to leave Kas here, perhaps able again to use his machine, no! But how, since I cannot?. . .

Tamisan looked to the stirring dreamer. The girl was struggling out of the depths of so deep a state of unconsciousness that she was not aware of what lay about her. In this state she might be pliable. Tamisan could only try.

Leaving Kas, she went back to the dreamer. Once more touching the girl's forehead, she sought to influence her.

The dreamer sat up with such slow movements of body as one might use were almost unbearable weights fastened to every muscle. In a painfully slow gesture, she raised her hands to her head, groping for the cap no longer there. Then she sat, her eyes still shut, while Tamisan drew heavily on her own strength to deliver a final set of orders.

Blindly, for she never opened her eyes, the dreamer felt along the edge of the couch on which she had lain until her hand swept against the cords which fastened the cap to the box. Her lax fingers fumbled and tightened as she gave a feeble jerk, then another until both cords pulled free. Holding those still in one hand, she slipped from the couch in a forward movement that brought her to her knees, the upper part of her body on the other couch, one cheek touching that of the unconscious Kas.

The strain on Tamisan was very great. She was wavering in her control now, several times those weak hands fell limply as her hold on the dreamer ebbed. But each time she found some small surge of energy which brought them back into action again so that, at last, the cap was on Kas, the cords which had connected it to the box in a half coil on which the dreamer's head rested.

So big a chance and with such poor equipment! Tamisan could not be sure of any results, she could only hope. Tamisan released her command of the dreamer who lay against the couch on one side as Kas half lay on the other. She summoned all that she had, all that she sensed she had always possessed, that small difference in dream power she had secretly cherished. Once more she touched the forehead of the sleeping girl and broke her dream within a dream.

It was like climbing a steep hill with an intolerably heavy burden lashed to one's aching back, like being forced to pull the dead weight of another body through a swamp which sucked one down. It was such an effort as she could not endure . . .

Then that weight was gone and the relief of its vanishing was such that Tamisan savored the fact that it did not drag at her. She opened her eyes at last and even that small movement required such an effort that it left her spent. She was not in the sky tower. These walls were stone, and the light was dusky, coming from a slit high in the opposite all. She was in the High Castle from which she had earned her way back to her own Ty-Kry in a dream within dream. But how well had she wrought there?

For the present, she was too tired to even think connectedly. Bits and pieces of all she had seen and done since she had awakened first in this Ty-Kry floated through her mind, not making any concrete pattern.

It was the mind picture of Hawarel's face as she had seen last while they marched toward the spacer which roused her from that uncaring drift. She remembered Hawarel and the threat the ship's Captain had made, which the Over-queen had pushed aside. If Tamisan had truly broken the lock Kas had set up to keep them here, then it would be escape. There was no strength in her. She tried to remember the formula for breaking, and knew a stroke of chilling fear when her memory proved faulty. She could not do it now; she must have more time to rest both mind and body. Now she was hungry and thirsty, with such a need for both food and drink that it was a torment. *Do they mean to leave me here without any sustenance?*

Tamisan lay still, listening. Then she inched her head up slowly to view the deeper dusk of her surroundings at floor level. She was not alone.

Kas!

Had she successfully pulled Kas with her? If so, was it the Kas that had no counterpart in this world and so was still his old self?

She did not have time to explore that possibility; there was a loud grating and a line of light marking an opening door. In the beam of a torch, stood that same officer who had earlier been her escort. Using her hands to brace her body, Tamisan raised herself. At the same time there was a cry from the far corner.

Someone moved there, raised a head and showed features she had last seen in the sky tower. It was Kas in his rightful body. He was scrambling to his feet and the officer and the guardsman behind him in the doorway stared as if

they could not believe their eyes. Kas shook his head as if
to clear away some mist.

His lips pulled back from his teeth in a terrible rictus
which was no smile. There was a small laser in his hand.
Tamisan could not move; he was going to burn her. In that
moment, she was so sure of this she did not even fear, but
only waited for the crisping of her flesh.

But the aim of the weapon raised beyond her and
fastened on the doorway. Under it, both officer and guard
went down. With one hand on the wall to steady himself,
Kas pulled along until he came to her. He stood away from
the stone, transferred his laser to the other hand and
reached down to hook fingers in the robe where it covered
her shoulder.

"On . . . your . . . feet." He mouthed the words with
difficulty, as if his exhaustion nearly equaled hers. "I do
not know how, or why, or who. . . ."

The torch, dropped from the charred hand that had
carried it, gave them dim light. Kas swung her around,
thrusting his face very close to hers. He stared at her
intently, as if by the very force of his glare he could strip
aside the mask her body made for her and force the old
Tamisan into sight.

"You are Tamisan—it cannot be otherwise! I do not
know how you did this, demon-born." He shook her with
a viciousness that struck her painfully against the wall.
"Where is he?"

All that came from her parched throat were harsh
sounds without meaning.

"Never mind." Kas stood straighter now; there was
more vigor in his voice. "Where he is, there shall I find

him. Nor shall I lose you, demon-born, since you are my way back. And for Lord Starrex, here there will be no guards, no safe shields. Perhaps this is the better way after all. What is this place? answer me!" He slapped her face, his palm bruising her, once more thumping her head back against the wall so that the rim of the Mouth crown bit into her scalp and she cried out in pain.

"Speak! Where is this?"

"The High Castle of Ty-Kry," she croaked.

"And what you do in this hole?"

"I am prisoner to the Over-queen."

"Prisoner? What do you mean? You are a dreamer; this is your dream. Why are you a prisoner?"

Tamisan was so shaken she could not marshal words easily, as she had to explain to Starrex. She thought, a little dazedly, that Kas might not accept her explanation anyway.

"Not . . . wholly . . . a dream," she got out.

He did not seem surprised. "So the control has that property, has it; to impose a sense of reality." His eyes blazed into hers. "You cannot control this dream, is that it? Again, fortune favors me it seems. Where is Starrex now?"

She could give him a truthful answer she was glad, as it seemed to her she could not speak falsely with any hope of belief. It was as if he could see straight into her mind with those demanding eyes of his. "I do not know."

"But he is in this dream somewhere?"

"Yes."

"Then you shall find him for me, Tamisan, and speedily. Do we have to search this High Castle?"

"He was, when I saw him last, outside."

She kept her eyes turned from the door, from what lay there. But he hauled her toward that, and she was afraid she was going to be sick. Where they might be in the interior of the small city which was the High Castle she did not know. These who had brought her here had not taken her to the core towers, but had turned aside along the first of the gateways and gone down a long flight of stairs. She doubted if they would be able to walk out again as easily as Kas thought to do.

"Come." He pulled at her, dragging her on, kicked aside what lay in the door. She closed her eyes tightly as he brought her past. But the stench of death was so strong that she staggered, retching, with his hand dragging at her, keeping her on her feet and reeling ahead.

Twice, she watched glassily as he burned down opposition. His luck at keeping surprise on his side held. They came to the foot of the stairs and climbed. Tamisan held to one hope. Now that she was on her feet and moving, she found a measure of strength returning, so that she no longer feared falling if Kas released his hold upon her. When they were out at last in the night, the damp smell of the underways wafted away by a rising wind, she felt clean and renewed and was able to think more clearly.

Kas had gotten her this far because of her weakness, so to his eyes she must continue to counterfeit that, until she had a chance to act. It might be that his weapon, so alien to this world and thus so effective, might well cut their way to Starrex. That did not mean that once they had reached him she need obey Kas. She felt that, face to face with his lord, Kas would be less confident of success.

It was not a guard that halted them now but a massive gate. Kas examined the bar and laughed before he raised the laser and sent a needle-thin beam to cut as he needed. There was a shout from above and Kas, almost languidly, swung the beam to a narrow stair leading from the ramparts, laughing again as there came a choked scream, the sound of a falling body.

"Now." Kas put his shoulder to the gate and it swung more easily than Tamisan would have thought possible for its weight. "Where is Starrex? And if you lie . . ." His smile was threatening.

"There." Tamisan was sure of her direction, and she pointed to where there was a distant blaze of torches about the bulk of the grounded spacer.

VII

"A SPACER!" Kas paused.

"Besieged by these people," Tamisan informed him. "And Starrex is a hostage on board, if he still lives. They have threatened to use him in some manner as a weapon and the Over-queen, as far as I know, does not care."

Kas turned on her, his merriment had vanished; his laugh was now a snarl and he shook her back and forth. "It is your dream; control it!"

For a moment Tamisan hesitated. Should she try to tell him what she believed the truth? Kas and his weapon might be her only hope of reaching Starrex. Could he be persuaded to a frontal attack if he thought that was their only chance of reaching their goal? On the other hand, if she admitted she could not break this dream, he might well burn her down out of hand and take his chances. She thought she had a solution.

"Your meddling has warped the pattern, Lord Kas. I cannot control some elements, nor can I break the dream until I have Lord Starrex with me, since we are pattern-linked in this sequence."

Her steady reply seemed to have some effect on him. Though he gave her one more punishing shake and uttered an obscenity, he looked ahead to the torches and the half-seen bulk of the ship with calculation in his eyes.

They made a lengthy detour away from most of the torches, coming up across the open land to the south of the ship. There was a graying in the sky and a hint that perhaps dawn might be not far away. Now that they could see better, it was apparent that the ship was sealed. No hatch opened on its surface, no ramp ran out. The laser in Kas's hand could not burn their way in by the method he had opened the gate of the High Castle.

Apparently, the same difficulty presented itself to Kas for he halted her with a jerk while they were still in the shadows, well away from the line of torches forming a square around the ship. Surveying the scene, they sheltered in a small dip in the ground.

The torches were no longer held by men, but had been planted in the ground at regular intervals, and they were as large as outsize candles. The colorful mass which had marked the Over-queen and her courtiers on Tamisan's first visit to the landing field were gone, leaving only a line of guardsmen in a wide encirclement of the sealed ship.

Why did the spacemen not lift and planet elsewhere, Tamisan wondered. Perhaps the confusion in the last moments she had been on board meant that they could not do so. They had spoken then of a sister ship in orbit above. It would seem that had made no move to aid them, though she had no idea how much time had elapsed since last she had been here.

Kas turned on her again. "Can you get a message to Starrex?" he demanded.

"I can try. For what reason?"

"Have him ask for us to come to him." Kas had been silent for a moment before replying. *Is he so stupid as to believe that I would not give a warning with whatever message I could deliver, or has he precautions against that?*

But can I reach Starrex? She had gone into the secondary dream to make contact with Kas. There was no time for such a move now. She could only use the mental technique for inducing a dream and see what happened thereby. She said as much to Kas now, promising no success.

"Be about what you can do now!" he told her roughly.

Tamisan closed her eyes to think of Hawarel as she had seen him last, standing beside her on this very field. She heard a gasp from Kas. Opening her eyes, she saw Hawarel even as he had been then, or rather a pallid copy of him, wavering and indistinct, already beginning to fade, so she spoke in a swift gabble.

"Say we come from the Queen with a message, that we must see the Captain."

The shimmering outline of Hawarel faded into the night. She heard Kas mutter angrily. "What good will that ghost do?"

"I cannot tell. If he returns to that of which he is a part, he can carry the message. For the rest . . ." Tamisan shrugged. "I have told you this is no dream I can control.

Do you think if it were, we two would stand here in this fashion?"

His thin lips parted in one of his mirthless grins.

"You would not, I know, dreamer!"

His head went from left to right as he slowly surveyed the line of planted torches and the men standing on guard between them. "Do we move closer to this ship, expect them to open to us?"

"They used a stunner to take us before," Tamisan warned him. "They might do so again."

"Stunner." He gestured with the laser. Tamisan hoped his answer would not be a headlong attack on the ship with that.

He used it as a pointer to motion her on toward the torch line. "If they do open up," he commented, "I shall be warned."

Tamisan gathered up the long skirt of her robe. It was torn by rough handling, frayed in strips at the hem where she could trip if she caught those rags between her feet. The rough brush growing knee high about them caught at it so that she stumbled now and again, urged on continually by Kas's pulling, when he dug his fingers painfully into her already bruised shoulder.

They reached the torch line. The guards there faced inward to the ship and in this crease of light, Tamisan could see that they were all armed with crossbows, not with those of bone which the black-dressed men had earlier worn. Bolts against the might of the ship. The answer seemed laughable, a jesting to delight the simple. Yet the ship lay there and Tamisan could well remember the consternation of those men who had been questioning her within it.

There was a dark spot on the hull of the ship and a hatch suddenly swung open. She recognized it as a battle hatch, though she had only seen those via tapes.

"Kas, they are going to fire." With a laser beam from there they could crisp everything on this field, perhaps clear back to the walls of the High Castle!

She tried to turn in his grasp, to race back and away, knowing already that such a race was lost before she took the first lunging stride. He held her fast.

"No muzzle," he said.

Tamisan strained to see through the flickering light. Perhaps it was a lightening of the sky which made it clear that there was no muzzle projecting to spew a fiery death across them all. But that was a gunport.

As quickly as it had appeared, the opening was closed. The ship was again sealed tightly.

"What?"

Kas answered her half question, "Either they cannot use it, or else they have thought better of doing so, which means, by either count, we have a chance. Now, stay you here! Or else I shall come looking for you in a manner you shall not relish; never fear that I can find you!" Nothing in Tamisan disputed that.

She stood; for after all, apart from Kas's threats, where did she have to go? If she were sighted by any of the guards, she might either be returned to prison or dealt with summarily in another fashion. She had to reach Starrex if she were to escape.

She watched Kas make good use of the interest which riveted the eyes of the guards on the ship. He crept, with more ease than she thought possible for one used to the luxury of the sky towers, behind the nearest man.

What weapon he used, she could not see; it was not the laser. Instead, he straightened to his full height behind the unsuspecting guard, reached out an arm and seemed only to touch the stranger on the neck. Immediately, the fellow collapsed without a sound, though Kas caught him before he had fallen to the ground and dragged him backward to slight depression in the field where Tamisan waited.

"Quick," Kas ordered, "give me his cloak and helmet."

He ripped off his own tunic with its extravagantly padded shoulders, while Tamisan knelt to fumble with a great brooch and free the cloak from the guard. Kas snatched it out of her hands, dragged the rest of it loose from under the limp body, and pulled it around him, taking up the helmet and settling it on his head with a tap. Then he picked up the crossbow.

"Walk before me," he told Tamisan. "If they have a field scanner on in the ship, I want them to see a prisoner under guard. That may bring them to a parley. It is a thin chance, but our best."

He could not guess that it might be a better chance than he hoped, Tamisan knew, since he did not know that she had been once within the ship and the crew might be expecting some such return with a message from the Over-queen. But to walk out boldly past the line of torches, surely Kas's luck would not hold so well; they would be seen by the other guards before they were a quarter of the way to the ship. However she had no other proposal to offer in exchange.

This was no adventure such as she had lived through in dreams. She believed that if she died now, she died indeed and would not wake unharmed in her own world. Her flesh crawled with a fear which made her mouth go dry and her hands quiver as they held wet upon the folds of her robe. *Any second now, I will feel the impact of a bolt, hear a shout of discovery, be . . .*

But still Tamisan tottered forward and heard, with alerted ears, the faint crunch of boots which was Kas behind her. His contempt for a danger that was only too real for her made her wonder, fleetingly, if he did indeed still believe this a dream she could control, and need not then watch for anyone but her. She could not summon words to tell him of his woeful mistake.

So intent was she upon some attack from behind that she was not really conscious of the ship toward which they went until, suddenly, she saw another of the ports open and steeled herself to feel the numbing charge of a stunner.

However, again the attack she feared did not come. The sky was growing lighter, although there was no sign of sunrise. Instead, the first drops of a storm began to fall. Under the onslaught of moisture from lowering clouds, the torches hissed and sputtered, finally flickering out. The gloom was hardly better than twilight.

They came close enough to the ship to board. When one of the ramps lowered to them, they stood waiting. Tamisan felt the rise of hysterical laughter inside her. *What an anticlimax if the ship refuses to acknowledge us!* They could not stand here forever and there was no way they could battle a way inside. Kas's faith in her communication with the ghost of Hawarel seemed too high.

But even as she was sure they faced failure, there was a sigh of sound from above them. The port hatch wheeled back into the envelope of the ship's wall and a small ramp, hardly more than a steep ladder, swung creaking out, dropped to hit the charred ground not far from them. "Go!" Kas prodded her forward.

With a shrug, Tamisan went. She found it hard to climb with the heavy, frayed skirts dragging her back. But by using her hands to pull along the single rail of the ramp, she made progress. Why had not the rest of the guards along that watching line of torches moved? Had it been that Kas's disguise indeed deceived them, and they thought that Tamisan had been sent under orders to parley a second time with the ship's people?

She was nearly at the hatch now, could see the suited men waiting in the shadows above. They had tanglers ready to fire, prepared to spin the webs to enmesh them both as easily handled prisoners. But before those slimy strands writhed forth to touch (patterned as they were to seek flesh to anchor), both of the waiting spacemen jerked right and left, clutched with already dead hands at the breasts of charred tunics from which arose small, deadly spirals of smoke.

They had expected a guard armed with a bow; they had met Kas's laser, to the same undoing as the guardsmen at the castle. Kas's shoulder in the middle of her back sent her sprawling to land half over the bodies of the two who had awaited them.

She heard a scuffle, was kicked and rolled aside, fighting the folds of her own long skirt, trying to get out of the confines of the hatch pocket. Somehow, on her hands and knees, she made it forward since she could not retreat. Now she fetched up against the wall of a corridor and managed to pull around to face the end of the fight.

The two guards lay dead. But Kas held the laser on a third man. Now, without glancing around, he gave an order which she mechanically obeyed.

"The tangler, here!"

Still on her hands and knees, Tamisan crawled far enough back into the hatch compartment to grip one of those weapons. The second she eyed with awakening need for some protection herself, but Kas did not give her time to reach it.

"Give it to me."

Still holding the laser pointed steadily at the middle of the third spaceman, he groped back with his other hand. *I have no choice, no choice; but I do!*

If Kas thinks he has me thoroughly cowed . . . Swinging the tangler around without taking time to aim, Tamisan pressed the firing button.

The lash of the sticky weaving spun through the air striking the wall, from which it dropped away. Then it struck one arm of the motionless captive, who was still under Kas's threat, and there it clung, across his middle, and on through the air until it caught Kas's gun hand, his middle, his other arm and adhered instantly, tightening with its usual efficiency and tying captor to captive.

Kas struggled against those ever-tightening bands to bring the laser round to bear on Tamisan. Whether he would have used it, even in his white-hot rage, she did not know. It was enough that the tangler made sure she could keep from his line of fire. Having ensnared them enough to render them both harmless for a time, Tamisan drew a deep breath and relaxed somewhat.

She had to be sure of Kas. She had loosed the firing button of the tangler as soon as she saw that he could not use his arms. Now she raised the weapon, and with more of a plan, tied his legs firmly together. He kept on his feet, but he was as helpless as if they had used a stunner on him.

Warily she approached him. Guessing her intent, he went into wild wrigglings, trying to bring the adhesive tangler strands in contact with her flesh also. But she stooped and tore at the frayed hem of her robe, ripping up a strip as high as her waist and winding it about her arm and wrist to make sure she could not be entrapped.

In spite of his struggles, she managed to get the laser out of his hold and for the second time knew a surge of great relief. He made no sound, but his eyes were wild and his lips so tightly drawn against his teeth that a small trickle of spittle oozed from one corner to wet his chin. Looking at him dispassionately, Tamisan thought him nearly insane at that moment.

The crewman was moving. He hitched along as she swung around with the laser as a warning, his shoulders against the wall keeping him firmly on his feet, his unbound legs giving him more mobility, though the cord of the tangler anchored him to Kas. Tamisan glanced around searching for what he appeared desperate to reach. There was a com box. "Stand where you are!" she ordered.

The threat of the laser kept him frozen. With that still trained on him, she darted small glances over her shoulder to the hatch. Sliding along the wall in turn, the tangler thrust loosely into the front of her belt, she managed to slam the hatch door and give a turn to its locking wheel.

Using the laser as a pointer, she motioned him to the com, but the immobile Kas was too much of an anchor. Dare she face the crewman? There was no other way. She motioned with one hand.

"Stand well away."

He had said nothing during their encounter, but he obeyed with an agility that suggested he liked the sight of that weapon in her hand even less than he had liked it when Kas held it. He stretched to the limit the cord would allow, so she was able to burn it through.

Kas spit out a series of obscenities which were only a meaningless noise as far as Tamisan was concerned. Until he was released, he was no more now than a well-anchored bundle. But the crewman had importance.

Reaching the com before him, she gestured him on to it. She played the best piece she had in this desperate game.

"Where is Hawarel, the native who was brought on board?"

He could lie, of course, and she would not know it. But it seemed he was willing to answer, probably because he thought that the truth would strike her worse than any lie.

"They have him in the lab, conditioning him." He grinned at her with some of the malignancy she had seen in Kas. She remembered the Captain's earlier threat to make of Hawarel a tool to use against the Over-queen and her forces. Was she too late? There was only one road to take and that was the one she had chosen in those few moments when she had taken up the tangler and used it.

She spoke as she might to one finding it difficult to understand her. "You will call, and you will say that Hawarel will be released and brought here."

"Why?" the crewman returned with visible insolence. "What will you do? Kill me? Perhaps, but that will not defeat the Captain's plans; he will be willing to see half the crew burned."

"That may be true," she nodded. Not knowing the Captain, she could not tell whether or not that was a bluff. "But will his sacrifice save his ship?"

"What can you do?" began the crewman, and then he paused. His grin was gone, now he looked at her speculatively. In her present guise she perhaps did not look formidable enough to threaten the ship, but he could not be sure. One thing she knew from her own time and place: a spaceman learned early to take nothing for granted on a new planet. It might be that she did have command over some unknown force.

"What can I do? There is much." She took quick advantage of that hesitation. "Have you been able to raise the ship?" She plunged on, hoping very desperately that her guess was right. "Have you been able to communicate with your other ship or ships in orbit?"

His expression was her answer, one which fanned her hope into a bright blaze of excitement. The ship *was* grounded, and there was some sort of a hold on it which they had not been able to break.

"The Captain won't listen." He was sullen.

"I think he will. Tell him that we get Hawarel here, and himself, or else we shall truly show you what happened to that derelict across the field."

Kas had fallen silent. He was watching her, not with quite the same wariness of the crewman, but with an emotion she was not able to read. Surprise? Did it mask some sly thought of taking over her bluff, captive though he was?

"Talk!" The need for hurry rode Tamisan now. By this time, those above would wonder why their captives had not been brought before them. Also, outside, the Over-queen's men would certainly have reported that Tamisan and a guard had entered the ship; from both sides, enemies might be closing in.

"I cannot set the com," her prisoner answered.

"Tell me then."

"The red button."

But she thought she had seen a slight shift in his eyes. Tamisan raised her hand, to press the green button instead. Without accusing him of the treachery she was sure he had tried, she said again more fiercely, "Talk!"

"Sannard here." He put his lips close to the com. "They, they have me; Rooso and Cambre are dead. They want the native . . ."

"In good condition," hissed Tamisan, "and now!"

"They want him now, in good condition," Sannard repeated. "They threaten the ship."

There came no acknowledgment from the com in return. Had she indeed pressed the wrong button because she was overly suspicious? What was going to happen? She could not wait.

"Sannard." The voice from the com was metallic, without human inflection or tone.

"Sir?"

But Tamisan give the crewman a push which sent him sliding back along the wall until he bumped into Kas and the bonds of both men immediately united to make them one struggling package. Tamisan spoke into the com.

"Captain, I do not play any game. Send me your prisoner or look upon that derelict you see and say to yourself, 'that will be my ship.' For this is so, as true as I stand here now, with your man as my captive. Send Hawarel alone, and pray to whatever immortal powers you recognize that he can so come! Time grows very short and there is that which will act if you do not, to a purpose you shall not relish!"

The crewman, whose legs were still free, was trying to kick away from Kas. But his struggles instead sent them both to the floor in a heaving tangle. Tamisan's hand dropped to her side as she leaned against the wall, breathing heavily. With all her will she wanted to control action as she did in a dream, but only fate did that now.

VIII

THOUGH SHE SAGGED against the wall, Tamisan felt rigid, as if she were in a great encasement of su-steel. As time moved at so slow a pace as not to be measured normally, that prisoning hold on her body and spirit grew. The crewman and Kas had ceased their struggles. She could not see the crewman's face, but that which Kas turned to her had a queer, distorted look. It was as if before her eyes, though not through any skill of hers, he was indeed changing and taking on the aspect of another man. Since her return to the sky tower in the second dream, she had known he was to be feared. In spite of the fact that his body was securely imprisoned, she found herself edging away, as if by the very intentness of that hostile stare he could aim a weapon to bring her down. But he said nothing and lay as broodingly quiet and impassive as though he had foreknowledge of utter failure for her.

She knew so little, Tamisan thought. She who had

always taken pride in her learning, in the wealth of lore she had drawn upon to furnish her memory for action dreaming. The space crew might have some way of flooding this short corridor with a noxious gas, or using a hidden ray linked with a scanner to finish them. Tamisan found herself running her hands along the walls and studying the unbroken surface a little wildly, striving to find where death might enter quietly and unseen.

There was another bulkhead door at the end of the short corridor; at a few paces away from the outer hatch a ladder ascended to a closed trap. Her head turned constantly from one of those entrances to the other, until she regained a firmer control of herself. *They have only to wait to call my bluff . . . only to wait . . .*

Yes! They have waited and they are . . .

The air about her was changing; there was a growing scent in it. It was not unpleasant, but even a fine perfume would have seemed a stench when it reached her nostrils under present conditions. The light which radiated from the juncture of the corridor roof and ceiling was altering. It had been that of a moderately sunlit day; now it was bluish. Under it her own brown skin took on an eerie look. *I have lost my throw! Maybe, if I could open the hatch again, let in the outer air . . .*

Tamisan tottered to the hatch, gripped the locking wheel and brought her strength to bear. Kas was writhing again, trying to break loose from his unwilling partner. Oddly enough, the crewman lay limp, his head rolling when Kas's heaving disturbed his body, but his eyes were closed. At the same time, Tamisan, braced against the wall, her full strength turned on the need for opening the door, knew a flash of surprise. Was it her overvivid imagination alone which made her believe that she was in danger? When she rested for a moment and drew a deep breath . . .

In her startlement, she could have cried out aloud; she did utter a small sound. She was gaining strength, not losing it. She breathed in every lungful of that scented air, and she was breathing deeper and more slowly, as if her body desired such nourishment. It was a restorative.

Kas, too? She turned to glance at him again. Where she breathed deeply, with lessening apprehension, he was gasping, his face ghastly in the change of light. Then, even as she watched, his struggles ended and his head fell back so that he lay as inert as the crewman he sprawled across.

Whatever change was in progress here affected Kas and the crewman, the latter faster than the former, but not her. Now her trained imagination took another leap. Perhaps she had not been so far wrong in threatening those on this ship with danger. Though she had no guess as to how it was done, this could be another strange weapon in the armament of the Over-queen.

Hawarel? The spacemen had probably never intended to send him. *Dare I go to seek him?* Tamisan wavered, one hand on the hatch wheel, looking to the ladder and the other door. If all within this ship had reacted to the strange air, there would be none to stop her. If she fled the ship, she would face the loss of the keys to her own world and might be met by some evil fate at the hands of the Over-queen. She had broken prison, and she had left dead men behind her. As the Mouth of Olava, she shuddered from the judgment which would be rendered one deemed to have practiced wrongful supernatural acts.

Resolutely Tamisan went to the door at the end of the corridor. It was true that she had no choice at all. She must find Starrex and somehow bring him here, so that they three could be together. They must win a small space of time in which to arrange a dream breaking, or she was totally defeated.

She loosened her belt a little so she could draw up her robe through it, shortening its length and leaving her legs freer. There was the tangler and Kas's laser. In addition, there was the mounting feeling of strength and well being, though an inner warning suggested she beware of over-confidence.

The door gave under her push and she looked out upon a scene which first startled and then reassured her. There were crewmen in the corridor. But they lay prone as if they had been caught while on their way to the hatch. Lasers (a slightly different pattern than that Kas had brought) had fallen from their hands, and three of the four wore tanglers. Tamisan picked her way carefully around them, gathering up all the weapons in a fold of her robe, as if she were some maiden in a field plucking an armful of spring flowers. The men were alive, she saw as she stooped closer, but they breathed evenly as if peacefully asleep.

She took one of the tanglers, discarding the one she had used, fearing its charge might be near exhaustion. As for the rest of the collection, she dropped them at the far end of the passageway and turned the beam of Kas's weapon on them, so she left behind a metal mass of no use to anyone.

Her idea of the geography of the ship was scanty. She would simply have to explore and keep exploring until she found Starrex. She would start at the top and work down. She found a level ladder and three times came upon sleeping crewmen. Each time she made sure they were disarmed before she left them.

The blue shade of light was growing deeper, giving a very weird cast to the faces of the sleepers. Making sure her robe was tightly kilted up, Tamisan began to climb. She had reached the third level when she heard a sound, the first she had noted in this too silent ship since she had left the hatchway.

She stopped to listen, deciding it came from somewhere in the level into which she had just climbed. With laser in hand, she tried to use it as a guide, though it was misleading and might have come from any one of the cabins. Each door she passed Tamisan pushed upon. There were more sleepers: some stretched in bunks, others on the floors, seated at tables with their heads lying on them. But she did not halt now to collect weapons; the need to be about her task, free of this ship, built in her as sharp as might a slaver's lash laid across her shrinking shoulders.

Suddenly, the sound grew louder as she came to a last door and pushed it. Now she looked into a cabin not meant for living but perhaps for a kind of death. Two men in plain tunics were crumpled by the threshold as if they had had some limited warning of danger to come and had tried to flee and fell before they could reach the corridor. Behind them was a table and on that, a body, very much alive, struggled with dogged determination against confining straps.

Though his long hair had been clipped and the stubble

of it shaven to expose the full nakedness of his entire scalp, there was no mistaking Hawarel. He not only fought against the clamps and straps which held him to the table, but in addition, he jerked his head with sharp, short pulls, to dislodge disks fastened to his forehead, which were connected to a vast box of a machine that filled one quarter of the cabin.

Tamisan stepped over the inert men, reached the side of the table, and jerked the disks away from the prisoner's head; perhaps his determined struggles had already loosened them somewhat. His mouth had opened and shut as she came to him as if he were forming words she could not hear, or could not voice. But as the apparatus came away in her hands, he gave a cry of triumph.

"Get me loose!" he commanded. She was already examining the underpart of the table for the locking mechanism of the straps and clamps. It was only seconds before she was able to obey his order.

Bare to the waist, he sat upright and she saw beneath, where his shoulders and the upper part of his spine had rested on the table, a complicated series of disks.

"Ah." Before she could move, he scooped up the laser she had laid on the edge of the table when she had freed him. The gesture he made with it might not have been only to indicate the door and the need for hurry, but perhaps also was a warning that with, a weapon in his hands, he now thought he was in command of the situation.

"They sleep everywhere," she told him. "And Kas, he is a prisoner."

"I thought you could not find him; he was not one of the crew."

"He was not. But I have him now, and, with him, we can return."

"How long will it take?" Starrex was down on one knee, searching the two men on the floor. "What preparation will you need?"

"I cannot tell." She gave him the truth. "But how long will these sleep? Their unconsciousness is, I think, some trick of the Over-queen's."

"It came unexpectedly for them," Starrex agreed. "And you may be right that this is only preliminary to taking over the ship. I have learned this much: their instruments and much of their equipment has been affected so they cannot trust them." Hawarel's face was grim under its bluish, dead man's coloring. "Otherwise, I would not have survived this long as myself."

"Let us go!" Now that she had miraculously (or so it seemed to her) succeeded, Tamisan was even more uneasy, wanting nothing to spoil their escape.

They found their way back to the corridor before the hatch while the ship still slept. Starrex knelt by Kas and then looked with astonishment at Tamisan. "But this is the real Kas!"

"It is Kas, real enough," she agreed. "And there is a reason for that. But need we discuss it now? If the Over-queen's men come to take this ship, I tell you her greeting to us may be worse than any you have met here. I remember enough of the Tamisan who is the Mouth of Olava to know that."

He nodded. "Can you break dream now?"

She looked around her a little wildly. *Concentration . . . no, somehow I cannot think so clearly.* It was as if the exultation the fumes of that scented air had awakened in her was draining. With that sapping went what she needed most.

"I . . . I fear not."

"It is simple then." He stopped again to examine the tangle cords. "We shall have to go to where you can." She saw him set the laser on its lowest beam and burn through the cords which united Kas to the crewman, though he did not free his cousin from the rest of his bonds.

But what if we march out of the hatch into a waiting party of the Over-queen's guards? They had the tangler, the laser, and perhaps the half-smile of fortune on their side. They would have to risk it.

Tamisan opened the inner door of the pressure chamber. The dead men lay there as they had fallen, and fighting nausea, she dragged one aside to make room for Starrex, who carried Kas over his shoulder, moving slowly under that burden. There was a fold of cloak wrapped about the prisoner to prevent any contact between the cords and Starrex's own flesh. The outer hatch was open.

A blast of icy rain, with the added bite of the wind which drove it, struck violently at them. It had been dawn when Tamisan had entered the ship, but outside now the day was no lighter; the torches had been extinguished. Tamisan could see no lights, as, shielding her eyes against the wind and rain, she tried to make out the line of guards.

Perhaps the severe weather had driven them all away. She was sure no one waited at the foot of the ramp, unless they were under the fins of the ship, sheltering there. That chance they would have to take. She said as much and Starrex nodded.

"Where do we go?"

"Anywhere away from the city. Give me but a little shelter and time . . ."

"Vermer's Hand over us and we can do it," he returned. "Here, take this!"

He kicked an object across the metal plates of the deck and she saw it was one of the lasers used by the crewmen. She picked it up in one hand, the tangler in the other. Burdened as he was by Kas, Starrex could not lead the way. She must now play in real life such an action role as she had many times dreamed. But this held no amusement, only a wish to scuttle quickly into any form of safety wind and rain would allow her.

The ramp being at a steep angle, she feared slipping on it, and had to belt the tangler, hold on grimly with one hand and move much more slowly than her fast-beating heart demanded. She was anxious that Starrex in turn might lose footing and slam into her, carrying them both to disaster.

The strength of the storm was such that it was a battle to gain step after step even though she reached the ground without mishap. Tamisan was not sure in which direction she must go to avoid the castle and the city. Her memory seemed befuddled by the storm and she could only guess. Also, she was afraid of losing contact with Starrex, for, as slowly as she went, he dragged even more behind.

Then she stumbled against an upright stake, and putting out her hand, fumbled along it enough to know that this was one of the rain-quenched torches. It heartened her a little to learn that they had reached the barrier and that no guards stood there. Perhaps the storm was a lifesaver for the three of them.

Tamisan lingered, waiting for Starrex to catch up. Now he caught at the torch, steadying himself as if he needed that support.

His voice came in wind-deadened gusts; it was labored. "I may have in this Hawarel a good body, but I am not a heavy-duty android. We must find your shelter before I prove that."

There was a dark shadow to her left, it could be a coppice. Even trees or tall brush could give them some measure of relief.

"Over there." She pointed, but did not know if, in this gloom, he could see.

"Yes." He straightened a little under the burden of Kas and staggered in the direction of the shadow.

They had to beat their way into the vegetation. Tamisan, having two arms free, broke the path for Starrex. She might have used the laser to cut, but the ever-present fear that they might need the charges for future protection kept her from a waste of their slender resources.

At last, at the cost of branch-whipped and thorn-ripped weals in their flesh, they came into a space which was a little more open. Starrex allowed his burden to fall to the ground.

"Can you break dream now?" He squatted down beside Kas, as she dropped to sit panting near him.

"I can . . ."

But she got no further. There was a sound which cut through even the tumult of the storm, and that part of them which was allied to this world knew it for what it was: the warning of a hunt. Since they *were* able to hear it, they must be the hunted.

"The Itter hounds!" Starrex put their peril into words.

"And they run for us!" Mouth of Olava or not, when the Itter hounds coursed on one's track, there was no defense, for they could not be controlled once they were loosed to chase.

"We can fight them."

"Do not be too sure of that," he answered. "We have the lasers, weapons not of this world. The weapon which put the ship's crew to sleep did not vanquish us; so might an off-world weapon react the other way here."

"But Kas . . ." she thought she had found a weak point in his reasoning, much as she wanted to believe he had guessed rightly.

"Kas is in his own form, which is perhaps more akin to the crewmen now than to us. And, by the way, how is it that he is?"

She kept her tale terse, but told him of her dream within a dream and how she had found Kas. She heard him laugh.

"I was right then in thinking my dear cousin might well be at the center of this web. However, now he is as completely enmeshed as the rest of us. As a fellow victim, he may be more cooperative."

"Entirely so, my noble lord." The voice out of the dark between them was composed.

"You are awake then, cousin. Well, we would be even more awake. There is a struggle here in progress between two sets of enemies who are both willing to make us a third. We had better travel swiftly elsewhere if we would save our skins. What of it, Tamisan?"

"I must have time."

"What I can do to buy it for you, I will." That carried the force of a sworn oath. "If the lasers act outside the laws of this world, it may be that they can even stop the Itter hounds. But get to it!"

She had no proper conductor, nothing but her will and the need. Putting out her hands, she touched the bare, wet flesh of Starrex's shoulder, but was more cautious in seeking a hold on Kas, lest she encounter one of the tangle cords. Then she exerted her full will and looked far in, not out.

It was no use; her craft failed her. There was a momentary sensation of suspension between two worlds. Then she was back in the dark brush where the growing walls did not hold off the rain.

"I cannot break the dream. There is no energy machine to step up the power." But she did not add that perhaps she might have done it for herself alone.

Kas laughed then. "It would seem my sealer still works in spite of all your meddling, Tamisan. I fear, my noble lord, you will have to prove the effectiveness of your weapons after all. Though you might set me free and give me arms, necessity making allies of us after all."

"Tamisan!" Starrex's voice was one to bring her out of the dull anguish of her failure. "This dream, remember, it may not be a usual dream after all. Could another world door be opened?"

"Which world?" At that moment her memories of reading and viewing tapes were a whirl in her head. The voiceless call of the Itter hounds to which *this* Tamisan was attuned made her whole body cringe and shiver and addled her thinking even more.

"Which world? Any one . . . think, girl, think! Take a single change, if you must, but think!"

"I cannot. The hounds, aheeee; they come, they come! We are meat for the fangs of those who course the dark runnels under moonless skies. We are lost." The Tamisan who dreamed slipped into the Mouth of Olava, and the Mouth of Olava vanished in turn, and she was only a naked, defenseless thing crouching under the shadow of a death against which she could raise no shield. She was . . .

Her head rocked, the flesh of her cheeks stung as she swayed from the slaps dealt her by Starrex.

"You are a dreamer!" His voice was imperative. "Dream now then as you have never dreamed before, for there is that in you which can do this, if you will it."

It was like the action of that strange-scented air in the ship; her will was reborn, her mind steadied, Tamisan the dreamer pushed out that other, weak Tamisan. *But what world? A point, give me but a decision point in history!*

"Yaaaah!" The cry from Starrex's throat was not now meant to arouse her. Perhaps it was the battle challenge of Hawarel.

There was a pallid snout about which hung a dreadful sickening phosphorescence, thrust through the screen of brush. She sensed rather than saw Starrex fire the laser at it.

A decision, water beating in on me. Wind rising as if to claw us out of the poor refuge to be easy meat for the hunter. Drowning, sea, sea, the Sea Kings of Nath!

Feverishly, she seized upon that. She knew little of the Sea Kings who had once held the lace of islands east of Ty-Kry. They had threatened Ty-Kry itself so long ago that that war was legend, not true history. And they had been tricked, their king and his war chiefs taken by treachery.

The Ill Cup of Nath. Tamisan forced herself to remember, to hold on that. And, with her choice made, again her mind steadied. She threw out her hands, once more touching Starrex and Kas, though she did not choose the latter, her hand went without her conscious bidding as if he must be included or all would fail.

The in Cup of Nath—this time it would not be drunk!

Tamisan opened her eyes. *Tamisan, no, I am Tam-sin!* She sat up and looked about her. Soft coverings of pale green fell away from her bare body. And, inspecting that same body, she saw that her skin was no longer warmly brown; instead it was a pearl white. What she sat within was a bed fashioned in the form of a great shell, the other half of it arching overhead to form a canopy.

Also, she was not alone. Cautiously, she turned somewhat to survey her sleeping companion. His head was a little hidden from her so that she could see only a curve of shoulder as pale as her own and hair curled in a tight-fitting cap, the red-brown shade of storm-tossed seaweed.

Very warily, she put out a fingertip, touched it to his hunched shoulder, and knew! He sighed and began to roll over toward her. Tamisan smiled and clasped her arms under her small, high breasts.

She was Tam-sin, and this was Kilwar, who had been

Starrex and Hawarel, but was now Lord of LochNar of the Nearer Sea. But there had been a third! Her smile faded as memory sharpened. *Kas!* Anxiously, she looked about the room, its nacre-coated walls, its pale green hangings, all familiar to Tam-sin.

There was no Kas, which did not mean that he might not be lurking somewhere about, a disruptive factor if his nature held true.

A warm arm swung up about her waist. Startled, she looked down into sea-green eyes, eyes which knew her and which also knew that other Tamisan. Below those very knowledgeable eyes, lips smiled.

His voice was familiar and yet strange, "I think that this is going to be a very interesting dream, my Tam-sin "

She allowed herself to be drawn down beside him. Perhaps, no, surely he was right.

PART TWO
Ship of Mist

Ship of Mist

TAM-SIN, she who had been born Tamisan, the dreamer, stood in the narrow slit of the craig tower. Below, the sea washed, tossing a lace of foam up so near that she might lean forward to gather the salt spinning into one hand. This was going to be a wild, storm-troubled night. Yet, for all the rage growing in the lash of water below, she felt no fear; rather excitement, as heady as thorson wine, warmed her scantily clothed, pearl-fair body.

Behind her, lay the room of her awakening: its nacre-coated walls, its shell bed, its hanging draperies and carpet of green-blue as much a part of the sea world as the people of the Nearer Sea were akin to the element guarding and encompassing their islands. Their sea was life, and what one feared the breath of life?

"My lady . . ." The voice came drowsily, lazy from that same shell bed, "it would seem that you seek . . ."

She turned slowly to face the man who still lounged at ease, the silk coverlet half drifting from his body.

"My lord," she raised her voice to a pitch above the ceaseless song of the waves, "I am remembering Kas."

His green eyes narrowed and that satisfied content which had been a part of his smile was gone. In his face, this new face, she saw the elements which perhaps only she could see: the stoical repression of Starrex, the bewilderment of Hawarel, those he had been in past and now must still carry in his mind.

"Yes, there is Kas." Now his voice had lost its first warmth, sounded tired as if he had been awakened from a pleasant half dream to take up once more some burden.

Half dream? What held them now was more than any dream. Tam-sin knew dreams; she had been able to summon and dismiss them at her own will, they and the people in them had been but toys with which she could play at desire—that is until she had dreamed for Lord Starrex and plunged them both into such a venture as she could not control. Fleeing that she had somehow brought them here: to new identities, new adventures, and—doubtless—new dangers. But where was Kas, her Lord's cousin and his enemy, who had striven to put an end to them both in two times, two worlds, and who must also have been wrenched with them into this, though not in their company?

The man sat up in the bed. His skin was as palely fair as her own. Where the cover lay against him that soft fabric seemed to impart a green reflection to his body. His hair was the red-brown of living seaweed, even as she could see her own in a polished mirror of silver metal on the wall.

"I am Kilwar, Lord of LochNar," he said slowly, as if

to assure himself of the truth of that identification. "What dream have you wrought this time, my Tam-sin?"

"That of the world in which the Ill Cup of Nath came not to the lips of these, our people, Lord."

"The Ill Cup of Nath, the betrayal of the Sea Kings." He frowned a little as if it were an effort to remember, not with Kilwar's memories but those of Starrex. "So that piece of black doing did not engulf Nath?"

"So I desired, Lord."

He smiled. "Tam-sin, if you can alter the writing of history then you are indeed a mighty dreamer. But I think that I shall find LochNar closer to my taste than was the world of Hawarel. Still, as you have said, there is the matter of Kas. And we shall have no easy dealings with that one. You did pull him with us?"

"We were tight-linked, Lord. We could not have come here was he not drawn with us,"

"But it would seem not so closely," Kilwar stood up. His body was not as sturdy as that of Hawarel, and the gill pockets on his throat formed a half collar of loose skin. Yet there was about him, bare bodied as he now stood, the same aura of command which had been Starrex's. "And," he added, "I do not altogether relish the thought that Kas is *not* here where I can keep an eye on him. Could he have gone back to the beginning?"

"Not so," Tam-sin was sure of that. "His dreamer awoke there, before I drew him through. No, he is linked too closely with us."

"My lady of power!" He crossed to her in two strides and her body melted against his, joyfully, in a way as if they were designed to do so by the very power which had given them birth. "You are very lovely," his breath was warm against her cheek. "And you are Tam-sin who has chosen life united with me."

She surrendered to his caresses, aware that Tamisan, the dreamer, now faded, that she was indeed Tam-sin and he desired her. Within her was a warm content.

His lips touched her closed eyes gently, right and then left. Then the spell of their closeness was broken by a mournful, hooting call.

"The signal shell . . ." He loosed his hold upon her. He was no longer lover, but Lord of the hold as he reached for shell-set belt and kilt of scaled skin. She held ready his sword, wrought from one of the huge, murderous saw snouts of a spallen, its toothed edges hidden in a sheath of the spallen's own tough hide.

As he belted it on, she herself tidied her short, sleeveless robe, pulled thread loops about the pearls of its breast fastening, took up her dagger of curved taskan tooth. While they dressed thus, hastily the boom of the shell horn sounded twice more, echoing through rooms carved from the very stuff of the sea cliff.

The part of her which was Tam-sin told her that the summons was such as might be a forewarning of danger. And with that thought came again a wondering concerning Kas and what mischief he might be about.

He had striven with such power as she had hardly been able to meet to kill his cousin during the first dream she had been required to set. With Starrex gone the fortune and power he held would fall to Kas. But in the Ty-Kry, Tamisan had first dreamed Kas had failed. Would he find here some more potent threat?

She followed Kilwar from the chamber. The walls beyond lacked the smooth casing of the living quarters, were rather rock, rough and natural, with narrow, twisting inner ways between the larger rooms. They descended steps worn into hollows by centuries of use. And the rock carried through to them the vibration of the waves beating beyond the wall to their left.

Tam-sin knew they were now close to sea level and she was close on Kilwar's heels as he passed through a tool-smoothed portal into a vast space which was rock roofed overhead, but into which the sea washed, forming a long ribbon between two level areas above the highest reach of the tides. A small ship rode the water there. Though the Sea People were at home in the waters, yet they also needed ships for the transport of their trade, and such a one was this. Men dropped from its deck, leaping expertly to the natural docks between which it now was anchored.

And other men, armed, yet with their swords and water guns still sheathed, saluted Kilwar as he passed through their lines to meet the seamen from the ship. They were all of the *Nath*, for though Land traders came, those did not use the inner harbors. Their leader held up his hand in a greeting which Kilwar acknowledged in turn.

Only four of them, that was not a full crew. Yet no more showed from beneath the deck. And there was about them a strain which Tam-sin picked up as easily as if they had come shouting alarm.

She knew that captain, Pihuys. Not a man easily shaken. A hunter of spallen in their own waters was not one to know fear as a side-by-side comrade. Yet that uneasiness she had sensed, it held the substance of fear.

"Lord . . ." Pihuys spoke that one word and then hesitated, as if what he had to say was such that he could not find the proper words with which to tell it.

"You have come," Kilwar moved to drop clan-chiefs grip on the other's shoulder, "with some news which is dire. Speak, Captain. Do the Land people show their teeth? But that would not rouse one who commanded at the Battle of the Narrows."

"Land scum?" Pihuys shook his head. "Not in whole truth, Lord. Though there may be some witchery of theirs behind this thing. It is thus . . ." He drew a deep breath and then spoke, with one word tumbling over the next in his haste to explain.

"We were examining the reefs off Lochack, for there were reports that spallen have come inward to those shallows for some reason. There was the mist as comes then before the true day and in the mist we found a deserted ship. It was one of the Land traders, and its cargo hold was full, sealed. I think that it had drifted from the eastern lands. Salvage it was, for there was nothing living on board. Yet the small boats were all in place. Since the land scum cannot live long in the water they would have taken those.

"Within there was even food from which men had risen hastily yet there were no signs of any battle, nor other trouble, no battering as if a storm had hit them. We thought that Vlasta had smiled on us, the ship being sound in every way and heavy laden with goods. So I left on board four men and we looped a tow to the *Talquin*.

"The mist continued very thick and, even though we held the ship in tow, we could not see her as we went, only the rope which held her. I had told Riker, who I left in command on board, to sound the shell at each turn of the sand glass. Three times he sounded; then, Lord, there was silence.

"We hailed and got no answer. Thus we swam back and boarded once again. Lord, my men were gone as if they had never been! Yet if they had taken to the sea there was no reason they would not have come to the *Talquin*. We found only the shell horn lying on the deck as if dropped."

"And the ship?"

"Lord, for the second time, I made an evil choice. Wund, who was brother to Riker, and Vitkor, his sword-companion, demanded that I let them take up vigil and discover what manner of strange thing this boat was. And to that I agreed. Once more we were mist-hidden and the horn stopped. Once more the men were gone." Pihuys opened his hands in a small gesture of helplessness. "So I swore that I would bring in this ship that those of LochNar could examine it. But when we went once more into the *Talquin* and the mist closed . . . Lord, it sounds beyond a man's belief, but the rope went slack and when we pulled it aboard it was cut!"

�֍ �֍ ▌▌ �֍ ✖

"A LANDSMAN'S SHIP," Kilwar repeated thoughtfully. "I know you must have searched her well each time."

Pihuys nodded. "Lord, any place a man could go within, that we sought. And the cargo hatch was sealed with an unbroken seal."

"Yet somehow, Captain, there is an answer to your mystery!"

The voice was high pitched and so unpleasant was its tone that Tam-sin looked over her shoulder to where another man had come out upon the cave dock. He walked clumsily, with a sidewise lurch, and his face had a petulant twist. Under that there lay a resemblance to Kilwar. And Tam-sin, with the part memories of this time, knew him, Rhuys, Kilwar's brother, whose injuries during the winter hunting of two seasons ago left him sour and sharp of tongue.

There was another stir of knowledge within her mind. In the craig castle, Rhuys was her enemy. Not openly, but with such an ill will as any sensitive (and above all a dreamer had to cultivate such sensitivity) could read. He did not even glance in her direction now, rather limped on to stand with Kilwar facing the Captain.

"Lord Rhuys," Pihuys's voice was far more formal in tone, "I can only tell of what I saw. We searched the vessel from bow to stem; the small boats hung in their lashings, there was naught living aboard."

"Naught living?" Kilwar echoed those words. "That is said, Pihuys, as if you have some explanation which is not of the living world."

The Captain shrugged. "Lord, we have lived in, by, and of the sea for all our generations. Yet do we not still come upon mysteries none of us, nor our records, can explain? There are great depths into which our species cannot venture. What may lurk there: who knows?"

"But this," persisted Rhuys, "is not a tale of the Great Depths, but rather of the surface, and of a Landsman's ship. They do not deal in any of our mysteries; they fear us." Tam-sin thought there was a thread of pride in that statement. Perhaps, because he had lost so much in his life, Rhuys clung to the thought that their race was feared by others.

"I tell only what I saw, what I heard, what happened," Pihuys repeated stolidly. And he did not look in Rhuys's direction at all, rather made a point of speaking directly to Kilwar. Rhuys was not greatly cherished within the hold of LochNar; his peevish temper too often flashed to life.

"I would have your chart, Pihuys," Kilwar said. "Perhaps the ship still floats free. You say the rope was cut, could it have been the work of a spallen?"

Pihuys half turned, gestured to one of his seamen. The man leaped back to the deck of the anchored vessel, returned with a coil of heavy rope slung over his shoulder. The Captain caught at the dangling end and held it out for their inspection. Even Tam-sin, knowing little of the ship's equipment, could see that end was cleanly cut, and it must have taken a sharp knife or hatchet to accomplish that so easily.

Kilwar ran his finger over the severed end. "This took strength," he commented, "as well as a sharp edge. Was it cut on board the ship, or when the rope lay between you and it?"

"Close on the ship, Lord, by the measurement," Pihuys answered at once. "There is no roughage as one would find at a saw-through. No, it was done by a single blow."

Rhuys laughed spitefully. "It could have been cut by a man who determined that the cargo was worth the risk of losing his comrades. If the Landsmen's ship was as intact as you say, it could easily be sailed to Insigal which, as all men know, is inhabited by those who are not too honest."

Pihuys, for the first time, faced Rhuys squarely. "Lord, if there had been any man hidden on board, him we would have flushed out. We know ships and on that one we even sniffed into the bilges. And if it is suggested that *my* men thought of playing such a trick . . ." The glare he turned now on Kilwar's brother was one verging on the murderous.

"Not so, Pihuys," Kilwar broke in. "No one would suggest that you or your men might be responsible for a ship taken to Insigal so that the salvage came not into our hands." He was frowning, but he did not glance at his brother.

Tam-sin sighed inwardly. Some time Kilwar would have to see Rhuys for what he was: a soured man, a troublemaker who stirred up many fires and depended upon Kilwar to see that he was not scorched when those burst into open flame. She could urge nothing on her Lord, that she knew. Rhuys was persuasive with Kilwar when he wished, and he hated her. She must allow no wedge to be driven between them.

"Bring me your chart," Kilwar was continuing. "Also, I shall ask of the Lord of Lochriss and him of Lochack, what they might have seen or had reported. For if you came across this derelict off the Reefs, that territory is well patrolled by their forces."

The chart of the reef territory was spread out on the table in the council chamber and Kilwar made a point of assembling there those Elders whose knowledge of the strange tales of the sea outrivaled the many accounts in their archives. He had Pihuys relate his version of the mist-concealed ship and then looked to the Elders.

"Has there been a like happening known?" the Lord of LochNar asked, when the silence fell after Pihuys' detailed report.

For a long moment no one answered. Then Follan, who all men knew, had made the eastern voyage a dozen times, arose and went to the map, using his forefinger to trace the line Pihuys had indicated.

"Lord, this has happened before, but not in these waters."

"Where and when?" Kilwar's question was brief.

"There is a place off Quinquare in the east in which ships have been sighted, yes, even boarded, to be found deserted. Nor has any captain been able to bring in those ships. At one time, this was so great a danger that men would no longer sail for Quinquare and that city's trade died, its people fled inland or overseas, and it became a shadowed ruin. But years passed and the ghost ships were not seen. So Quinquare arose again, yet never was it the great city it had once been."

"Quinquare," Kilwar mused. "That is a full sea away. But such ships have not been seen on *this* coast?"

"That is so," Follan replied. "Lord, I do not like it. Just so acting were the ghost ships of Quinquare. If some power holds them that now lies on our lee, then it is trouble indeed."

"Lord, the message hawks . . ." He who had charge of those swift flying birds moved to the table, one on either wrist. The birds looked about them with bright and fierce eyes, moving their feet uneasily on the heavy gauntlets covering the Hawkmaster's wrists. They were sea eagles, able to wing tirelessly over the waves, bred for intelligence, and trained to carry the messages from one craig-island castle to the next for the Sea Kings.

Kilwar drew a small piece of cured sea snake skin and inked on it coded words. When he had done, he took each bird in turn to fasten his message in the tube bound to one leg.

"Release them now," he ordered. "And be alert for any quick return."

"Lord, it is done."

"Meanwhile," Kilwar said, "let our battleship be made

ready. We shall seek out this ghost vessel for ourselves, if it still floats and seeks men as a bait lies within a trap. Pihuys, what manner of seal lay upon the cargo hatch? Did you know it?"

"Lord, it was of this design," the Captain had picked up another square of snakeskin and the writing stick Kilwar had dropped. He sketched in some lines. "I have not seen it before," he added as he put aside the pen and pushed the sketch over to his Lord.

Tam-sin moved forward a pace or so, in spite of Rhuys's glare, to peer down over Kilwar's shoulder. She drew a gasping breath when the significance of those lines became clear. Tam-sin of LochNar would not have recognized it, but Tamisan of Ty-Kry knew . . . And she saw, almost felt, the sudden tensing of Kilwar's body as he made the same identification.

"It would seem, brother," Rhuys said, "even if the brave Captain knows not this symbol, she who shares your bed does."

The six-point star with a jaggered bolt of lightning through it, Starrex's own badge out of Ty-Kry, the real Ty-Kry from which they had come. No, there was no mistaking that!

TAM-SIN DID NOT ANSWER THE WORDS Rhuys had made into an accusation. She was sure that Kilwar himself had recognized instantly that sign of his own House in the other tune before they had been caught, by Kas's planning, in these dreams. She would leave it to him to say yes or no. But it was Follan who spoke first, with a gravity which seemed a part of his personality.

"Lady Tam-sin, is this sign truly known to you?" She studied him, not sensing any of the hatred which her sensitive's power could pick up from Rhuys. And that part of her which was Tam-sin knew that Follan had been her friend from the beginning in this place, for she was not born of LochNar but had come from a small, less important craig keep which was nearer to the land.

"It is known to both of us," Kilwar replied before she could summon words. "It is the sign of a land house, one in its time of no little power. And now it can be the sign of an enemy." He was thinking of Kas she was certain. Could it be in *this* dream world Kas was Lord of Starrex's clan, should that clan exist at all? "I do not like it being a part of this ghost-ship matter."

Kilwar's answer drew their eyes from her. She caught only a malicious glance from Rhuys and her chin lifted determinedly as she allowed herself a return stare. Rhuys could not make trouble between this Kilwar and her, no matter how he had been able to deal in the past with that other Tam-sin who had given her form and body here. There was such a tie between this Sea Lord and herself that none standing here could understand nor trouble.

"Landsman!" the Captain exploded. "They are ever a threat to us and whyfor? We do not want their territories ashore, and we do not forbid them the sea when they gather courage enough to venture out on it! Then why should they set themselves against us as they are ever minded to do?"

"They have a greed born in them," Follan answered. "What they have is never enough, always they want more. The High Queen likes it not that our lords do not bow knee in her court nor send her gifts. Also, they say that because we can live where they dare not, for the sake of their lives, venture . . ." his hand arose to finger the edge of his now closed gills, "we are not of their species. And what they do not understand, that they hate and fear. Nor can we say that we do not do the same upon occasion. This was a Landsman's ship, therefore it is natural that it bears a House seal."

"Bait for a trap." Rhuys lurched forward another step so that he stood to Kilwar's other hand, flanking him on the left as did Tam-sin on the right. "This ship could be the bait of a trap, brother. Have not already six of our men gone into it and not come out again? What they may want is for us to try it farther, losing more men each time. It would be better to use sea fire and destroy it utterly . . ."

"Thus making sure," Pihuys commented dryly, "that we destroy also any means of learning where are our men and whether we can find them once again."

"Do you think they still live?" Rhuys flung at him. "Do not be a complete fool, Captain!"

Pihuys's hand went to the hilt of the knife at his belt and Rhuys smiled. That he had deliberately provoked the Captain for some purpose of his own Tam-sin had no doubts.

"Be quiet, Rhuys." Kilwar's voice was calm but the tone of it was such as to raise a flush on his brother's bitter face. "We shall," he gave the final word, "await word from Lochack and Lochriss; if they have further news of this ship, it would be well to have it. Then, at sunrise we shall take out the battleship and see what we can discover. Meanwhile, have you aught in the way to offer as advice, Elders, Captain, do you think upon it so that when we gather for further council that we may listen."

They went, silently, as men who had much upon their minds. Kilwar watched them through the doorway, his hand still resting on the chart. Only Rhuys did not move.

"I still say it is a trap."

"Perhaps you are right, brother. But we must make sure of what kind of a trap before we attempt to render it useless. And who set such a trap off Quinquare in years past? We have no touch with the northeastern lands now, not since they were overrun by the Kamocks, who care nothing for the sea, and will not let traders into the borders of the lands they have seized. It might well be that whoever devised a way of leveling Quinquare has, because of those very Kamocks, changed his arena of action hither. Yet I cannot see the profit in this thing. They do not loot ships, it would seem, unless that bark was emptied and the hatch resealed, which I do not believe. Pihuys is too experienced a seaman not to tell between the riding of a ship in ballast and one which is well laden. Therefore, it seems a very elaborate trap indeed for the catching of a handful of venturesome seamen who lay aboard what they believe to be a derelict."

"Six men from a crew of ten, brother, is no small catch," Rhuys returned.

"Not by our counting. But if this game is played long . . ." Kilwar frowned. "Let me but hear from Lochack and Lochriss and we may know a little more. If the messages come I shall be in our chamber." He held out his hand and Tam-sin laid her fingers lightly on his wrist, as they both turned away from the table, leaving Rhuys alone.

Nor did they exchange any words until they were once more in the chamber where they had awakened together. Once there, Kilwar walked to the window slit and looked out.

"There is a storm coming fast," he observed. "It may well be that no ship can sail no matter how pressing the need."

"Kilwar."

At the sound of his name, he swung about to face her. Tam-sin looked quickly right and left. She had a queer feeling that even here, they were overlooked, perhaps spied upon. Yet the part of her who knew this keep well recognized no such form of spying was possible.

"The seal . . ." she continued.

"Yes, the seal." He came closer as if he, too, had that sense of being under observation. "You told me before that these dreams made us the people we would have been had history taken a different turn in the past."

"That is what I believed."

"You say now 'believed,' have you then changed your mind?"

"I don't know. I have no sea people in my ancestry. Have you, Lord?"

"Not that I know of. Yet it would seem that there is my House here, yet I am no longer a member of it."

"There is Kas."

"Yes, Kas. Could he be Clan Lord then by some quirk of fate? Is there any way you would know, Tam-sin?"

She shook her head. "Lord, as I told you, in our first venture, these are not ordinary dreams wherein I can influence the flow of action. I myself am enmeshed in them, which is not natural. I can break the dream, or so I hope, but as you know there must be the three of us together to do this thing. And we have not Kas."

"Unless he is a part of this ghost-ship mystery and in searching out its secret we can fasten on him," commented Kilwar. "Meanwhile, I am not a man of uncontrolled fancy, but I sense trouble here, even as it awaited us at the court of the High Queen."

"Watch for Rhuys," she gave the warning which seemed most important to her. "He is a bitter man, and, like Kas, he resents that you have what he lacks. Kas wants your clan leadership, your wealth. Rhuys wants the same, but with it burns resentment that you are a whole man, and he is maimed and cut off from a full life."

"Part of me, that which is native here," Kilwar said slowly, "resents that saying. But you are right. Ties of blood hold him fast so far; after all we are brothers. But brother-hate can be worse than many other rages. And you he hates even more. To him our mating is a shameful thing because you are a Tide-Singer and of a lesser House. Also he would have kept me if he could from any heir."

"Tide-Singer . . ." Tam-sin repeated slowly and searched the memories of this personality. Yes, she was indeed a Tide-Singer, once she released the memories of Tam-sin, knowledge awoke in her. It was strange knowledge, alien to any she knew. She must search those other memories, find more about this power which was of a different race and time.

There was a fierce blast of wind fingering at them through the window slit and Kilwar quickly drew the shield across the opening.

"A storm indeed," he observed.

But Tam-sin thought that one hardly less fierce might even now be gathering strength within this very pile.

❈ ❈ IV ❈ ❈

THE STORM battered and worried at the craig keep throughout the night. Tam-sin slept only in snatches, awakening at intervals to hear the drums of fury without. Twice as she did so, lying tense and shivering, Kilwar's hands sought her and she found comfort in his nearness and touch.

She tried to search the memories of Tam-sin and discover what powers that other whose form she now wore had. Once she had been a dreamer, then a Voice of Olava in a different world wherein she had fronted the anger of the High Queen; now she was a Tide-Singer, one who "sang" the fish into the nets, could "see" from a distance any ship of the Sea Kings. In each life, she had talents which were not those of the common sort.

A Tide-Singer might follow a ship with her mind, if she were linked with any on board it. But she could not pick out such a ship unless those ties existed. And she herself must be given time to absorb from the Tam-sin personality what she could now put to use.

"Lord," she whispered, "what think you lies at the heart of this matter?"

"Any guess could equal mine," he returned in a murmur no louder than that she had used. "But I am uneasy that the cargo seal was the one I know."

He fell silent then and she lay as quiet, with her head upon his shoulder, knowing that, even as she, he sniffed danger for them ahead.

But they spoke no more and when the first gray light appeared around the edge of the shutter he had pulled across their outer window, he slipped from the bed, arousing her in an instant.

"Lord, let me go also when you hunt this derelict."

"You know I cannot. By the Law of these folk I am constrained not to take any female into what might be battle."

That lay within the Tam-sin memory, too. Yet to have him vanish now was more than she thought she could bear. To be alone . . .

As Tam-sin arose to face him, she read in his face that he could or would not go against the customs of the Sea People.

"You know," she said, her lips feeling stiff even as she shaped those words, "that if aught happens to you and I am not near, then this dream will never be broke."

Kilwar nodded. "I know. But there lies no other answer. I must, being who I am, follow this course. You are a Singer, you can link with me."

"Well enough, but I will have no power to aid, even if my thoughts ride with yours and I learn that dire fate befalls you."

She turned away, not wishing him to read what might be written on her face. There was no appeal from his decision, from the customs of the Sea Kings. Kilwar would ride the waves when the storm had blown itself out. And she would be left alone . . . here.

Yet later, she was able to master herself and stand outwardly unmoved to watch him aboard the battleship, his liege men in their scaled armor and their sea given weapons raising a salute as he swung to the deck. And Tam-sin watched the ship loose off its mooring ropes, to slide under the direction of the helmsman into the passage leading to the sea.

The storm had indeed blown itself out. Also the birds had returned at an hour after first light, each bringing a message. The ghost ship had been sighted by those of Lochriss, who had lost four men to its mystery. But Lochack reported no such haunted vessel. However, each keep lord would now join with Kilwar at the Reefs.

Tam-sin watched the ship bearing her lord slip into the open beyond the anchor cave. There a weak sunlight made brighter scale armor, and the banner of LochNar was the scarlet of new-shed blood as the wind played with its folds.

She still watched, until that vanished. Only then was she aware of Rhuys, who was not looking toward the going of the battle vessel, but rather regarding her through narrowed eyes. His stare was boldly measuring, as if she were some spell book whose hidden secrets he would make his own.

Tam-sin returned that study with a level gaze. Rhuys's lips parted, for a moment she expected him to speak.

But he did not, merely hunched his shoulders as if to face into a stiff sea wind, and limped away, his back turned insolently upon her, leaving her without any form of courtesy, to return to the inner ways alone.

She held her head high; no one lingering here among the women who had watched their men sally forth on such a dubious mission must think that she felt aught of embarrassment at this open flaunting of her rank within LochNar.

Instead, returning to the inner passages, she sought one with a narrow, steep stair hacked out to rise and rise, past all the levels of the keep, until she came out on the crown of the craig. There, though the wind whipped her, she cupped her hands about her eyes and searched for last sighting of Kilwar's ship. But it must now have drawn farther out, enough to be hidden behind the rising craig of Lochack which stood between this keep and the norther reefs.

Seabirds called and shrieked about her, swooping to search among the storm wrack piled below for the debris of the storm, fish or other food things, entrapped by high waves washing among the sharp lacework of the rocks. As she looked down, she could see many of the women and children of LochNar were already busied there, seeking the sea's lavish bounty even as did the birds. But Tam-sin had no mind to join them.

Instead, she settled down with a rise of rock to her back, her arms about her knees, crouched small under the freshness of the wind, her eyes still on the sea. Again, she searched diligently the memory of Tam-sin, putting into order all she might learn from this other self of hers.

There was much to astonish her therein. Even as the occult learning of the Voice of Olava had come to her in the last dream, so now did seep or rush into her mind those talents which were Tam-sin's. Some she pushed aside, working ever to find what might serve them best now. But for the moment she did not try linkage with Kilwar, rather .she wished to learn what she might against that time when such linkage became vital.

"My Lady."

The voice startled her so quickly out of that study that she gave a gasp as she turned her head. It was the Elder Follan who had followed her here. And he was watching her with an intentness which matched that Rhuys had earlier turned upon her, yet this study had no twinge of malice such as she knew moved Rhuys whenever he thought or looked at her.

"Follan," she asked, "what else do you know of these ships of Quinquare?"

"No more than I told our Lord, Lady. It was a puzzle which had no ending that I have ever heard."

"But how can men vanish from the deck of a ship, one in tow, and no way known?"

"I do not know. With Landsmen . . . yes, a sudden panic, a quick squall which might threaten a ship with upturning . . . even a madness of mind to grip one and all, sending them plunging to their deaths. There is such a madness which comes with the eating of spoiled grain. Men can list such explanations. But those would not account for what happened to Pihuys's men. And the Captain is a wary and careful ship master. There might be some hidden place on board which searchers could not find . . ."

"With what menace in that?" Tam-sin urged when Follan hesitated.

"Lady, there are a many things in this world, or in the sea of which there has never been any report. But . . ." again he paused and then added somberly, "Lady, you are faithful to my Lord in all things and his chosen. Now I must warn you: walk carefully."

"Well have I guessed that, Elder. I am not loved elsewhere in LochNar."

There was a shadow of relief on his face as if he were glad that she accepted his warning so promptly.

"There is always talk," he said. "And for thoughtless hearers talk holds a shadow of truth, or so they believe. You are an out-craig, and there are those who believe, and now say, that our Lord could have done better. Nor does one who is a Tide-Singer seem close to others."

"Follan, my thanks for your plain speaking. I had already known there were those who wished me away from this place. But I had not thought they were becoming so open."

Her hand clenched tightly. Rhuys had supporters, but had she ever believed that he did not? What sort of tale could he spin for her undoing? What if Kilwar did not return?

"You are our Lord's chosen," Follan returned. "As such, Lady, you have only to command, you will find the most of us ready to harken to those commands."

She smiled a little thinly. "Elder, such words are as a shield and a blade to me. I only hope that I shall not have to take up such weapons."

But his expression remained troubled. "Lady, walk

carefully. After our custom, the Lord Rhuys commands while our Lord is gone. He is maimed and we would not choose him Sea King, but that fact adds to his desire to give orders while he can."

V

TAM-SIN LAY WITHIN the shell bed. Her eyes were wide open, but she did not see the intricate mosaic of shells set in the ceiling over her. Rather, she drew upon that other sight of hers so that Kilwar was before her, standing brace-legged on a ship's deck which was never still. Around him wreathed tendrils of fog, gray as the bones of men long dead.

So clearly was he in her mind that it seemed she need only reach out her hand, which arose a little from the bed cover at her thought, and lay it upon the well-muscled arm of the Sea King, to make him turn and look eye to eye with her. Yet, there were distances separating them in body, if not in mind.

"Kilwar," her lips shaped his name, though she did not speak it aloud. And she was sure that somehow, he heard her summons, soundless, as it was, for his head turned a little as if to glance over his shoulder.

But at that very moment, he started and his body tensed.

So Tam-sin was aware he must have heard something which she did not. For it was the nature of this mind-linkage that it could not carry any sound, only sight with it. Sight, and a kind of nonverbal communication which she was still hesitant to use, lest she distract him from what must be his primary concern. Another man loomed out of the wreathing mist, and Tam-sin could see it was Pihuys, even though his image wavered and did not show as plainly as that of Kilwar, perhaps because there was no true linkage.

The Captain waved an arm toward the left, as if calling his Lord's full attention to something there. And, when Kilwar strode to the rail to peer into the ever-thickening fog, Tam-sin could see it, too . . . the narrow prow of a vessel piercing the folds of the mist as a needle might prick cloth.

Yet the strange vessel did not keep its course, but shifted with every wave. And she could believe there was no helmsmen in control. She saw Kilwar's head turn again, the movement of his lips. Men appeared on the deck behind him, a small boat was loosed, lowered over the side. So her Lord had indeed come upon the ghost ship of the mists!

At that moment, a stab of terror struck into her so deeply that she lost control. Kilwar, the mist-hung ships—all were gone and Tam-sin lay panting, her palms damp, her mouth feeling dry. This fear . . . she assessed it as well as she could. It was not the normal fear of one who faces an unknown danger. No, it was a panic which she had not felt before. As if there was some charnel house emanation from the strange vessel which had struck directly at the seat of her own sensitive talent.

No, she must go back, see Kilwar, even though her flesh crawled and her body shook as if she lay bare under the ice-rimmed wind of full winter.

Kilwar! Once more she strove to steady herself, to push away the fear and renew the linkage. There was . . . death? No, something else, but as devastating for her kind, which crouched waiting on the half-visible ship. Tam-sin knew that as well as she had seen a monster rise up behind the rail, reach forth claws to capture its prey.

Kilwar! Tam-sin summoned her nearly demoralized forces, built his image in her mind. There was a queasy shaking of the world, and she was back, but in a different place. For with the Sea Lord, she stood on what could only be the deck of the derelict.

It was a vessel, she judged from what the fog would allow her to see, of a size between that of Pihuys's ship and the battle one her Lord commanded. Nor did it have the clean lines of a sea-folks' design, but was rounder, fashioned to carry more cargo than any Sea King's possession. There was a hatch before Kilwar, the rope fastenings of which were stoutly tied and impressed with a seal as big as her palm. When Kilwar went down on one knee to inspect the pattern on that, she was not in the least surprised to see the impression Pihuys had drawn for them.

Kilwar gestured, gave orders, she could not hear. Men climbed from the boat below, spread out, going in pairs and with drawn weapons, to the search. As Kilwar himself ventured into the officers' quarters drawing far sight with him.

There was the table, bolted to the floor for safety in

times of storm. A single-backed chair, a bench, and against the far wall a bunk covered with salt-stained crimson cloth. On the deck rolled a jar which had dribbled its contents long since in a meaningless, sticky swirl across the planks. And there was a rack in which hung swords, none missing; set upright below those a stand of double-headed boarding axes. But there was no trace of any living thing save Kilwar and the men who had come with him. And, as the Sea King sat in the chair and men reported to him, coming in pairs, Tam-sin could tell from his expression that he was learning nothing save that which Pihuys had already reported: the ship was empty.

Yet, that menace which she had felt with the thrust of panic still lurked here, and she held linkage only by all the willpower she could summon. It seemed to her unbelievable that she did not sight some lurking thing which was more substance than shadow. Yet, for all the determined use of her powers, she could fasten on nothing concrete, save the knowledge that it was indeed present.

The last pair of searchers had reported. Now Kilwar sat, elbow planted on the table, his firm jaw supported by his fist, a considering look about him. When he spoke, Pihuys made a gesture of dissent. It was apparent he launched into some vehement argument. But Kilwar cut him off with a word or two. And, looking beyond the Captain, he pointed to two of the waiting warriors, both of whom the Tam-sin part of her recognized as being men long battle-bound to their Lord. At his gesture, they raised naked blades to salute him.

Once more, Pihuys made protest but at Kilwar's manifest order, he tramped from the cabin. With him went all but the two the Sea King had selected. Tam-sin could guess what Kilwar's orders were. He, himself, chose to remain on board the haunted ship, seeking to solve its mystery. Again, that panic overwhelmed her so that her talent failed, returning her to the keep and to another battle with that strong fear.

This time, her struggle was more protracted. Perhaps her will had been a little weakened in the first encounter. Yet she fought valiantly, with all the strength she could summon. When she at last won to Kilwar it was to see a shadowed cabin. Two ship's lanterns were set on the table, the light flaring low within them, giving radiance only to the section immediately about them. She could see Kilwar who was still, or again, seated in the chair.

On the board before him lay not only a bared sword, but two of the double-headed axes, also placed close to his hand. The rack wherein those and the swords had been was now empty. Tam-sin guessed that he had taken the armament, determined that no one, or nothing, could secretly equip itself from that collection.

His attitude was one of listening, though she believed he had not yet heard anything suspicious but waited for such to manifest itself. Now and then, his mouth opened and she believed that he called to his men, doubtless checking them at sentry posts without.

It seemed as if time dragged on thus forever. The lantern light flickered. Sometimes Kilwar arose to his feet and tramped back and forth. When he did so, he went sword in hand, as if he did not intend to be caught unawares by the unknown enemy.

Suddenly, he shouted again, whirled to the table and

snatched up one of the waiting axes with his left hand. Then he leaped into the shadows beyond the reach of the lantern light. The deck, was he bound for the deck?

That must be so, for now Tam-sin saw a curtain of mist, silvery light. This was no normal mist, that she knew, for within it were small motes of glitter which were like insects flying back and forth. Through this blundered a dark form, staggering. The shadow man fell just as Kilwar broke into the thickness of the mist. He made a second leap, until he stood one foot on either side of that supine body, his sword ready to slash, and his head a little bent as if he had difficulty in seeing.

At that moment, the terror which had exiled her twice struck full. Tam-sin was swept into a darkness of sheer horror, racing ahead of that which she dared not see, could never hope to imagine until, at last, she knew nothing at all, taking a last refuge in mindlessness.

❊ ❊ VI ❊ ❊

"LADY!"

It was a calling from far off; she would not listen. Here was safety . . . there . . .

"Lady!"

Tam-sin became aware of her body, though not yet would she open her eyes. Memory had returned to her bringing the last mind picture of her Lord wrapped round by that mist sparkling with unholy light. But there was a hand on her shoulder and for the third time the voice came urgently:

"Lady!"

Reluctantly she opened her eyes. Althama, who was her own waiting woman, leaned over her, her face showing distress. Behind her shoulder, Tam-sin saw Follan. That the Elder would come thus into her inner chamber argued some dire happening.

Tam-sin sat up. "Our Lord . . ." she croaked the words as if for too long she had been without speech. "He faces the danger."

"Lady," Follan replied somberly, "word has come by hawk that when he of Lochriss and he of Lochack came to the meeting place, our Lord was gone to gather with two of his men, and the derelict drifted, empty of life."

"He is not dead!"

"Lady, they have searched the ghost ship once again. They found no life, no sign of any on board her."

"He is not dead," she repeated sharply. "For that I would know, Elder. When one is mind-linked and death comes, then there is such a shock of loss as no one can mistake. I stood mind-linked when our Lord went to battle . . ."

"To battle what?" Follan demanded eagerly. "What saw you then, Lady?"

"Naught but a mist filled with whirling specks of light. But it was not of any energy that I know. And I was cut off—"

Follan shook his head. "Lady, the news has been too clear. Our Lord is gone from us, dead or no, yet he has gone. Now it is Rhuys's day, for when the message came he proclaimed a regency. A man of twisted body may not rule the keep, but he can hold the power until time passes and men at last agree our Lord is truly dead."

"But I shall say that our Lord lives."

"Lady, which one of the men now pledged to Rhuys will harken to an assurance they believe you make only to hold sway here? Rhuys has spoken much during the past hours. It is his tale that you have laid a bewitchment upon our Lord since your first meeting, and that it is because of this bewitchment, Kilwar went to his death. He tells a logical story and one those without your talents can well believe."

Tam-sin ran her tongue across her lips, lips which suddenly felt dry. She could, indeed, see the logic in Rhuys's argument and what had she to stand against it? She was a Tide-Singer right enough, but those who had not such gifts were wary of the ones who had, resenting often their own lack.

"What would he do with me?" she asked directly of Follan.

"Lady, there are already two guards without your door. What lies in his mind I cannot say, save that it means no good to you."

"Yet you came hither to warn me."

"Lady, I have known you since the first day my Lord went wooing. You are his chosen and to my mind you have never worked any mischief. Now you say my Lord lives, but where is he?"

He leaned forward, his eyes holding her. There was something fierce and demanding in his gaze. Just so did the sea eagles look upon one.

"I do not know, only am I sure he is not dead. And now there is that I must do . . . go in search of him. We have been mind-linked; there must lie some trace on board that evil ship which I can trace. But I cannot do it from here. And you say there are guards without the door . . ." Now she looked swiftly to her maid.

"Althama, how much will you serve me?" Tam-sin demanded bluntly.

"Lady, I am your woman," the maid replied simply. "What is your wish is my desire."

"Will they let you go forth?"

"I think so, Lady. After they make sure that I am no messenger."

"What do you plan?" the Elder wanted to know.

"That which is my only hope. Follan, you have ever shown yourself a true liege man to my Lord, how stand you for me?"

"You say our Lord is not dead, and yours is said to be the talent which can separate life from death in such matters. Lady, I am with you. What *is* your plan?"

"There is this," she looked again to Althama, "I can use my talent to set upon me the look of Althama. Such a disguise cannot be long held, but perhaps it would get me out of here. And that she may not be held by Rhuys for my escapement, I shall leave her bound upon this bed. How say you?"

The maid nodded vigorously. "Lady, if you can do this thing, then do it speedily. There are many whispers among the women and some of them are ill to hear. Lord Rhuys holds power now and you he fears and hates. But where will you go? There cannot any ship set forth from here without the knowledge of those who will speedily tell him of it, or prevent its sailing."

"I will not go by ship. And, Althama, neither shall I say how I go, thus they cannot press you for such an answer. Put on the pretense of hatred for me, saying that I am wild of thought because of my Lord's loss and that you believe I have taken the Dark Road of self-destruction because of my love for him and my fear of Rhuys. To think that I fear him so much will be pleasant hearing for that one."

She arose from the bed and it was Follan who made

tight the bonds about Althama's wrists and ankles, also putting a gag of cloth within her mouth, but in such a way that she could work that out and then call to the guards for deliverment.

Tam-sin set on the maid's kilt and then she stood with closed eyes for a long moment, willing upon herself the dream talent to be what she was not. She heard a gasp from Follan as she opened her eyes once again.

"Lady, had I not seen this, I would have said it could not be so."

"I cannot hold the illusion long," she told him. "Let me get to the beach where they glean among the storm wrack."

"That I can insure you will do," he replied readily. So, wearing the illusion of Althama, she went along the corridors a respectful two paces behind the Elder who brushed past the guards as if they were unseen. Down they traveled by a narrow stair, and then by a wider one. She could hear now the calls of the women who were busy with the storm gift upon the shore as they came out into the open. There, Tam-sin hurried before the Elder as if, having been somehow kept from this treasure hunt, she was now the more eager to reach the debris. But since all that nearer the keep entrance was already well swept she needs must hunt farther toward the point.

Once there, she clambered up over a tumble of rocks which were water washed to find beyond a pocket of cover wherein but two women tugged and pulled apart the water-sodden strands of weed to see what might lie within its broken folds.

Follan caught up with her. "Lady, there is no ship to be launched from here."

She nodded. "Well do I know that, Elder. But I have my own talents and such can bring me to where my Lord disappeared." She went again toward farther rocks about which spray tossed, wetting their surfaces and streaming from their sides.

As Tam-sin climbed up on the outermost of those, she looked down and back at Follan.

"Elder, what will Rhuys do if he finds you have given me such countenance."

Follan smiled wryly. "Nothing. I shall be witness to your giving yourself to the sea, Our Mother, in your frenzy of mind. But be sure of this, my Lady, Rhuys will not find it easy to rule in LochNar, regnant or no. And I shall not give *him* any countenance at all."

"Good friend," Tam-sin smiled a little unsteadily. Follan was not a man easy to fathom but that he had done this for her, that was enough to give near kin-kindness. "Say what you will, but perhaps not the truth."

She unfastened the kilt, to stand bare of body save for a belt which held the long-bladed knife Kilwar had given her at their choosing. Then she swung to the sea and, cupping her hands about her mouth, she sent forth a high ringing call. Three times did she so call, and at the third she saw the distant form leap above the waves for an instant and knew that she had been heard and answered.

Content for so much, Tam-sin slid into the embrace of the sea, choosing well her moment that she might not be crushed between wave and rock, and began to swim. She was not far beyond the rocks when those she had summoned flanked her on either side, their round, bluish bodies only half seen. She flung out a hand to each, felt that hand seized in a gentle but firm grip by mouths which were armed with wicked teeth, but whose weapons would never be turned on one who had the secret of their calling. Now she was drawn forward at a speed no swimmer, not even the sea-born of the keeps could equal. She needed no ship to reach the Reefs with these at her service.

❈ ❈ VII ❈ ❈

AT INTERVALS, Tam-sin swam by herself but the loxsas still flanked her, ready to offer help when she tired. That weak sunlight was gone and the sky, whenever she arose to the surface for a sighting, bore the deep purplish red of the afterglow. The water world through which she now headed was as known to the Tam-sin part of her as her own room in the Hive of the dreamers from which the other person in her had come. Though there were dark bulks which plowed these ways, yet none would turn toward her with the loxsas on watch.

Those were of high intelligence, but of a thinking pattern so alien to her own that it was a difficult effort to contact them. So the messages of such communication were necessarily very limited. They knew where she would go, the why was not needed for they would ask no explanation of her.

The moon arose and once more she was towed by her finned companions. Then, out of the waters, whirled two more of their kind swiftly and efficiently taking their places to offer her the same aid.

She was hungry and thirsty, but the needs of her body could be set aside for now. Let her but reach the Reefs and she could relax the inflexible will which kept rein on the loxsas and carried her along.

Time ceased to have any real meaning. Tam-sin felt as if she had so traveled for hours without number. Then she sighted, during a surfacing, the dark bulk of a ship. For a single wild moment she thought perhaps this was the ghost vessel, until she heard the sound of a gong ring across the water and knew that it must be one of those set on guard by the Sea People.

At this moment, she had no desire to seek out any ship save the ominous one which drifted in the billows of the fog. Should she chance to be picked up by Kilwar's own vessel there was good chance of being taken into custody by those among the crew who might be Rhuys's men. For she never doubted that he had his spies on board. And, were she to hail the battleships of either Lochack and Lochriss, the result might well be the same in the end. Therefore, she must head for the Reef itself and there await a chance to find the ghostly sea trap which had taken Kilwar's party.

The loxsas angled left now, drawing her away from proximity with the ship. And they swam underwater, where at night they could not be detected. There arose rocks high before them, and the girl knew she had reached the roots of that wall whose jaggered crest formed the surface Reefs. Getting the loxsas to loose their hold she swam slowly toward that and, sought hand- and footholds to raise her out of the waves and into the night air which was so frosty cold on her bare skin that she gave a gasp as she crept up the jaggered surface. Huddling below the crest line where the movement of her body might well reveal her to some keen-eyed watcher, she breathed deeply to loose the action of her gills and return once again to that of her lungs.

From this point she could see lights on three ships. They were apparently riding at anchor well off the danger of the Reef. There was no mist and she began to wonder if the ghost vessel itself had something to do with that as a cloak for the evil which undoubtedly inhabited it.

Her eyes could not serve her now; she must seek with that other talent, search out through the cloak of the night for the mind to which she could link. There was a faint in-and-out pattern which she caught first, but did not attempt to clarify. That was loxsas' thoughts and of no value to her. Farther, wider, she must spread her net, hoping to catch in it the faintest flicker of Kilwar to guide her. But it would seem that she could not find . . .

She had pushed near to the limit such a seeking could go if it were unfed by linkage. Then she tightened her hands into fists, her head whipped left, to the north. Again she summoned the full of her power and sent it probing in that direction.

Not true linkage, no. It was like finding only an end of a raveling thread when one sought the whole piece of weaving. But there was enough to assure her that in that direction lay her field of search. So heartened, Tam-sin slipped once more into the water, her sea guard closing in about her without her call.

Her escort had grown to six now. The loxsas had a vast curiosity, especially about men. It was well known that they often accompanied Sea People at a distance, merely, it would seem, to watch their actions. That they came so close to her was because she had used the old summoning. Now they sped along beside her, and her sea ears caught the faintest traces of their shrill cries which, as their thoughts, sped in and out of her own range of consciousness. Their sleek bodies, twice as long as her own, made a formidable ring of defense, but that they would serve her so once her goal was found, that she knew could not happen.

Since they swam now below the surface and towed her at the speed they could easily maintain, Tam-sin left her transport to her companions and centered all her mind upon picking up and holding that trace which had lured her in this direction.

It was not a true linkage, that she already knew. Rather it was closer to seeing a thin shadow in place of the substance of a man. But she knew that she was not mistaken, some form of contact with Kilwar endured.

Only that grew no stronger, as they went, though she had expected it would. And in that she was disappointed. Finally, she loosed her ties with the loxsas and swam to the surface. About her . . .

Her heart raced with mingled triumph and apprehension. The mist lay heavy, a rolling fog. It hid the surface of the sea so that she could not tell now east, west, north, or south. The loxsas who had last borne her company raised their snouts free from the waves and faced ahead. She strove once more for communication and got a faint

reassurance. The fog did not baffle the sea creatures—
there was a man-made thing there.

That could only be the ghost ship! With all her will,
Tam-sin sent forth her desire—to come beside the thing
hidden in the mist. But, to her astonishment, for the first
time the creatures refused their help.

She could sense their protest even though she could
not hear their supersonic voices, nor meet them squarely
thought to thought. Whatever swung with the roll of wave
within the fog frightened them.

Just as it frightened her. Yet she would not yield to
that fear and she swam resolutely ahead, aware that the
loxsas, upset, flashed around her at a distance, striving to
herd her back to what they considered less dangerous
territory.

It was only the strength of her will which made them
reluctantly give way. Now they no longer flanked her,
rather drifted back, following her at a distance which grew
the greater as she kept determinedly on. Their breed
feared nothing in the sea as she well knew. So that this
present uneasiness of theirs was a warning of what she
deliberately took the wild chance to face.

Here, the fog was so thick that it seemed a wall to
ward her off. She dropped below the surface where she
could not see it. Ahead, ahead was a trail of phosphorescence outlining what could only be the keel of a ship.
That phosphorescence was a warning in itself, for it was
born from the shells of those creatures who lived best on
wood long washed by salt waves. And for so many to gather in one place meant that this ship had been far too long
at sea . . . no attention given to the cleaning of its hull.

Tam-sin headed directly for the source of the wan light. She knew that the loxsas had dropped completely behind and her all thought was for how she might win aboard. Unless there remained some line dropped along the side she might not be able to win to the deck.

Surfacing once more, she raised her head, treading water, one hand against the weed-grown side of the derelict. As far as she could see there was no rope or trailing line here. The anchor chain?

She paddled toward the stern and there she saw it, heard it, too, rasping along the wood it had already polished bare of weed and shell. The anchor was gone, but the chain still hung as if weighted, near enough so that Tam-sin managed a push upward to hook a hand in a half-open link.

It was a difficult climb and one which left her breathless. However, she reached the opening where the chain fed in. That was too small for even her slight-boned figure to use, so she sought for a hold above and, gasping with effort, at least swung over a splintered rail onto the deck. The mist hid all from view except for perhaps an arm length away. She crouched to listen, with her ears, not her mind.

VIII

THERE WAS LIFE HERE, she could sense it. But it was as alien as that of the loxsas, overlying and near smothering the traces of Kilwar which she sought. Of one thing was Tam-sin sure, she would not find anything in the common cabins and passages of the wallowing vessel. The searches which had been made there had not been slighted. There was naught left for any seeker to find.

Yet something brooded here . . .

The girl's bare feet were silent on the deck as she crept forward, her knife ready in her hand. To draw that was only instinct for she was sure that what lurked in hiding was nothing one could overcome by any blade, no matter how skillfully wielded.

Not in the ship, then where?

The curdling of the fog cloaked near all the deck save that which was immediately about her. Though she listened, all she could hear was the slap of waves against the vessel's side, the scrape of the anchor chain rubbing ever back and forth like a pendulum.

There was something in the mist, close to the deck. Very slowly, Tam-sin edged toward that shadow. This could only be the edge of that hatch so battened down and sealed. With her left hand resting on it, slipping over the web of ropings that kept it secure, she made the circuit of the wide square. This was the only place they had not searched, those who had been drawn into the trap of the ghost ship.

Because the lashings were taut and looked undisturbed, because of the seal, none boarding the derelict had given it a second thought. But it was the only place left to hide whatever made the derelict a menace.

Tam-sin had reached the seal. It was near as wide as her palm, and, through the wan light which seemed a part of the fog itself, she could indeed see that impression of the House which Starrex ruled in the real world.

Tam-sin sank to her knees. The deck was runneled with damp, perhaps condensed from the fog. And there was a cold which made her shiver. But she raised the seal where it crossed the final knotting of the ropes and gave it a hard tug.

It seemed to her that something in the crisscross of ropes had yielded to her grasp. She pulled again, harder. The seal slipped free and rope ends fell away, far too easily. This had not been truly sealed after all, merely the appearance of being so had been craftily given.

She worked hurriedly, throwing off the latchings of the hatch. Whether she would have the strength to raise the cover was another problem. It was divided into two leaves, which split down the middle. Putting her knife between her teeth for safekeeping, the girl hooked fingers in that center crack and heaved with all her might.

She nearly lost her balance as the half she worried at arose swiftly as if it were far lighter than she had thought it, or as if she had activated some spring to aid in the opening. From the void below, burst a light: pale, greenish, and wholly unpleasant. And with the light there arose a stench, the foul like of which she had never been forced to inhale before.

Choking with nausea, Tam-sin fell back, waiting for whatever horror might then dare to show. But there was nothing save the light and the smell. With one hand over her nose to ward off all she could of the latter, Tam-sin once more approached the half-open hatch.

She made herself look down, though all her sensitive's warnings, every fiber of her body, opposed that act.

What she saw she could not first understand, the horror of it was too great. But she forced herself to study the contents of the hold below, catalogue them with her mind.

Immediately below the center break of the hatch was a long box or coffer. And in that lay a man. At his head rested a globe of light from which spread the greenish illuminance. But . . .

On either side of the open coffer were tumbled . . . bodies! Tam-sin pressed her hand, knuckles hard against her lips, so stifling a scream. Some sprawling there must have been old, the skin was only parchment stretched over bone, husks of what had once been men. But slumped against that open coffer, close by the head was Kilwar! And with him his liege men, beyond those three others which must be some of those Pihuys had sent on board, though they had a curious sunken and wasted look and she was sure they were dead.

Kilwar! Her seeking thought probbed into mind of the limp body. No, not dead!

But how could she get him free of that pestilent prison?

The ropes which had lashed down the hatch! She caught at the fog-wet lengths, striving to knot the longer together. The meaning of what she had uncovered she did not know, but that there might be very little time left for Kilwar, of that she was sure.

Tam-sin made fast her rope to the nearest deck rail, testing each knot as she came back along her improvised ladder to the edge of the hatch.

She had to face now what was the greatest test of all: she must descend herself into that charnel house and seek to rouse Kilwar and his men, if those still lived. And it took all her resolution to climb over and work her way down the ropes.

It was when she stood over the Sea Lord that she realized whatever power this terrifying trap was rousing. For that was the sensation she caught, something horribly sated stirred from a gluttoned sleep. She would be caught in turn . . . only the fact that it had feasted well had so far served her.

Reaching down, she caught at Kilwar's sword. It was far heavier than her knife and she drew it awkwardly, not being schooled in the use of such a weapon. The light, that was growing stronger. She glanced to the globe, saw a swirling deep inside.

There was . . . life!

The globe . . .

Something closed upon her, wrapped her around as if to smother, driving air from her lungs, leaving only the nauseating stench which made her retch. It would . . . take . . . her!

She dug fingers into Kilwar's shoulder, shook him. There was still a spark of life flickering in him, of that she was sure. He must awaken, help himself. For she now faced a power which far outreached any she had fronted, in dreams or out.

"Kilwar!" Tam-sin shrieked his name, felt him stir feebly. She could not pull him nearer to the rope; he was too heavy for her as a dead weight. Instead, he toppled a little toward her, driving her back against the side of the coffer. For the first time, she saw directly the face of the man within it. Saw and knew . . .

Kas! Was he dead, drained of life force as the others here, or did he sleep?

The globe pulsated with light. A vast, arrogant confidence spread from it to her. This thing had never known defeat, it had gathered its victims as *It* chose and none could stand against it.

Tam-sin drew upon that part of her which was dreamer, Tide-Singer. The thing was not man as she knew it, but something far beyond any classification her knowledge could offer her. Only to find Kas lying here . . . in a queer way that steadied and strengthened that part of her which had never been defeated either.

It was the globe which fed, fed the man it guarded or itself? There was no sign of corruption about Kas's body.

She thought she even saw his breast rise and fall in a very shallow breathing.

The globe . . .

That which abode within it was growing stronger—ready to overpower her. Tam-sin reversed the sword she still held. Though the sharp-toothed edges cut painfully into her flesh, she raised it high, and brought the pommel down on the globe.

That did not shatter as she had hoped, though under her blow the light whirled malignantly and she swayed under return blow of willed force. A second time she struck at the bubble, blood from her scored hands making the blade slippery in her grip.

It would not break. And in another breath, perhaps two, she would be overtaken by its power. What . . .

Once more, Tam-sin reversed the weapon, the blood flowing down her wrists. She had only a second left, and a wild guess which was only that. Holding the sword as best she could, she aimed the point straight down, into the breast of the man in the coffer, realizing that she had no other choice.

❊ ❊ IX ❊ ❊

THERE WAS A HOWLING SCREECH which did not burst from Tam-sin's throat, mainly because she could not at that moment make a sound. All sense failed her under a vicious blow. She reeled and fell among the tangle of bodies, clinging desperately to the spark of life within her.

The howling was a torture to her ears. And there was surge of light as blinding. She moaned feebly. No longer could she muster any strength, she could only endure as best she might.

There was movement beside her.

The thing in the coffer, she had not known in that back lash of power whether she had struck true or not. No, *no*, and no!

Somehow, Tam-sin drew on her last dregs of strength. She struggled up, loathing what lay beneath, about her. The light, it no longer seared her tearing eyes. It was flickering in the globe as if it, too, now fought extinction.

That terrible hate which had struck at her . . . she was

free of it. Tam-sin set one hand to the side of the coffer, her fingers clamping on the edge. And by that hold she fought to draw herself upright again.

That within the globe coiled back and forth as might a serpent sore wounded. She longed for an ax and the power to strike without mercy or hindrance.

"Tam-sin!"

Though the howling had lessened, she could barely hear her name. Rather she was staring down into the coffer. There Kilwar's sword stood hilt upright, caught between the ribs of the sleeper. But this was no sleeper . . . the flesh fast shriveled, dropped away, to pull skin tightly over bones.

"Tam-sin," there was an arm around her shoulders as she fought the heaving nausea which gripped her.

"Kas," she pointed a shaking hand into what lay there, now with the seeming of a man many months dead.

Anger, incredulous anger, impotent anger. Though she felt an arm about her, she could not look away from the globe. That was no longer a perfect sphere of light, it bulged as if that which lay within were fighting to be free.

"Out," she mouthed the word twice before she could say it aloud, "out."

The arm about her was drawing her back toward the rope, away from the coffer, the globe. The greenish glow in that still writhed, but its struggles were weakening. Another's hands swung her around to face the rude ladder, lifted her body from the noisome mass on the floor. Only half conscious of what she did, Tam-sin gripped the rope.

But there was no strength left in her. To climb . . . she could not make it.

"Tam-sin, climb!"

The sharpness of that order broke through the daze, long enough for her to weakly strive to obey. There was someone still behind her urging her up. Somehow, she gathered a last spurt of both courage and energy and fell out upon the mist-clouded deck.

There was not even strength enough left in her now to raise herself from where she lay,

"Stay!" Again that sharp order. "I go for Trusend and Lother."

Her eyelids dropped, never had she been so tired. That which now fought in the globe had seemed to suck from her all energy and purpose. She no longer cared, it was enough to be out of that pestilent hold, into the sea wind.

But at length, she edged around so she might see the hatch. The rope was drawn very taut, and it moved in little jerks.

A head arose over the hatch edge and a man stood on deck.

Kilwar. She did not even feel relief at seeing him. Too much had gone from her. He turned and began to pull on the rope, until a second head drooped limply into sight. Then he drew that still body to fall beside her own, and once more disappeared into the depths. Only to bring out a second man as unconscious as the first had been.

Hard upon their rescue there came a flare of eye blinding light. Flames spurted up from the hatch, clawing spitefully at the rescuer as he drew the second man to safety.

"Fire!" Kilwar shouted. "By the Face of Vlasta there is no fighting this!"

He stooped and caught at her, dragging her to her unsteady feet "Get you down," he had pulled her as far as the rail.

As she clung to that, she watched him jerk at the open cover of the hatch, hacking at part of it with a sword. Then he drew the length of seasoned wood to the rail, heaved it over. Having seen it hit the waves, Kilwar turned and shook Tam-sin.

"Get down! I will lower them to you. Hold them on that raft."

Somehow, she was able to leap out and down, cleaving the water not too cleanly, but welcoming the wash of the cleansing sea about her body. She swam for the raft and worked her way up on it. Then Kilwar lowered the bodies of his liege men to that half-awash surface, leaped to swim and join her where she lay flat, one hand locked upon each of the unconscious men's belts.

Behind the mist glowed as if it, also, had caught fire. Tam-sin watched dully a line of flames creep along the rail she had left behind only moments earlier. And something, perhaps the heat of the burning ship, was conquering the mist, drying it away as they bobbed off from the side of the ghost vessel.

Kilwar unhooked her fingers from the belts, rolled the bodies together in the center of his improvised raft.

"That," he gestured toward the burning ship, "should bring them to investigate. We can hold here until that happens."

"The fire . . ." Tam-sin watched the destruction of the ghost ship with no emotion. Feeling seemed to have been wrung out of her by the experiences of this night.

"The thing, that which rested in the globe," he told her, "it broke its dwelling place, and this is the result."

There was something else she must tell him, but her mind seemed unable to think logically. Something important, but she was too spent to care.

"Rrrruuuu!"

Out beyond the derelict someone had sounded a shell horn. Kilwar rose to his knees, balancing carefully on the bobbing raft. He sent back a call as ringing as the blast of the horn. A second later, a shout answered him.

"Tam-sin," his hand was warm and gentle on her shoulder, "they are coming for us."

She could not answer, even when he raised her head to rest upon his knee. Through the haze of fatigue she saw one of those others Kilwar had saved, turn his head, look to his Lord.

The mist was fast going. She could see the wink of a star overhead. While the fierce burning of the ship sent a full light over the water. The nose of a ship cut into that light, heading toward them.

She was hardly conscious of being hoisted aboard, carried to a bunk where Kilwar left her, a soft quilt pulled over her. He was back before she was aware fully that he was gone, holding a goblet. Bracing her against his shoulder, he put the container to her lips, and, because she was too tired to protest, though she smelled the strongness of the wine it held, she swallowed what was liquid fire.

"The . . . the thing," she half whispered. "If it got out . . ."

A nightmare shadow built in her mind. What if the

thing, now freed from its container, could follow to haunt them?

"It is dead, or at least it is gone," he reassured her quickly. "Now sleep my lady, and know that naught can harm us here."

She allowed him to lay her back on the bunk. Sometime she must sort out what had happened. Now she no longer cared, and sleep waited.

❈ ❈ **X** ❈ ❈

THERE WAS AN EDGE OF GRAY LIGHT spreading from one of the cabin windows, touching upon Kilwar as he sprawled in a chair, his head thrown back, his eyes closed. Tam-sin watched him sleep as she marshaled a host of broken memories from the immediate past: the ghost ship, and what lay in its hold. Once more, she looked down upon one who seemed to sleep under the baneful light of that globe.

Kas!

Then only did she understand what might have come from her attack upon that sleeper. The three of them were bound together in this dream which existed seemingly beyond her control. And if Kas was dead . . .

But the evidence of her eyes, the body which, when she had used the sword, certainly had withered, shrunk into the corpse of one who had been dead, not for moments, but for days, or longer. Could this have been the same ship which had haunted the coast off

Quinquare? If that was so, then Kas on this plane had been dead for a long time, or in a half-life secured by the globe.

What matter of strange and frightening sorcery lay behind what had existed in the hold of that ship?

Kilwar stirred, his eyes opened, and he straightened in the chair. Then he looked quickly to her and from somewhere Tam-sin drew the strength to smile.

"My Lady!"

He was quickly at her side.

"My Lord!" She warmed to his concern, felt his need of her as an anchor in the midst of so much she could not understand.

"You dared to go . . . *there*." He caught her hands, held them in a grip too tight for comfort, but she would not have it otherwise.

"When there was such a need, how else could it be?" she asked. "But it was your strength that got us forth in the end, Kilwar. What was that thing?"

He shook his head slowly. "That I cannot name. It . . . it *fed* . . . upon the life force of those it took. And it had many victims."

Tam-sin shivered, remembering what had lain about that coffer. Now she slid her tongue over her lips. If he did not know, she must tell him at once. And it was a thing which laid heavy on her.

"Kilwar, did you see what lay within the coffer?"

"Another of the dead . . ."

"Not wholly . . . I think. Not until I slew it with your sword. Kilwar, it was Kas who lay there."

"Kas!" He stared at her. "You saw him so?"

"I saw him, knew him. He was not changed as are you and I, but wore the face I first knew. And . . . do you understand, Kilwar . . . I killed him!"

The astonishment had not left his face.

"Kas?" he repeated wonderingly. "But that ship, it must have voyaged so for a long time."

She knew a sudden sickness rising in her as the full meaning of what she had witnessed flashed into her mind. Kas transported to this dream world, imprisoned in his counterpart here, part of a dead-alive body ruled by the globe thing! Had he been conscious of what had happened to him? No, she could not, dared not believe that!

Kilwar's arms were about her, drawing her close to the warmth of his body, as if he would keep her safe even from her thoughts . . . those thoughts now spinning out sheer horror.

"If that was the Kas in this world, then you had no part of it."

"But, Lord, it was my power and will which brought us here."

"Out of very certain death," he reminded her. "I do not know what was the reason for the death ship. Since the globe strove to keep alive the counterpart of my cousin, perhaps he was the one who fashioned such a trap in the beginning. It must have been that the two were close linked for as you slew him, then the globe went wild. It was a murderous being whatever its nature. And the blame for none of this can you take upon yourself, Tam-sin."

"But I brought him here . . . to *that* . . ." her voice was near a whisper.

"You brought us all to what meant safety as you could

see it. Kas on this plane must have dealt with devilment, or he would not have been linked to that eater of men's life force."

"We cannot be sure." She wanted to be comforted, to believe that Kilwar had guessed rightly, but how could they ever know?

"I was there, remember," he brushed her hair from her forehead with a tender hand. "I was the prey that thing sought. If it meant slaying half a hundred men and them all blood kin to me, then I would have given the order, for that unclean thing was not fit to endure in this world. It had slain and slain again, ruthlessly and for a greed which sickens a man to think on. Kas, dead or alive, was what tied it to that trap. Do you think that any will say that his death under those circumstances was not merited?"

"You do not yet understand," Tam-sin tried to pull out of his hold. "Kas is dead . . . I cannot now break this dream! We can never go back."

The expression smoothed from his face, even his eyes seemed turned inward. He knew now, and he would not, could not forgive what she had done. They were lost in a dream . . . there would be no return to Ty-Kry where he ruled a sky tower kingdom.

"This is so, you are sure?" his question came evenly, in a voice as expressionless as his face.

"It is so," she replied desolately. She had hated Kas for what he had tried to do, his plot to see Starrex dead within some dream she herself had spun. But she should have preserved him, if she could, that they might return.

"So be it!"

Kilwar was smiling, his face lighting as she had never seen Starrex appear.

"Do you not remember, my Tam-sin? In that Ty-Kry I was but half a man, tied to a body which would no longer obey my commands. As Harawel, I was half a man in another way, for there was a simplicity of thought in that one which I could not live with for long. But here," his head lifted proudly, "here I have what I sought! Do I think the past is better than the present? Not so! I am lord in LochNar and I have my lady. If Kas is dead, then let us accept that as a fact and turn our faces to the future. Look," gently he lifted her higher, took her up and bore her to the cabin window.

There was the sunlight topping the waves without. A dark body leaped from the water, hung a moment in the air, its snouted face turned in her direction and Tam-sin had no doubt that the loxsa had seen and recognized her.

"Tam-sin, this is another day. We have won from the night of mists into the day which is given us to use . . . that we shall do. Do you regret the past?"

"No!"

Nor did she. Dreamer she had been, but whether this was a dream without substance in which they were now entirely entrapped she no longer cared. Perhaps her real body lay in Ty-Kry's tower, but she refused to believe that that was real . . . not now. She was Tam-sin and this was Kilwar not Starrex; and they were both free to follow, not the devious path of a planned dream, but life itself. She laughed joyfully until Kilwar's lips closed upon her own and another kind of happiness followed.

PART THREE
Get Out of My Dream

Get Out of
My Dream
❖ ❖ ❖ ❖

EVERY WORLD had its own rites, laws and customs. Itlothis Sb Nath considered herself, in position of a Per-search agent, well adjusted to such barriers and delays in carrying out her assignments. But inwardly, she admitted that she had never faced just this problem before.

Though she was not seated in an easirest which would automatically afford her slim body maximum comfort, she hoped she gave the woman facing her the impression she was entirely relaxed and certain of herself during their interview. That this . . . . this Foostmam was stubborn was nothing new. Itlothis had been trained to handle both human and pseudohuman antagonism. But the situation itself baffled her and must not be allowed to continue so.

She continued to smile as she stated her case slowly and clearly for perhaps the twentieth time in two days.

Patience was one of the best virtues for an agent, providing both armor and weapon.

"Gentle Fem, you have seen my orders. You will admit those are imperative. You say that Oslan Sb Atto is one of your present clients. My instructions contain authority to speak with him. This is a matter of time, he must be speedily alerted to the situation at his home estate. That is of utmost future importance, not only to him, but to others. We do not interfere on another world unless the Over-Council approves."

There was no change in the other's expression. By the Twenty Hairs of Ing! Itlothis might as well be addressing a recorder, or even the time-eroded wall behind the Foostmam.

"This one you seek," the woman's voice was monotonous, as if she were entranced, but her eyes were alert, alive, cunningly intelligent, "lies in the dream rooms. I have told you the truth, Gentle Fem. One does not disturb a dreamer. It would be dangerous for both your planetman and the dreamer herself. He contracted for a week's dreaming, provided his own recorded background tapes for the instruction of the dreamer. Today is only the second day . . ."

Itlothis curbed a strong desire to pound the table between them, snarl with irritation. She had heard the same words, or those enough like them to seem the same, for six times now. Even two more days' delay and she could not answer for success in her mission. Oslan Sb Atto *had* to be awakened, told of the situation on Benold, then shipped out on the first available star ship.

"Surely he has to wake to eat," she said.

"The dreamer and her client are nourished intravenously in such cases," the Foostmam replied. Itlothis did not know whether she detected a note of triumph in that or not. However, she was not prepared to so easily accept defeat.

Now she leaned forward to touch fingertip to the green disk among those she had spread out on the table. Her polished nail clicked on that ultimate in credentials which any agent could ever hope to carry. Even if that disk had been produced off world by an agency not native to this planet, an agency which held to the pretense of never interfering in local rule, yet the sight of it should open every door in this city of Ty-Kry.

"Gentle Fem, be sure I would not ask you to undertake any act which would endanger your dreamer or her client. But I understand there is a way which such dreaming *can* be interrupted . . . if another enters the dream knowingly to deliver a message of importance to the client."

For the first time, a shade of expression flitted across the gaunt face of this hard-featured woman, who might well have played model for some of the archaic statues Itlothis had noted at this older end of the city where the sky towers of the newer growth did not sprout.

"Who? . . ." she began and then folded her lips tightly together.

Within, Itlothis felt a spark of excitement. She had found the key!

"Who told me that?" she finished the other's half-uttered question smoothly. "Does it matter? It is often necessary for me to learn such things. But this can be done, can it not?"

Very reluctantly, the other gave the smallest nod.

"Of course," Itlothis continued, "I have made a report to the Council representative of what I wish to do. He will send the chief medico on his staff, that we may so fulfill regulations with a trained observer."

The Foostmam was again impassive. If she accepted that hint as a threat or a warning, she gave no sign that Itlothis's implied mistrust caused her any dismay.

"This method is not always successful," was her only comment. "Annota is our best 'A dreamer. I cannot now match her skill. There are unemployed only . . ." She must have touched some signal, for there flashed on the wall to her right a brilliant panel bearing symbols unreadable to the off-world agent. For a long moment, the Foostmam studied those. "You can have Eleudd. She is young but shows promise, and once before she was used as an invasion dreamer."

"Good enough." Itlothis arose. "I shall summon the medico and we will have this dream invasion. Your cooperation is appreciated, Foostmam." But not, she added silently, your delay in according it.

She was so well pleased at gaining her point that it was not until the medico arrived, and they entered the dream chamber, did Itlothis realize that she was facing a weirder adventure than she had in any previous assignment. It was one thing to trace a quarry through more than one world across the inhabited galaxy, as she had done for a number of planet years. But to seek one in a dream was something new. She did not think she quite liked the idea, but to fail now was unthinkable.

The dreamers of Ty-Kry were very well known.

Operating out of the very ancient hive presided over by the Foostmam, they could create imaginary worlds, adventures, which they were able to share with anyone able to pay their high fees. Some of the dreamers were permanently leased out to a household of the multi-credit class inhabiting the upper reaches of the sky towers, where their services were for the amusement of a single individual or house-clan. Others remained at the Hive, their clients coming to them.

While entwined mentally with a dreamer, that client entered a world seeming utterly real. And an action dreamer of A rating was now fashionably expensive. Itlothis surveyed the room in which her quarry now lay lost in his dream.

There were two couches (the Foostmam was over-seeing the preparation of two more which would crowd the room to capacity). On one lay a girl, thin, pallid of skin, half her head hidden in a helmet of metal which was connected by wires to another such covering Oslan's head where he rested on the adjoining couch. There was also an apparatus standing between their resting places hung with bottles feeding liquid into the veins of their arms.

Itlothis could see little of Oslan's face, for the helmet covered it to nose level. But she identified him. This was the man she had hunted. And she longed to put an end to her frustration at once by jerking off that dream cap, bringing him back. Only the certain knowledge that such an action was highly dangerous made her control her fingers.

The Foostmam's attendants had set up one couch beside the dreamer and a tech made careful linkages of wires between that of the cap now worn by the girl, and the one waiting to be donned. While a second couch was placed beyond Oslan's, another cap adjusted to match his.

That uneasiness was growing in Itlothis, akin now to fear. She hated beyond all else to be under another's will in this fashion. On the other hand, the need for bringing Oslan back was imperative. And she had the medico to play guard.

Though she showed no outward reluctance as she followed the orders of the Foostmam, settled herself on the waiting divan and allowed the helmet to be fitted on, yet Itlothis had a last few moments of panic when she wanted to throw off that headgear, light and comfortably padded within that it was, to run from this room . . .

They had no way of telling into what kind of an adventure Oslan had been introduced. No two dreams were ever alike and the dreamer herself did not often foresee what pattern her creations would follow once she began the weaving of her fantasies. Also, the Foostmam had been careful to point out that Oslan had supplied the research tapes and not relied on those from the Hive collection. Thus, Itlothis could not know what kind of a world she might now face.

She could never afterward be sure how one *did* enter the dream world. Was there a moment of complete unconsciousness akin to normal sleep before one opened one's eyes upon . . . this?

Itlothis only knew that she was suddenly standing on the rough top of a cliff where rocks were wind-worn into strange shapes among which a flow of air whistled in queer and mournful moaning. There was another sound also, the drum of what she recognized as surf, from below.

But, she *knew* this place! She was at Yulgreave, on her own home world! She need only turn away from the sea's face to see the ancient, very ancient ruins of Yul in all their haunted somberness. Her mind was giddy. She had been prepared for some strange, weird dream world, then she had been abruptly returned to the planet of her own birth! Why . . . how? . . .

Itlothis looked for Yul, to make sure of her situation.

But . . .

No ruins!

Instead, heavy and massive towers arose unbroken, as if they had grown out of the cliff's own substance, as a tree grows from the earth, not as if they had been laid stone upon stone by man or manlike creatures. The ancient fortress in all its strength was far more imposing in every way than the ruins she knew . . . larger, extending farther than the remaining evidences of her own age suggested.

And, remembering what her own time deemed Yul to be, Itlothis shrank back until her shoulders scraped against one of the cliff pinnacles. She did not want to see Yul whole, yet she found she could not turn away her eyes, the dark rise of tower and wall drew her.

Yul, Yul had been in ruins when the first of her own species had come to Benold's world a thousand planet years ago. There were other scattered traces of some very ancient civilization to be seen. But the least destroyed was Yul. Yet, eager as her own kind had always been to explore the mysteries of those who had proceeded them in ruler-ship of any colonized world, the settlers on Benold did not willingly seek out Yul. There was that about the crumbling walls which made them uneasy, weighed so upon the spirit of any intruder that sooner or later, he withdrew in haste.

So, though it was viewed from a distance, as Itlothis viewed it now, and tri-dees of it were common, those were all taken from without. Why had Oslan wanted to see Yul as it might once have been?

The puzzle of that overrode much of her initial aversion. That this dream had a real purpose she guessed. It was not merely a form of pleasant escape. The girl moved away from the crag against which she had sheltered and began to reconsider her mission.

Oslan Sb Atto, he was heir to the vast Atto holdings, after the custom of Benold. Thus, when Atto Sb Naton had died six planet months ago, it had been very necessary that his heir take up Clan-Chief duties as soon as possible. His brother, Lars Sb Atto, had hired Itlothis's agency to bring back with the utmost dispatch the heir who had cruised off world. Later, when the continued absence of the Atto heir had taken on political ramifications, the search became a Council matter.

But why had Oslan come to the dreamer's planet, sought out the Hive, and entered a dream set on his own home world in the far past? It was as if he, in turn, might be searching something for importance. Itlothis thought this the truth.

What *did* he so hunt?

Well, the sooner she discovered that, the sooner they would both be freed to return to the right Benold and Oslan's duties there. Though Itlothis hated the very thought of what must follow, she began to walk toward Yul, certain, as if Oslan himself had told her, that there lay the core of this tangle.

At least the visible forms of life familiar in her own time had not altered. Overhead, swooped the seapars, their crooning cries carrying above the boom of surf, their brilliant orange, blue, and green plumage bright even on this day when the sun was cloud-veiled. Among the rocks grew small plants, almost as gray-brown as the stones about them, putting out ambitious runners toward the next cupful of soil caught between the crags.

Itlothis kept a wary watch on Yul. Though its walls were now entire, its towers reaching high, unbroken, she could detect no sign that it was any more inhabited than in her own time. No banners were set on those towers, nothing showed in the windows, which were like lidless eyes staring both seaward and toward the rise of sharp hills to the west.

Yul lay on the edge of the Atto holdings. Itlothis had seen it last when going to confer with Lars Sb Atto before leaving Benold. They had flown hither from Killamarsh, crossing the mass of ruins to reach that inner valley beyond the hills.

In fact, the House of Atto could claim this cliff and the ruins had they so wished. But the ill repute of Yul had made it no man's territory.

Determinedly, Itlothis scrambled over the rough way, listening to the cries of the seapars, studying the grim pile of Yul. She had thought that, plunged into Oslan's dream, she would meet him immediately. But apparently, that did not follow. Very well, she must hunt him down, even though the trail led to Yul. For the belief that it did grew firmly in her mind, in spite of her desire to be elsewhere.

As she approached the now unbreached outer wall, the huge blocks of its making added to her uneasiness. There was a gate in that wall, she knew. Oddly enough, it did not face the interior of the land, but the sea. And, if she were to reach that, she must follow a perilous route along the verge of the cliff.

There was no road, nor even path. That there had been none such had always baffled the experts among her own people. Why had the only gate not fronted on some road impressive enough to match the walls? Also, there was no trace of harbor below, no sign this had ever been part of a port.

Itlothis hesitated, surveying the way before her with a doubt which began to shake her self-confidence. She had initiated this quest believing that all her experience and training prepared her for any action. After all, she was a top agent, one with an unbroken number of successfully concluded cases behind her. But then always she had been operating in a normal world . . . normal as to reality, that was. Here she felt more and more cast adrift, all those familiar skills and safeguards challenged.

In any *real* world . . . she drew a deep breath. She must make herself accept for the present that this was a real world. If she could not regain her confidence she might be totally lost. After all, many of the planets on which she had operated with high efficiency had been weird and strange. Thus, she must not think of this as being a fantasy Benold, but rather one of those strange worlds. If she could hold to that, she must regain command of the situation.

The way ahead was very rough and she did not know whether the strip was under observation from Yul. She kept glancing up at the windows, to see nothing. Yet she could not escape the feeling she was being watched.

Setting her chin firmly, Itlothis crept forward. The space between the edge of the cliff and the wall seemed very narrow, and the thunder of the surf was loud. She set her back to the wall, slipping along sidewise, for she had the feeling she might tumble and fall out and down.

There were many upward jutting rocks and by each she paused. Then she crouched into hiding, her heart beating wildly, her breath shallow. For more than seapars now soared over the waves!

Whatever the thing was, a flying craft perhaps, it came at such speed as to make her wonder. And it was homing on that sea gate toward which she crept. Like an arrow shot from some huge primitive bow it sped into that opening with the same unslacking speed.

Craft . . . or some living monster? Itlothis could not be sure which. She had a confused impression of wings, the body between them shining with metallic brilliance. Man-made . . . or living?

She was startled by a flicker of movement overhead and glanced up. There, well above her, she was certain that someone, or something, had moved into a window opening.

Itlothis leaned far back against the rock which sheltered her. Yes, head and shoulders were framed in the window opening. And, by comparison of size, either the stranger she sighted or the window itself was far out of proportion, for the body was dwarfed by the frame about it.

He, he was climbing out on the sill!

The girl gasped. Was he going to jump? Why?

No, he was moving cautiously, hunkering down to swing over. Now he appeared to find some support for his feet. But how did he *dare?* He was pressed tightly to the wall, inching down, with hands and feet feeling along the stone for grips.

Itlothis was tense with empathy for the strain of that descent. That he was able to find a way seemed to her a miracle. But he moved surely, if slowly, seemingly certain he could find the holds he sought.

The sight drew Itlothis from her shallow hiding place to the foot of the wall immediately below where he hung so perilously. She lifted her own hands to skim that surface, unable by eye to distinguish any break in it. Then her fingers dropped into a kind of niche cut so cleverly that it must have been fashioned for no other purpose than to so afford an invisible ladder for a climber.

She stepped back a little the better to watch the man descending the wall. There was a familiar look about his head, the set of his shoulders. Her eyes trained to value such points identified him.

Oslan!

With a sigh of relief, Itlothis waited. Now she need only make contact, explain the need to break his dream. Then they could return to the world of reality. For the Foostmam had admitted that Oslan's desire held the dreamer's efforts in balance; that, whenever he wished, he could awake.

Perhaps he had already completed whatever purpose had brought him to this ancient Yul. But at any rate,

Itlothis's message was important enough to keep him from lingering any longer.

Having made sure of his identity, she noted he was wearing clothing alien to any she had seen. The covering clung tightly to his body but was elastic, as if fashioned from small scales, one fitted to slightly overlap the next. Only his hands and his feet were bare. The exposed skin was brown enough to match the stone down which he crawled.

His hair made a smooth cap, dark enough to show better. Itlothis knew, though she had not yet seen his face, that he had the well-cut features of his clan; he could be counted handsome if in the tri-dees she had seen there had been any expression to lighten a dull, set countenance.

Still a way above cliff level, he loosed his hold, ending his descent with a leap. He breathed heavily as he landed. Itlothis could guess the cost in effort of that long trip down the wall.

For a moment he remained where he was, gasping, his hands and feet both resting on the ground, his head hanging as he drew air into laboring lungs.

"Clan Head Oslan," Itlothis spoke with official formality.

He flung up his head with a jerk, as if he had been so hailed by some monster out of the sea below. His gaze centered on her as he scrambled to his feet, planting his back against the wall. His hands balled into fists, prepared to front some attack.

She saw his brilliant green eyes narrow. There was certainly no lack of expression in his face now! No, what she faced was raging anger. Then his eyes half closed, his fists fell to his sides, as if he saw in her not the danger he had expected.

"Who are you?" His question came in almost the same monotone as the Foostmam used, his voice might be willed not to display any revealing emotion.

"Per-search Agent Itlothis Sb Nath," she replied briskly, "Clan Chief Oslan, you are needed."

"Clan Chief?" he interrupted her. "Then Naton has died?"

"In Ice Month Two, Clan Chief. You are badly needed on Benold." Itlothis was suddenly struck by the oddity of their present position. They *were* on Benold. A pity the dream world was not the real one. It would save so much valuable time.

"You have not only clan affairs to settle," she continued, "but there is a need for a new treaty over the output of the mines, a Council affair much pressed by time."

Oslan shook his head. Once more a look of mingled alarm and anger crossed his face.

"No way, no way, agent, do you get me back yet!" He moved closer.

In spite of herself, Itlothis, to her annoyance, retreated a step or two.

"Now," he said with a whip-crack note in his voice, "get out of my dream!" It was as with each word he aimed a stun bolt at her.

However, his open opposition brought a quick reaction. Itlothis no longer retreated, standing firm to meet his advance. This was not the first time she had faced an unwilling quarry. And his negative attitude steadied her.

"This is a Council affair," she replied briskly. "If you do not . . ."

He was laughing! His head was flung back, his fists resting on his hips, he laughed, though his amusement was plainly fired with anger.

"The Council and you, Per-search agent, what do you propose to do? Can you now summon an armsman to back you—*here*?"

Itlothis had a momentary vision of yet another couch, another dreamer, if any such could be crowded into the Hive chamber, an armsman ready to be transported. That was utterly impossible. On this case she did, indeed, have only herself.

"You see," he took another step closer, "what good is any Council authority here? The Council itself lies uncounted years in the future."

"You refuse to understand," Itlothis retained her outward calm. "This is of the utmost importance to you, also. Your brother Lars, the Council, must have your presence on Benold by High Sun Day. I have the necessary authority to get you on the nearest hyper ship . . ."

"You have nothing at all!" Oslan interrupted her for the second time. "This is my dream and only I can break it. Did they tell you that?"

"Yes."

"Well, then you know. And you are my captive here, for all your powers and authorities, unless you willingly agree now to let me send you back."

"Not without you!" Even as she retorted, Itlothis wondered if she were making some fatal choice. However, she had no intention of giving up as easily as he seemed to think her willing to do.

"Do you wish to be cited as relinquishing your

clanship?" she added quickly. "In this matter, the Council has extraordinary powers and . . ."

"Be quiet!" His head turned slightly toward the walls of Yul. So apparent was his listening that she did also.

Was that deep humming note really a sound, or a vibration carried to them through the rock on which they stood? She could not be sure.

"Back!" Oslan flung out his arm and caught at her, to drag her to him until they both stood pressed to the wall. He was still listening, his face grim, his head at an angle, as he stared up at the outer defenses of Yul.

"What is it?" Itlothis asked in a whisper as the moments lengthened and he did not change position.

"The swarm. Be quiet!"

Highly uninformative, but his tension had communicated to her the necessity for following his order. This was Oslan's dream and he had come out of Yul, therefore he plainly had knowledge she lacked.

There came a burst of light, like that of an alarm flash, aimed at the air over the sea. Another and another, issuing from the cliff-facing gate and shooting over the waves so rapidly Itlothis could not see more than what seemed bails of fierce radiance. Then these were gone, quickly lost far out over the water.

As he stood body against body with her, Itlothis felt the tension ebb from Oslan. He drew a deep breath.

"They are gone! There will be a safe period now."

"Safe for what?"

Oslan looked straight into her eyes. Itlothis did not quite like that searching stare, it was as if he wished to read her thoughts. Though she wanted to break free, she could not. And her failure brought resentment. She did not wait for him to answer her question but repeated her own message as bluntly as she could.

"If you do not break the dream, now, you will lose Atto. The Council will confirm Lars as Chief in order not to waste time."

His smile was tinged with anger as his laughter had been.

"Lars as Chief? Perhaps . . . if there is an Atto left for him to rule over."

"What do you mean?"

"Why do you think I am here? Why do you think I crossed half the star lanes to find a dreamer to put me in Yul's past?"

His stare still held her. Now his hands fell on her shoulders and he shook her, as if that gesture would emphasize his words.

"You think Yul is a ruin, a masterless place in our own world. Men have repeated that since the first of our kind explored Benold. But Yul is not just tumbled walls and a feeling of awe. No, it is the encasement for something very old . . . and dangerous."

He believed this, she read the truth in his voice. But what? Itlothis did not get a chance to ask her questions, words poured out of him now in a torrent of speech,

"I have been in this Yul. I have seen . . ." he closed his eyes as if to shut out some sight. "Our Yul above ground may be three-quarters erased by time. Only that which is the heart of Yul is not dead. It lies sleeping, and it begins to stir. I tell you I have speculated on this for some years, searched out all accounts. A year ago, I dared take a scanner within for a reading. I sent the data to the central computer. Do you want to know the verdict, do you?" He shook her again. "Well, it was that the new mine tunnels spreading east had alerted, awakened something. That thing is ready to *hatch.* . . ."

Itlothis realized that he believed so fervently in what had brought him here that she could raise no argument he would listen to, the fantasy possessed him.

"To hatch," she repeated. "Then what is *it*?"

"That which once filled Yul with life. You have just seen its swarm take flight. Well, that is only a thousandth part of what Yul can produce. Those flying things are energy and they feed on energy. If one came near you, your body would crisp into ash. There are other parts to it, also." She again felt him tense. "That which lies in Yul can appear in many forms, all utterly alien and dangerous to us.

"Men, or beings not unlike men, reared Yul, made those other cities we can trace on our Benold. Then . . . *that* came. Whether it sprouted from some experiment which went wrong, or broke through from another dimension, another world . . . there is no record.

"Only those who found it made it a god, fed it with life energy until it was greater, the absolute lord of the planet. Then it blasted away the men it no longer needed, or thought it no longer needed.

"But when there was no more life energy, it began to fail. Instead of spanning the planet, it was forced back to this continent, then into Yul alone. It knew fear then and prepared a nest. There it went into hibernation . . . to sleep away the years."

"But the mine-search rays awoke it. Those fed it new energy. It grows again. Benold has new food for it. And . . ."

"You must warn the Council! Wake us."

He shook his head. "You do not understand. This monster may not be destroyed in our time. It can feed upon the minds of those who face it, empty their bodies of life force. There is no shield. Only in the past can it be defeated. If its nest is sealed against it, then it will starve and die. Benold will be free."

Itlothis was shaken. Oslan must be mad! Surely, he knew this was a dream! What could they accomplish in a dream? Perhaps if she humored him a little . . .

"I gathered all the reports," he continued. "I brought those to this dreamer. They can use such research to back a dream. Clients are often interested in the past. I had her concentrate on my readings."

"But this is a dream!" Itlothis protested. "We are not really on Benold in the far past! You cannot do what. . . ."

This time the shake he gave her was savage. "Can I not? Watch and see! There are dimensions upon dimensions, worlds upon worlds. Belief can add to their reality. *I* say that this is the Benold which foreshadows the Benold that is now." Oslan swung away from her to face the wall. "It has sent out its feeders, it will be concentrating only on them. This is my time!"

He reached above for a hold, began to climb.

Itlothis moved too late to prevent him. She could not leave this madman here. If she went with him, agreed outwardly that what he said was true, might she lead him to break the dream? Ever since she had entered this fantasy she had felt at a disadvantage, shaken out of her calm competence. She now could only cling to the hope that she could influence Oslan in the future if she kept with him.

She sat down on the rock, pulled off her boots. With her fingers and toes free, she searched for the wall hollows, started up the wall of Yul.

Luckily, she possessed a head for heights. Even so, she knew better than to look down. And she feared and hated what she was doing. But, determinedly, she drew herself up. Oslan was already at the window. Now he reached over to aid her. And they pushed from the wide sill down into a shadow-cornered room.

"Best you did come," Oslan remarked. "Otherwise *that* might sense your presence. You must be quiet for you cannot begin to imagine what your folly in entering my dream might cost you."

Itlothis choked down her anger. This was a madman. He could not yet be influenced by any argument, no matter how subtle. So she offered no protest, but crept after him along the wall, for he shunned the center portion of the chamber.

The stone-walled, ceilinged, floored room was bare. What light came issued from the window behind them. Oslan did not head to the door Itlothis could sight on the other side. Instead, he halted halfway down the wall, and felt above him at the full stretch of his arms, as if seeking another place to climb.

However, he did not swing up as she half expected him to do, to no purpose, since, the ceiling, though well above their heads, appeared entirely solid. There sounded a grating noise. Three massive blocks before which he stood thudded back, to display a very dark opening.

How had Oslan known that to be here? Of course, in a dream, an imagined wall passage was entirely possible. Only the seeming reality of this shadowed room continued to war with logic. How *could* a dream appear so real?

"In!" he whispered. When she did not move at once he jerked her into the hidden way. She tried to break free as the blocks moved to seal them in a dark which was more horrible because now she was conscious of an intangible sense of wrongness, that which dwelt in the Yul she knew.

"Here is a stair," his grip on her wrist was mercilessly tight. "I will go first, keep hand on the wall beside you."

Now he loosed her. Itlothis heard only the muted sounds of his moving. There was no way back, she had to follow orders. Setting her teeth, more afraid than she had ever been in life, Itlothis cautiously slid one foot forward, feeling for the drop at the end of the first step.

Their descent was a nightmare, which left her weak of body, drenched with sweat. That there was any air to fill their lungs was a minor marvel. Still always the stair continued.

Oslan had not spoken since they left the room above. Itlothis dared not break silence. For about her was the feeling that they now moved, in a caution born of intense fear, past some great danger which must not be alerted to their presence within its reach.

A hand on her arm brought a little cry from her.

"Quiet!"

His grasp drew her beside him. There, her bare feet

sank into a salt cushion, as if centuries of dust carpeted this hidden way. Once more, Oslan was on the move, towing her with him. In the utter darkness, she was content to cling to him as she dared not think or face what might happen if she were to lose contact.

Finally, he dropped his hold and whispered again: "Let me go, I must open a door here."

Trembling, Itlothis obeyed. An oblong of grayish light appeared ahead. After the complete dark of their journey this was bright. Across it moved a dark bulk of what must be Oslan. She hurried to follow. They stood in what was nearly twin to the room far above, save that its ceiling was much lower and one full wall to the left was missing. Thus, they could look out into a much larger space. That was not empty. What light there was, and Itlothis could not locate the source of that wan glow, made clear a massive park of wheeled vehicles jammed closely together.

Oslan paused, his head turned a little to the right as if he listened. Then he beckoned to her, already on his way toward the outer area.

There was only a narrow space left open around the wall through which they could move. Oslan hurried at the best pace he could keep in such cramped quarters. Now and then, he paused to inspect one of the strange machines. Each time, seemingly unsatisfied, he pushed on again.

At last, they reached another open wall and there he halted abruptly, his nostrils expanding as if he caught a warning scent. She had seen a vast hound do so on settling to hunt.

Here was another of the strange vehicles directly

before them and Oslan made for its control cabin. When Itlothis would have gone after him he waved her back. A little mutinous, she watched him climb into the driver's seat, study a control board.

The rigid line of his shoulders eased. He nodded as if in answer to his own thoughts, then beckoned again. Itlothis wriggled through to join him. The seat on which she crawled was padded, but both short and narrow, so his body pressed tight to hers. Oslan hardly waited for her to settle before he brought the palm of his hand down on a control button.

There was an answering vibration, a purr, as the vehicle came to life, moved forward, down the open way it faced. Itlothis waited no longer for an explanation.

"What are you going to do?"

"Seal the nest place."

"Can you?"

"I will not know until I try. But there is no other way."

There was no use in trying to get any sense out of him while he was so sunk in his obsession. She must let him follow his fantasy to the end. Then, perhaps, he would break the dream.

"How do you know how to run this?" she asked.

"This is my second such visit to Yul. I came at an earlier time in the first part of my dream, while there were still men serving *Its* needs."

He had been two days deep in the dream when she had located him and she supposed a dream fantasy could leap years if necessary. That did have some logic of its own.

The vehicle trundled forward. Now the passage began

Andre Norton

to branch, but Oslan paid no attention to the side ways, keeping straight ahead. Until a rock wall blocked them. At that barrier, he turned into the passage at the left.

This new way was much narrower. Itlothis began to wonder if sooner or later they might not find themselves securely caught between the walls. From time to time, Oslan did stop briefly. When he did so, he stood upon the seat, reaching his hands over his head to run fingertips along the ceiling.

The third time he did this he gave a soft exclamation. When he sat down he did not start the vehicle again. Instead, he crouched closer over the control panel, peering at the buttons there.

"Get out!" he ordered without looking up. "Go back, run!" Such was the force of that command she obeyed without question. Only she noticed, as she jumped to the floor, his hands were flying over the buttons in a complicated pattern.

Itlothis ran, back along the corridor. Behind her, she heard the vehicle grinding on. As she turned, pausing, she saw Oslan was speeding toward her, the machine moving away on its own. Satisfied he had not deserted her she began to run again.

He caught up, grasped her arm, urging her to greater efforts. The sound of the vehicle receded. They gained the mouth of the main tunnel. Oslan pulled her into that, not lessening his furious pace as he pounded back the way they had come. The fear which boiled in him, though she did not know its source, fed into her, making her struggle ahead as if death strode in their wake.

They had reached the cavern holding the machines

when the floor, the walls, shook. There came a roar of sound to deafen her. After that, darkness . . .

Something hunting through the dark . . . a rage which was like a blow. Itlothis hid from that rage, from the questing of the giant anger. Shaking from fear of that seeking, she opened her eyes. Inches away from her face was another's which she could see only dimly in this light. She wet her lips, when she spoke her voice sounded very thin and far away: "Clan Chief Oslan . . ."

She had come here hunting him. Now someone, some *thing*, was hunting her!

His eyelids flickered, opened. He stared at her, his face wearing the same shadow of fear as possessed her. She saw his lips move, his answer was a thread of sound. "*It* knows! *It* seeks!"

His mad obsession. But perhaps she could use that to save them. She caught his head between her hands, forcing him to continue to look at her. Pray All Power he still had a spark of sanity to respond. Slowly, with pauses between words, summoning all her will, she gave the order:

"Break the dream!"

Did any consciousness show in his eyes, or had that same irrational and horrible fear which beset her now, driven him into the far depths of his fantasy where she could not reach? Again Itlothis repeated those words with all the calm command she could summon.

"Break the dream!"

The fear racked her. That which searched was coming nearer. To lapse herself into madness, the horror was worse than any pain. He must! He . . .

There was . . .

Itlothis blinked.

Light, much more light than had been in that cavern below Yul. She stared up at a gray ceiling. Here was no scent of dust, nor of ages.

She was back!

Hands had drawn away the dream helmet. She sat up, still hardly believing that she, they, had won. She turned quickly to that other divan. The attendants had removed his helmet, his hands arose unsteadily to his head, but his eyes were open.

Now he saw her. His gaze widened. "Then you *were* real!"

"Yes." Had he really imagined that she was only a part of his dream? Itlothis was oddly discomfited by that thought. She had taken all those risks in his service and he thought she had only been part of his fantasy.

Oslan sat up, looked about as if he could not quite believe he had returned. Then he laughed, not angrily as he had in Yul, but it triumph.

"We did it!" He slammed his fist down on the couch. "The nest *was* walled off, that was what made *it* so wild. Yul is dead!"

He had carried the fantasy back with him, the obsession still possessed him. Itlothis felt a little sick. But Oslan ·Sb Atto was still her client. She could not, dared not, identify with him. She had performed her mission successfully, his family must deal with him now.

Itlothis turned to the medico. "The Clan Chief is confused."

"I am anything but confused!" Oslan's voice rang

cut behind her. "Wait and see, Gentle Fem, just wait and see!'"

Though she was apprehensive during the hyper jump back to Benold, Oslan did not mention his dream again. Nor did he attempt to be much in her company, keeping mostly in his cabin. However, when they reached the spaceport on their home planet, he took command with an authority that overrode hers.

Before she could report formally, he swept her aboard a private flyer bearing the Atto insignia. His action made her more uneasy than angry. She had dared to hope as time passed that he had thrown off the effect of the dream. Now she could see he was still possessed by it even though this was not the Benold the dreamer had envisioned.

As he turned the flyer north, he shot a glance at her.

"You believe me ready for reprogramming, do you not, Itlothis?"

She refused to answer. They would be followed. She had managed to send off a signal before they raised from the port.

"You want proof I am sane? Very well, I shall give you that!"

He pushed the flyer to top speed. Atto lay ahead, but also Yul! What was he going to do?

In less than an hour planet time, Itlothis had her answer. The small craft dipped over the ruins. Only this was not the same Yul she had seen on her first flight to Atto. Here only a portion of the outer walls still stood. Inside those was a vast hollow in which lay only a few shattered blocks.

Oslan cut power, landed the craft in the very center of the hollow. He was quickly free of the cabin, then reached in to urge her out with him. Nor did he loose his hold on her as he asked:

"See?"

The one word echoed back hollowly from the still standing outer walls.

"What . . ." Itlothis must admit that this was a new Yul, but to believe that action taken in a dream on a planet light years away could cause such destruction. . . .

"The charge reached the nest!" he said excitedly. "I set the energy on the crawler to excess. When the power touched the danger mark it blew. Then there was no safe place left for *It* to sleep in, only this!"

She had, Itlothis supposed, to accept the evidence of her eyes. But what she saw went against all reason as she knew it. Yet whatever blast had occurred here had not been only weeks ago, the signs of the catastrophe were ages old! *Had* they been sent eons back in time? Itlothis began to feel that *this* was a dream, some nightmare hallucination.

But Oslan was continuing:

"Feel it? *That* has gone. There is no other life here now!'"

She stood within his hold. Once in her childhood, when she was first being trained for the service, she had been brought to Yul. Then only just within the outer wall, beyond which few could go, and none dared stay long. She remembered that venture vividly. Oslan was right! Here was no longer that brooding menace. Just the cry of seabirds, the distant beat of waves. Yul was dead, long ago deserted by life.

"But it was a *dream!*" she protested dazedly. "Just a dream!"

Oslan slowly shook his head. "It was real. Now Yul is free. We are here to prove that. I told you once, 'Get out of my dream' I was wrong; it was meant to be your dream also. Now this is our reality . . . an empty Yul, a free world. And, in time, perhaps something else."

His arms about her tightened. Not in anger or fear. Itlothis, meeting that brilliant green stare holding hers, knew that dreams, some dreams, never quite released their dreamers.

PART
FOUR
Nightmare

Nightmare

"BUT I KNOW nothing of this sector." The youngest man in the room squirmed slightly in his easirest, as if that half-reclining seat, intended for maximum comfort was now giving more than minimum unease.

"Which is precisely why you are necessary for the operation," came a cold-tinged reply from one of the three facing him, the Trystian whose feather crest held the slight fading of age.

"A Terrian of a wealthy clan, touring this sector," the man to the Trystian's left elaborated, "could visit Ty-Kry, order a dreamer's services without comment or questions being asked in the wrong places. It is well known that our multi-credit class are ever avid to try new experiences. Your background would be impeccable, of course."

Burr Neklass shrugged. He had never had any quarrel with that department of the service. Any background they supplied could be combed and recombed with impunity for the one using it. He would be provided with a life history dating back to the moment of his birth and it would be a flawless one. That was not the base of his present uneasiness.

Being who and what he was, he now came out frankly with that basic argument

"I am not an Esper."

"You were chosen for that very reason," Hyon returned. "Anyone testing Esper, and do not consider for a second that they will not investigate you thoroughly, would have no chance."

"So I'm just bait." Again Burr hunched his shoulders against the easirest. "And it appears very expendable bait."

Grigor Bnon, the only true human on that inner council, smiled. It seemed to Burr there was an implied taunt in the curl of his lips as he did so. Bnon had a reputation, which it was said he delighted in, of being utterly un-human when it came to assignments.

"Very good bait," he said softly now. "According to the record you are just the type meant to this trap, whatever it is or however it works."

"Thank you so much, Commander!" Burr snapped. "And what if I say 'no'?"

Bnon shrugged. "There is always that, of course. And it is your privilege."

"And you want me to do it," Burr returned silently. "You have been waiting a long time to catch me a hair's space off orders, either way, 'yes' or 'no,' you'll have me." There was a sour taste in his mouth which could have come from biting hard on that realization.

"So I go in without any backman, then what if I turn up dead? Will you know any more than you do right now? You haven't been able to monitor these dreams in any way . . ." His sentence had a slight lift which made it half-question. If they could monitor, get him out before the final fatal minute, that would put a different face upon the whole operation.

"Not in the way you think," the third of those facing him spoke for the first time. Outwardly, he was so humanoid that Burr might have accepted him for a Terran-descended colonist. Only his strange pupilless eyes and the fine down which covered the visible portions of his skin named him alien. "But there will be a backup for you. To have another man killed uselessly would avail us nothing at all."

"I am grateful to hear that," Burr put what irony he could in his reply to Corps Master Ulan.

Ulan appeared not to hear him. "We shall provide the dreamer you know; I have been informed that you were fully briefed, that these dreamers are either hired or purchased from the Hive. On the death of any purchaser, the dreamer must be returned, half of her price being repaid to the clan-family of her owner. If she is rehired, then it is for an agreed-upon time only.

"Osdeve, Lord of Ulay, purchased a ten-point dreamer two years ago, He was in the last stages of kaffer fever. Two days ago he died. This dreamer, Uahach, must now be returned to the Hive. It is the general custom that once an out-dreamer so returns, she is not resold for at least a year, since each owner or hirer programs the dreamer to his taste and she must have a rest before such reprogramming.

"However, the Foostmam of the Hive is not one to suffer idle minds. She will allow Hive dreaming for Uahach, providing that the one who purchases the girl's time is willing to accept any dream and does not require a certain briefing.

"You will be a tourist, wanting simply to try a dream as part of your travel experiences. Therefore, Uahach would answer your purpose as well as any other. You have heard of her and can ask for her with an excellent reason . . ." Hyon paused for breath and Burr shot in his question. "How did I hear of her if I have never been in Ty-Kry before?"

"Osdeve was off planet three years ago. He visited Melytis. As the person you will be on Ty-Kry, you made his acquaintance there. In fact, he spoke so much of dreaming that you came to Ty-Kry lured by his stories."

Burr was frowning a little. He had no doubts about their meeting in Melytis, that would be so expertly documented that it would stand now for the truth. But he was puzzled concerning another point.

"This Uahach, how can you be sure of her?"

"She is an agent . . . or will be by the time she returns to the Hive," Bnon explained. "With some plasta buildup, she'll be Uahach; she *is* an Esper and has been undergoing dream study for some time. We had her long before the assignment computer selected you."

And this unknown "she," Burr accepted, was taking even a far greater risk than they expected him to accept. Dreamers were born, though they underwent vigorous training to achieve the status of A or E, ready to guide someone through their imagined worlds.

"Yes, she is one of us," Hyon once more took over. "And her being unattached at this moment is what brought us together. We had to wait for just such a circumstance. Five deaths and no answers!" For the first time, the Trystian showed outward emotion. "There is too leading a pattern: two diplomats; an engineer who had made recently a discovery, which left him so wealthy that he was about to set up his own research laboratory; two men of great possessions whose dream deaths brought about almost galaxy-wide confusion. Someone is troubling waters in order to collect the flotsam of such storms."

"Maybe they all had weak hearts . . . I hear that action dreams can be tough to take," Burr suggested, though he did not believe his own words.

Bnon snorted. "You do not Hive-dream if you do not present a certificate of health to the Foostmam on your first visit They may not follow up what happens to the owner of a dreamer, but one-time dream excursions within the Hive are well supervised·so that this sort of thing does not happen. They want no accusation of killing off their clients. It would be ruinous for their business."

"Yet it has happened," Burr pointed out. "Five times."

"Five times within the space of one planet year," agreed Hyon.

"But if these deaths are arranged, aren't they playing it reckless?" Burr mused, more to himself than the other three. "I should think they would be waiting for the authorities to do some investigating."

"The planet authorities," Hyon returned, "have done what they could. But they cannot shut down the Hive, nor are they even allowed to screen the dreamers, that could be fatal. And Ty-Kry is dreamer-oriented. The dead were all from off planet and such as would not cause any local stir. In fact, Villand and Wyvid were both traveling incognito and not officially. But the authorities were enough concerned to call us in, a step which is revolutionary as far as they are concerned, as the locals resent to a high degree off-world contacts. They made the proviso when they did that we were *not* to appear there officially either, and they will give no open help to any investigation we might start."

Burr grinned without mirth. "Do they know about your planted dreamer?"

"No. And they are not to know either. The Hive has a monopoly on its product. To learn that a dreamer might be created by artificial means would turn the whole planet hostile. There is a religious significance to the existence of these girls and that we dare not meddle with."

"But what would make me so important they would try their game a sixth time?" Burr wanted to know.

"Burr Neklass has become owner of an asteroid which is nearly pure Bylotite," Hyon answered.

Burr's eyebrows lifted in unbelief. "*Is* there any such thing?" he asked wonderingly.

"It exists, yes. And it is under the guardianship of the Patrol. All rights are now on record in your name. You have no near family, and . . ." Hyon paused as if to give extra emphasis to what he would say next, "one of your partners in Neklass Enterprises has been approached, very cautiously but with enough seriousness to be understood, to discover whether, at your death, the Bylotite will be included in your general estate. I do not doubt that there is already on record, perhaps not on Ty-Kry as there would be too pointed, a will ready to turn this estate over to whoever makes the highest bid for your life."

"Fine, you do have me well hammered in, don't you?" Burr scowled. "So, I'm good bait for murder. All right, when do I lay myself all ready and waiting on the Hive altar?"

"You will be briefed at once," Hyon said. "Then you will take your own space cruiser to Ty-Kry. There, you will proceed to make yourself very visible as a man of great wealth who wants to try the unusual. I think there will be no difficulty in your finding the Hive welcoming and you will then ask for Uahach . . ."

"And get down to a good death dream," Burr finished for him. "Thank you, one and all, for this exciting assignment. I shall remember you in my dreams!"

HER FIGURE hidden in a dull gray sack of a robe, her hair cut so close to her head that it seemed less than half a finger in length so that the dream helmet would fit more easily, the slight figure sliding out of the carrying chair could have been any age from pre-teen to elderly. Her face was blank of any expression as she moved with the air of one still inhabiting those dreams which were her trade. The guard flung open the door and she stepped into the noiseless, curtained secrecy of the Hive.

As she moved down the central hall, her eyes kept their fixed stare, but inwardly she was recognizing that which she had never seen before, but which the intensity of a mind-to-mind briefing had made plain to her. She was not Ludia Tanguly any longer, but Uahach, an A dreamer with a ten-point rating. And it had been two years, a little more, since she had left the Hive to which she now returned. Luckily, they had been able to so dip into the dreamer's mind that her double was familiar with all she saw, knew well the routine for returning.

Uahach turned toward a door to her right and stood, impassive, waiting for the spy ray to announce her. When the barrier split in two, she entered.

The room was small, containing only two chairs, not easirests but of the archaic hard-seated kind. It would seem that the Foostmam made no concessions of comfort for those who sought an interview. A memory control stood between the chairs, within easy reach of the ruler of the Hive. And there was a blank screen on the wall to one side. The Foostmam herself sat waiting Uahach's arrival. She gave no verbal greeting, only raised a hand to signify that the dreamer might sit in the second chair.

"You have not come very speedily," the woman observed. "Your late lord died four days ago." Her tone was monotonous. If she meant her words as a question, they did not carry that inflection. And if she offered a reproof for tardiness, that, too, could only be guessed at.

"I was not released by my Lord's heir until an hour since. I then vision-messaged at once," Uahach's own voice held the same absence of meaningful accent. She had let her hands fall limply in her lap, sitting as one who had been under orders all her life.

"True. It was necessary for the Hive to remind the Lord Ylph that our contract was only with his predecessor. His reluctance to release you has been duly noted in the records. Perhaps he had thought to bargain . . . because of your rating and the satisfaction your Lord took in your dreams. We, however, do not bargain. And you are returned. Your dream records have been fed into the archives. For the present you are on inactive status. The Lord Osdeve required much research; it may even be necessary for you to undergo an erase." Now there was a faint shadow of some emotion in the Foostmam's eyes. "The records must be studied to the full, I do not wish to order an unnecessary erase."

Uahach remained outwardly impassive, but inside her instinct for self-defense awoke. Had the Corps Master foreseen that? To undergo an erase would negate everything she was programmed to do. If that happened, she would become Uahach in truth.

"There is this . . ." the Foostmam's thin mouth snapped out each word as if she cut it free with a knife. "We are getting more and more of a new type of client, off worlders who seek sensations strange to them. The lore you studied for Lord Osdeve was largely action adventure. And you might be a Hive dreamer for a length of time, serving these newcomers. They would not find what you had to offer too familiar."

"I am a Ten Point," Uahach said.

"And so above Hive service?" The Foostmam nodded. "It is agreed. Yet you must be rebriefed before you are again hired for outside. Be assured that you shall not be downgraded in the least."

"I shall be guided by you in this as in all else," the girl gave the conventional answer. So Bnon had been right, already the first move of her game had been made.

"You are a true dreamer," the Foostmam replied with her conventional dismissal words. "I have given you the Chamber of the Mantled Suxsux. Dial what you may need. Your credit is unlimited."

Uahach arose and raised one hand to touch her forehead, the Foostmam replying with a perfunctory copy of that gesture. To be told that her Hive credit was unlimited meant that she was still rated a very valuable piece of merchandise. As she moved along the hall, ascended the twenty steps to the next floor, she was already planning what she must do now. And since the Foostmam had suggested that she was to be hired in Hive service, she had every right to start learning all she could.

The library of tapes owned by the Hive was the most spectacular collection of general information gathered anyplace in the galaxy except at Patrol Headquarters. Travelers' tales from thousands of worlds, history, strange stories, anything which could enrich the worlds the dreamers created for their clients, was at the call of those within the Hive. But was there any method of locating the special tapes either of the suspected dreamers had called upon? That was one fact they had not been able to ferret out for her. She knew the names of those dreamers, Isa and Dynamis. Both were action dreamers, neither one supposedly of ten-point rank, and both never hired outside the Hive. Uahach's memories, which had been sifted as well as the Patrol science could manage, had supplied a hazy picture of Isa. Dynamis was totally unknown. She was young, one of the Late Dreamers, whose talent developed enough to be measured only when she entered adolescence and not in early childhood when most of them were found and brought in for training.

Isa had survived the two dreams which had killed her clients . . . but just barely. She was, by all accounts the planet law enforcers passed along, now a near vegetable. Dynamis had had better luck. Though it had been necessary for her to undergo, the Foostmam had sworn, a lengthy period of reeducation.

The dreaming itself was not too complicated an affair, though it was particular to this world. Linked by a machine which capped both dreamer and client, the dreamer entered into a hallucinatory state in which the client partook of vigorous action, some type of which he selected in advance. He could so return into the past, explore other worlds, venture into the speculative future. If a lengthy dream was desired, both dreamer and client could spend as long as a week so engaged, fed intravenously. And at any point, the client could demand to break the dream.

Yet, five men had dreamed themselves into death, and had not awakened. Once, perhaps twice, a faulty machine, a weakened heart, or some natural fatality could have occurred, but five were far too many.

The Foostmam had had, as Uahach well knew, every machine tested before the authorities. She demanded, and in this she was backed by those same authorities, certificates of health from every would-be client. And those were the result of examinations which could not be faked. The law in Ty-Kry had no wish to continue a scandal which was growing far too fast for comfort. The dreamers, long in use by the natives, had recently become a prime tourist attraction, the worth of which the rulers of the planet fully recognized.

Yet, in spite of all such safeguards, one dreamer was brainwashed into idiocy and five men were dead. Five men whose deaths could be turned to the credit of others off world. Suspicion was heavy, now there must be proof.

She came to the door bearing the painted design of

the fabled creature the Foostmam had mentioned, and knew the chamber to be one of coveted single rooms within this warren. She was, indeed, being shown that her value to the Hive had in no way diminished.

Though the room was considered luxurious by any dreamer who had not been quartered in one of the sky towers of the Lords, it was a small one with few attractions. There was a couch formed of piled cushions covered in dull greens and grays; nothing must distract the attention of a dreamer, lure her attention from her work. Against one wall was a reading screen with a slitted block before it into which any tapes she desired could be fitted. On the opposite wall was a small board with a row of buttons; she could there order the bland, nearly tasteless food high in protein and nourishment which was the usual meal of her kind.

A curtain hung before a small private bathroom. That, too, was gray, as was the thick carpet on the floor. Uahach sat down on the divan, wondering if the Foostmam had some hidden method of viewing the chambers of her charges. That point certainly could not be overlooked, and she must never be off her guard.

There was a thick silence here, not a single sound came from without, though the Hive was crowded. Again, the dreamer must be able to study undisturbed by any-thing outside her own cubicle. Probably they did not find silence oppressive. To them, dreaming was life and the world outside those they themselves created did not exist except as a shadowy and uninteresting place.

She went to dial for a drink, accepting the small cup of hot liquid gratefully. Her mouth felt parched and she was aware of that usual reaction to coming danger. The familiar dryness of her tongue and lips, the moisture of her palms were warnings for her to exert the techniques in which she had long been schooled.

Waiting was always difficult. If one could plunge straight into the indicated action, one lost oneself in that. But to have to sit and wait . . . How long before the other player Hyon was putting on the board arrived? She would not even know who he was, nor how much she could depend on him. And she did not like working in the dark. This was far outside of any operation of which she had before been a part. And she found she enjoyed it less with every passing minute.

❋ ❋ ▐▐▐ ❋ ❋

"SO I ASK for this Uahach."

The Foostmam's hands rested on the edge of her memory control board. She favored Burr with an unwinking stare so devoid of any personality, he began to wonder if the ruler of the Hive was now caught in some dream herself. Then she spoke, without any warning inflection in her voice.

"You say that the Lord Osdeve spoke of her. Yes, she was on lease to him. But you must understand, Lord, she is still unbriefed in a new series, for she has only returned to the Hive two days ago. You would not be able to choose your subject matter. . . ."

Burr opened his belt pouch, produced a silvery credit plate.

"I'm not asking for a series to be arranged just for me. In fact, I am only curious to see how this dreaming of Ty-Kry works. Any briefing she had had for Lord Osdeve would be all right as far as I am concerned. It is merely that I would like to try it as an experiment, you understand."

The Foostmam's stare had shifted for several breaths to the credit plate. Burr himself had never handled such before: unlimited credit, a promise to be accepted on any planet where the Council had an Embassy.

"For a single dreaming time," the Foostmam said, "the price is higher, since the dreamer has no security factor for the future."

Burr shrugged. "Price does not matter. But I want Uahach. Osdeve had plenty to say about her dreaming when I saw him last."

The Foostmam again favored him with that blank expression. But her hand went to one of the buttons on the small control board and pressed two. A pattern, not a face, flashed on the vision screen. She eyed it and then her hand closed over the credit plate.

"She has not yet gone through debriefing. Very well, if you will accept Osdeve's series, it can be done. You have your certificate of health and stability?"

He produced a second piece of perforated plasta. She accepted that to push into a slit on the control board. There was a relay of clicks and the pattern on the screen changed.

"What is the danger in dreaming?" he decided to come openly to the point. As an off worlder, unfamiliar with the processes of the Hive, Burr believed that he could ask such a question as a matter of routine.

"A ten-point A dreamer," the Foostmam returned, "can produce so vivid a dream that its reality entirely grips the client. In such cases, any strain on the heart or the mind can prove to be a very serious thing. Therefore, we naturally wish to know that this will not happen. We will also have a Medic standing by. But the final choice anywhere in the dream to leave is always for the Client to exercise. If you dislike the dream, you will it to end. Since you will be mind-linked with the dreamer, your will instantly records with her and she releases you."

"The danger then must be slight," Burr prodded.

"It has been so." Apparently the Foostmam was not going to say anything about the recent fatalities in the Hive. "When do you wish to call upon Uahach's services?"

"How about right now?" Burr pressed. "The rest of this Five Days I guest with Lord Erlvin and I believe he has made arrangements I cannot alter."

The Foostmam held his credit plaque between thumb and forefinger. She was again fixed of eyes, but Burr was sure she was no longer studying him, rather thinking deeply.

"Uahach is free, that is true. But there must be our own preparations to be made. At the present, all our interior dream rooms are occupied. But if you will choose to return past nooning it can be arranged."

"Good enough." Burr reached forward and plucked the credit plate from her fingers. She had continued to hold that as if reluctant to lay it down. He wondered fleetingly just how many such plaques she had ever seen. Galaxy-wide complete credit vouchers could not be too common.

He nooned in the best of Ty-Kry's restaurants. And he ate sparingly, selecting from a list which had been supplied him along with the plaque which had so entranced the mistress of the Hive. All that could possibly be done to ensure his own safety (outside of actually canceling the operation entirely) was accomplished. But he did face the unknown, and a threatening unknown.

When he returned to the Hive he was shown directly to a room occupied nearly to the full extent of its area by two couches. Between them stood the machine of linkage and there was already a girl stretched on the right-hand couch, her face masked past nose level by a helmet. Its twin awaited him. The dreamer was breathing in slow, regular breaths and Burr wondered if she were already asleep.

Two attendants, one of whom wore the insignia of a Medic greeted him and, within moments, Burr was installed on the other couch, blindfolded by the padded helmet. He drew a very deep breath of his own. There was no pulling back now; this was it!

He blacked out with a queasy feeling of whirling out and out through space itself. Then there came a burst of light as if he lay under the warmth of a sun, helmetless and in the open.

Burr sat up slowly, surveying the country about him. He had not expected this . . . this freedom of body, the absolute reality of all he could see. Experimentally, he pulled at a tuft of gray-green grass. It resisted and then gave way, so that roots and reddish soil parted company. He . . . this . . . was so *real!*

Around his present position small hills or mounds arose to make a wall about a cup of lower land in which he crouched. On the top of each was embedded a standing stone, weatherworn, but certainly never so regularly placed by any natural means. The country bore no resemblance to any he had ever seen before.

Burr got slowly to his feet. An A dream promised straight action adventure. This landscape had a certain grim and threatening appearance, but as far as he could see, he was alone in it and there was an absence of any life signs. No bird wheeled overhead, no insect buzzed or flew. This was being on a deserted stage before the curtain arose and the play began.

The nearest of the rounded hills attracted him. From its summit surely he would be able to see more than he could in this hollow. And toward that block-crowned summit he climbed.

The tall mound was covered with grass of the same gray-green shade as the tuft he had pulled. And it was both steep and slippery, so he stumbled and had to clutch at the grass to keep from slipping back into the spot where he had entered this hallucinatory world.

Once on the crest he turned slowly, facing outward, trying to get an idea of the country. The hills with their pillars continued on into what he guessed was the north in an unending series. But to the south there were only a few before they gave way to a wide open land in which were embedded a number of stones, tumbled together in a manner which suggested they were very ancient remains of some building or buildings, long reduced to a rubble, either by time itself or some ancient disaster.

There was a deep, quiet brooding over this stark world. Yet from somewhere came a vibration which could be felt rather than heard. It was almost as if the land itself were breathing, slowly, heavily.

Burr had a desire to shout, to make some sound which would rip away that quiet. He mistrusted all he saw with more than the mistrust which warnings had set in him. This was . . . dangerous, in a way he could not grasp.

His hand went to his belt, or where his belt should have rested, instinctively hunting a stunner such as any prudent man wore in strange territory. But his fingers swept across bare skin and, for the first time, he looked down at his own body.

He was no longer wearing the rather fantastic suit which had been designed for Burr Neklass, multi-credit man. Instead, his body was darker of skin where it was clearly visible. He did have on a pair of breeches of a steel-colored material, seemingly elastic and fitting nearly as tightly as that same skin. On his feet were coverings feeling as soft as if fashioned of cloth, but soled with thickness of a dull red material, while the upper part of the shoes(?) were stitched with glittering red thread to mark each hidden toe plainly.

Above the waist he had two belt straps, not for about his waist, but reaching one over the right shoulder and one the left. Where those crossed on his breast they were united with a palm-sized plate of silver metal in which were set colored stones ranging in shade from a deep red to a brilliant orange. About each upper arm was a wide band of the same silver, one bearing all red stones, the other yellow to orange. It was to Burr the dress of some off-world barbarian, in spite of the obviously fine workmanship, and certainly one he had never seen before.

Movement among the rumbled blocks of the ruins sent him ducking prudently to shelter behind the monolith which stood beside him on the hilltop. For the first time, he realized his folly in making so open an appearance there. Something was flitting from cover to cover among the stones, moving so fast he could catch only a confused glimpse of it. He could not even be sure it was humanoid.

There were plainly no weapons furnished him in this dress. Now, as he knelt behind the stone, Burr gazed around him for some possible way of arming himself. Finally, he pried loose a small rock which he held in his hand.

A usual client of any dreamer was prepared for the nature of the dream, since he had indeed ordered it. But Burr must accept the programming which Osdeve had ordered and what had been implanted in the pseudo-Uahach.

Therefore, he did not know what to expect, except trouble. And perhaps that was flitting toward him even now.

IV

THERE WERE MORE than one . . . Burr drew a deep breath, his grip on the stone so tight that the rough surface scored his fingertips. One hid behind two blocks still piled one on top of the other, a second moved, with the same fluid speed, more to his right, gone to cover before he had more than an impression of raw color, an acid blue which flashed swiftly among the stones.

That they hunted him, he somehow knew. Perhaps Osdeve enjoyed this type of thrill . . . chase, choosing, because of the infirmities of his final years, a physical-combat type of dream.

Burr glanced over his shoulder at the procession of mound-hills filing on to the far horizon. He could retreat perhaps, play what he was sure would be a deadly kind of hide-and-seek, through that countryside. But that would only prolong whatever action lay in this dream. No, he would stay where he was until he was sure that the danger ahead was too much for him to handle.

Perhaps they had lost sight of him and their impatience was enough to bring them out. For they were moving again, this time farther into the open. There, some distance from each other, yet in an even line, three oddities stood statue still, as if by freezing they could also conceal their presence.

For an off-world traveler, Burr had long lost the ability to be surprised by any alien difference from his own norm. But these were unusual enough to rivet his attention.

It was hard to judge sizes from this distance, but he believed that all three of them were taller than himself. And they were birds, or at least birdlike in form. Their bodies, perched on long, thin legs, were covered with a vivid blue or green feathering (there were one green and two blues) which fluffed into plumes for tails. Their heads were unusually large, bearing tall crests of feathers, large eyes, and murderous appearing bills with points like Harkiman short swords. These outsize heads were connected to the bodies by long and very supple necks which were bare of the feathering, showing instead an expanse of scaled skin.

There was nothing reassuring about them. Rather Burr *knew*, just as he had been sure he was the quarry of a hunt, that they were deadly enemies to his own kind.

Now they were no longer so still. The green one dropped its head, a fraction, straightened its neck. Thus it pointed directly in Burr's direction. The man began to suspect that perhaps his lingering here had been the wrong choice after all. Yet the speed with which the bird things had transversed the ruins made him sure that any race between them would end fatally for him.

Was this how those others had died? Had they been

hunted, perhaps not by those feathered monstrosities before him, but by other enemies? He remembered the warning of the Foostmam: he could wake . . .

The green bird took a flying leap which lifted it from among the blocks, moved it as if it were a chess piece in action to the crown of a nearer hill, slightly lower than that on which Burr had taken refuge. No use trying to play hero, this was a time to wake.

Instead of his directive being answered by an instant cancellation of the hunt menacing him, there was a quiver of light through the air. Point deep in the earth beside his sheltering monolith stood a spear, its shaft still vibrating a little from the force of the throw which had hurled it there.

Instinctively, Burr's hand went out to tighten on that shaft. And the same time, he was startled by a shout from the north. The head of the green bird snapped around, its intent gaze now in that direction. Burr wrenched the spear out of the ground. But overriding all else in his mind at that moment was that the cancellation demand had *not* worked!

So, he balanced the spear in one hand. This was it! He could well have been abandoned here. And the pseudo-Uahach who got him into this could not get him out. His stubborn refusal to be downed took over. Someone had thrown him a weapon, though it appeared a very paltry one taken in connection with the size and swiftness of the enemy. And someone had drawn the bird's attention . . .

Burr edged around, trying to keep an eye on the birds as well as discover who had come to his rescue, if only momentarily. At the same moment, the green bird gave vent to the first sound he had heard it make, a shrill, ear-tormenting scream. It sprang directly into the air from the stand it had taken on the other mound.

And, though it seemed wingless and unable to fly, that prodigious leap carried it directly to another mound, this even with the one on which Burr crouched, but still a short distance away. It no longer watched him, rather continued to look to the north.

Though he felt he dared not glance away from its two companions still among the ruins, he had to know who, or what, the thing was now moving to attack.

The body of the bird tensed, its long legs just a little bent. Burr was sure it was about to launch a third spectacular leap. If so, it was a fraction late in coming to that determination. Something whirled through the air. The weighted ends of a long cord snapped about the legs just under the bird's body, the force of their passage wrapping the limbs tightly together. The bird crashed with a fury of squawking, its head bobbing up and down as it tore at that prisoning cord with its wicked bill. As it writhed on the ground, a second weighted cord whirled, wrapping about its neck with force enough to completely overset it and bind its head partly to its body.

Burr slued around to watch for its companions. They had vanished, though they might be using the cover of the mounds themselves to come to the aid of their half-bound fellow.

"Come!"

That was no scream from the bird, it was a clearly distinguishable word in everyday Basic. Burr turned again. Two mounds away, a figure stood waving him on.

The newcomer was cloaked, a hood pulled well down so he could distinguish little more than it had at least a general humanoid shape. And since there was nothing else to do, he obeyed, running down one slope and up the next at the best speed he could manage, while the corded bird continued to screech.

He was gasping as he fought up the last incline. A hand shot out from under the edge of the cloak, caught his arm and jerked him on, so that both of them were able to dart behind the monolith on this mound.

"That whip-round will not hold the qwaker long." Burr was looking eye to eye with a girl. She pushed back her hood, showing hair pulled tight into a clasp high near the crown of her head, flowing freely from that down to her shoulders. And that hair was a dark blue. As with Burr, the skin she bared as she shrugged the cloak back on her shoulders to free her arms was dark brown. And under her slanting blue brows her eyes shone like fiery sparks of orange flame.

Burr balanced the spear thoughtfully. "I would not say this would be too effective either," he commented dryly. "What now, do we run?"

He had no idea from whence this female had sprung. She seemed to have saved his life for the moment at least. Now she was shaking her head so that upheld plume of hair swished back and forth whispering against her hooded shoulders.

"That is what they wish. They can move faster than any man. No, we change . . ."

"Change what," he repeated.

"Change our dream site. Give me your hand!" Her

fingers closed about his in a grip which had no gentleness in it. With the other hand, she made a sweeping gesture.

The world reeled and Burr closed his eyes to fight nausea, for this instability was outside of any state of consciousness he knew. When he made himself look once more he was standing on a beach of yellowish sand against which washed, with turgid slowness, a vast body of water that might even be a languid sea. But his hand was still clasped in hers and he caught what might be a sigh of relief. Then she dropped her hold and moved a little away.

"So . . ." she said as if to herself, "so far that they cannot alter."

"What is all this?" Burr asserted himself to demand, and his voice came out almost embarrassingly loud above the slight whisper of the wavelets.

"Listen," she turned a little to fix him with a very direct gaze, "they have us locked somehow. When you tried to break, I could not make it. Do you understand? They have us both locked in this dream, and it is only partly out of Uahach's memories. The ruins were hers . . . and the qwakers. They actually exist, or did exist, on Altair IV. But they are not hostile. Now . . ."

"Uahach's memory," Burr caught the part that he understood the first. "Then you are . . ."

She laughed harshly. "I am your backup, the dreamer. But I am now caught in my own snare. You gave the signal to wake, I would have obeyed. But there was a barrier. However, they did not, as least yet, manage to inhibit movement within this dream. We are now here," she gestured to the beach, "instead of dodging qwakers back on those hills. I do not know if they can control us within the dream, or just keep us here. But we dare not count on any safety."

Burr tightened hold on the spear shaft. He understood her well enough. They were caught in this exceedingly real dream and at present, there was no escape. "Can you keep doing this . . . move us around if they threaten us?"

She shrugged. "Some. I can call on Uahach's memory in a little. But if they force me to reach the end of those, then . . ." she shook her head. "Beyond her memory, I have no pattern to follow. I knew of this sea in this particular dream. There are perhaps four other sites we can switch to.'"

"And after that," he finished for her, "we will be really trapped?"

Slowly she nodded, and echoed him. "Really trapped."

V

BURR examined the point of the spear, which he still held. The metal was three-ridged, though dull of color. He had been schooled in the use of such barbarian arms as the sword, dagger, and primitive weapons which fired projectiles. But he had never attempted to use such as this before.

"You know this dream," he said slowly, "what is the pattern Uahach set in it for Osdeve? Can you see that ahead enough so that we will know what might come up next?"

"So far, it is the same, as to background, even to the qwakers. However, there are subtle alterations. The qwakers were meant to be hunted, not to hunt. Osdeve enjoyed such hunts. Here . . ." she hesitated. "Be warned— he was dreamed here to meet with Sea Rovers and join them on an expedition against the ancient sea Lords of the Isles. There were three such episodes within the dream: a hunting of the birds, the sea voyage, and at last the venture to take him to the Tower of Kiln-nam-u. Each has potential danger if the dream does not proceed as it should. Now there is a pressure which I do not understand . . ."

She spoke slowly, a slight frown marking her forehead.

"You understand that you are now a different personality, Your name is Gurret and you are the Warrior of the Right."

Burr scowled. "How much of this . . ." he began.

"The dreamers create a form of reality," she struck in before he could complete his question. "You are a part of this world, which is an ancient time on Altair IV, yet not quite that either, since each dreamer adds her own touches. I am Kaitilih, a War Woman of the Left. Traditionally, we would have been enemies. But it seems that Uahach altered that point also. By her plan, we are united on a quest whereby, is the manner of legends on each world, we must find certain things. Having these in hand we are to return to the Three Towers and there . . ." She smiled faintly, "I gather from dreamer memories, our reward would be spectacular. Of course, even though there was a strong element of risk in this dream, Osdeve was at no time in great danger, just enough to satisfy his need for the action he craved. But now, with the alterations, I cannot foresee what may lie ahead within the general frame of the original dream."

"If we are warriors," Burr returned, "why no real weapons?"

"Because this quest was meant to be a testing. I carried the spear, the whirling cords, but neither was used. It was set on you to go bare-handed."

"You snapped us out of that attack. Can you dream up

a stunner, or something better than this?" Burr banished
the spear.

Slowly, she shook her head. "I can add nothing of
my own, only use the material provided from Uahach's
memory. You know I am not a trained dreamer. And . . ."
she turned her head to look up and down the deserted
beach, "there is pressure on me. There is someone else
who meddles and changes so subtly that I cannot trace
that interference to its source. Just as the hunt in the hills
was reversed. I believe we can look for other reverses to
come."

"Fine!" Burr snapped. "Best if we stuck it out right
here while you try to break the dream."

"We cannot halt the flow of action," the dreamer
replied. "We have to play the pattern through to the
end."

Burr knew she was speaking what she believed to be
the truth. So roles were reversed so far in the dream.
Might they then take it that that would continue?

"Two more pieces of action then. What should they
be?"

"You are to light a beacon of the drift," Kaitilih, as she
had named herself, motioned toward the bone colored,
sea-cured wood which was caught among the shore rocks.
"This should be done at twilight. Then a boat will come in
from a raider named the Erne. You have already, or
Gurret has, contacted the Captain of the Erne, promising
him rich loot at the Sea Keep of Eastern Vur. All you
want from Vur is the Cup of Blood that Death kept in
hiding there. There will be great peril, but the Erne will
be lucky, getting in and out without dire mishaps. With

the Cup in your possession you can then bargain with that which holds the Tower of Kiln-nam-u—"

Burr laughed harshly. "This is like some tale for a child's reading screen! Do you mean that Osdeve actually wanted to live out this wild nonsense?"

"It is not a story, but a legend with a core of truth," the girl corrected him. "Much research was done to provide the very old bones of a hero tale with the proper background and contemporary details. Part of it is history. There *was* a Gurret who was the first Supreme Arms Lord of half his world. And he gained that position because he pursued such a quest. The dreamers are adept in returning to the past, not only of their own world, but any other planet whose history appeared in their study tapes."

"But if it *was* . . . *is*, history, then how can it be altered? I gather I was supposed to do something else upon awaking than run from those qwakers as I did."

"Yes. You were to capture two who would then make you free of their nest place. There in the debris you would find a very old cylinder of metal in which lay a map of Vur . . ."

"It's unreasonable!" Burr interrupted. "I can't believe that any adult would be serious about this . . . even if it is supposed to be history!"

"I assure you Osdeve was. As a man who had lost much use of his own body he craved this outlet as a drug addict craves the powders which will give him entrance to another world for a space. This was Osdeve's last dream before he died and it was the most elaborate and complicated one Uahach was ever called upon to plot, for he had good warning that he was very close to the end."

"I thought that anyone in poor condition was not allowed to dream," Burr countered.

"An off worlder, yes. But a native of Ty-Kry is not bound by such rules. Some have chosen to die in dreams."

"But that . . . I thought that was impossible. It was because men died that we are here."

"Then the situation was entirely different. Those victims were off worlders, known to be in good health, and they had not signed any dismissals. Also the dreams they had selected were not dangerous ones."

Burr shook his head. "But a man can be dreamed to death?"

"If that is his recorded desire. And it must be recorded and certified by the Lords in Council, also the First Person of his name clan. It is not permitted to any off worlder."

"All right," Burr knew that she was doubtless well schooled in this dreaming business. "But this dream has been already altered. I did not get that map or whatever that Gurret is supposed to have. What if I don't build the signal fire and the raider does not come? Will that break the dream?"

"I don't know. Perhaps you will be forced to take the next step."

Burr dropped down on the sand, balanced the spear across his knees as he sat cross-legged. "That I do not believe."

She seated herself a little away, her head bared to the sea wind which tugged at the length of her hair. "Good enough. We can so test the strength of what stands against us." Her reply was calm.

Some moments later he broke the silence between them with a question:

"You still cannot wake?"

"No. And there is this also," she hesitated as if considering the wisdom of telling him, then she added: "I am no longer in command."

"What does that mean?"

"Just what I have said. Before, I was aware of what lay before you . . . us. Now," she lifted a handful of sand and let it shift through her fingers, "I cannot be sure of the future. It is . . . blurred . . . is the best word I can find to describe it. As if you might take one picture and lay another over it so that two different scenes strive to cancel out each other."

"Then there is another dreamer?" Burr asked.

"I cannot be sure. Only that the dream I knew is being overlaid with another and . . ."

She was gone. Burr stared at the place on the beach where she had been sitting. There was still a vague depression in the sand. But Uahach, or Kaitilih (whoever she was) had vanished before his steady gaze, winked out in an instant!

He got to his feet, still staring, and reached forth with the butt of the spear to touch with caution that slight mark in the sand. No one . . . nothing there!

That this was of her own doing he doubted. The other pattern she had sensed over the dream which had been Osdeve's . . . had that strengthened to obliterate her, take over his own future?

She had saved him from the qwakers. It might be that he was *not* to be saved from the next ordeal of the ancient legend. But she had said he must light the beacon to bring in the ship, and that he could refrain from doing.

In fact, he was going to get away from here right now! Though he could not travel Uahach's instant roadway, he could move away from what was suddenly a treacherous shore inland, give himself time to find some way he could defeat the unknown dreamer, since he had not the slightest hope, he thought, of his signal to wake being answered . . . except by refusal.

VI

BURR faced sharply away from the sea. Before him the land was wooded by small, dense appearing clumps of what was either very tall brush, or stunted trees. The leafage was thick and dark in coloring, making each copse appear like a blot. There was something sinister about that landscape. Whereas the mound country had seemed eerie and alien, this gave him the impression of being actively threatening in a manner he could not define.

Also, he had to struggle against a very definite and growing compulsion *not* to head inland. Perhaps the new dream pattern was trying to force him to light the shore beacon, follow the original dream into the raid on Vur. Now Burr set himself to a grim battle of wills, fighting his way on.

The same tough grass which had clothed the mounds covered the ground, and the long, sharp-edged ribbons of that tangled about his feet, jerked him nearly off balance, as if it were moved to make this journey as difficult as possible. He only knew that he *was* advancing against the desire which fought him, and for the moment, that was all he could hope for.

Such was the foreboding atmosphere of the region ahead that he expected any moment to see some peril leap or slink out of the tree blots avid to do battle.

Choking for breath, Uahach-Kaitilih-Ludia (who *was* she in truth?) swayed back against a support she could feel but not see clearly, and tried to regain full consciousness. She was no longer on the seashore. Nor had she been summarily returned to her couch in the Hive. No, she was back again on the mound where she had entered the dream. Beyond, her she saw the man crouched against the monolith, the qwakers about to leap for his perch. Her hand had already gone to her belt to free the throwing cord.

Only . . . this was wrong!

Her thoughts were hard to order into clarity. She must save the man.

But it seemed to her that the whole scene before her quivered. It had none of the in-depth reality of the first time.

Her will sharpened and her mind awoke fully. No instinctive action . . . This was not her dream, but that other's. She was being presented not with the man who was her companion in their adventuring, but a dream simulation.

The qwaker leaped, its bill flashed down, transfixed the chest of the man whose fending blow had been easily deflected. She heard his sobbing cry, the triumphant screech of the qwaker. But she was fighting her own battle, the one to tear the false dream to pieces.

Now the whole scene rippled, fought desperately to remain, tore, like rending cloth, from top to bottom. In that instant, she caught a single glimpse of a shadow form far removed from her own place, but operating on what must be another plane. She saw the enemy, but she could neither identify that lurker, nor even discover where was its normal position.

Dying man and qwaker vanished, the mound melted into a mist which thickened about her, so that she breathed faster and faster in frantic gulps of air. For it seemed that she was being enclosed in a monstrous blanket of damp. If she did not fight . . . bring her own natural Esper powers as well as all she had learned from Uahach to the highest pitch, she would meet death here.

This was a dream, an illusion. And a spinner of dreams could not be caught in another's dream, not without her full consent. Therefore, she could not be killed unless she accepted the illusion. She forced herself to breathe deeply and slowly, to fight the evidence of her eyes. She was not enmeshed in the enemy's dream, but a part of the one whose pattern lay deep in her own mind! That only was truth!

The mist rolled back. She knew a moment of triumph which she would not yield to. This happening was beyond the knowledge she had acquired from Uahach, beyond any records she had had access to. Only it was plain that, in spite of the enemy's efforts, a hallucination could not be held once she knew it for what it was. She was so armed, but what of Burr?

They had been separated deliberately, and she believed that he could well be governed by the other dreamer, strong as his will might be. He had no Esper talent or he would not have been chosen for the part he was playing, he lacked her only weapon.

There was only one hope for them both, she must find Burr. Only together did either of them have a chance.

The mist had rolled back a little, but not enough for her to see the country now about her. She could only be sure that her instant defense, her refusal to be caught in the reaction of the mound duel, had broken the pattern the other had set. She had only one way to find Burr—that was, by concentration of will. They had been on the shore . . . she shut her eyes and concentrated on the shore even as she had on that first move which had so swiftly snapped them from one point of the altered dream to the next. Shutting her mind to every outward sight, every inward fear, she pictured the shore as she had seen it last, and fiercely willed herself to he there again.

There was that sense of weightlessness, of sharp pain. She looked about her. Yes, here was the sand, the turgid wash of tideless ocean, the rocks . . . But one portion of the beach was exactly like the next. And there was no Burr.

She had half expected to see him busied erecting the beacon. For she was sure that the other dreamer still tried to move within the general framework of the original dream. But there was no sight of him.

Swinging around, she faced inland. There was nothing pleasant about the landscape. She was chilled by the sight of those trees, the outlines of which against the lighter grass had hints of strange shapes. As if the trees could dissolve their nature at will and assume other and far deadlier forms.

Nothing there . . .

Yet she could feel·. . . What did she feel? A very vague tugging as if a cord as light as a thread spun out from her body and was anchored to some object out of sight but among those threatening trees. That must be Burr and he had left the shore, was striving in his own way to break the threat of the dream by moving directly against the future she had sketched out for him.

That he had been able to do so surprised her. She had been sure that any dream will strong enough to snap her back at the beginning of all action would have had no difficulty in moving Burr to the new pattern. He had made himself vulnerable by playing the role of client, so accepting the original dreaming.

Perhaps it was the struggle she had fought her way through which had served him indirectly, removing a greater part of that unknown other's will from him. Thus he had had a chance to change course.

At any rate, they must come together or they would have no chance at all now. For client and dreamer were bound indissolubly together and entered and exited so or not at all. While all she had to follow was that very tenuous sense of a tugging, resolutely, she began to walk inland.

The sky was darkening. She believed that night was not far off. In the true dream, they had spent that night on board the Erne. But this was the new pattern and what dangers could be fashioned to attack any wayfarer in the dark? The rising wind was chill, she drew her cloak more closely about her, but she kept on, hoping that her guide would not fail.

It was getting dark. Burr had avoided the scattered copses of trees, making detours to skirt even the shadows they threw upon the ground. He was very tired, not of the walk itself, but rather from the constant struggle against the will which would enforce his return to set the beacon. That came now in surges of strength which were more disquieting than the first steady pressure, for there were intervals between, as if to encourage him to hope that he had won, then a blow sharper and more insistent. And that other seemed untiring, so that Burr wondered how long it would be before he did turn, and start back to pile the drift, light the beacon, and bring down upon him some fate he was only too sure awaited him in the altered dream. Since the qwakers had nearly finished him, he thought he could well expect no friendly Sea Rovers, but perhaps men equipped with steel and a strong desire to have his life.

Still he kept on his feet and moving, in spite of those blows. Then he raised his head and looked more closely at a copse to his left. That was altering in outline . . . There was something very wrong about it

VII

A FIGURE AROSE from the half crouch which had made it so resemble the other stands of stunted trees. It was larger than human but the outline was so disguised that Burr was not sure whether he faced some large beast or a sentient being. In the swiftly descending twilight, it was only a black bulk. And, oddly enough, as he neared it, that bulk appeared to draw in upon itself, shrinking in size so that at length it was no taller than he.

Burr gripped the spear tightly. The thing, once it had strode into his path, made no other move. But he had no doubt that it represented an enemy force. At least it was not a qwaker. But what other dangers might walk these lands he did not care to guess. Though he had faced perils without number before, there was that in this adventure which was unlike any operation of which he had been a part. Those had been in a real world wherein he could assess in part the dangers. But this was a country born of will and mind . . . whose will and mind? By her own account not entirely that of the psuedo-Uahach.

Yet now he did not try to evade meeting with the thing awaiting him. It was better to look fear directly in the face rather than let his imagination supply him with details.

All at once, the figure moved, shrugging away folds of a dead black cloak. There was enough light remaining to show him clearly face and head.

She was back!

A welcoming hail was already on his lips when he slowed to a stop. Though every detail of her features and her movement of head were the same as he had seen before, yet . . .

The girls hand appeared, waved to him imperiously. Burr remained where he was. Only now the pressure which had been against him ever since he had left the shore had veered. Now it would urge him forward to join this Uahach. And that very alteration in the unseen will warned him off.

"Come." She spoke the same word which had been her first greeting to him. Once more she beckoned and there was a frown, which might have been fostered by impatience, on her face.

He planted the spear butt down in the ground, tightened both hands upon it, as if by this he could anchor himself against obeying that summons.

"Who are you?" he asked.

"I am Kaitilih." Her voice held the same timbre, was no different in his memory from the tone she had used as they sat together on the shore. It was only that persistent forward urge which warned, and in this place he would heed any warning, no matter how small.

"You are not!"

"I am Kaitilih . . . come." It was as if she had not even heard his denial. "Night falls and in it there prowls that which will imperil us. We must find a shelter . . . Come!" Her command was reinforced by a sudden surge of compulsion, so strong it nearly tore him from his spear anchorage, to send him stumbling on.

"You are not she," he repeated; though what if she was? Burr was uncertain, could only depend upon that revulsion stirring within him for a guide.

"I am Kaitilih!" Now she raised both hands to pull back her hood. "Look upon me, fool, and see!"

Burr steadied. Her mistake that. For a moment, she had slipped out of her dream disguise. That was *not* the girl from the shore.

"You are not Kaitilih," he was convinced now.

She stared at him, all emotion smoothed from her face. Then she reacted so quickly that he was only half prepared. Her right hand swung up to hurl something at him. He was aware only of a flash of light, but his trained reflexes had not been lost even in the dream world. For he hit the ground, rolled, and was up again with the practiced swift and fluid motion of an expert unarmed fighter.

Something struck behind him and from that sprang a burst of fire. Burr leaped, not at her, but to one side again, as again her hand moved. This time, with the flash, came a sensation of burning close enough to touch him.

Then her face convulsed into an ugly mask, she spat in his direction. Her cloak whirled up as if the material had a life of its own or was controlled by her will alone. It wrapped tightly about her, transforming her into a dark pillar, hiding once more her head in shapeless folds.

That column of darkness began to sink into the ground, swiftly disappearing. At Burr's side, a patch of grass was charred and small red embers glowed there. But she was gone.

An acrid odor arose on the night air. However, save for the shadows of the trees, he seemed to be alone.

"Gurret?"

Spear ready, he wheeled about. There was another shadow advancing toward him.

"Gurret," there was recognition in that. But he was not deceived. She thought to play the game a second time, did she?

Once more, Burr saw her face clearly. Even in this twilight, her features had a kind of radiance which made them plain. He readied himself to again avoid attack.

"It is no use," he said, "you are not Kaitilih."

"No," she agreed, "but I am she who dreams."

Burr eyed her warily. There was indeed a subtle difference (one he could not put name to even in his mind) between this girl and the one who had vanished as if the earth had opened under her feet.

"If you are . . . the dreamer, give me proof."

"What proof can I offer?"

"Tell me . . . where did you go . . . and why?"

She did not try to come near to him. "Where did I go? Back to the beginning of the dream. Why? I know not that, save that the one who seeks to change our venture would have me believe that you were dead."

"She nearly achieved that purpose. If a man can be brought down by a dream weapon." He used the point of the spear to stir the charred grass.

The warning which had been so alert in him when he had fronted that other one was lulled. "How did you return?"

"By my will." Uahach seemed confident of that. "What was not real fled when I willed it."

Burr shook his head. "Shadows and dreams . . . how can a man fight them? At least your double had a weapon which could do this." Once more he plodded the scorched earth and ashes of grass. Then he told her of that other who had taken her form.

"The other dreamer," Uahach returned. "You did not follow the pattern, now . . ." She drew a deep breath. "That having been broken, the other can substitute her own."

"So we will not know what to expect?" he caught the significance of her uneasiness.

"Perhaps so. There is one last thing we may try . . . to go on to nearer the end of the dream, try to hasten its conclusion. Before she gathers her forces and builds up a greater command of the dream design we might break free from there."

"Can you do this?"

"I do not know. At least she could not hold me with her illusion when she returned me to the mounds. Perhaps she cannot hold the two of us if we will the end. It is not easy to retain any pattern, though I do not know if it has ever occurred that the client strove to alter it for himself. I am your dreamer, thus tied to you . . . if we two work together we may be too strong . . ."

"You think we can . . . go ahead?" Burr demanded.

"We can try." But he thought there was a shade of hesitancy in that reply.

"And what is your choice?"

"The Tower of Kiln-nam-u."

She held out her hand, even as the other had done. And the likeness of their gestures was so alike, that, for a breath or two, he was almost hesitant to approach and take it . . . lest he indeed had been deceived for a second time. But here there was none of that pressure, the choice clearly remained his.

He took the two strides to her side and felt her grasp close about his fingers. The touch of her flesh was a little chill, and he sensed through that contact, slight as it was, the whole tension of her body, the concentration building in her.

"Think," she said with sharpness, "of a tower by the sea, the same sea we looked upon . . . think of it!"

He did not know the tricks and shifts of an Esper mind, but if it would help he could at least think of a tower. And he summoned as best he could a mental picture of one . . . archaic by the standards of his own world, but at least matching in part the ruins he had seen from the mounds. Burr closed his eyes better to build that mental picture and then was no longer aware of her touch, rather of something which burned high with an almost consuming force, as if great energy struck full on the flesh-and-bone link between them.

VIII

SO THIS WAS THE TOWER and Uahach's efforts had brought them to the end of the dream. Burr stared at the edifice before him. For a long moment, the mental concept he had built in his mind lay like a misty illusion over the reality. Then that was gone and he faced the place native to the dream world.

It was set so that rising pinnacles of a cliff sheltered two of its walls on the sea side, those forming a right-angled corner into which ancient masonry had been carefully fitted in a way so that not even time itself could level it. For there was about this erection such a heavy feeling of age as to lie almost a visible shadow.

For a space which Burr counted as possibly two ordinary stories in height, there was no break in the stone, the blocks showed no openings. Above that space existed a triangle of wedge-shaped windows set in a diamond design, giving upon utter blackness, for no bit of the sunlight penetrated those deep holes.

That was another startling shift. They had left night

behind them on whatever journey their united will had energized. It was, he thought, now near midday.

The stone from which the Tower was built was a dull red in color unlike the rock of the cliffs which half sheltered it, which were a yellow brown. While caught in the crudely smoothed surface of the blocks were sparks of glittering crystals which reflected the sun, so that the edifice appeared necklaced with gems.

"KiIn-nam-u," Uahach dropped her hold upon his hand. "So much have we won."

"And what was Osdeve set to do here?" Burr wanted to know.

"He was to anoint that block." His companion pointed to one of the stones, reaching near to Burr's shoulder in height, seemingly a well set part of the foundation of the Tower. "With water from the Cup of Blood. Then would issue forth the Thing which has always dwelt within and with it he bargained . . . for the Rod of Ar . . . that he might rule."

"Since we don't have this cup," commented Burr, "can't we just break the dream now?"

When she did not answer he glanced from the Tower to her.

Her face was set, her eyes not seeking his, nor even the tower itself, but rather as if she looked beyond or through all which lay before them.

"I . . . can . . . not . . ." Her words, separated by forced breaths (she might have been at the end of a long, hard flight) came in harsh whispers.

"If we have reached near the end of the dream . . . and cannot break it? . . ."

"Then we shall be forced into the other's chosen pattern, here and now," she gave him the bitter truth.

Burr accepted her reply as being correct. All right, so they could not break the dream (the dream Osdeve had set up), but must follow another . . .

"You know all Uahach knows. You must have if they briefed you." He continued. "Is this ever done?"

Now her head did turn a fraction so her wide eyes met his.

"To my knowledge, which is Uahach's in truth, such a transference is unknown. She is a ten-point dreamer . . . the Hive knows no higher class on its test scale . . ."

"Yet there must be one, or we would not be caught. Have you any way of locating the source?"

The faint shadow of shock which had been in her eyes faded. She wore an intent expression, but not that of one wrapt in concentration.

"I could try. They . . . she . . . must reach us here sooner or later. The dream must come to a definite end or the Medic at the Hive will know there is trouble. They . . . the Foostmam, if she is a part of what we seek, would never dare not to allow him to intervene. We certainly lie in proper dream sleep now . . . back there. Therefore, since our dream is timed, whoever would spin the new pattern must move fast. We have cut out the midportion of Osdeve's adventure, brought it close to the end. I can do no more than wait for the next move, and that will be theirs."

Burr did not like it. Patience was a tool he had had to cultivate in his own operations. But those had dealt with the real world and he had then had a measure of control over the future. He had waited out attacks before, but always the opponent had then been working within a framework he himself could understand. This nebulous kind of battle irked him.

"Is there any way we can arrange a defense in advance?" he pressed her.

She did not reply, instead her hand came up to signal warning. A second later, he staggered under a blow which was not really physical, although it felt as if some giant fist slammed between his shoulder blades giving him a massive thrust forward toward the Tower. At the same time, Uahach's hands went to her head and she cried out in pain.

On . . . that force wanted to push Burr on, to slam him bodily against the block of stone. But he had his wits about him now and he dug in with the spear again to anchor him. His body swayed back and forth under the unseen blows, but he held fast, his mouth set in a grim line.

His companion fell to her knees, her hands still over her ears, tears edged from her eyes. She moaned, that sound oddly echoed by the rocks about them. It was apparent that, even as he, she fought against some compulsion which was nearly too great to withstand.

The Tower blurred before Burr's eyes. Or was it that the block Uahach had earlier indicated moved? On. Whatever strove to control him now wanted to hurl him on, into a dark slit opening there. If it was a door, its outline was a very uneven one, following the natural cracks between the stones.

Burr stood fast. He was not going to obey. Uahach said they had reached near the end of the proper dream;

therefore, he would not accept any new pattern. He summoned all the stubbornness of will which he had ever shown, used that as an armor against this beating.

The girl was slowly rising to her feet. Her face, wet with tears, still showing pain lines, had also set (though he did not realize the likeness) into a determination matching his own.

That irregularly framed hole at the base of the Tower was completely open. Uahach said that in the proper dream the Thing, as she called it, had come forth to bargain with Osdeve. Well, Burr did not have the mysterious Cup of Blood it wanted. And whatever rode him now wanted him to go in, not wait here.

As in the wedge windows above, the sun did not enter that opening, even though it made the Tower plain to the eye to the very edge of the jaggered doorway. The darkness lying beyond the threshold of that had a tangible quality which held out all natural light.

Was the Thing coming now? And now would it react to the fact Burr did not have what Osdeve had used to summon it? He wavered forward one bitterly contested step as the compulsion dealt an even more severe blow.

It wanted him in. Therefore, that was where he was *not* going!

For the first time during their struggle Uahach spoke. "That other dreamer must fight hard to hold us both." She had regained much of her air of command as well as mastery over herself. "When I raise my hand, try to move back . . . try with all your might!"

She was again watching the Tower with a fixed stare, her body stiff. Then her hand arose. Burr threw himself back, putting into that action every bit of stubborn strength he possessed.

A cord might have snapped. Burr lost his feet, struck the ground with a force which half stunned him, then rolled. The girl stood straight, a defiant pillar between him and the hole he had no doubt was a trap. But he felt a release which left him weak.

Uahach's figure wavered. Once more she sank to her knees, as if pressed so by a punishing weight. Before he thought, Burr dropped the spear. And, getting to his feet, leaped to cover the distance between them. His grip closed tight and steady on her shoulders, holding her so as she went limp.

IX

WHAT FILLED THE ATMOSPHERE about them was a malignant and petulant anger. Burr could not have told why he was so sure of that disembodied emotion, he only knew that he was. And from that sullen rage he gained a fraction of confidence. The other had not expected such a forceful defense from the two of them, for the moment it was defeated. But only for the moment . . . of that Burr was also sure. There was a sudden end to the manifestation of the unknown's will, even the anger winked out.

Uahach drew a deep breath, nearly a sob.

"She is gone," her voice was ragged, drained.

"Will she try that again?" Burr asked.

"Who knows? At least she still has power enough to keep us here."

"You are sure?"

"Do you think I have not already tested?" the girl flashed at him. "Yes, we are fixed here, in Osdeve's dream. What new pattern may have been devised I cannot guess."

Burr looked to that irregular gap in the Tower wall. He had half expected it to close now that the pressure on him to enter had been withdrawn. However, it remained not only open but with an ominous kind of threat lying within its thick blackness. He wanted to go and thrust the spearpoint deeply into that. But another part of him shrank from advancing any closer to the enigmatic fortress.

"Is there any way," he continued to explore possible avenues of escape or means of defense, "for you to continue improvising from the end of Osdeve's own dream?"

She shook her head. "I am not a true dreamer. Since I am Esper, I could pick up just Uahach's experiences, relive those. But these dreamers of Ty-Kry are born with different talents, and those talents are fostered by training from the moment their abilities are recognized. Many of them actually have very little real life apart from their dreams. I know only what my briefing, which was thorough just as to Uahach's past, could give me."

"There is no way then." But Burr refused defeat. He was not to wait here tamely for what the unknown could bring into being as a threat against them.

"I do not know . . ."

At first, her words hardly pierced through the milling thought in his own mind. But when their meaning did reach him, Burr turned on her swiftly, his controlled anger at the whole situation making his demand explosive in force.

"You may not know, but you are speculating . . . about what?"

"There is this, and it will be highly dangerous. She will make a move soon, you must have felt her rage when she could not force us to her desire. If we let whatever menace she sends against us develop fully, then there is just a chance I can connect with the thread of her dream weaving. But the dream then must be hers . . . not mine, nor a hybrid one which is half and half."

"So you may be able to find the connecting thread . . . what then?"

"Just this, if I can fasten to it firmly, we can force our way out These dreamers are fully programmed in one important factor . . . they must break the dream on the client's order. I could not do that for you because this unlooked-for situation had arisen. The dream was second-hand and it was already overlaid, before I tried, by a blanketing force from another and very powerful dreamer."

What she said made sense to Burr, after a fashion. But he did not like it at all.

"How far must the new dream go before you have a chance to do this?"

She did not meet his gaze. "I am afraid far enough to make the situation highly dangerous. You will have to face whatever peril she introduces, and hold it, until I have located the dream thread and can anchor us to it."

There was a kind of desperate logic in that and Burr could understand what she suggested, even though it was far outside his experience. That the result of such action would be perilous he had no doubts at all. But neither had he any other choice that he could see.

"We wait then—until she moves." That was not a question but a decision on his part. Then he did add a question, "Can you guess who 'she' is? The Foostmam?"

"No. She trains dreamers, but she is not known to be

a dreamer herself. You understand, many dreamers are almost completely locked away from reality; they must be tended as one tends an infant. Those who so protect and care for them are not dreamers for that very reason. There are two dreamers in the Hive who had their clients die. One was herself maimed in the dream world so that she lives, but just that . . . her dreaming mind is either dead or so shocked it cannot be reached.

"The other dreamer is unusual in that her potential was never realized until she reached adolescence. This *has* been known to happen, but very rarely. Any family which has produced a dreamer in the past knows the signs to watch for in early childhood and are eager to find one of their clan house with the ability. It means a large sum of credits for them. So a late developer has been found now and again, but it is an uncommon happening."

"You think this is the one?"

Uahach shrugged. "How can I tell? Two men died in dreams she spun for them and she was not shocked herself. Those are the only facts I can give you."

"Have you seen her? Talked to her?" Burr pressed.

"No. The Hive keeps all their dreamers of higher rank separated. A dreamer not in service is expected to build up her dreaming ability by the garnering of information, using the stored tapes to gather material for her dreams. It is a very lonely life for those who wake."

"Each of those dead men provided reason to wish them dead," Burr commented. "Either their wealth or their offices made them vulnerable. So if someone could tamper with a dreamer, perhaps even provide the proper background tapes . . ."

The girl was already nodding. "Yes, it could be done. Each one of us hides in his or her inner mind some personal and private fear. If the nature of that fear was known and it could be materialized to the highest wave . . ."

"They could well die, or wake raving! But that information would have to be supplied by someone close enough."

"What of your fears?" she asked.

"They provided me with a tight background for identity," Burr mused. "But hardly recorded anything such as that."

He paced up and down beginning to wonder. Could a dreamer herself shift out of a man's mind his greater fear and then materialize it?

As he turned to face the girl once more, he saw she had changed position, her eyes fixed on the dark hole which remained open in the Tower. The tense rigidity was back in her figure. He needed no more warning than that.

There was something coming, their enemy once more moved. But so far, all Burr could see was that deep darkness within. Breathing a little quickly, he came to stand shoulder to shoulder with Uahach. He wanted to ask if she could give any hint as to what to expect, but feared to break her concentration. She had already made it plain to him that he must stand up to anything which awaited them long enough for her to reach the dream line lying behind it.

There was a curdling crawl of the black shadow. Some of it licked forward like a black questing tongue, striking out into the light and air in a pointed ribbon of darkness.

Instinctively, Burr retreated, drawing his companion with him.

There was something about that evidence of strange life which churned his stomach, made his flesh roughen as if he stood in the midst of an icy blast.

The point end arose from the ground, weaved from side to side, as might the head of some reptile. Now there were bulges there. These popped with an audible sound to display red coals of eyes.

Burr could not identify the thing and, though the sight made him sick in an odd way he could not define, he fought to subdue his fear. Perhaps, since the unknown dreamer did not have any briefing as to his private fears she was producing now a fragment of her own most morbid imagining.

The black ribbon flowed forward slowly. Its head had stopped weaving, those coal eyes were centered on Burr. If the head was narrow, the bloated body coming into view through the hole door was slug fat, with a quivering hump forming most of it.

"No!"

The girl beside him cried out, raised her hands as if to push the crawling monster back into hiding. Her face was a mask of disgust and terror, the fear taking over.

❋ ❋ **X** ❋ ❋

BURR GUESSED what had happened. The enemy had not struck at him, but rather at Uahach, perhaps because already the opposition was aware that in such a battle as they faced, the girl was the stronger opponent.

A fetid odor wafted from the crawler, thick and loathsome enough to make Burr gag. He had put out his left hand to grip the girl's shoulder, and could feel the shudders running through her. Though this crawling monstrosity was unknown to him, it was not to her.

"Hold on!" He gave her a shake. "It is a dream . . . remember . . . a dream!"

She could not still her shivering, but he saw her head move. It was plain that she was in no condition at this moment to do what must be done . . . trace that thread of communication with the other dreamer.

Burr raised his hand from the roundness of her shoulder, grabbed for the throat buckle of the bulky cloak she wore. His fingers freed the latch and he gathered the long folds of material swiftly into his grip.

"Stand back!"

Setting the spear between his knees, he took the cloak into both hands. The material was very closely woven, yet silky to the touch. He shook out the length and then, with what skill he could summon, he sent the outer edge snapping up in the air, spinning the goods out and down.

The folds settled over the crawler, masking the creature from view and, before the thing could free itself, Burr sprang forward to stab down again and again at that bulk heaving under the cloth. In his head, not his ears, shrilled a thin screaming which shook him, but not enough to make him retreat. There were growing splotches on the cloak, evil-smelling liquid oozing through the slits the spearpoint made.

Yet it would seem that the thing could not be killed for there was no end to the movement under the torn and befouled cloak. Burr stabbed . . . stabbed. Could *not* the Thing be killed?

Once more, he sensed the rise of strange fierce anger in the very air about him. But at last, the monster no longer moved. Burr drew back warily from the bundle of stinking cloth, his spear ready for a second assault.

Uahach breathed in deep gasps, but when her eyes met his this time there was recognition in them.

"Were you able to get anything?" He thought that a very vain hope. She had been too shaken by the emergence of the crawler.

But she nodded. "Something . . . not enough. I must try again. That . . . I did not expect *that*." Still shivering she pointed to what lay hidden from their eyes.

"That was your fear."

She shook her head. "Not mine . . . hers . . . Uahach's! It seems they implanted more than her memories in me."

For a moment, there was silence between them. That attack had been cunningly organized . . . not to get directly at Burr, but rather remove the support of his true dreamer. If he had been killed, it would have served a double purpose. But now, he was convinced that the girl with him had as much to fear as he did. And when she spoke, Burr knew that she realized that in turn.

"To shake me," she spoke in a voice hardly above a whisper. "With me held, then you can be easily taken, or so she thinks!"

"What will she send next?" He knew the folly of asking that even as he voiced the question. Esper talented this pseudodreamer might be, but to be able to outsee the enemy dreamer was too much to expect of anyone.

There was a noise, not issuing from the dark bowels of the Tower but rather from the rock cliffs. Burr slued around, and his breath caught in his throat.

Perhaps the enemy did not have the proper knowledge of his personal fears, but what had been conjured up now, what was scrabbling over the waste of rocks would awaken sick fear in any one in whose veins even a trace of Terran blood now flowed.

Each planet has its own perils. But there was one overriding one which had led in the past to two desperate measures, the actual deliberate burn-off by force of whole worlds which had been infected, lest a horrible death spawned on the surface somehow be carried on to blight more of the galaxy.

This . . . this *Thing* which lurched with purpose

toward them . . . Burr had seen its like in the tri-dees of warning each agent must memorize in first training. The mewling creature must once have been human, or humanoid enough to interbreed with Terrans. For their species alone in the galaxy was susceptible to what it harbored within it. And it was an added curse of that rotting disease that those victims who harbored it were driven in turn to infect their fellows. Touch, a whiff of breath from their half-dissolved throats . . . a myriad different things could transmit the virus . . . a virus which had a deadly life of its own, feeding not only on the victim's body, but on his liquifying mind, so that it learned from its carrier where and when it could be most likely to pick a fresh victim.

The creature, dead as a man knows death, yet stumbling on, powered by the will of the thing which had killed it so horribly, lurched toward them. All Burr's instincts lay toward flight, even though he knew it would do no good. Once the thing was set on their trail, it would tirelessly follow. Since it was already dead, no weapon save a burner beam could destroy it. And it was a menace to both of them. So it would seem that the dreamer was now determined to slay them together in a single supreme effort.

Burr kept telling himself that this was a dream, that only his own acceptance of such action as being reality could give the thing the power of killing. But his indoctrination against the disease went so deep that the logic of that argument was far too feeble.

The sea . . . the sea was behind it and here the cliff was high. If there was only some way of hurling it back

over that rise they could gain time, for it would take long
for that broken, eaten body to climb such a barrier and be
after them.

Burr, gritting his teeth, took a couple of strides
forward and snatched up the cloak which hid the battered
monster, paying no attention to the noisome mass
beneath.

"You have another weighted cord?" he said over his
shoulder.

She did not answer and when he looked around, he
could see his companion was caught again in a trance
state. Apparently this time unaffected by the loathsome
thing tottering inexorably toward them, she was striving to
trace the nightmare creature back to its creator.

Dragging the torn, stained cloak, Burr leaped to her
side. She did indeed have one of the weighted cords in a
hook on her belt. He jerked it free, nearly dragging her
from her balance by that sudden grab. Her attention did
not shift to him, but he did have the cord in his hands.

Burr swung around to face the shambling horror. The
weighted cord was a weapon new to him, but it was all he
had. To let the thing come near enough to spear would
avail him nothing for that body, until its legs rotted away
under it, would pursue, it would even crawl as long as its
bone-arms lasted.

He whirled the cord about his head as he had seen the
girl do. This was such a slim chance, but the only one. He
loosed the thong . . . to see it pass out through the air. It
caught about the thing a little lower than hip-high, just at
a moment when the thing teetered on a rock from which
it could leap out and land close to them.

However, instead it fell under the impetus of the weighted cord. Instantly, Burr moved, flinging the cloak over the floundering thing much as he had done over the slug-creature. It fought the folds of cloth. A limb which was half bone, protruded through from one stained slit, but Burr was ready.

Twisting the spear, he jabbed fiercely with its butt at the fighting thing. Twice his weapon thudded home, rolling it back toward the edge of the cliff. With a mighty effort, for it had somehow gotten to its knees again, he sent the spear in a third blow, into which he put all of the strength he could muster, straight into the middle of the muffled shape.

This time, he hurled it well back. For a second or so he was afraid not far enough. Then, as it fought to rise, to balance, it teetered farther back and was gone . . . down into the sea beneath.

XI

"IT IS GONE for a moment." He could have shouted that in his relief.

But when he looked to Uahach again, he saw she had not turned her head a fraction; she could not have witnessed his small victory. Her lips moved though . . .

"Come."

She had not spoken that word aloud, he had only read it with his glance. Her left hand made a vague motion away from her body as if seeking something to grasp. Burr plunged forward and gripped her fingers within his. Had she done it . . . found the link with the enemy? . . . Could he dare to believe? . . .

The world of the Tower was blotted out by a burst of utter darkness, if one could imagine dark snapping instantly into being. Burr could not even feel if he was still hand-linked to the girl, that he had any anchor at all. There came a sensation of rushing through that darkness . . .

Was this how a dream ended? His lost feeling awoke new fear. Suppose they were now caught within this place of not-being . . . held forever here. Twice there were flashes of sight, a misty uprise of tower and rocks. Burr had the sensation of being drawn in two directions. And there came a pain in that which was not of body, but struck rather at some innermost core.

The dark held steady now. And the sensation of passage through this space was more intense. Then came a break in the blackness. What lay there, clothed in mist, was not rock or tower, rather a body stretched out on some support which did not come into visibility at all. And he was drawn to the side of that body.

This was a dreamer, her head half masked in the helmet which reinforced and held the dream intact.

And now Burr was aware of a strong emotion. Not the anger which had struck at him before . . . no, this was the need for action, imperative and demanding. It came not from the dreamer, but from somewhere about him.

He watched a hand materialize out of nothing, its fingers crooked as if it would claw at the helmet of the sleeper. And at the same moment there was a wordless demand . . .

"Now! Give me . . . now!"

In him arose, without his conscious volition, an answer to that cry. He must give form and substance to that clutching hand with every particle of energy he could summon. There was a swift outrush of such strength as he did not even know that he could produce until he felt it drain from him.

The hand grew denser, more real. Still he was being

drained, as it began to descend with infinite slowness, moving in small jerks as if fighting its way against some defensive covering, down toward the body of the dreamer.

He could not continue to give, yet he must! For unless that hand completed its mission, he would be lost indeed. Burr did not know how he could be so sure of that, he only knew that he was certain of it as if it had been part of his briefing.

Slowly the hand moved . . . so slowly. He was so weakened by the drain it caused that he felt now only a tatter of man which any wind might bear away.

The crooked fingers straightened a little. They no longer resembled claws. The forefinger turned, pointed to the breast of the sleeper.

Burr held on. This was such a battle as nothing in his past had prepared him to wage. It all depended upon that finger . . . the touch . . . but that must come soon, very soon!

Still in jerks, as if the energy which powered it flowed and ebbed, the hand continued to descend. Then, the forefinger touched the misty figure of the dreamer, which had not taken on any substance at all during the long space of time, or so it had seemed to Burr, since he had come to its side.

The dreamer writhed. The finger could have been a point of steel well aimed. Then the mouth, showing beneath the rim of the helmet grimaced, lips moving as if spewing forth some curse. Yet Burr could neither hear nor read words.

Again dark snapped down and he was . . . lost . . .

Something stung with a sharp stab of pain. And that

pain had not been in his innermost self . . . no, he had felt that in his body. The virus ridden horror? His imagination painted a picture of that climbing doggedly up the cliff, coming to embrace him—to . . .

Gasping, he opened his eyes. A man wearing the badge of a medic leaned over him, watching him with a steady, measuring gaze. Burr blinked and blinked again. He felt dazed, unable to put name to this place at first.

"You'll do . . ."

Even those words spoken in Basic sounded queer and far away.

His whole body was stiff as he raised his hand jerkily. The helmet was gone. He was back! Recognition came now with a warm rush. He levered himself up on the divan.

"Uahach?" Burr got out the name in a shaken voice.

"She'll do," the Medic reassured him. "Close thing there though . . ."

"The other one!" Burr remembered. "The other dreamer . . ."

He saw the Medic's eyes narrow. The man was attached to the Council HQ here, he would have been briefed before this experiment.

"She . . ." a voice as weak as his own brought Burr's head around.

Dreamer's helmet had been shed. A thin girl with cropped hair of dull brown, her wan features sharp as those of a famine victim, sat on the side of the other divan. Her slender arms were folded over her middle and she was so different from the fighting Kaitilih he had known in that other place that it was almost impossible to equate this wan and drab other being with his companion.

"Come . . ." Uahach attempted to rise to her feet, wavered and fell back. The Medic turned quickly.

"Lie still!" he ordered.

"No!" her answer came as emphatically, "We must . . . go . . . to . . . *her* . . . now!"

Burr wavered to his feet. He was as weak as if he had come out of the nightmare of the tower world sorely wounded.

"She's right," he said. "It has to be finished."

He was glad when another man, wearing a guard's side arm, stepped into his line of vision, put out a hand to steady him. While the Medic, though looking as if he highly disapproved of the whole affair, was aiding Uahach up.

"Where is she?" It was Burr who asked that.

"Lost . . . there. . . ." Uahach's faint answer did not quite make sense.

As the Medic supported her from the room, the Foostmam stood just outside the door, facing them with an expressionless face. She made no move to step aside, barring their way.

"By order of your own lords," the Medic snapped, "give us free passage."

"The Hive cannot be forced!" the woman retorted sharply.

"In this case, yes." The Medic gave a jerk of his head which brought another guard into sight "Step aside, or be put aside."

A spasm of pure hate contracted her features. "You take too much on you, off worlder. The Hive cannot be so used."

"As you have used it for murder?" Burr asked.

She swung around to face him, her face once more expressionless.

"That is not the truth. I have already been proven, by your own methods of questioning, blameless."

"But you harbor a dreamer who is not . . ." the Medic retorted. "Now we go to face her. And later, there shall be inquiries as to her briefing, Foostmam. Perhaps you shall discover those who may give the Hive a darker repute than it now has."

"The Hive is innocent. Dreamers cannot kill. . . ." Her armor of defense remained undented.

"I can testify," Burr said, "that they can try . . ."

His weakness was ebbing, he was able to stand now without the support of the guard.

Uahach had said nothing during their exchange. Her face was set, her body once more rigid as it had been when she had thrown all her power into the search for their unknown enemy. The Medic glanced at her and then nodded.

"Step aside!"

This time, the Foostmam shrugged and obeyed. They proceeded down the hall, around into a second corridor. The ruler of the Hive must have followed them for now her voice was raised in a new protest.

"There are no dreaming rooms here. . . . You must not enter the private chambers!"

The Medic did not even answer her. His arm around Uahach kept her on her feet. Burr guessed that the draining of the girl's Esper power to effect their return had been far more serious than his own ordeal. Yet she moved forward now as if driven by the need to find the source of the energy which had attempted to lock them into the dream world.

She swayed to a stop before a door at the far end of the corridor, putting out her hand to rest fingertips on the closed portal.

"Inside . . ." Her voice had gained no strength.

XII

AT A GESTURE from the Medic, the guard who had loomed over the Foostmam set his palm on the seal of the door. For a moment or so it would seem, it had been locked against any outside interference. Then it began to roll aside, slowly and grudgingly.

From inside came a noise, a kind of mewling such as a sick animal might make. The Medic, staring over Uahach's head, showed such shock that Burr moved up beside him. Instantly, the man pushed Uahach back, flung out an arm to bar Burr's advance.

"Close that, damn you!" he ordered. And the guard, wearing the same expression of shock and horror, slammed the barrier to. But not before Burr had had a single glimpse of what half lay across the divan within, was making an effort to rise, its blind, eroded face turned questioningly toward those it wanted as prey.

It was not as far gone as the horror which had bunted them on the cliff. But there was no mistaking the signs of the same dread disease. Burr made a quick move to support Uahach as the Medic rounded on the guards with a series of orders.

And it was Burr who led the girl back to the dreaming chamber. As he settled her on the divan and sat beside her, his arm about her shoulders, she spoke slowly:

"It . . . recoiled. What she dreamed against us became a part of her."

"How could that happen?" Burr asked. He tried not to remember what he had seen in that room, what must now be destroyed without mercy and as swiftly as possible.

"I don't know," Uahach returned. "But I think that she was not a true dreamer, not one such as they have always known on Ty-Kry. And she has been using her powers deliberately to kill. They said that she was a late developer . . . perhaps she was something else, a mutant of the dreamer stock. But I believe she was striving to send that crawling death against us even as we broke into wakefulness. Then, somehow, the force returned upon its sender. They called her Dynamis. We must find out now from whence she came, and who stands, or stood behind her."

"Not our job," Burr told her. "Let the regular hounds take over that coursing now."

Uahach sighed. "We must report . . ."

"That much I agree upon. But let the Organization take over then. We are entitled, I am sure, to hazard leave."

"And, by the way," he added a moment later. "What is your real name? I refuse to settle for either Kaitilih, as good a fighter as she was, or Uahach, a dreamer . . ."

She shivered. "I am *not a* dreamer!" It was as if with that statement she thrust aside all which had menaced them, up to and including that last burst of horror found in the Hive chamber.

Burr smiled. "That you are not! They say that Avalon is an excellent leave planet. But I'd like a name to enter on the request token."

"I am Ludia Tanguly," she answered. And her voice was firm. "Yes, indeed I *am* Ludia Tanguly!" It was as if she must affirm that identity and make sure that nothing remained of Uahach.

Burr nodded. "Very well, Ludia Tanguly, it is now our duty to get to HQ, to give recorded statements and then . . ."

She straightened up within the half circle of his arm as if new strength flowed back into her. "And then . . . *I* shall think about your suggestion," she ended firmly.

Knave of Dreams

ONE

THE ROOM was large enough to breed shadows in its far corners, for the one light came from a globe set in the middle of the long table. The woman who occupied a canopied chair of state could be distinguished only with difficulty by staring straight at her cloaked form. Though the room was warm, she had drawn the furred garment close about her as if she were chilled.

However, the men, seated in less impressive chairs, were far enough into the glow of light for their features to be clearly visible. There were four of them, and they ranged in age signs from youth to more than middle years. For the moment, they were silent, as if each were brooding upon some thought he did not want—or feared—to share with the rest of the company.

To the woman's right, the black-and-white robe of the Chief Shaman identified Osythes, a representative of Powers Unseen (but not unfelt) at this gathering. Beyond him was the slightly younger Privy Councillor Urswic.

These two represented age and a conservative caution, to balance the youth and impatience facing them beyond the limited source of light.

Prince Berthal sat there, his tunic glittering as he shifted impatiently, uneasily; the heraldic symbols emblazoned on his chest displayed glints of gemmed splendor. His neighbor was the least impressively clothed, for his tunic carried only the badge patch of the Household. Yet his face had a trace of arrogance that marked him as no common servant, but one who had a right to address those about him with equality. He was Melkolf, a delver into new ways of thought, an experimenter whose recently discovered knowledge made him a power to be reckoned with.

They all turned their faces now a fraction toward the canopied chair, as if willing its occupant to speak. Perhaps their concentration did act upon her, for she leaned a little forward as if to see them better.

Now her features were illuminated. She was old, her dark skin drawn tightly over the bones of cheek and jutting nose. But her eyes were not those of one entirely in command, reminding the other that it was *her* will that was paramount in their venture, whether they would have it so or not.

"You are certain?" The Empress spoke directly to Melkolf.

"The proof has been shown, Your Splendor Enthroned," he replied with complete confidence.

Berthal once more shifted in his chair. Osythes's wrinkled, large-veined hand, resting on the table top, began a tapping of forefinger, his thumb ring glinting red and green as the light caught the jewels in it. He might have been measuring the number of words spoken or the passing of time.

Urswic, although an elder usually taking a conservative course, reinforced the Younger Melkolf's statement, though there was a ring to his words as if he did not do so with entire willingness.

"There were three exchanged, Your Splendor Enthroned. All succeeded."

Once more, a moment of silence fell, then was broken by Osythes: "This is wrong, an evil thing—"

The Empress's eyes fastened upon him alone.

"There are small evils and large. You yourself, Reverend One, have correlated the prophecy of what will happen to this land if matters proceed as custom decrees. My son lies on his deathbed. He breathes, and only while he breathes do we have this small space of time to amend or prevent that darkness which Ochall and his slave Kaskar will bring upon us.

"Can you deny that what they would accomplish is an evil," she continued, "a very large evil, enough to engulf all that my lord Hunold, my son Pyran, have wrought? Sometimes we have no choice between good and evil; rather, there is set before us a small ill and a great one. And in this hour we face that."

Osythes's eyes no longer met her fierce ones. His forefinger moved upon the table, tracing signs no man, except perhaps himself, could read.

"You speak only what is true, Splendor Enthroned. Still, the deed is evil." Then Osythes, the Shaman, was silent, as if withdrawing from what they were about to do here.

"You are sure"—this time Urswic spoke, addressing Melkolf—"that you have the right man selected?"

Melkolf shrugged. "Ask that of His Reverence, the Shaman. It is *his* knowledge that searched the worlds for us."

"Yes." The Shaman did not raise his eyes from his moving finger. "He who is twinned to Kaskar has been found. The dream sending has been very clear—it is all recorded."

"You see?" Melkolf demanded. "All is ready. We have only to move. And by the latest reports, we must move soon. His Supreme Mightiness fails fast. Ochall has his man in the outer chamber there. The moment breath fails, Kaskar will be heralded as ruler. And, think you, when that is done, any of us here will be safe for even a portion of an hour?"

Berthal ran his tongue over his lips. He glanced uncertainly at the Empress Quendrida in her cave of a chair. His fingers dropped below the edge of the table to close upon the hilt of a ceremonial short sword.

"For all Ochall's impudence," the old Empress said, "he will not move openly against *me*. But there are hidden ways—yes, I do not doubt that he intends to dispose of all opposition with his usual efficiency. And with Kaskar entirely in his power, there is no limit to what he can do. To see all that I and my lord have fought for, all that Pyran labored to make stable, go crashing down because of this—this man—!" She beat her first upon the table top, her voice rang deeper in an intense note.

"If the death of one man of whom we know naught, except that he exists, can save our land, then, to me, that death is a deed of worthy cause!" Her gaze centered again upon the Shaman as if demanding some answer from him. But he did not speak.

"Very well. Let it then be done. And as soon as possible. There is one other who must know—"

They all stared at her, startled.

"The Duchess Thecla. She is on her way here now for the ceremony of betrothal—to Kaskar. That she comes unwillingly and under threat, we are all aware of. However, she loves her country and would not see it under Ochall's fist—so she comes. We need Olyroun, but we shall not overrun it as Ochall would do. Thecla is well beloved. Her people would rise, even if it meant the blotting out of their land.

"My Eyes and Ears have sent me many reports. Already, there is unrest in Olyroun. Rumors spread that Thecla comes under duress to this matter of a future wedding. Therefore, we must assure her that she does not have to see in Kaskar her betrothed—"

"Splendor Enthroned"—it was Urswic, the Councillor, who dared to speak as his mistress paused for breath—"is this wise? Need she know? When all will be done perhaps before her arrival?"

The Empress nodded. "She must know. She must understand what we are doing for the sake of the land. This will make her more amenable afterward to the suggestion that she be joined with Berthal. Let Kaskar die without her understanding and she may depart to Olyroun, there to make some other alliance that will not be to our liking. But if she is assured that she need not hand-fast with Kaskar, in her relief she will look to

Berthal. It will be your duty"—now those hawk eyes were turned upon the Prince—"to woo her with that skill that I have heard much of—"

He flushed and his lips parted as if he would reply, but the Empress was already continuing: "You, Osythes, will bring her to my private chamber upon her arrival. I shall make plain to her what we do and why. I ask no other to say such a thing. Kaskar—" She hesitated for a breath's space, and then spoke on. "He is the son of my son in body, though surely not in mind or spirit. I could well believe in the ancient tales of possessed ones. How Ochall wrought this change in him I do not know. Perhaps that should be the subject of your searching, Master," she struck out at Melkolf. "Does Ochall also have the use of some machine which he may put into operation to change the spirit of a man? Or, Osythes, can he call up the Power Unlimited to do such a thing?"

"Perhaps he can," the Shaman answered quietly.

Quendrida stared at him, shock showing for the first time on her face. "You mean that, Reverend One!" Her voice held the same astonishment.

"In one way of thinking, yes, Splendor Enthroned. There are things of the mind that can overrule the identity of a man. Just as Melkolf can use his machine to exchange the spirit of one person into the body of another in an alternate world, Ochall is not of the Enlightened Ones. However, that does not mean that he may not have learned some trick of mind control that he has used to override the inner man in our poor Prince and make Kaskar only an echo of himself."

Councillor Urswic leaned forward. "But if that is so—

could such an enthrallment not be broken? Why have you not said this before? As an Enlightened One, you could have—"

"Done nothing," Osythes interrupted him. "That which was free once in Kaskar was long ago killed. Do you think"—he lifted his head, looked from one pair of eyes to the next in that company—"I have not tried? I do not know what power Ochall has called upon, but it is such as cannot be broken now. But think not so ill of Kaskar, for he is but a helpless tool in the hands of a determined and evil man. And now we plot his death—and the death of another, who is wholly innocent. Also, we say that this must be done for the good of Ulad."

"You know that it must—" There was almost a pleading note in the Empress's voice.

Osythes nodded. "As you say, Splendor Enthroned, it must. Yet that does not make this deed any the less evil when it shall be weighed against us as we come to the Final Gate of all." He raised his hand and covered his eyes, his shoulders hunched under the heavy folds of his black-and-white robe. "I offer what excuse I may to the Power Unlimited in the name of all of you. Still, it will weigh—"

Now it was Melkolf's turn to move in his chair. There was a faint expression of distaste on his sharp features, as if Osythes were uttering nonsense that the younger man found hard to endure.

"Then we are to move at once?" he asked.

The rest looked to the Empress. A moment later, she inclined her head in a nod, though her expression was troubled and she watched Osythes with a fraction of uncertainty she had not shown earlier.

"Reverend One?" Her mention of his title was half question.

Osythes dropped the hand that had masked his eyes. "Splendor Enthroned, the coordinates have been already sent to the machine. The dreams have prepared the selected one with linkage and for the necessary manipulation within his own time world."

"What is he there?" Berthal showed some curiosity. "Is he a ruler, one who will be missed? If we have our counterparts in these alternate universes—and we must or the experiments would not have worked—do they live lives such as we do? Is there another Berthal who is a Prince, and a Reverend One"—he nodded to Osythes—"a Councillor—a—"

"Circumstances alter with the world, Prince," Melkolf answered. "I think there are very few princes or emperors left in the world to which we send Kaskar."

"Then how do they govern?" Berthal asked.

"Through representatives elected by the people, I believe. We have only a few scattered readings picked up from our subject there. He is not connected with the government. He has been a student; now he seeks work—"

"And such as he is Kaskar's twin?" Berthal laughed. "No prince but a commoner who must work with his two hands to earn his bread? I wish that Kaskar knew! I wish I could tell him—" He laughed again.

"This is not amusing!" Quendrida's tone was cold, the snap of a lash. Again the Prince flushed. "You speak of a man who must die, and you do not jeer at death. From what Osythes has told me, this one who is not tied to

Kaskar is far more worthy of wearing the Imperial Crown than he who is of my own blood. I wish that we might save him, but there is no way. Yes, Master, let it *be* done and speedily—while the Emperor, Kaskar, still lingers. We must not hesitate too long."

"The deed is—evil—" The Shaman drew a deep breath. "Yet the foreseeing is also evil. It is true we have no choice, but to say yes—that I cannot do. Agree you will. As I have agreed in spirit, may the Power forgive me!"

"It is agreed then?" The Empress kept her eyes away from Osythes as she asked.

The "yeses" from Melkolf and Berthal came quickly and firmly, followed by that of Urswic.

"Then I say it be so," Quendrida ended. "Make ready, Master. And that speedily. As you have pointed out—our time is very short."

Three of the men arose and bowed formally to the old Empress, withdrawing with some haste back into the shadows beyond the reach of the globe. Osythes remained where he was.

"My friend"—the Empress put out her hand toward him—"do not believe I cannot understand what lies in your heart now. It is through the Power Unlimited that this person to be sacrificed was found, and through your direction that he was entangled in the destiny of Ulad. Duty is a harsh mistress. I have spoken words that my heart would not have owned had there been any other way to achieve that which had to be done. Now I condemn one of my own blood because he is unworthy, because he would be only the face behind which an utterly evil and vicious man would rule. This is not easy—But it is what

I must do so that all that has been built of peace and goodness here be not destroyed.

"When my lord came to the throne, you will know what measure of hardship there lay in this land. Small lord warred against his neighbor, famine and death stalked hand in hand. No man, woman, or child was safe. My lord used what forces he could summon to counter this chaos. He brought you and the other Enlightened Ones, and set up the Groves wherein you might teach your ways of peace and fulfillment. He tamed the outlaw lords, he fostered the trade of cities, he made Ulad a bright and smiling land.

"And after him, Pyran carried out his father's work with the same will and dedication. But this wasting illness which was sent upon him, sapping his body and then his mind—that defeated him. Then came this devil Ochall who made himself so strong that he put hand upon the High Chancellor's key and none dared say him no. And Kaskar—Ochall enfolded Kaskar as a swamp serpent enfolds its prey, crushing out of him everything except his own will.

"I was in deepest despair, for I knew, as well as your foretellings could say, what would come to Ulad when Kaskar ruled. Then Berthal and Urswic brought Melkolf to me, and I learned to hope. Not for my own line—for now we perish—but for the land which was our duty to protect. Yes, I live by duty, not by my heart, old friend. And if indeed that fact weights ill upon me when I reach the Final Gate, then I can offer no other excuse for all the acts of my life."

The Shaman lifted his eyes, and there was a sadness in them.

"Lady," he said quietly, "I was at your hand-fasting to your lord, at the naming of our dear lord-in-chief who now lies so spent and helpless, at the naming of his son who is now a lost one. I know well that what moves you to this lies as heavily upon your shoulders as does the ancient Power weigh upon mine. We made our choices long ago and we must live by them. I do not doubt that this act will save the Ulad which your House brought into being. And I shall entreat the Power that good may come from ill, for there is no other way—"

"No other way," she echoed. "Now I must go to Pyran and watch the life ebb slowly from him, praying for him to live, in spite of all his pain and torment, until we can make safe his country. And upon me that weighs heavily also."

She pressed on the wide arms of the thronelike chair, levering up her body as if her limbs were so stiffened she found movement hard. Osythes also arose, but he made no move to help her, knowing well that her fierce pride would not allow her to acknowledge the infirmities of her aged body.

With effort, she stood erect, and now her back was very straight, her head, bound with an embroidered scarf over which was set a small diadem of Presence, held high. She walked toward the shadowed end of the room, moving with purpose, Osythes near but not touching her.

Another dream! Ramsay Kimble sat up in the bed on which sheets were rumpled and tangled as if he had been fighting some hard-pressed battle against it. He was sweating, though the night was rather chilly; his black hair was pasted across his forehead. He looked around him, half amazed to find that he was really here, in his own well-known bedroom—not in that other place that had been so real. Then he snapped on the reading lamp and reached for the notebook and the pen placed to keep the pages open at that point.

"Get it down right when you wake up"—that was what Greg had told him last week. "The longer you wait, the more the details can recede." Ramsay set the notebook on one knee and began to write.

"Big room," he scrawled, "machines of some sort— never saw them before. Two men—" He must remember details. "One young—queer clothes—a kind of body suit something like a leotard, close-fitting, all over—color—" Ramsay closed his eyes and tried to center a memory that was already growing fuzzy around the edges. Yes! "Color green—dark green. Over the suit a kind of loose-fitting vest—sleeveless—fell to about the mid-thigh—but not really a vest because it was not open in front. There was a design on the chest—looked like gems and gold—very intricate—" Only he could not remember more than the general impression of that.

"The other man—a little older—body suit, too—gray, and over it some type of jacket—but also gray—no fancy trimming except a small patch of red on the right-hand side of the chest. Both men dark skinned—but not blacks—dark hair and eyes, too—Indian?" He underlined the questioned word. "Man in gray busy with the machines, going from one to another. Feeling of excitement—as if they were very tense about something that was going to happen. Impression that this was another room in the same building or place I dreamed about before. Old man not there, though. What came through most was *their* feeling—all tense—as if a lot depended on what they were going to do."

He did not add his last impression as he closed the book and laid it down—the impression that he had an important part in what was going to happen. Of course, that was normal. It had been *his* dream.

Ramsay snapped off the light, thumped the pillow straight, and lay down. There was a streak of moonlight reaching from the window. He lay watching it with no desire to go back to sleep now.

Perhaps, he was feeding all this from his own imagination because of Greg Howell's interest. Subconsciously, he wanted to please Greg, maybe make himself important, so he dreamed. But he was sure these were not ordinary dreams. In the first place, they were like fragments of a play. He saw a bit here and a bit there—though the plot eluded him. They seemed to be in a kind of sequence, though, and the reality of the people moving through the scattered bits of action, the background, was certainly stronger than he had ever found in any dream before.

Greg had been excited, of course, because of his project, and because Ramsay was half Iroquois. He kept talking about how an Indian had to dream up a spirit guide or something of the sort before he was considered a man. Sure, that happened in the old days. But a medicine dream, as far as Ramsay could learn through reading, was about an animal or some kind of object a man could afterward claim as a totem. This collection of strange scenes certainly could not be included under the heading of any ancestral memory.

The Dream Project at the university was new, and Greg was all wrapped up in it. They worked on dream telepathy—with a control studying a picture and the dreamers trying to pick up what he saw. But Ramsay had not been interested. After all, he had graduated and it was time he was working. There were no funds to expand the project—

If he had only *not* mentioned it to Greg when these dreams began! Ramsay grimaced at the moonlight. Now Greg was after him all the time—keep an account, try to find out what spiked them. Certainly nothing he saw on TV or read or encountered during the days had any relation to these dreams. Greg had questioned him exhaustively, and they were both convinced that that was so. Then— why did he dream? And they—the dreams—grew more vivid and real each time. He had felt in this last one as if he could reach out and tweak the coat or vest or whatever it was that the man in green had been wearing.

Ramsay was oddly restless, as if the excitement he had sensed in the two dream men were beginning to infect him also. There was no chance of getting back to sleep; he was sure of that.

He pulled out of bed and went to the window. The bit of moonlight had vanished; so had the moon. There were clouds rolling up. Ramsay shivered and glanced back over his hunched shoulder. He had an odd sensation of being watched, which intensified as the moments passed. All his imagination! This settled it! He was through trying any more experiments with Greg.

Thunder muttered low in the distance. Ramsay began to dress with a furious haste which a part of him did not understand. He could not stay in this room another minute! He looked at his wristwatch. One o'clock. It was Greg's night to monitor at the lab. All right. He, himself, would go over there right now and say he was through—

As Ramsay tightened his belt, he shook his head. Why was it so necessary to talk to Greg now, at this hour of night? He must be going crazy—those dreams—Yes, maybe if he told Greg it was over, he could come back and get some reasonable sleep. He had that appointment to see the personnel manager at the Robinson place at ten tomorrow. And he was not going to blow that. Tell Greg that he was finished, come back and take an aspirin, and get a good night's sleep.

He was down the hall, realizing he was nearly running, yet unable to account for this urgency that moved him. Ramsay only knew that he must get out of the apartment, down to the lab. He found the car keys clenched in his hand, though he did not remember picking them up.

Outside, the banners of the storm were very dark across the sky. He got in the car in the parking lot, was pulling out before he forced himself to take it slow. There was no need for all this hurry. Why—

But there was! The unease inside him was growing, insisting on speed, while the unease itself was swiftly developing into a kind of fear that made him glance twice into the back of the car, almost expecting to see someone crouched there behind him, willing him to hurry.

What had happened to him? He had to see Greg— find out if this was some normal reaction to the type of intensified dreaming he had been doing. But—this was not the way to the lab! He should have turned right at

Larchmont, and he was two streets past now. Now he deliberately swung left into Alloway, which would take him straight on up to the lake and the park.

He did not want to go that way—what made him—?

Fear dried his mouth. His hands were on the wheel of the car, his foot on the gas—but he did not want to go this way! Yet he could not will himself to turn, to elude the control that made him drive on and into the dark.

The storm broke, and it was a furious one. Driving rain walled him in; his headlights could not cut far through that flood. The sensible thing was to pull up and wait, but whatever possessed him now would not allow that. He could no longer see the lights of any house—or street lamp. He must be already approaching the park, and the road was climbing. Its curves were not to be negotiated in the rain, not such a rain as this.

Still, he could not stop.

The headlights picked out dimly the white paint of the railing to his left, he was above the river ravine here with a drop—

Then—

In the faint reach of his headlights a figure. Ramsay yelled involuntarily, swerved to avoid the floundering shape. The car skidded straight for the fence. There was a crash. He had a last moment of utter fear when he knew that the car was going over and down.

❊ ❊TWO❊ ❊

SCENT—THE SCENT of flowers. Ramsay was aware of that first. He might be slowly climbing some steep hill out of the darkness into a garden. Yet, this scent was more concentrated, stronger than the fragrance of any garden he could remember.

He tried to remember more, then was chilled by a flash of fear as his mind sluggishly fitted together events of the immediate past. That mountain road in the dark, his skid as he fought to avoid the man caught in his rain-dimmed headlights. He must have gone over.

Flower scent—a hospital room?

Now he tried to feel some pain, some sign that he had been smashed up in a wreck. There was nothing. Again fear struck—hard! A broken spine? Complete paralysis? His acute terror at that thought made him afraid to try to move arm or leg.

As he lay, immobilized by his own dark suspicion, sound returned, as scent had earlier. Very near him, a

313

voice spoke, but he had no understanding of the words. There was a rhythmic pattern to the flow of those sounds which was not unlike a chant.

Slowly, Ramsay opened his eyes. He was lying on his back, yes. But above him was no hospital ceiling; it could not be. Arches swept up, to meet in peaks, and from the center of those peaks, hung a chain with a pendant in the form of a cage of elaborate latticework holding a globe of light. Though its glow was not brilliant, Ramsay blinked and blinked again.

He could catch designs in color that were painted or inlaid between the arches with a flamboyance and richness unlike anything he had seen before. The chant continued at his right.

Ramsay edged his head around, seeking the source of it. The flower scent was almost overpowering. He could see a massing of blooms near him. They must be banked against the bed on which he lay, but—why—?

Beyond that massing of flowers, someone was kneeling. Ramsay could make out only a rounded head, the suggestion of shoulders, for the figure was enshrouded by thick veiling, completely hiding it from his sight. Only hands, small dark hands, were raised to the level of his vision. Clasped between those was some object that glinted when the light reached through the encircling fingers.

He tried to understand the words the veiled figure was saying. But there was not one word that he knew. There were only sounds. What *had* happened?

Now he was determined to test the mobility of his body.

Try his right hand— To his overwhelming joy, he

could raise his hands. Though it moved oddly, stiffly, as if it had lain in one position long enough to cramp a little. As he raised it, he dislodged whatever his fingers had been clasped about, and that in turn slid across his body into the bank of flowers.

The veiled figure started—went silent—pulled away from his side—stood up. The veil fluttered as one hand lifted it and revealed the face underneath.

A girl—but one he had never seen before. Yet there was something familiar about her face. If he had not seen her exactly, he had seen someone like her in cast of features, dark color of skin. In the dreams!

He was back in the dreams again. Perhaps, he was actually in the hospital and unconsciousness had returned him into that series of subconscious-triggered imaginings that had grown so vivid over the weeks just past.

However, Ramsay was shaken out of his own thoughts by the expression on the face of the girl. She had eyed him first with—he supposed fear would be the best description. Now that was easing, and there was something else, though he could not read the emotion that made her eyes narrow a little, her lips press tightly together.

Her skin was smooth and delicately flushed beneath the brown. She could have been full-blooded Amerindian, except that she lacked the width of cheekbones. Rather, her face was a delicate oval, her nose high-bridged, perhaps a fraction too prominent for real beauty. But her eyes were the most remarkable of all. As Ramsay gazed straight into them, they seemed suddenly to grow larger and larger, until, in an odd way, he was aware only of them.

Then there came a delicate touch against his cheek. He realized she had lifted one hand, her fingertip sliding down to rest at the pulse point of his throat.

"Kaskar?" A single word asked as a question.

Only it was one Ramsay could not understand. This was the most vivid dream he had ever had. Could it be born from some drug, used to help his hurt body, that had this effect on intensifying his dream?

He found that he could not willingly break the gaze with which her eyes held his. She might have been probing him in some way, trying to awaken a response that she needed desperately.

Then, once more, he saw her frown of surprise. Whatever response he could not give had alerted her to danger. He knew that as well as if she had audibly warned him of peril. She glanced to right and left and then back to him. The finger which had sought for his pulse was now set to her lips in a gesture that he could readily understand.

She drew her veil tightly around her, though she did not hide her face, and pressed out of his range of sight in a quick movement. Because she had made him deeply aware of some peril, he obeyed her command and remained quietly where he was.

But where was he?

The ornate ceiling above him, the flowers, their scent now so strong as to make him feel rather sick— He tried to deduce what these meant. Ramsay did not remember ever being aware of smells in a dream before. While the touch of the girl's finger on his cheek and throat—somehow he could still feel it.

Where was he? What had happened?

Desperately, he recalled as best as he could those final few moments before he had crashed out into the dark maw of the river gully. The rain, that figure blundering into his headlights. Both of those were clear. But no clearer than this present scent about him. Only, this could not be real!

Wake up, he told himself firmly. Wake up—right now!

If this dream was drug-induced, would such tactics work? It seemed not. He was not waking; the flowers, the place remained. Would the girl come back? What had she said? Ramsay tried to shape the word correctly with his lips but not utter it aloud—

"Kaskar." Was Kaskar a person, a state of bodily being, a place? What was Kaskar?

And why should he lie here?

He brought his right hand up into his line of sight. The skin was certainly a shade or two darker than usual, and on the thumb was the wide band of a ring, a ring with an elaborate casing of what must be gold holding a dark stone-carved intaglio, as if meant to serve as a seal. There was a band of gold about the wrist also, folding in the bottom of a sleeve of a rich coppery shade—a color he had never worn in his life.

Always before in dreams, he had been aware of others, but never of his own body or clothing. In those dreams, he had seemed a disembodied spirit of some type, watching the action before him, but not caught in it. But this reality of the hand with its ring and wristlet was awesome.

There was a flutter of movement; he looked up quickly. The girl stood there again. Now her hand advanced to clasp his with a commanding firmness, pulling toward her. Her message was clear enough. She wanted him to get up and come with her.

Ramsay levered himself up. That stiffness that had cramped his hand and fingers seemed to have spread throughout his body. He realized he had not been resting on a bed's comparatively soft surface, but rather on a long slab as hard as stone, over which there was only a thin draping of crimson cloth.. At head and foot stood candlesticks as tall as himself when he at last reached his feet, where he wavered unsteadily, clutching at the flower-rimmed slab to keep erect. Each of those sticks held a candle as thick as his forearm from which thin ropes of scented smoke coiled lazily.

Again the girl tugged at his hand, urging him away from the slab—back into the shadowy space beyond the reach of either overhead lamp or candles. He was startled to see four men, their backs to him, one at each corner of the place where he had lain. Their heads were bowed, their hands clasped upon the hilts of swords which rested, bared point, on the pavement.

None of them stirred as Ramsay lurched forward in obedience to the girl's guidance. As he passed the nearest man, he could see that, though the man's eyes were fully open, he stared only at the sword hilt in his hands with a curious fixed intensity. Yet this was no statue, but a living man. Ramsay could see the rise and fall of his chest as he breathed.

Their complete stillness, the fact that they were ignoring any movement made by Ramsay and the girl, did not strike him as peculiar. After all—this was a dream.

And in a dream one expects the unusual. What bothered him was the continued feeling that this whole episode was far too vividly detailed. His dreams of the past few months had never equaled this.

All four of the men, Ramsay noted, were dressed much like those he had seen in the lab scene, with form-fitting undersuits and loose vest jackets coming to mid-thigh. Their undersuits were a dull black, the overvests gray with a large device of red stitchery spread almost completely across the chest. He looked down at his own body to find it clothed in a similiar fashion but with other colors.

The undersuit, which appeared to have all the elasticity of a finely knitted garment, was the coppery color. His vest, a deep gold with a red breast device, was embellished by what could only be small gems sewn into a highly intricate piece of embroidery. On his feet were smooth, soft boots, ankle high and of the same coppery shade.

The girl had drawn her veil back over her face, and now only the hand that gripped his so tightly was still in evidence. Like his own, her thumb was encircled by a massive ring bearing a blue engraved stone. But she wore two other rings as well. One on the forefinger was formed as an odd mask of a horned creature in gold, the eyes green gems; the other, a wide band around her little finger, had a deeply incised design which Ramsay could not distinguish. Otherwise, she was only a moving shadow among other shadows as they drew farther away from the light around the slab on which he had awakened.

They passed pillars, which he could only half see in the gloom, to approach a wall covered with stone panels carved with figures he could not clearly distinguish. The girl went to the middle one of these and thrust the fingers of her other hand into a deeper portion of that carving. Perhaps she released some fastening, for under her touch, the tall length of the panel swung outward like any other ordinary door. Thus they came to a narrow flight of stairs lighted by a globe at the top.

There was a hallway at the head which the globe more fully illuminated. It ended in a door resembling those Ramsay had always known. This his guide pushed open, that they might enter a chamber far more clearly lighted than the scene in which he had awakened.

His interest won over his conviction that this was some drug-induced dream. Instead of any uneasiness, he felt an avid and growing curiosity about what would happen next. As the girl dropped his hand, left him standing just within the chamber, he stared about him.

There were some features of the room he found familiar. These had appeared in early dreams, such as those that had been dominated by an elderly man wearing a long black-and-white robe.

The walls were paneled, covered here and there by long strips of what must be embroidery. The subjects were plainly fanciful, with oddly shaped and improbably colored vegetation and beasts which were not of the world Ramsay knew. There was a fireplace with a large hearth on which crackled a fire that did not a quarter fill its black cavern. Flanking that stood two long seats covered with a stiff cream-white cloth on which was sprinkled a glitter of gold dusting.

A long table with carved legs stood between him and the fireplace. On that was a medley of things, including bronzed candlesticks, goblets, a plate with what he thought were apples, though they were very large, and the like.

Except for the long seats, there appeared to be no chairs. However, here and there were piles of large square cushions made of different materials in colors that blended subtly. The light came from four of the suspended globes in their filigree containers.

The girl had gone to the nearest of the long seats. Now she lifted the veil that cloaked her so thickly from head to foot. She drew it up from her feet and shoulders and tossed it across the end of the divan before she turned to face Ramsay straightly.

Her dress was akin to his own clothing, except that her overvest was near ankle length. It was split on either side, so that when she moved one could see, more than thigh high, those limbs covered by the lighter, clinging undergarment. The color she had chosen was a rich green-blue, near the shade of the gem in her thumb ring, in startling contrast to the cloak veil she had shed, which was an ashy gray.

The embroidery on her breast was in silver, the design being far simpler than that which he himself wore. It showed only the head of a cat, the eyes of which were yellow gems, perhaps as large as his own thumbnail, having a bar of light across the surfaces, as if they were indeed the living eyes of the creature they represented.

Her hair was thick and black, cut short and kept sleekly in place by a silver band that held another smaller cat's head just above and between her eyes. It was an *outre* dress, but it became her. And there was about her an aura of presence, as if she had been used to giving orders all her life and having them unquestioningly obeyed.

She was still watching him with that searching, measuring look, which was a reflection of the gaze she had turned upon him when he had first seen her, when there came a faint rapping sound. Without turning her head, the girl spoke. Her voice carrying, Ramsay was sure, the inflection of a question.

She was answered by a voice which came more faintly. At that, she spoke again and, to Ramsay's right, a second door opened to admit another woman. Though she wore clothing not too different from the girl's, it was plainer and of a dullish russet brown. The cat's head was repeated on the tunic vest, only in a much smaller size and lacing the gemmed eyes. Her face was plump and broad of feature, her short hair coarse, having only a russet ribbon to control it.

She halted just within the door which she had closed behind her—her attention on Ramsay. Her generous mouth fell open in the most exaggerated expression of surprise he had ever encountered. For a long moment she simply stared. Then the girl spoke, swiftly, her words sliding into one another, so that Ramsay could no longer separate one strange sound from the next.

As she talked, the woman's gaze shifted from Ramsay to the girl, then back again, her first complete astonishment fading as the girl continued. Then the girl looked once more at Ramsay.

Slowly, as if determined to make him understand, she touched the cat's head on her breast with a ringed forefinger.

"Thecla," she pronounced. That must be her name. She was waiting now for some response from him. Was he Ramsay Kimble in this dream? But, of course, who else could he be—no matter how he was dressed or how bizzare the circumstances surrounding this encounter.

In turn, he pointed to himself. "Ramsay Kimble," he replied.

Again, the older woman displayed confusion. She shook her head violently and spoke that same word the girl had used earlier:

"Kaskar!"

It was if she were trying to deny the identity he had claimed and force upon him another.

"Ramsay Kimble!" he returned, more loudly, and with all the emphasis he could center on those two words.

Thecla made a gesture that Ramsay read as urging the woman to understand him. Then she pointed at her companion and said: "Grishilda."

Though such manners were not of his own world and he was a little surprised himself at his instinctive response, Ramsay inclined his head in a slight bow and repeated: "Grishilda."

The one he addressed came closer. Her survey of him from head to toe and back again was both searching and slow. Then she shook her head, threw up both hands.

"Kaskar!"

Thecla smiled, the first time he had seen her expression lose all tenseness. It was as if the reaction of Grishilda were in some way amusing.

However, Grishilda, herself, broke into rapid speech, her air that of one raining questions, without pausing for a breath to catch any answer. Again the girl gestured—this time raising her hand palm up as if to urge silence. She spoke a single sentence. Grishilda gave a quick nod and hurried toward the door where she had entered. There she tugged a small bar into place, effectively locking it.

Thecla beckoned to Ramsay, bringing him to join her on the long seat by the fireplace. What followed was a language lesson. First, she pointed to the objects in the room, repeating words which he echoed as best he could, though she often corrected his pronunciation. There was about her an air of urgency, as if they must learn how to communicate as quickly as possible for some reason. And he caught her uneasiness.

A long dream, he thought fleetingly. And the most consecutive as to action he had ever had. This very strangeness gripped his complete concentration, and he gave himself to following Thecla's lead as best he might.

Ramsay did not know how long they sat there, repeating words. He was more tired than he had realized when Grishilda broke in upon their study session, bearing a tray on which she had two brimming goblets, small squares of what looked like a yellowish bread, as well as one of the huge apples sliced into several portions.

The drink was, Ramsay decided, some kind of unfermented fruit juice. The squares were slightly sweetened, more than the bread he knew, but less than the cake of his waking world. The firm-fleshed apples were the most refreshing of all.

They ate and drank. Thecla stretchd wide her arms and made a comment to Grishilda. Then she touched his own hand lightly.

"Sleep—Sleep—" She repeated the word she had pantomimed some time before with closed eyes and her head resting on one palm.

Ramsay almost laughed. Sleep, was it? He was asleep— and dreaming. Could you sleep within a dream? Apparently, Thecla believed that you could. But, of course, she was a character in his dream, not in the least real.

He nodded to show he understood. She motioned to Grishilda.

"'Grishilda—take—sleep—'"

The russet-clad woman nodded emphatically and beckoned. She did not lead him to the door she had so cautiously barred, but back to the passage through which they had come from the place where he had "awakened" (if one could awake into a dream). Ramsay wondered if he was now to be returned to the flower-encircled slab and the four unseeing watchers.

However, Grishilda turned left, pressed open another panel, and so brought him into a small room in which there was a bed, not unlike a stripped-down cot, with only a single covering folded at its foot.

Here was no window, but a slit high in the wall through which, apparently, some air found its way, for the room was not too musty.

Through the slit came now a sliver of daylight, enough so that, when Grishilda abruptly left him, Ramsay could see to slip out of the stiffly fashioned vest-coat. Then he lay down on the cot, dragging the cover up over him.

Oddly enough, he did feel sleepy. But he did not yield to that. There was too much to think about. And since he no longer had the stimulation of Thecla's language lessons, his self-erected barrier against doubt began to melt away.

He knew enough of Greg's research—had listened to tapes and seen dream telephathy in action—to realize that this adventure of his was certainly unique. But to believe, to accept it as real was a step he shrank from. There was too much that could not be explained in any logical fashion.

Now Ramsay began to reconsider every small detail of what he had seen since he had first opened his eyes. That slab on which he had lain, with the tall candles and the seemingly entranced guardsmen—the whole scene haunted him somehow. He had seen its likes before. Not in any dream, no— Had it been on TV, in a film? Not in real life, no.

Ramsay began a methodical memory search for the answer. Perhaps if he could identify one small bit of this whole episode, he could unravel it all. Where *had* he seen such before?

A picture— It must have been a picture. All right. What picture? When and where? He tried to visualize a book, turning the pages, looking for that all-important illustration. No use. That did not work.

Maybe it had not been in a book, but a magazine.

Now his memory picture produced larger pages, began to turn them as he searched. Yes!

Ramsay sat up on the cot. He had remembered!

That—that had been a bier, the kind a king or some royalty personage would lie on in state. Guardsmen at the four corners, the candles. A little different from the picture he could now recall, but enough like it to make him sure he had hit upon the truth.

That meant—he was dead!

But he wasn't! He was sitting right here. Anyway, in his own waking world, Ramsay Kimble would never have been laid out in state with guardsmen and those candles, with a strange girl like Thecla coming to mourn him. He might have been in a funeral home—in a casket—yes. But not with all those trimmings.

However, he could not rid himself of the idea that that had been the way that a dead man might be treated. And this Kaskar—he knew now from Thecla's tutoring that Kaskar was a proper name. Kaskar was the man she had expected to find lying on that bier—a dead Kaskar.

He was not Kaskar! He was Ramsay Kimble, a perfectly normal American who had gotten mixed up beyond his depth in a screwy research project of some sort and was now having hallucinations. Yet, he had never been involved in the drug scene. If some dude wanted to blow his brains clear out of his skull, popping uppers, downers, all the rest was just the way to do it the quickest. No, he was not on drugs, and he had been all laid out for a funeral—

Ramsay drew a deep breath and tried to control hands that were suddenly shaking. This was the time to wake up. And the sooner the better. Let go, dream, let go!

☀ ☀ **THREE** ☀ ☀

BUT THE NIGHTMARE part was that Ramsay could not wake up!

The small, dim room remained as clear as ever. He pinched his own arm viciously. That hurt—but he did not wake. Fear dried his mouth, made him gasp for breath. He was fast caught in his hallucination!

"Don't panic now!" He said the words aloud, as if the very sound of them in his ears could somehow calm him. He had to get hold of himself, rationalize in some way what was happening.

But there was no way to rationalize all this!

Ramsay looked about him, at those solid walls, at the slit through which a scrap of daylight reached him. He stood up and jerked at the cot bed, bringing it as close to the wall under that slit as it could be moved. Then he mounted on it, tried to see out. He could sight another wall some distance away that was bathed in sunlight. But there was nothing else to be seen, except an ordinary-looking strip of blue sky.

A suspicion possessed him, and he went to try the door. But Grishilda had not locked it. He was able to peer out into the narrow corridor. There, at the end, were the steps leading down to where Thecla had found him. In the other direction, nearly within his arm's reach now, was the door to the chamber where he had been with her. However, he had a strong feeling that to prowl about on his own would be dangerous.

He had to do something! If he just sat and thought—he'd go completely crazy! He had to *know* where he was and how he got here. For somehow, the reality of his surroundings had impressed themselves on his mind. If this was not a dream, then something completely beyond understanding had occurred. They had to *tell* him!

Ramsay took a hasty step toward the door to Thecla's chamber. But he did not raise his hand to the latch. Thecla had definitely dismissed him. Until he knew more, he would abide by the rules she had apparently set. And to know more he must be able to communicate.

He returned to the cot and relaxed on it. Now he began to mumble the words she had impressed upon him, summoning with each a mental picture of explanation. He knew the names of each piece of furniture in that chamber, and the words for simple action, but he needed more vocabulary. And, against his will, he was growing tired now. Suppose he did sleep—would he then dream himself back into the normal world?

That was the last thought of his waking, but his sleep was dreamless, or else he did not remember what dreams he had had when he awoke to a slight shaking and opened his eyes to see Grishilda bending over him.

"Come—" She shaped the word with extravagant lip movements, as if to make her order perfectly clear.

Still sleep-dazed, Ramsay sat up. The woman had looped over her arm the richly embroidered vest-coat he had discarded, and she was watching him impatiently.

They went back once more into the chamber where the girl had taught him words, but there was no sign of Thecla. The older woman did not linger there, but beckoned him on into a second room.

Here the walls were tiled with shining pale-green blocks through which was a drifting of silvery motes. And in the center of the chamber a tub, like a small pool, had been sunk. It was now filled with water, and he caught a pine-like scent.

On a bench at one side lay a pile of what could be only towels. And the other appointments of a bathroom were enough akin to those of his real world that he was able to recognize them at once.

"Wash—" Grishilda waved a hand toward the waiting bath. Then she pointed to a pile of fresh clothing at the other end of the bench from the towels. "Clothes—on." She made gestures of dressing.

But how did one get out of this skintight under-clothing? Ramsay could see no form of opening at all. He pulled it a little away from his throat, and it snapped promptly back. Then he heard a sound that could only be laughter.

Grishilda, her mouth stretched in a wide grin, advanced on him. Her hand reached to his right shoulder, pressed there for an instant, and there was an even splitting of the fabric, peeling open across his chest.

"So—" she said, and guided his own fingers to a button-like spot imbedded in the fabric. Then she turned briskly and left him to it.

Ramsay had peeled off the undersuit before he was aware of the long mirror panel. But he caught a glimpse of his movements in it and, once stripped, went deliberately to stand before it. Even though he had somehow known that he would not look exactly like himself, what he saw there was a shock.

His features were the same, but he missed the small scar along his cheekbone that had marked his encounter with a wooden splinter the summer he had worked with the logging crew. His hair was brushed back and fairly short in front, down to his neck in back. And he wore around it a broad band of what could only be gold, set with red stones. Also—his ears—he had on stud earrings of large red stones.

There was no trace of beard on his face; in fact, he had very little hair anywhere on his body. And across his chest was a red pattern, a tattoo, his rubbing finger advised him, in the form of a fierce-looking bird, perhaps an eagle or hawk, its beak half open, its wings mantling.

So—this was Kaskar! The dead Kaskar, except that he was Ramsay and he wasn't dead in the least.

He pulled off the headband, detached the earrings. But he couldn't wipe away the bird which was a part of his very skin. For the rest, he thought he looked much as he always had.

But he wanted to know—he *had* to know!

Ramsay lowered his body into the water. There was a bowl of some solid green substance—reminding him of jade—and in this was a soft cream that gave off the pine scent. He scooped out a generous fingerful, and when the water touched it foam appeared. Soap! So equipped, he proceeded to luxuriate in the largest bath he had ever seen.

As the water cooled, he came out and rubbed dry with the waiting towels. Then he investigated the pile of clothing. These pieces were different in texture and embellishment from those he had discarded, being far less rich.

The undersuit he fumbled his way into and sealed via shoulder button was the same dull russet shade as that of Grishilda's over-robe. And the vest-coat that went over it was green, with no elaborate spread of thread and gem across the chest. Rather, there was only a small patch of a silver cat's head near the shoulder to the right. It was shorter, too, than his golden tunic had been, by at least three inches.

He made no move to pick up either the headband or the earrings he had shed. And he was standing before the mirror, sleeking down his hair with his hands, since a brush was one appointment he had not found, when Grishilda came back. This time, Thecla accompanied her.

The girl was dressed much as he had seen her the night before, but her expression was less serene. She came directly to him, surveying him from head to foot, as if there were something very important in the appearance he made.

"Trouble—" she said. "You—go—with Grishilda—go to Kilsyth. They hunt for Kaskar—find"—she shook her head vehemently—"find—kill!" She repeated that word, stabbing a pointed finger at his breast as if that were a knife. "Ochall—angry—hung—you must go."

Before Ramsay could either protest or question, her hands on his shoulders pushed him back and down on the bench. Grishilda rustled forward, a box open in her hands. She held it ready, and Thecla frowned at the contents, which appeared to be a selection of tubes and jars.

The girl selected one of the tubes and uncapped it. Inside was a thick pencil-like projection. She took Ramsay's chin in a firm hold, turning his face more to the light, and with swift strokes marked his brows with the pencil. With another tube she dabbed along the line of his hair, and finally smoothed his face with a cream. Then she gestured him toward the mirror.

She had not made any great changes with her cosmetics, but the effect startled him for the second time. His skin was much darker in shade, his brows thicker, nearly meeting above his nose. His forehead was lower, and somehow his whole face was coarser, appeared older.

"Good, good!" Grishilda complimented the girl on the effect.

But Thecla shrugged. "Little," she said, "But all one can do. Listen!" She caught Ramsay by the sleeve, drew him away from the mirror. "You must go—with Grishilda. At Kilsyth safe—there I come. You learn speak— Grishilda teach. Must not be taken by Ochall—or"—she hesitated—"others. We plan—you do. Eat—go—" She made shooing motions with her hands.

Ramsay wanted to protest. But her uneasiness was so manifest that he knew he would have to trust her. For she was able to convey to him not by her scattered words, but rather by some reaching of emotion that she was in deadly earnest. There was a direct danger to him here, and her plan was his only hope.

He ate hurriedly of food from a tray in the outer chamber. While he chewed and swallowed, Thecla walked up and down, talking to the older woman. Perhaps she was giving orders, but she spoke so fast Ramsay was not able to catch more than a word or two. Twice Grishilda seemed to raise a protest, but was straightway overruled.

At length, the older woman pulled a cloak around her shoulders and signed for Ramsay to put on another. Then she pointed to him and a small chest sitting on the floor. It had a rope handle on its top, and he understood that he was to carry it.

"You"—Thecla once more addressed him directly—"Grishilda's man—servant. She goes to Kilsyth—safe there."

"Thank you," Ramsay said, "but why—"

"Do I do this?" She completed the sentence for him swiftly. "You know later. Learn—speak—then we talk, I tell you. You stay here—Ochall—others find—like Kaskar—you then be dead."

That she thought her fears were based on truth he was certain. And he could not produce any protest she might heed or understand. Better go along with this, at least for now, until he could learn enough of their language to find out just what was going on, where he was, and perhaps even why.

He was turning away, having picked up the chest in his right hand, when Thecla caught his left, holding it tightly between both of hers. Ramsay was startled, even more than when he had seen the changes they had made in him reflected in the mirror. For there actually seemed to be a kind of energy flow that spread from those two palms clasping his fingers so tightly, passing into his own hand and arm.

Nor was that contact a physical sensation alone for, at the same time, there built up in his mind a need for haste and caution, a warning of danger, the suggestion that he must follow any leads Grishilda might give him or else be betrayed in some way to an unexplained, but very real peril.

"All right," Ramsay said in answer to that mental warning. "I will do as you say." Some of his answer was in her tongue, some in his.

She nodded vigorously and dropped his hand, breaking the communication, so odd because he never had known it before. He wished that she had continued, if only for a short space. Perhaps so he could have learned more—But he guessed that now haste was imperative, and he turned obediently after the woman, out of the door Grishilda had fastened so carefully at their first meeting.

They came into a wide corridor, carpeted and paneled, with globe lights at regular intervals along its length. Grishilda walked fast, suggesting with a gesture that he keep behind her, the proper attitude, he suspected, for the servant role he was now playing.

Twice they passed others, both times men wearing a shorter vest-coat resembling his own. But those tunics were yellow and the small badges on them the red hawk or eagle which he bore concealed on his skin. Each of the men glanced at Grishilda, but neither spoke. And Ramsay thought they did not really see him at all, as if a servant were beneath any curious notice.

The hall gave upon a wide stairway, beneath that a broader corridor. At the door at the end of that stood two guards whose clothing matched that of those who had been beside the bier. One stepped forward as if to question them. But Grishilda held up her hand imperiously. Grasped in her fingers was a square of silver bearing the outline of a cat's head, this one also with jeweled eyes. The guard drew back, leaving their way open.

The other guard opened the door and Grishilda sailed on, Ramsay in her wake. They were outside in growing dusk now, though still within the confines of whatever building this was. Three of the barriers surrounding them were formed by five-story structures; the fourth was merely wall. However, sitting within a few strides of the door was a vehicle unlike any in Ramsay's experience. It had a passenger compartment perched on three stilt-like legs, from which a mounting ladder hung. Grishilda hurried to that, and Ramsay, in his role of servant, had wit enough to step out faster, be there in time to assist her up the steps.

Once inside, they found seats and Grishilda buckled a wide belt around her, Ramsay following her example. Only a portion of the space apparently was for passengers, and he deduced that there must be a separate section which sheltered the pilot or driver.

Then he grabbed at the edge of the seat and gulped, for the vehicle rose straight up with a lurch that unsettled his stomach. Grishilda showed no surprise; in fact, when she eyed him, her preoccupied, worried look vanished for a second or two, and she smiled.

Leaning forward a little, her ample middle compressed by the belt, she said: "We fly—"

However, this was unlike any plane of his own world. He had not noted any blades aloft such as a helicopter possessed, nor were there, to his recollection, any visible wings. And they had not taxied for a normal takeoff. There would not have been room enough for one in that courtyard.

Only they *were* flying, and when he pressed closer to the window panel at his right, he could see a blaze of lights spread beneath. There was no doubt that they had taken off across a city of no mean size.

Without a watch, Ramsay had no way of judging time, but it was not too long a trip until they set down, with some of the same speed as they had been airborne. Grishilda freed herself from her seat belt, and, as the door in the side of the cabin opened automatically, the ladder slipped out. Ramsay descended, set the chest on the pavement, and turned to aid her.

They were only two in a crowd of passengers arriving in such small flyers. The people as they alighted swarmed on toward a large building, and Grishilda set off in the same direction. Ramsay followed, trying not to be noticed as he glanced quickly right and left at those about him. The clothing seemed standard in general, the only differences being in the length of the vest-coats. Those worn by women varied in length from below the knee to level with the ankle, and were all slit up the side to the thigh. The ones worn by the men were as short as his own (and those were the soberest, less ornate kind) or as long as the one he had worn as Kaskar. There was a show of rich embroidery and some gems on the longer tunics. The wearers of these usually had one or two attendants in shorter tunics. Earrings were visible, but the headbands were plain and much narrower than the one he had worn, being fashioned of thread-worked strips of cloth rather than precious metal. When they came to the building, Grishilda waited for him to draw level with her.

"Go through," she told him. Ready again in her hands was the same silver plate she had shown to the door guard. Now she wove a path through the crowd until they reached a latticed gate. Beyond that were a series of capsule-like objects, strung together bead fashion. Doors in their sides gave access to an interior where four travelers might sit.

Grishilda showed her plaque to the gateman. He studied it, then reached behind him and pulled a length of chain. Within a moment or two, a man in a matching uniform came running. He in turn eyed Grishilda's passport, if that was what it was, and then bowed his head, said something in a low voice, and led the way down the line of bullet-shaped carriages to one which he opened with a flourish, waiting only until they were inside to close the door firmly.

Ramsay's companion dropped her cloak with an audible sigh.

"Good. Safe here. Alone—no one else—"

There were four seats, half reclining. She selected one, seated herself, and again adjusted a seat belt, waving him to the one beside her. But Grishilda was not relaxing for any trip. Instead, she was about to fulfill Thecla's command that she teach their tongue to this pseudo-serving man.

And Grishilda had the firmness of one who knew well her duty and had no intention of shirking it. Ramsay found himself already at work before the car in which he sat began to vibrate, and he believed they were on their way. There were no windows to give glimpses of the country and perhaps so distract him from his lessons. And the woman worked hard.

She not only pursued the method of pointing and naming some object, but she produced from the chest a series of pages loosely ringed together at one corner. Whether this passed as a book Ramsay could not tell—but he concentrated on learning with almost the same fervor as she did on teaching. Perhaps if he could learn enough to understand, he could also discover the nature of this strange—dream? Somehow he was not so sure that it was a dream. Though he could not imagine what else held him.

His mouth was dry from repeating words, though his vocabulary had greatly expanded, when Grishilda turned to press a button on the wall near her hand.

"We shall eat," she told him, "drink. This is tiring—to teach one from the beginning."

Within moments, the wall of the compartment before them opened in two narrow slots and covered trays slid forward to rest upon a shelf which then bore them within reach. Ramsay snapped up the cover of his and found, in sections, a square of the yellowish cake bread, something that appeared to be dried fruit (slightly shriveled pears and peaches), and a larger portion of thick stew. In addition, there was a tube from which Grishilda skillfully twisted the top, demonstrating how this was done. Inside that a dark liquid sloshed.

Ramsay spooned up the stew. It had an odd flavor which was not altogether to his liking, but he was hungry and this was food. The drink was tart, he thought perhaps some form of fruit juice. He ate and drank with a will, though Grishilda named all the dishes and made him repeat those after her, shaking her head at times, as she had all through her lessons, at his faltering attempts to give just the right accent to some syllables.

Though he might not be able as yet to please his instructress's ear when it came to accent, Ramsay was learning. He could understand, if she spoke slowly enough, longer and more complicated sentences. They had finished the meal and pushed the tray shelves back into the wall before he took the initiative with a question:

"Where are we going?"

"To Kilsyth, the place of my lady when she wishes to be private, away from all. It is over the border, out of Ulad."

"We are in Ulad?"

"Yes. We go now to Olyroun, which is my lady's own country. Though they plan to take it from her." There was a bitterness in her tone.

"Who does so?"

"Those of Ulad. They wish a hand-fasting with the heir to Ulad. My lady likes it not. But if she goes by her own wishes, then Ulad will seize power and Olyroun will be swallowed up. If she hand-fasts, then perhaps she still can hold rule, see that her people are not just servants to the Empire."

"This heir to whom she must be hand-fasted—who is he?"

"He is—was Kaskar."

"But—" Ramsay digested that. "Kaskar was—is dead."

"I know not the inner plan of this," Grishilda said frankly. "I can tell you only what my lady has said, what I have seen with these two eyes of mine. When we came unwillingly to Lom, where rules the Emperor, my lady went to wait upon the old Empress. Her Splendor Enthroned, Quendrida, told my lady some secret which lightened her heart. When she came back to me, she said there was naught for us to fear, she would never be forced to accept Kaskar.

"Shortly, thereafter, came the news that he was dead, quickly through some failure of his heart. Then they bore him into the Resting Place of Kings for a space, before they would set him in the tomb of his House. My lady is not an Enlightened One, for she could not leave her country and go into a Grove, setting aside all things of this world. She had a duty first to her House and her people. But the Way of the Enlightened Ones has already beckoned to her, and a little of their knowledge has been given her.

"Thus, hearing that Kaskar was dead, she went to petition that he not be weighed too harshly at the Final Gate, and that perhaps mercy would temper justice when he stood there. Then she found—you—"

"I am not Kaskar."

"So my lady swore. And because she possesses the Knowledge, I do believe her. Also, there was a great outcry when the bier was found empty and the guards enspelled— But that—" She smiled. "That last was my lady's doing. How else could she have gotten you away? I do not know your secret, but she does. Now she says that

you are in danger. Not only does Ochall seek you, but
there are others of nearly as great power who wish Kaskar
dead as much as Ochall wishes him alive."

"And who is Ochall?"

She stared at him for a long moment before she
answered. "Stranger, I do not know what you are, or
whence you have come. But my lady has given me assurance
concerning you and has said that what you ask of me that
I *can* answer I should. But if you know not of Ochall, the
Will of Iron, the Heart of Stone, that is hard to believe.

"He is High Chancellor of Ulad and, since the
Emperor has ailed in mind and body for some years, he is
all-powerful. Kaskar was his thing to be ruled, not his
Prince to have rule. All well knew that when the breath at
last left the Emperor, then Ochall would command,
behind the screen of Kaskar, a will-less prince who was his
creature. Now, Ochall believes that the Prince perhaps
did not die in truth, but lay drugged and has been taken
away by those who have good reason to want him kept
from the throne. But the High Chancellor has no proof.
And those others, those perhaps who have the most to
gain by Kaskar's death—my lady fears that they mean to
make his death a true fact—to be able to show a body to
the people."

"But I am *not* Kaskar!" Ramsay repeated. "And how
did I get here?"

Grishilda shook her head. "I do not know. Though
perhaps my lady does. But such information must be part
of that secret that the old Empress entrusted to her. When
my lady comes to Kilsyth, she can answer your questions,
the ones I do not understand. It is true that you are not

Kaskar. For now a different person looks from his eyes, speaks with his tongue. That this is true—it is a thing to marvel at. But because you look like Kaskar, you walk in danger until this matter is righted. That is why my lady sends you to Kilsyth, where you may lie in safety until she comes."

Ramsay shook his head. This was unbelievable— without logic, the deepest sort of hallucination. Yet, it was plain Grishilda believed that what she said was the entire truth as she knew it. And he must learn from her all that he might, hoping to stumble on the reality behind this wild experience.

FOUR

THE VIBRATION CEASED as if the train (if that was what one might call their present vehicle) had halted. Grishilda put a hand within one of the slits of her overvest and once more produced the silver plaque with the cat's head.

"We are at the border," she said. "This, my lady's own token, will take us through without question. But"—she turned her head and pointed to one of the seats behind her—"since you play the liege man, play it well, wait humbly on me, who am First Companion to my lady."

Ramsay got her point and quickly changed to the seat behind his supposed employer. He hoped no one would ask him any questions that would make his tumbling tongue betray him.

The door through which they had entered slid aside. A man wearing a tight cap that was nearer to a hood, bearing a cat badge on its front, looked in. Grishilda said nothing, merely held up the plaque. The intruder blinked and then bowed his head, and the door slid shut again.

"Good!" That word exploded from Ramsay's companion, as if she had been holding her breath to expel it. Maybe she had not been as confident as she had claimed to be. But Ramsay waited until the train was in motion again before he rejoined her at the front of the car.

"Do we go far?" he asked.

"Not so. Shortly, we shall reach Matering which serves the Hill Province as a station. There will be one waiting for us there. Kilsyth was once a hunting lodge, before my lady came to rule. Those of the Groves do not kill; they maintain life. Thus, there are hunters no longer at Kilsyth, only those who are protecting the life of the Vorst Forest, not draining its strength. Now—" She pursed her lips, and there was a small frown crease between her eyes. "Listen well, man who is not Kaskar. You cannot play the servant at Kilsyth, for those who live at the lodge would speedily know that you were not one of them. Thus my lady has used her wits and thought of yet another role for you. But you must understand and be able to act it well. You are now Arluth, and you come from Tolcarne—which is overseas.

"Those of Tolcarne follow the old ways, and House battles House in deadly feud. It is a wild country, and blood spills easily there. As Arluth, you are of my lady's blood, but four generations separated from her House. And you are the heir remaining, whose life must be protected lest your House die and there be no male left to stand before the Heart of the House on High Days. You lie under blood ban of a mighty feud and so have come into hiding with the welcome of my lady. Do you understand?"

Wilder and wilder, mused Ramsay. Though what Grishilda said was easy enough to grasp.

"Yes. I am Arluth and am in hiding because I have enemies from some feud."

"Thus," Grishilda swept on, "you will be at Kilsyth, and our men there will have excellent reason to beware of any stranger who might come seeking you. They will believe him either a blood enemy from Tolcarne or else a bought killer hired by such. So, if any of Ulad suspect and send after us, their coming will be known. You will have good excuse to keep indoors—in the Red King's chambers to which there is only one door, since Guron the Red had good reason to fear a killer himself. As soon as my lady can, she will come to us with what she has learned."

The plan sounded very neat and logical, if anything in this maze that had caught him could be termed that. He was to lie low in this Kilsyth place, guarded by men who would believe that a hired gun was out to get him, and wait out the coming of some explanation.

What secret had this old Empress confided to Thecla that might even begin to explain what had happened to one Ramsay Kimble? He used to think he had a vivid imagination, but he could not now summon any idea of his own to mind. There was nothing to do but drift with the tide of events until he had some fact he could seize and work from.

It was morning when they alighted from the bullet car. Ramsay could see nothing that might suggest an engine or motive power. And the series of bead-like passenger vehicles ran not on wheels but rather slipped along a groove in the ground, which took the place of the rails of his own world.

The roofs of a town rose beyond. Pulled up to the platform where they had detrained was a small wagon to which was hitched—Ramsay took a closer look. They were not a team of horses, but large wapiti, elks of his own world! There were two in harness side by side, and a third to the fore as a leader. A man sat on the high seat holding the reins of the beasts, which were snorting and tossing their antlered heads as if they had little liking for the proximity of the train. But it was already gliding on.

Ramsay picked up the chest by its woven handle and followed Grishilda, who was heading for the elk-drawn wagon. He helped her aboard onto a padded seat and sat down beside her. The driver, having noted they were in place, loosened the reins, and the elk frisked off at a smart pace.

They did not turn into the road leading to the town, but rather paralleled the groove of the train track on an unpaved lane. Ahead, to the right, Ramsay could see the dark smudge of what was certainly a forest, though there were fenced fields now bordering the way, and ripening crops in the fields.

The train track curved away from them. Now, on the left, was scrub land covered with a thin growth of bushes and brush, with here and there a tree in advance of a distant wood. The wapiti had fallen into a steady trot, but the wagon seemed to have little in the way of springs. Its passengers were jostled back and forth on the bench until they both took firm grip of its edge and tried to hold stiff against each bump and lurch.

The lane itself was growing narrower, assuming the look of a couple of well-worn ruts rather than a real road.

They left the last of the fields behind, and came into the fringe of the forest.

Here they trundled over drifts of long-dead leaves, and there was the smell of growing things. Ramsay thought he could identify pine scent, and he was sure he saw maple, oak and birch trees. The wapiti of the team were larger and heavier than any he knew of in his own world, but the trees and vegetation appeared very similar. He could *not* have drawn this all from his imagination, no matter how deeply his so-called subconscious might be mining memories to reinforce any dream.

They were out of the sun into a greenish gloom. At first, Ramsay was glad to have drawn away from the heat. Then he became aware of a subtle oppression, a blight upon his spirit, as if the woods about them rejected his kind. Birds called and could be seen in flight among the trees. And there were chattering squirrels giving audible voice to their annoyance of this intrusion. But there was something else—old, formidable—

Ramsay shook his head to deny his own fancy. He had said nothing to Grishilda since they had left the station. In fact, he was less aware of her presence now than he was of his own rising uneasiness.

As the track curved to the right, they penetrated deeper into the green gloom, which he liked less and less. He had had few experiences of any life in the wild, only his logging venture and a couple of camping trips in well-supervised national parks. There, he had never sensed this watching—waiting—Suddenly he caught sight of a monolithic pillar of red stone standing like an upright spear amid the green. He could not believe that that was some freak of nature. As he turned to ask Grishilda about it, he saw her hand loosen hold on the seat, rise quickly breast high, while her fingers and thumb curled into a fist, except her forefinger and little finger which she pointed at the rock. And she was muttering some words he could not catch.

"What is that?"

Her frown grew stronger. "It is of the First Ones—back there—hidden—is one of their Power Places. We do not go there. Nor do we talk of them." The look she shot him was forbidding.

Obediently, he held his tongue. If he was to be Arluth, he had better follow any local customs. And he wondered how much longer they were going to bump through this wilderness. His arm ached from trying to keep his place on the seat, and he was tired—

Yet the journey seemed to be endless. Once or twice, the wagon pulled to a stop, allowing the team to blow and paw for a period of rest. But their driver never addressed any words to his passengers, and Grishilda was as silent. Ramsay was afraid to speak, lest his unfamiliarity with the language betray him to the stranger holding the reins.

Finally, there was a break in the green wall. The wapiti plunged out into a sunlit space, bellowing as if glad to see the end of their journey.

Here a low house and outbuildings filled at least three-quarters of a glade. The walls were of the same red stone as the pillar Ramsay had seen in the woods, but this was a dwelling with narrow latticed windows and a plank door with huge hinges and latch. The roof was slated, and on the slates around the eaves was a green of velvety growth.

The wagon pulled to a halt before the door, which opened before they had climbed down from the wagon. A woman stood there. The sleeves of her underclothing were rolled well up, and a belt about her overtunic had pulled up those skirts also, as if to free her body for some labor. She was thick of body, short, and her face broad, with a flattened nose, so unlike Thecla in feature that she might have been of another race, though her skin was the same even brown. Her hair was black, but she did not wear it short as did both Thecla and Grishilda. It was braided, and the braid was wound about her head, with a couple of burnished copper pins, their heads carrying small drops of the same metal, that both anchored and ornamented.

She made a low bow to Grishilda, and then looked uncertainly at Ramsay. Grishilda spoke a couple of sentences which Ramsay did not understand at all, and now the woman acknowledged him with the same gesture of deference.

"This is Emeka, wife to the head forester, also the keeper of the lodge. And she is a woman of Zagova, so she does not speak our tongue except brokenly. I have said to her that you are my lady's far kin. Later, I shall give her the story my lady has arranged."

They entered a long room in which a huge fireplace yawned directly opposite the door. This interior was full of shadows because the narrow windows did not admit much light. The floor was blocked with slate, and the stone walls had hangings of a rather coarse weave on which were painted symbols and designs Ramsay did not recognize.

There were three masks of burnished copper riveted

to the wide mantel of the fireplace. And he recognized in them realistic representations of wolf, stag, and wild boar—the curving tusks of the boar giving that mask a wicked, threatening appearance.

The furniture was massive and looked as if it had been there for centuries—the wood darkened by the passing of time. Two high-backed benches flanked the fireplace, and there were several stools, a long table, and some chests and cupboards against the walls.

A few moments later, leaving Grishilda, Ramsay was ushered up a crooked-stepped stairway and through a door into a chamber, where the massive furniture below was echoed by a bed with carved posts, two cupboards, a table, and some stools. The hangings here were painted with various animals as realistically portrayed as the copper masks. And there was a stuffy, musty smell, as if this room had been closed for some time.

Emeka bustled past him to fling open both of the latticed windows, letting in air and a small measure of light. Then she bowed again and was gone. Ramsay explored a little, discovering behind one of the hangings a primitive kind of bathroom—with water running constantly through a stone opening in the wall, as if piped from some spring. It could be caught and held in a basin as large as a small bath by inserting a waiting plug in the floor groove. But any bathing, Ramsay decided, would have to be done quickly before the overflow from the pipe flooded the place.

He was more interested in the bed, for he could not deny that he was sleepy. Sleep—there was always the chance that if he wooed it hard enough, he would awake once more in his own rational world. Now he undressed and crawled into the cavern of the bed. The linen was not musty; in fact, it smelted agreeably of some flower or herb. He settled his head on the pillow with a sigh.

This time, he did not lie awake trying to find some answer to what had happened. And if he dreamed during the sleep into which he fell, he had no remembrance of it upon awakening.

Ramsay was aroused by a knocking at the door. There was still the glow of sun outside the narrow windows. As he sat up in bed, he pulled the upper cover about him. For a moment, all the words with which Grishilda had pounded his mind during their journey deserted him. He could not recall the simplest of expressions. Then he got control of himself and climbed out of bed, padded across the wooden floor, and lifted the hatch of the single door.

A man waited without, a huge copper jug held in both hands, giving off steam, while over his shoulder was draped what could only be fresh clothing.

"Your liege man, lord—" The newcomer jerked his head in a rough salute.

His own clothing was brown, with a green vest-coat, the ever-present cat-head badge, this time of copper, fastened near his shoulder. It was apparent that he was ill at ease; perhaps he had never before played the role of body servant. But he dumped the heated water into the waiting basin and Ramsay, taking the hint of overflow, made haste to use it. The forester had gone back into the bedroom to lay out the garments he had brought. Like his own, they consisted of an undersuit of brown, an overtunic of green, but they were fashioned of somewhat finer material. The cat badge was embroidered in copper thread and had the eyes worked in with glistening green.

"The Lady Grishilda, lord." He spoke slowly, as if he, too, hunted words in a foreign tongue. "She asks your gracious presence. There has come a message—"

Ramsay expressed his thanks and dressed quickly. The man had left him alone in the room where the dying sunlight of late afternoon no longer reached as far. A message? Ramsay thought that could come from only one person—Thecla. And he trusted that he would have a chance soon to ask her all the questions that had been gathering in his mind for what now seemed days.

He found Grishilda seated on a stool by the table below, over one end of which was stretched a cloth of a deep cream shade. Laid out on it were plates, spoons, a two-tined fork, and a knife with a matching handle.

She arose at his coming and inclined her head, giving the impression, Ramsay thought, that she greeted one who was her superior in rank. But he returned her unspoken greeting with a bow he had copied from that of the forester. "Lady—"

She smiled. "You are very gracious, my lord. Will you not sit and eat? This is no city feasting. But it has a flavor and appeal of its own."

The stool she indicated stood at the head of the table. Ramsay took his place there while Emeka and a younger girl of much the same cast of features hurried forward to serve them.

He found the food, as Grishilda had promised, both flavorsome and good. There was half of what was clearly some small fowl, steeped in sauce, a dark bread, honey still in the comb, sweet potatoes, beans—both cooked with a flavoring new to him. Again, the food reminded him of his own world, and it was these similarities that really troubled him the most, relatively unimportant though they were.

"You have a message, lady?" He could wait no longer.

Grishilda nodded. "It came by bird wing, as my lady always sends word to the lodge. She is on her way, but since she must go by Irtysh, her own home, she will be delayed. The Ears and Eyes of Ulad watch her—of that she is certain. Though whether they suspect—" Grishilda shrugged. "On suspicion only, they dare not detain her. Since Kaskar is dead, there is no betrothal, so she has every right and need to withdraw to Olyroun. We may expect her in two days—perhaps even less."

Two days—for Ramsay that time appeared to stretch far too long. And he discovered, as hour followed hour, that impatience could indeed eat at a man. Grishilda warned against any straying from the lodge, even going out from its doors—lest he be marked, though she was also vehement that any intruder would be quickly located and reported by the foresters.

The lodge was kept by Emeka's family—which consisted of her husband, who had driven the wapiti wagon; her eldest daughter, whose husband was acting as Ramsay's rather unhandy servant; and two younger children, a boy and a girl, who peered very shyly at the visitors now and then through a window or from a doorway, apparently much in awe of Grishilda and perhaps of Ramsay, who had reported kin, if distant, to the ruler of their land.

There was little to do but try to perfect his grasp of the language, in which Grishilda patiently concurred, and to discover from her all he could concerning the situation of this land, of the tangle about Kaskar and how it affected Thecla herself.

He learned that Olyroun was both independent and small. In spite of the greed of Ulad for its wealth of minerals, which the natives mined only frugally, Olyroun's independence had perhaps persisted mainly because it also sheltered a powerful and awesome group of what he guessed were religious leaders—the Enlightened Ones. From Grishilda's comments, Ramsay gathered that they possessed some form of mental power that completely overawed the common people. And had Ulad thrown her might against a country sheltering them, she would have raised a hornet's nest among her own countrymen.

However, lately the Empress-Mother of Ulad had had as an adviser one of these Enlightened Ones—Osythes. And the councillors of Olyroun were afraid that the balance of this unseen power might shift to their neighbor. In addition Ochall had reorganized much of the army, letting go the volunteers from the various steads; in their place, employing mercenaries from beyond the borders, men who fought not from any inborn loyalty but for the one who paid them. And from some source, Ochall apparently had gathered unlimited funds to do exactly that.

With mercenaries under his banner who had apparently no fear of the Enlightened Ones, and with all men knowing that Kaskar was just his creature and that upon his accession to the throne, Ochall would be the real ruler—Olyroun was threatened indeed. So much so that Thecla had had to make the hard choice of marrying the weak and controlled heir.

"To the Grove she went," Grishilda said. "And there she spoke freely with a Listener. The Listener read the foretelling, and there was only one road—that she wed with the heir of Ulad. Otherwise, there was destruction to all. For the Enlightened will not use their power to save any nation, taking sides one against the other. To do this, they say, will lead only to their Power fleeing from them. They will advise, but they will not support any who turn to them. Every man and woman must make decisions for himself—herself. Yet, my dear lady must have had some warning—for she went to Lom as one in triumph rather than despair."

"But you said," Ramsay pointed out, "that an Enlightened One now advises the Mother Empress of Ulad. If they do not take sides—"

"It is so. He can advise. *Advise*, not *act* for the good of Ulad. But we do not know what he advises. For the Enlightened Ones do not see our lives as we do. They follow some greater pattern visible only to those passing through the mysteries. And oftentimes, their advice may lead a man to sorrow for himself. Still, they claim that in that sorrow lie the seeds of a greater good to come. So it is not every man or ruler who will ask for a foretelling. My lady did so because she is fearful for Olyroun. I know not what they told her, only that she was shown her choice."

Grishilda was correct in her guess about when her mistress would arrive at Kilsyth. But Thecla came not by the wapiti wagon, but in an airborne flyer, which touched down neatly in front of the lodge just long enough for her to disembark, then rose immediately, to be lost from sight as it shot away over the forest straight toward the setting sun.

Grishilda, with a cry of welcome, ran forward, catching one of her mistress's hands, first kissing it and then holding it tightly to her breast. Tears welled from her eyes. At that moment, Ramsay realized that, in spite of her outward calm during the past few days, the woman must have been inwardly racked with uneasiness for the girl she so plainly loved. Thecla kissed her cheek and patted her shoulder with her free hand. But her own eyes glistened, as if tears she did not shed had begun to gather there. Then she looked beyond to where Ramsay stood, and her hand went up in a small salute.

He bowed, but did not move toward them. Impatient as he was, he must leave the initiative now to the girl. This was not the time to marshal all his questions.

They did not get to that until after the evening meal, after Emeka and her eldest daughter had cleared the table and the forester family had all withdrawn to their own quarters at the rear of the house. Thecla watched the door close behind the bowing Emeka and then she swung at once to Ramsay.

"Our forest dress becomes you, cousin," she commented. "But we have little time. I have consulted again with Adise—"

He heard Grishilda draw a whistling breath that made Thecla glance at her.

"Yes, I have been to the foretelling once again, my dear friend. And—" She lifted both her hands, let them fall limply to her lap. "It remains the same, even with Kaskar gone. Olyroun must wed with Ulad, in order that the future be safe for my people. Which means, of course, Berthal, cousin to Prince Kaskar. Well, I have heard naught to his discredit, though little to his credit either. At least he is no creature of Ochall's. But enough of what may be my future—it is yours we must deal with." Again she addressed Ramsay directly.

"Do you know how I came here?" he demanded bluntly.

He did not really expect an affirmative from her, but she was nodding.

"Yes. I was sworn to secrecy before it happened. But I am now absolved of my oath—by Osythes and, indirectly, by the Empress. They were afraid of you—deathly afraid. It is a matter of strange import." She hesitated and then plunged on. "It seems that there are realms of knowledge which even the Enlightened Ones know little about. And in Lom, a young expert in such matters, Melkolf, first got the ear of Berthal and then the Councillor Urswic. They took him to the Empress.

"It is proved that there are many bands of worlds which exist side by side, though they are walled from each other by some form of energy. In some, our counterparts live lives different from ours because in those worlds the action of history has moved in another pattern. This the Enlightened Ones have long known, just as they deduced also that, in places, the walls between these worlds grow thin at times, worked upon by some unknown energy. So may a man or a woman fall through, vanish from their own time into this other.

"All this Melkolf also knew, though he is not an Enlightened One, for he works not by mind control, but through certain machines he has been years in building, it being his desire to travel from one world to another. However, he had good reason to fear Ochall, and so he came to Berthal with a plan. It was this: if they could locate in one of these many other worlds the twin to Kaskar, then they could send the personality of the prince into the body of that stranger and arrange his death. Thus would Kaskar—tied to the other—also die—apparently of the failure of his heart—leaving no mark upon him.

"Three times did they do this with criminals condemned to death. But they needed Osythes's aid, for the one on the other plane must be linked in preparation through a series of dreams—"

"Dreams!" Ramsay burst out.

"You dreamed, did you not?"

He nodded, but she continued before he could speak.

"Osythes foretold—he agreed that you could be controlled into a fatal accident, drawing Kaskar with you into death. Melkolf set up the machine. They felt they were justified because of Ochall and what would happen to Ulad if Kaskar came to the throne. But it did not work as they had planned. Kaskar died, and you came to take his body. And Osythes says that this happened because they interfered with your life plan and that you still had a pattern to complete.

"Now, with Kaskar's body gone, Ochall is like a wild man. He believes that the Prince was only drugged and that he is being kept hidden somewhere. For this, Melkolf has no answer. But now Berthal, and Urswic, Melkolf, too—they hunt you eagerly. If they have their will, they will put an end to you—"

"Can I get back—" Ramsay brushed aside her warning. The story was so fantastic that somehow he had to accept its truth, odd though that reasoning might seem. He was here, and he had awakened in a dead man's body.

"That I do not know—" Thecla answered honestly.

"But I must!" And he made of those three words a promise to himself and to those who heard him now.

✹ ✹ **FIVE** ✹ ✹

RAMSAY was on his feet, his back to the open cavern of the fireplace, his attention focused on Thecla.

"Can this Melkolf reverse what he has done?" he demanded of the girl.

"I do not know. Dream sending—this is of the Enlightened Ones. And I have seen it in action many times among our own people. Foretellings that have come to pass—those, too, are common. But to use a machine—" She shook her head. "There, Melkolf has ventured into new ways. I know only that it was his machine, combined with the dreams, that altered the planes so that Kaskar died—and you live. Though that was not what was intended.

"Osythes and the Empress—" She continued slowly. "They want you gone, for you are now a threat to all they would accomplish. But neither will raise hand against you to achieve that desire. For Berthal, Urswic, and Melkolf, I cannot promise as much. They might willingly slay to cover their secret. And Ochall—if he could lay hand upon you—" Thecla shivered. "He could make you into such a weapon as would wipe out all who oppose him."

"Do they know that you helped me out of Ulad?"

"Osythes must guess; Ochall certainly knows that the guards were under hallucination that night. But he blames Osythes. Only not even one of his Power can move against an Enlightened One. But naught has been said to me. Nor will it when I fulfill the destiny marked out and hand-fast with Berthal. I am now too precious to their plans—"

Thecla's gaze was level. She was stating a fact that she believed; Ramsay had no doubt of that.

"If I could get to that machine—" he began again, half to himself, speaking aloud his thoughts.

"I know not what you could do," Thecla replied frankly. "The secret of it lies with Melkolf alone. However, it might well be that, in order to protect their own plan, they would be willing to return you to your world."

"They have hinted this to you?"

Thecla shook her head. "I cannot speak for any of them. But if you return to Lom, then you will be within reach of Ochall. And of him, I have no doubts. Kaskar was his creature, well controlled. As he made of the Prince his tool, so could he also you."

Anger was building in Ramsay. Wild as her story was, it carried belief with it. At least, the very fact that Thecla accepted it in entirety was somehow convincing. That he had been used to further an intrigue in another state of existence, callously, without his knowledge or will, chilled hot anger into an icy determination that from now on Ramsay Kimble was not going to be a puppet to be marched about at the whim of these who dared to entrap strangers for their own purposes.

"I want to go back to Lom." He did not make that into any question. He stated a determined fact. "I must get to that machine—"

Thecla stood up. "It was in my mind that this would be your answer. Though it is the most dangerous act you may choose. However, I shall not speak against it. For, though I am no Enlightened One, I have a feeling that this is the path for you.

"But, since it is one of peril, we must move with caution—"

"We?" he echoed. "I will not depend upon any more help from you." He supposed he should be grateful for all she had already done, giving him this respite, a safe way to hide out for a space from what seemed to be two determined organizations, neither one of which meant him any good. But he chafed at any more limitations being placed on his own action. Unfortunately, at the moment, he had no idea what form that action would take, nothing with which to counter any plan she might have concocted, since she knew the truth. He only felt resentment that he would be in any way bound to a plan that was not of his own devising.

Thecla shrugged. Some of the animation had gone from her face. "Walk openly, to your death, then, stranger. Or worse than death if Ochall's searchers gather you in. Do you know enough of our world to take your place among its people and not betray yourself in a thousand ways, great and small, to the first to observe you closely?"

He rebelled against the logic of that, but he could not

deny that she was correct. He spoke the language—after a stumbling fashion—only due to her orders and Grishilda's patient help. But the customs in general usage, even the small ingrained habits of everyday living—she was right; he could make a fatal error at any time.

"So now you understand?" Thecla must have read realization in his expression. "It is only if you understand, and agree to be guided by me, that you can return to Lom. Though that is great unwisdom. It would be better to remain here for a space, then depart overseas, where all strangers have odd habits and so are not greatly remarked if they dwell among the natives, being outlanders—"

"I have no intention of remaining here—nor even in Lom! I *will* get back to my own world!"

"Fair enough. If it can be done. You shall accompany me to Lom as Arluth within the disguise we have already devised. A Feudman goes masked, by the old custom. And I have no male kinsman, which is of importance in betrothal, for there is no one of my blood to stand as my champion at that time. This is an ancient form, long a form only. I would have had to choose someone of Berthal's kin for this ceremony. But with a cousin from overseas, that is no longer necessary. You have learned our speech fairly well—now you must learn our customs, what is the role of a Feudman—that you may pass undetected in Lom."

Thecla could not linger at the lodge. She stayed the night and was picked up in the morning by one of the flyers. But before the end of that day, another sky ship dropped a man on their doorstep. He was plainly past middle age, his black hair frosted by strands of gray, a star-shaped scar on his chin below one corner of his mouth.

He saluted Ramsay in an offhand manner, his dark eyes sizing up the younger man as if he must learn all he could by such measurement.

"Yurk," he introduced himself, "Commander of Her Own Guard. Also once out of Tolcarne Overseas."

Yurk became his instructor. Whether or not Thecla had entrusted her Guardsman Officer with the truth, Ramsay was never to know. For Yurk never mentioned his lady after that first moment of their meeting. Instead, he concentrated completely on the task he had been sent to do—making Ramsay into the best imitation of a Tolcarne lordling he could.

The overseas country, Ramsay was told, was in the same chaotic feudal state that Ulad had been in before the rise of the old Emperor and the subjection there of unruly and riotous nobles. There was no central power to bring order into Tolcarne; rather, each House had its own territory. And while House might ally with House for protection, for some more ambitious raid upon a mutual neighbor, or for some temporary benefit to both, such alliances seldom lasted more than a few years, or maybe for a single generation.

The idea of a personal feud was a fearsome part of the general unrest. One branch of a House might assault another in hope of coming into full control. And once a feud was officially proclaimed, those caught within it could openly hunt or be hunted. However, when a House was reduced to a single male, that survivor was encouraged to forget honor and retire to some point of safety while negotiations to settle the dispute were in progress. For the complete stamping out of any of the Houses was, oddly enough, against the highest code which these semi-barbarous people bound themselves to follow.

For such a House representative to flee abroad was not uncommon in the least. When he appeared in public, he went masked and unarmed, that state meant to protect him against any paid retaliation.

Neither Tolcarne nor Ulad had always been in such a state of flux, Ramsay discovered, by what he hoped was adroit questioning. There had once been a worldwide civilization with a central government under stable rule. But a sudden and dramatic change in basic trade—brought about by the discovery of a new and far more effective metal—and a bitter dynastic struggle had broken down that concentrated rule.

Countries on both continents turned to war, first over the supplies of ore of what sounded like fissionable materials. There followed the horrors of some kind of atomic conflict, and then a dark age.

Ulad, in the space of three generations, was lifting itself out of this dark past. But the success of its struggle depended upon the defeat of Ochall, who still had the feudal state of mind, and saw only warring conquest as the answer for a strict rule.

Tolcarne had produced no leader as yet who had been able to win any loyalty from more than one or two Houses. Thus, the land remained buried in the morass of petty wars. And since wars defeat trade, few merchants ever ventured now to its shores. In fact, Tolcarne was to Ulad and Olyroun largely legend.

But to Yurk, its ways had once been his life, and he recalled old customs and ceremonies, drilling into Ramsay all that he could during the days and nights that followed.

They were not to have too long a time for such study. Ten days after Thecla had returned to her own capital, a flyer dropped in with an urgent message that the party at the lodge move on to Irtysh, where she now held court.

Again, Ramsay changed clothing. That which had been a forester's uniform was laid aside for a dull red undersuit, an overvest-tunic of a lighter shade of the same color. The breast badge was that of a broken sword, encircled by a wreath of oak leaves. In addition, there was a mask that hid his face from upper lip to hairline, attached to a tight-fitting cap, which covered his head completely, rather like a skier's helmet. This had, at the crown of his head, a tuft of upstanding feathers dyed in the same silver as the embroidery of his badge. When he looked at himself in the mirror, Ramsay believed that his present barbaric figure could certainly not be recognized by any who had known Kaskar. At least, not as long as he kept the mask firmly over his face, though it was uncomfortable to wear, and he disliked having his vision limited by the eye slits.

With Yurk and Grishilda he embarked to fly over the long reach of the forest, and then above cultivated fields and several small towns. Unlike the bullet cars of surface transportation, these aircraft had windows, and one could push against them for some glimpses of the land beneath—as the flyer did not soar too high.

Irtysh, itself, lay at the beginning of the mountain foothills, well into the heart of Olyroun. It was in the mountains that the mines lay. And the only year-long passable road from those mines ran through Thecla's ancient city, which was built more like a fortress than the usual capital. Her palace and headquarters of her government resembled most an eight-sided castle, enough like those of his own world for Ramsay to identify.

The flyer carried them over the clustered buildings of the city to land on the wide roof of one of the sentry towers, where a small guard awaited them. They saluted Yurk, seeming to pay little attention to his companion. Grishilda, her fingers closing on Ramsay's arm, drew him to one side, through a doorway in a nearby turret, where a narrow stairway coiled dizzily down into a not-too-well-lighted interior.

The inner part of the castle was, to Ramsay, a bewildering maze of passages, doorways (nearly always closed so one could not guess the nature of the areas behind them), steps up, stairs down. At last, the three emerged into a section where the walls and pavement were no longer dank stone without covering.

Here ran soft carpeting, and wall hangings of painted designs, more stylized than realistic. Not that Ramsay was given any time to survey this art, for Grishilda urged him on as if they were now running some real race with time.

At a door, she finally came to a halt, tapping on its closed panel. It was flung open by a man wearing the same servant's garb that had clothed Ramsay on his escape out of Lom. The man bowed, edged out after they entered, and closed the door firmly behind him. The carpet here was flowered, muted lavenders, golds, roses on a background of spring green. And panels of similar flowers gathered into loose bouquets with silken threads covered the walls, except on the far side, where there were tall windows open to the day.

Thecla sat by the window directly opposite the door, a table before her, its surface crowded by a collection of yellow painted chests, each open, and each full of what seemed separate sheets of paper, though they were thick and coarser in texture than any Ramsay knew.

She had been engaged in stamping one such sheet with her thumb ring, having first impressed that upon a crimson pad shaped in the form of a cat's head and, rimmed in silver. At the sight of them, she pushed aside the waiting pile of papers and arose.

"There has been a message." She wasted no moment in any greeting, as if she must let them know immediately of some dramatic happening. "They have found a body that they claim to be Kaskar's. Melkolf and Berthal supplied that. Once more, the plans for his funeral are in progress. And I have been summoned for my role therein. Nor will I be allowed to return—that I know—until they have their way of me and I am betrothed to Berthal. But whether or not things will go so smoothly as they desire—that is another matter.

"Ochall has withdrawn into Vidin, officially to gather Kaskar's own liege men to see him to his tomb. Vidin," she said to Ramsay in explanation, "lies under the rule of the Emperor's heir though Kaskar spent as little time there as he could. He had no taste for the duties of rule, liking only what he deemed its pleasures and privileges—which he cultivated in excess. However, that Ochall has tamely accepted Kaskar dead and ready to be buried I cannot believe to be true.

"I have had a private message from the Empress Quendrida that the Emperor may depart to the Final Gate at any moment. With Ochall absent, then they will move at once to proclaim Berthal, even if Kaskar be not yet buried. Lom is filled with rumors and counter-rumors. There is much unrest, and the Empress has summoned the Life Guard into field duty order. She had laid it upon me to come at once. The betrothal with Berthal will follow immediately upon his proclamation."

She spoke evenly, as if this whole matter had no bearing upon her future; rather, that it was already a matter of the past, sealed into the unchanging wall of history. Ramsay felt a sudden urge to protest. How could Thecla accept as perfectly natural this arrangement of her future, as if she were a thing to be commanded, rather than a person with desires, doubts, wishes of her own? In his own time and world, there were few vestiges of royalty. And those rulers remaining were much more free to be themselves, not stiff symbols of history and duty ever walled from ordinary men. Thecla to him now was no symbol of rule; she was a person, a singularly attractive and intelligent person, who had moved on his behalf, though she had had no reason to aid him from the danger devised by those whom she knew much better, those same forces with whom she now proposed to ally herself without any question of their right to demand this of her.

But he could not summon any words to dispute her choice. The very calmness of her speech, her acceptance of things as they were, defeated him before he could even find the words.

"Grishilda, as the Mistress of my body women, you

will, of course, once more accompany me to Lom. And you"—she nodded to Ramsay—"for I have told the Empress by message that you have arrived in Olyroun and are kinsman to me through my great-grandfather's daughter who married into the House of Yonec. At this moment, you are the only kinsman of my blood, and since Ulad wishes to keep to all the old ceremonies it can resurrect (which is ever the way of a new House), you are acceptable to approve my hand-fasting. You need only remember that you are also a Feudman, not to be seen without that mask. Nor can you lay hand to any weapon. But doubtless Yurk has made this all clear to you?"

"Yes—"

Thecla waited no more than for that single word of assent from him.

"Very well. I am giving you for servant one of my guard who is familiar with the ways of Tolcarne. His uncle is one of the few merchants who still ventures there for trade. He will gossip and his talk will bear out your position among those of Ulad. But since he has not himself been overseas, he cannot challenge any small slip of bearing you might make.

"This much I shall do: My party will carry you under their approval into Lom, into the palace. You must thereafter be on your own. If you can influence Melkolf—well and good. But I would advise you not to move with any haste, and to take very good care."

"My lady, it is folly!" Grishilda burst out. "If he goes to Lom Court as one you vouch for and then is uncovered! My dear lady, this is a matter of too much danger for you!"

"It is by the word of Adise that I do this," Thecla answered quietly.

"Oh, these Enlightened Ones!" Grishilda made a repudiating gesture with both hands. "My lady, I know you will listen to them and obey. But they say frankly that they care not for a single person, only for what they deem the good of all. They would sacrifice even you in some plan of theirs!"

"That could be the Truth," conceded Thecla. "But in this case, Adise gives me bond-word that I shall not lose by supporting the one who moves in Kaskar's place."

"Bond-word?" Grishilda repeated. "Bond-word from an Enlightened One? My lady, seldom have any of our people heard that."

"Just so. And this I will do as I have been advised, and we shall see what comes of it. Now to practical matters of the present. We go by flyer in the morning. This night, cousin, you shall stay in the north tower, better aloof from all save Cyart who is to be your liege man. It is custom anyway that you come not much into open company."

A short while afterward, Ramsay stood by a window, wishing he could shed the confining masked hood, which was overwarm and chafed around his throat. But he knew from Yurk that that was not done unless he was entirely alone. And the man Thecla had assigned to him moved about the room behind. He should be planning what he would do when they reached Lom. Only he knew so little about what he might find there it would be better to wait and see what fate would toss him as a chance.

Oddly enough, in spite of what seemed incredible to the sensible Ramsay Kimble he had been—and would extend every effort once more to be—he was accepting the fact that this *had* happened. He moved through no dream or hallucination. No, he was here in a world perhaps parallel to what he had always known—first tied to it by dreams, and then in a body not his.

That any machine could accomplish what Thecla calmly believed Melkolf's could do—Only he understood from Yurk's comments upon the past state of civilization that this world had once reached a standard undoubtedly in advance of any his own had ever known. There could well be reason to believe that Melkolf had rediscovered some principle those supermen of long ago had once put to use.

There remained only that he must discover whether such a machine would work two ways, whether Melkolf could be confronted and forced to return Ramsay. And since the party of which that scientist was a full member certainly did not want his presence here, they ought to be only too glad to send him back. For their purposes, Kaskar was now dead. Berthal ready to take the throne. Ramsay was a threat; he might even be able to exert a little blackmail on his own behalf, working through either the old Empress or this Osythes. He would just have to wait and see.

Waiting took him into the air again the next morning aboard the largest flyer he had yet seen. Thecla and Grishilda had a cabin to themselves near the fore of the machine. Ramsay sat surrounded by the men of her bodyguard, Yurk to his left. But he did not try to make any conversation as they were carried steadily to the southwest and Ulad.

Ramsay was not even aware that they had crossed the border until suddenly he saw other flyers in the air bracketing them, flying an escort of honor. They ate once and, as evening began to close in, he caught the first flash of the lights of Lom—the spread of the city across the plain beneath.

When they landed, it was outside the walls of Lom Palace, where a saluting guard awaited them, together with an old man in black-and-white, and another in almost as long a robe of yellow; both were bowing to welcome Thecla.

Ramsay started at the sight of the black and white robe. That was the man he had seen twice in dreaming. He could only be Osythes, the one responsible for enmeshing him in this coil. He wanted to be angry at the sight of the other's thin face, the brush of his white hair. Only it was not quite anger Ramsay felt now, rather excitement, the impatience of one who must act. And Osythes could be the key to that action.

❈ ❈ SIX ❈ ❈

RAMSAY had tossed aside traveling cloak, unfastened the throat latch of that bonnet with its mask, behind which sweat gathered on his forehead. However, he knew better than to discard that headgear, for Cyart still bustled about the suite of chambers that had been assigned to Thecla's kinsman. Also— Ramsay studied first one wall and then the next with suspicion. Perhaps this civilization had not yet advanced to the refinement of "bugging" a room when those in power wished to check on its inhabitants. But that did not mean that he could not be under some form of surveillance, if only through a secret peephole. This palace was the kind of medieval looking structure that made one think instinctively of secret passages, spy holes, and all the other aids to a court intrigue.

So, best to continue to wear his mask, no matter how hot and confining it seemed. If there *was* some spy crouching behind the hanging-covered walls, there was no use in exciting a report that Kaskar had again returned— this time alive.

The chamber was luxurious. One of those long couches, covered with a thick green fabric, balanced piles of wide cushions scattered across a similarly shaded carpet to serve as chairs. And there were small tables, each bearing numerous figurines, bowls, cups, which Ramsay guessed were for display, not use, since they were of precious metals or carved from what looked like semiprecious stones.

Long windows to his left gave not on the outer world but on a narrow balcony above a court. He caught words of command from below. A squad was being put through some drill there.

Somewhere within this pile must lie that lab that he remembered from the last dream in his own place and time. After Cyart had stowed away the baggage Ramsay had brought from Olyroun, Ramsay dismissed the man, wishing he dared take the servant enough into his confidence to ask him to keep his ears open, report anything he heard that might point to the direction in which Ramsay must search. Only he dared not risk any such suggestion.

He sat down on the couch, realizing only too well just how difficult this was going to be. Of course, he could attempt to cultivate Melkolf, but Ramsay doubted his ability to do that without raising any suspicion. Having never before played the part of a detective, he did not have the slightest idea how to begin. Instead, he strove to recall every one of those dreams that had tied him in to this wild venture. Perhaps somewhere hidden in his own memory he could find a possible clue.

The first one— That had been entirely of Osythes, the old man in his full black-and-white robes, seated in a chair with a tall, carved back, his head resting against it so that his chin was pointed up a little, his eyes closed, a certain rigidity and tenseness of his figure suggesting, as Ramsay guessed now, complete concentration. In that dream, Ramsay had seemed to watch the Enlightened One through some window, as if between them at that moment there were a pane of clear glass.

Try as he would now, he could bring to mind only Osythes, the chair, that sense of deep involvement in thought that the Shaman had projected. Ramsay had not been in any way an actor in that dream, only an onlooker.

That first contact must have signaled the point when Osythes, searching for Kaskar's "twin" on some other world plane, had at last discovered Ramsay. Then, there had been no suggestion of foreboding. He himself had awakened from the dream only curious. So his curiosity had led him to mention it to Greg, mainly because it had been clearer, remained more firmly fixed in his mind, than any dream he had remembered having before.

Now Ramsay saw Osythes in a chair—was the Shaman perhaps dreaming also? Or was the priest forcing his personality to search beyond this plane of existence? What next?

The second dream—Osythes had been in that also, but not passive, seemingly asleep in his chair. Instead, he had stood, his eyes open, in his hand a round, glittering object, like a mirror, from which light reflected. The Shaman had held it carefully, moving it back and forth, until the flashes it reflected had struck straight into Ramsay's own eyes. This time, there had been no feeling of a protecting wall between them; rather it was as if

Ramsay himself, without power of motion, were in the same strange chamber with Osythes.

The chamber? Ramsay closed his eyes now, bent his powers of concentration on trying to recall—not the Shaman with his flashing mirror, but what stood about him as a frame.

Walls—yes—and with hangings on them—much like the hangings of the walls that covered this chamber here and now. What were the designs on those hangings? Not those of animals and birds such as Ramsay would see if he opened his eyes; rather lines of black and white, the same colors as the Shaman's robe. They had formed geometric patterns. But he could not see them except very hazily, and it required a terrific effort of will to recall them at all. The flash of the mirror into his eyes had tended to center his attention only on the Shaman.

Now—the third—Osythes again, but beside him two others. One was a woman, and she was seated in a chair that had a heavy canopy over her head. That shadowed her figure so much that he could make out but little of it. On the other side of that chair was another man. He was much younger than the Shaman, wearing all gray, both undersuiting and vest-coat—bearing a hawk-eagle on his badge on his shoulder. Osythes had pointed the way; this was Melkolf bringing science to carry on what mental powers had begun.

That suggestion fitted—very well. Ramsay believed that now he could recognize the face of the enemy.

Three dreams. The fourth—? Osythes no longer occupied the scene here, nor was the woman in the canopied chair visible. Ramsay could see only Melkolf, the scientist, clearly defined against a shadowy background. He was engaged in fitting a box with a rod into the square top of a large apparatus that stood shoulder-high before him. Ramsay drew a quick breath— *That* must be the machine Thecla had spoken of.

He struggled to concentrate on it, but to do so was like watching an object through a wavering wall of water. One moment it was clear, the next it was hidden by a rippling. It was not the machine, however, he realized quickly, that he must deal with. No, rather the room that held it. What was that like?

Walls—stone, no hangings such as had existed in the first two dream pictures. But the stone was lighter in color, too. And there were other fittings in the room aside from the cube where Melkolf worked. Unfortunately, in some manner, Ramsay's attention had been concentrated mainly during the dream on the scientist. Had he been already so tuned in to whatever had been used to contact him that he had been linked at that moment to the exclusion of all else?

Not quite, for there had been a fifth dream before the final one from which he had been awakened to serve the purposes of Melkolf's companions. In that, he had been going down a long hall, before him the black-and-white robe, the Shaman's white head, holding his attention. Osythes approached a section of wall with a large panel that bore the hawk-eagle painted on it in gold.

The Shaman glanced hastily from high to right and back again as if to assure himself that he was alone. Ramsay suddenly wondered about this dream. It was unlike the others in that neither Melkolf nor the Shaman was facing him, or using either the mirror or the box. Rather, this was as if Osythes might not have been thinking of his prey at all. Then how had linkage occurred? Was it done because, once, having touched Ramsay through some control he evoked by an Enlightened One's mental range, the Shaman had inadvertently opened a door for Ramsay that could be a two-way one, enabling his victim also to spy upon him?

At any rate, Ramsay watched the Shaman lift old, heavily veined hands to touch the outer tips of the gilded bird's spread wings. He appeared to exert heavy pressure. Then, in answer, the panel split down the center. Osythes stepped through that opening quickly, bundling his robe about him tightly as he went.

He had to move quickly indeed, for the paneling snapped shut again as if the mechanism that controlled it were on a tight spring. Then had followed a change in the dream, a shifting of background.

Once more, Ramsay saw what must be the laboratory, this time from a different angle. Osythes went before him, descending a stairway into what must be, in comparison with the Shaman's slightly stooped figure, a large area. The equipment housed there was in startling contrast to the medieval appearance of the rest of Lom Palace. Ramsay recognized nothing he saw, but it startled him with the feeling that all these installations were centuries in advance of anything he had seen, either in a dream or in reality, in either Ulad's city or his own home.

Centuries ahead? Or aeons behind, Ramsay wondered now. That story Yurk had told him—of a highly technical civilization that had vanished in a chaos of worldwide war. Suppose Melkolf, a man with what passed at present for scientific training, had found some very ancient storage place, or just the knowledge to reproduce such experimental equipment? That could be the answer.

Osythes reached the floor of the lab now, walked across it. Melkolf and Berthal suddenly came into view, as if the Shaman had raised his voice to summon them.

Though the dreams had always been vividly realized as to sight, Ramsay had never heard anything during them. Now, he longed to have that second sense added as he saw the three men conferring together. He might not hear their words, but he was able to pick up a sense of excitement, of need for action. As Osythes turned, the other two accompanied him. Then—

Ramsay shook his head, opened his eyes. That had been when he woke up. And there had been only one more dream, that which had been his undoing, after which the compulsion to drive to the mountain and his crash must have been exerted. He remembered Melkolf in that and the man he knew now to be Prince Berthal— cousin to the helpless Kaskar.

That last dream held nothing he could now put to advantage. All he really had was the secret panel that led to the lab. But could he openly tour what might be miles of corridors within this pile, seeking one panel with a gilded bird on it? There could be more than one, since the hawk-eagle was the badge of the ruling house.

What about by night? Were there then sentries on duty along the corridors? How long would he have to hunt? In what direction? Ramsay's frustration sent him pacing restlessly back and forth, tugging at the throat latchet of his hood. He longed to skin that and the mask off, but he did not quite dare.

Melkolf, Urswic, and Berthal—Thecla had warned him that those three might take matters into their own hands, making sure that Kaskar, or what seemed to be Kaskar, might never rise to trouble them again. Osythes and the old Empress were opposed to such a drastic step. Ramsay began to concentrate on the Shaman.

From what Grishilda had said, these Enlightened Ones did not take much note of the needs of the individual. They dealt with matters of the future, how men and events might be manipulated in the present to bring about the results they had decided were the most beneficial. Apparently, Osythes had been of the belief that the removal of Kaskar, which would immobilize Ochall's plans to rule Ulad through a puppet, was of great importance.

But would Osythes support a mock Kaskar in his demand to be sent back to where he really belonged? And if the Shaman was friendly enough to exert himself on Ramsay's behalf, did he have enough control over the Empress's party to enforce such a move?

Thecla was housed in the so-called Yellow Tower, and its position in relation to his own chambers he had discovered easily enough through Cyart. After all, he was Thecla's proclaimed only kinsman. As such, surely he had reason enough to seek her out. Perhaps she could solve a few riddles for him. It would do no harm to see her anyway.

Ramsay rebuckled his hood, surveyed himself in the mirror to be sure that his Kaskar features were truly in eclipse. He thought that he made a rather sinister appearance in this suiting of dull red, the hood and mask concealing most of his face. A picture from a book flashed into his mind, that of a medieval headsman in part so appareled, waiting for the reluctant approach of a victim.

However, he was equally sure that even Kaskar's hostile grandmother could not recognize him at present, and that he dared venture out. In spite of his grim appearance, as a Feudman, he was unarmed by the standards of the world, and thus harmless. The customary short sword did not swing from the belt tightened about his vest-coat.

Beneath the feud mask, Ramsay grinned a little. To each world, its own arts. He had listened to Yurk carefully, leading the veteran soldier to accounts of his own past campaigns against mountain outlaws. Karate skills were seemingly unknown in either Ulad or Olyroun. Ramsay flexed his hands now. At least he carried a secret protection. For he already knew, from some research at the lodge when he was totally alone, that the skill in his memory could be grafted on to this new body. He was a little slower, a little less tough. But he had been working on that, too.

Now as he stepped into the corridor, he walked with purpose. However, his attention was not only just for the guard who might dispute his way, but also for the wall panels. Here they were designed with arabesques in complicated patterns, no hint of any bird about them. As he turned into another corridor, which should lead directly to the Yellow Tower on a level below Thecla's suite, Ramsay saw that the panels gave way to a series of shallow niches, in each of which was poised the figure of a small, monstrous-looking animal. The company of figures were all different and all highly fantastic. Ramsay thought that they, like those pieces on display in his own chamber, had been fashioned from semiprecious stones, quartz and perhaps jasper—but he knew so little of the subject he could not be sure.

There was no door at the end of the hall, only an archway, elaborately trimmed with gilding over a smooth, brown-red surface. This opened upon a stairway. There, he met his first guard. But Ramsay did not alter his stride, which was that of a man who knew exactly where he was going and expected no trouble in reaching his goal.

When he had passed and was climbing the stairs, Ramsay gave a sigh of relief. The man had saluted him with raised hand, which Ramsay, after a fraction of a second, had replied to with a flick of his own fingers in what Yurk had impressed upon him was the acknowledgment of Tolcarne between one class and another.

He had to restrain his desire to hurry. Something about roaming these corridors gave him a naked, exposed feeling. He would have to get over that if he was to go hunting his split-bird door panel. Now he wanted most of all to see Thecla.

A second guard stood before her door. Set there to do her honor, Ramsay hoped, and not as a barrier to any meeting with her kinsman from overseas. It seemed that his hopes were sustained, for the man saluted and then himself rapped at the door.

Grishilda opened it. Seeing Ramsay, she gestured a greeting, stood aside to let him in. But her face was expressive, and though he could not quite understand what she was trying to signal, he guessed that wariness on his part was needful.

Thecla stood rather demurely beside that same long divan on which he had had his first language lesson. Facing her was Berthal, the splendor of his person somehow too ostentatious when matched to either Thecla's quiet elegance or the good taste of the room's furnishings.

"Ah, kinsman!" Thecla smiled. Ramsay might have been the one person above all now in Lom whom she was wishful to see. "What fortune that you have come at this moment, Arluth. Prince Berthal, this is my blood-kin out of Tolcarne, the Master-in-Chief of the House of Olyatt. Arluth, this is Prince Berthal."

Yurk had schooled Ramsay well. No Master of a House in Tolcarne considered an Imperial Prince, heir or not, more than his equal. He would acknowledge such an introduction with a salute only slightly more deep than he had that of the guardsmen. Ramsay performed exactly as Yurk had taught him.

Berthal frowned. Thecla, in spite of the sober set of her lips, watched them with amused eyes. Ramsay decided that she was enjoying the reaction of the Prince to such offhand familiarity as he seldom met.

"We give you welcome, Master." Berthal's voice was cold. He was already using the royal "we," though he had not been proclaimed, Ramsay noted. "It is indeed fortunate that you have arrived in so timely a fashion that you may serve Lady Duchess Thecla as kin-witness."

"It is always fitting," Ramsay replied carefully, wanting no slip of word or accent to betray him now, "for kin to stand by kin in any matter."

"Just so." Berthal was frankly staring at him. "My lady says you are new come out of Tolcarne."

"Yes." Ramsay kept his assent as curt as he could.

"Then you must have been highly fortunate, Master, to find a ship. Few take the western sea roads these days."

He was probing, Ramsay knew.

"Few. But some still want the trade in sea-ivory and gold. All merchants are not timid of heart where there is a profit to be reaped. The fewer the ships, the higher the reward in the markets of Olyroun."

"Yes," Thecla stuck in. "My people bid high on any such cargo nowadays. Were there less unrest in Tolcarne, there could be much trade between us, benefiting both. Perhaps someday, a man with the wisdom and spirit of your own reverend grandfather will rise there and the turbulence be quenched. But, Berthal, greatly do I thank you for your pleasant welcome—" She waved her hand to indicate a bowl of deep green in which were arranged a thick cluster of lilies of the valley which gave off a sweet perfume. "And assure Her Splendor Enthroned that I shall indeed be honored to attend her at the fourth hour after noon."

This was so evidently a dismissal that Berthal could not linger now without seeming rudeness. But he shot Ramsay a glance as he passed which suggested that he had no desire to leave the Outlander here. Thecla waited until the door closed behind him. Grishilda came swiftly then from the next room and stood with her ear against the panel, listening.

Ramsay wasted no time.

"How well do you know this palace, lady?" he asked.

"Not as well as that of Irtysh, yet it is not new to me. When I was small, my mother brought me hither on visits.

The old Empress is her great-aunt. Why?"

"Is there a corridor you remember where the wall panels are painted with the badge of the Imperial House—laid on in gold?"

"Yes, such leads to the private apartments of the Empress. There are ten such panels, five to a side. What are you seeking?"

"The way to what Melkolf hides. I remember it from one of the dreams through which they caught me."

She bit at her knuckles, her eyes still on him, but as if she did not really see him at all, rather considered some thought.

"And if you find this place? Then what can you do if Melkolf refuses to use his machine to return you?"

Ramsay shrugged. "How do I know? But perhaps there is something to be learned if I can reach there. Lady, do you think Osythes would back me?"

"I do not know. It depends upon what the Enlightened Ones' policy is concerning the future of Ulad. I know that the seeress, Adise, of my own land has a foretelling that your presence here will make a difference. If it is such a difference as will defeat Osythes's plans, then he may be brought to consider such support."

"And could he in turn influence Melkolf?"

"If he wishes. A true Enlightened One can use his mind as a weapon, to bring about any result he chooses. However, very few are the times they will do so. There must be a very powerful and compelling reason. I do not know what your presence will mean to Osythes. And I warn you about hunting out Melkolf without being sure you do have such backing."

Ramsay shook his head with determination. "I am not going to just sit and wait," he declared. "Let me find this lab, then perhaps I can make terms with Melkolf myself. It is a secret—therefore, he is vulnerable—"

"So are you," Thecla pointed out swiftly. "Inconvenient people, who know more than they should, might—and sometimes do—vanish. Of course, I do not think he would move while my betrothal is not yet carried through. They dare not openly meddle with my avowed kinsman, whose presence is needed to make such a ceremony legal. Yes, perhaps you are right in your daring. This may be the time that you should discover whatever there is to be found. Perhaps the more you know, the more you can impress Osythes."

It seemed she had argued herself from her first hostile position to a reluctant agreement.

"I shall give you reason to go there. Grishilda, bring me the casket of gifts for Her Splendor Enthroned.

"It is customary," Thecla continued, speaking to Ramsay, "for the betrothed-to-be to bring a gift to the eldest woman kin of the House. Since Her Splendor Enthroned holds that position, I shall send you with it. Carry it openly, and all will pass you according to custom. Now—you will descend the stair without to the level of your own chamber, but where the corridor forks just beyond your room, take the right-hand way and keep straight ahead. This reaches across the length of the castle between the Yellow Tower and the Red, in which Her Splendor Enthroned resides. There you should find your wall."

She handed him the silver box Grishilda had brought, waved away his thanks. However, she followed him to the door of the chamber and, before he went out, laid her hand upon his arm.

"Take care, Kinsman Arluth," she said softly. "You walk between enemies who are very lightly tethered, and your path is rough."

"That I know. But for your good wishes, lady, I thank you—"

"Perhaps you may have little to thank me for. Wait until you are safe and then speak so. For only then will such return have meaning."

The note in her voice suggested that she was far more uneasy than her words might suggest.

Ramsay found his way easily, holding the casket plain to see in his hands as she had ordered. So it was very little time before, with his heart beating faster, he came into a short length of hall with the panels he remembered from his dream. He strode swiftly along it, delivered the casket to the lady-in-waiting who answered his rap on the Empress's door. She did not ask him to enter and, relieved that he so easily escaped the scrutiny of one of those he had to fear, he hurried back to the panels. Judging by his dream, the one he wanted was the third from the other end of the corridor, on the left-hand side as one approached the Empress's tower. He halted before that, glanced up and down much as Osythes had on that other occasion. There seemed to be no one in sight. And though he listened for several long moments, Ramsay caught nothing but the sound of his own rather fast breathing.

He raised his hands to set his thumbs against the tips of those upheld wings, exerting pressure as he had watched the Shaman do. For a long moment, he feared he had counted wrong, or else this way was sealed. Then, with a small, rusty rasp, which sounded as loud as a gunshot in his ears, the panel parted.

Quickly, Ramsay forced his way into the space beyond, before the hidden door could snap together again.

❊ ❊ SEVEN ❊ ❊

HE STOOD on a small platform above a flight of steep stairs, but he was not in the dark. At regular intervals along the wall were blocks that glowed with a bluish-tinged light he had seen nowhere else in the palace. Under that radiance, Ramsay's own hands took on an oddly unpleasant look, as if the dark skin were shriveled and age-touched.

For a long moment he did not move, striving to use his ears to learn whether he had any guard to fear at the foot of those stairs for they turned at a landing about ten steps down, and he could not get a glimpse of what lay below.

Not only was Ramsay now enwrapped by silence, but the feeling grew upon him that he had taken a step away from the world of the living into one of preserved and awesome age. He shivered—not from any chill, but because the very walls here radiated an alienness that was counter to all he had met in this world. All had been strange, yes, but there was also a human cast to that strangeness. Here he felt as if he had invaded a place never meant for his species.

Ramsay tried to shrug off his uneasiness. When he had come into Ulad, he had certainly suspended logic. But to allow his imagination full rein was to lead into sheer superstition. Cautiously he began the descent, one step at a time, wondering, as he planted each foot firm, if he might be so alerting some system of alarms which he himself could not hear. However, he had to take that chance.

He had reached the landing now, made the right-angled turn, and he could see the foot of the stairway. It was lighter down there. The glow was not the blue of these wall lights, but that of the normal globes. And certainly, no one was in sight. What or who might lurk in hiding he could not guess; no sound reached him at present.

As he went, he flexed his hands, wondering if, when faced by an attack, his Kaskar muscles could respond to his Ramsay mind fast enough to aid him. If he had only had more time to discipline this new body into his service!

From the bottom of the stairs, he looked through an open doorway into a room where there was no sight or sound of any occupant and which his first glimpse told him was what he sought, the lab of his dream visits. Yet, as Ramsay edged within, he kept his back to the wall, facing outward into the center of the area trying to be alert to any sudden rush and yet study the massed machines.

Even in his own time and space, he knew very little of such establishments. How could he judge now whether this was all of Melkolf's own devising, or some legacy from that higher civilization of the past? For the aura of age clung here. What drew most of his attention was that huge metal cube into which his dream self had watched Melkolf fit the rod-on-box equipment. With a darting glance right and left, Ramsay assured himself that he must indeed be alone here. He left his defensive half-crouch by the wall and sought a closer look at that mass of burnished metal.

It was easy enough to find the slit near the top where Melkolf had inserted his hand instrument. That, with its upward-pointing finger of stiff wire (or else another like it), was still within the socket.

Ramsay put out his hands toward it and then drew back. No, he wanted to know more before he tried anything. He began to circle the cube. The top was on a level with his shoulder, and it was about six feet long on a side. The one that had been turned toward him as he entered had only one break in its surface—the gap into which what Ramsay now termed to himself "the finder" had been fitted.

The next side was totally smooth. However, when he reached the one directly opposed to the finder, he discovered a row of dials, below them levers on which one might comfortably rest a fingertip. Two of those, at the far end, were illuminated from within, as if to prove that the apparatus was in working order. Ramsay wondered what would happen if he suddenly pushed down all the levers, but he was not fool enough to try.

All right—so this, according to what information he had been able to gather, was what had transported the personality and memories of one Ramsay Kimble into the waiting body of Prince Kaskar. Only it had not been meant to be used that way—at least Melkolf had not intended to do so.

Suppose the Uladian scientist had been working with

some device which he had *discovered*, one which had been built by an entirely different race? What purpose had the thing served for them? Ramsay had a momentary fantastic flash of suspicion—suppose it was intended for some medical use, to transfer a personality from a dying body into a fresh young one? But there was no point in speculating about what it might do—he must concentrate on what it had done, with him as unwilling victim.

He had found this machine, was sure that he had discovered the medium of his exchange. Only that did him little good, unless he could learn how to manipulate it (and he was very doubtful of that), or unless he could force Melkolf himself to reverse the process.

The atmosphere here in the lab was stuffy; there were strange and unpleasant odors that made him cough. Ramsay fumbled with the buckle of his hood and jerked it and, the mask off, shook his head to enjoy the sudden feeling of freedom that gave him. He continued his trip around the square, finding the fourth side to be as smooth of surface as the second. Was it the finder that controlled his presence here in this world? Suppose he worked it loose—then what would happen?

"Stand still!"

Ramsay's hand, reaching toward the finder, froze in midair. He had heard no one approach, but he had been criminally reckless in not being alert. The puzzle of the cube had taken him off guard. And he had no doubt that whoever had given him that order and now stood behind him was armed. "Rabalt, take him!"

A line snaked out of the air, flickered within Ramsay's range of vision, and settled on his outstretched arm immediately tightening in a painful grip. At the second that one end of it closed upon his flesh and held him prisoner, there was a jerk on its end, a pull sharp as to nearly drag him from his feet to sprawl backward. But he managed to turn and yet keep his balance.

The man who drew the line so taut wore the uniform of a guardsman. Behind him was Melkolf. In the scientist's hand was a glass tube ending in a bulb about which his fingers were curled. That this was a weapon, and a powerful one, Ramsay had no doubt.

Quickly, the man who held the line flipped the other end at Ramsay, holding by the center of its length. As if the cord were a living thing with instinct or intelligence, it swung directly through the air to clasp Ramsay's left wrist as effectively as it had already caught his right.

The guardsman might have been more intent upon making the proper throw than he was on the identity of his prisoner. Now when he looked directly at Ramsay's face, his own eyes went wide.

"The—Prince!" he cried out.

"Not so!" Melkolf snapped. "He is a creature of Ochall's under illusion to make us think so. Now he is powerless. You may go, Rabalt. This, I shall handle. But tell my Lord Councillor Urswic and the Prince Heir that this one has been found here. That is of utmost importance."

He reached out his hand, and the guardsman, if a little reluctantly, gave the loop of the cord into his grasp, though never did Melkolf allow that other weapon to waver from its aim on Ramsay. Without looking again at the captive, Rabalt disappeared up the stairs in haste, either agog to carry out his orders or because he found the lab itself an intimidating place to be. Melkolf waited, apparently wishing to make sure that the other was gone. Then he spoke again.

"You are very wise to surrender—" With the glass tube he executed a small movement, as if to be sure Ramsay was aware of it. "This will destroy a man far quicker than any steel blade or air bullet. Those who went before us had weapons making ours as clumsy-seeming as stone and wood spears. Kaskar is safely dead. He is not going to rise from the tomb again."

Ramsay found his tongue. "You can make sure of that in another way. Send me back!"

Melkolf smiled slightly. "But that is just it. I would, with every good wish, if I could. But I cannot."

Ramsay nodded to the machine. "Then this will work only one way? You cannot reverse it?"

"Oh, it could be reversed easily enough. But the fact remains that Kaskar is dead and buried. Do you not understand, you barbarian fool? Kaskar was in your body when it died, and that body is safely buried!"

Ramsay stared at him. Why had that thought not occurred to him? The stupidity of his own simple plan to return struck him speechless. Then he summoned the will not to allow this man to know how that struck home.

"If Kaskar was in my body, then where was I? There must have been some time lapse. I found myself awakening on Kaskar's bier—"

"Yes, that has been our puzzle. Where *were* you during two days between the time when our unesteemed prince had his fatal attack and you came into residence in his carcass? An interesting problem. But of no consequence now. What remains is that, of present, Kaskar is safely dead, in two time worlds, and he is going to remain that way. There will be no resurrection to delight Ochall, that I assure you. And your foolish return to Lom will avail you nothing at all but—"

"My murder?" Ramsay somehow found the words, maintained with effort his outward composure. Melkolf indeed had the upper hand, for Ramsay did not doubt that he could easily be put to death here, and no one would ever be the wiser. Nor would his body turn up later to make trouble for his murderers.

"Murder? One cannot slay a dead man." Melkolf laughed. "Had you a single wit in your head, you would have kept away, once you escaped. The Duchess arranged that, did she not? Well, she cannot speak of it, nor will she, knowing that Olyroun is the prize in the end. You will simply disappear. Using that"—he nodded at the cap-mask Ramsay had discarded—"someone will walk away from here and take ship to return to your homeland of Tolcarne. You have made it very simple for us, have you not?"

"No, he has not!"

Another man stood on the stairs, his long black-and-white robe giving bulk to his body. Melkolf shot a quick glance over his shoulder.

"How did you—" he began, then bit his lower lip as if those words had been shaken out of him by surprise and he wished he had never uttered them.

"How did I know, Melkolf? I was on my way to Her Splendor Enthroned's apartments and met your messenger on his way. It needed very little persuasion to learn from him what had happened here. And what has been done is not in the least simple, Melkolf."

"How so?" demanded the other defiantly.

"The very fact that Kaskar's body drew this other is a thing we must know more about. Did it happen in the first exchanges you made?"

"No—"

"Then why should it in the most important one? There is always a meaning behind such things. We only follow paths which we choose for good or ill, that is our free choice. But we have not made those paths—do you understand me?"

"That is the talk put about by your Enlightened Ones. He is here because of some misfunction of the machine!" Melkolf scowled.

"But I thought you were certain of the functions of this machine of yours. Have you not shown us in private many wonders you have learned from your discovery of ancient and forbidden knowledge—"

"Forbidden by whom?" Melkolf flared. "By small-brained men who feared what they could not understand!"

"In the past, by men who understood very well, well enough to have survived a world gone mad," Osythes returned coldly.

"Legends—"

"All legends lie coiled around a core of truth. But we do not argue history now. This man's fate is something that I do not understand; he is not to be lightly handled!"

"I do not intend to handle him at all," countered the other. "I will use this"—again he indicated his weapon—"and there will be nothing left to handle."

"No? What essence came to inhabit Kaskar's body? You may destroy flesh and blood, bone and sinew, but there remains a part that cannot be destroyed—"

"I do not believe you." Melkolf spoke firmly. "I believe what I see, what I can touch, hear—"

"If you believe what you see—there is Kaskar." Osythes pointed. "Touch him, listen to him. He is what your machine has created. Do you deny that?"

"No—"

"Is he also the Kaskar who was—?" persisted Osythes.

Ramsay listened to this exchange with growing surprise. Just what was the Shaman trying to establish? That if Melkolf disposed of him, he would continue to haunt a lab in Lom? That sounded as impossible as everything else had been since he had had his first dream.

"No! Kaskar's dead!" Melkolf stated that fact now with all the emphasis of one who was determined to hold onto at least one truth in a rapidly shifting play of suggestion.

"I agree. Kaskar is dead. But this man"—Osythes indicated Ramsay—"is someone, something else. And we must know more about him. Since he has flaunted certain laws of existence which were believed to be firmly set—"

"You mean the Enlightened Ones want him?" Melkolf demanded.

"His existence has not been reported to the Grove." For a moment, a shade of disturbance showed on Osythes's face.

"Then he need not be."

"Who is Adise?" Ramsay shot that question into their duet. He had no intention of standing there tamely while they decided whether or not he was going to be killed for what might be a second time, if one counted by bodies.

It was as if some potent voice had sounded out of the air, striking both of his opponents dumb. Melkolf stared, but Osythes blinked. Then the Shaman answered his question with a second.

"Where did you hear of Adise?" However, he gave Ramsay no chance to answer; instead, he swept on to reply to himself. "Then the Duchess—"

"What about the Duchess?" demanded Melkolf. "She brought him here—why?"

"If she were not the ruler of Olyroun, she would have entered the Grove. Her testing in the potentials of the true talent were high. Now it seems she has contacted the Enlightened Ones if Adise has been mentioned to this one."

"Well, who is Adise?" Melkolf sounded defiant now.

"She is a Foreteller. I wonder—" Osythes looked more disturbed. "But I have no message, no sign from them. No." He pointed to Ramsay. "We must keep him to hand, safe. Do you understand? I must wait for a message. And do not think you can daunt the Enlightened with any tricks." His voice sharpened and deepened as he spoke. "This man is under protection—"

He raised his hand and pointed his thumb bearing a heavy ring at Ramsay's head, moving that thumb in a small tight circle.

"You can't. This matter comes before the Council—" Melkolf protested.

Osythes simply stared at him, full faced. The scientist's scowl deepened, but he looked sulky also. As if he had been bested at last.

"Keep him in the cells where you had the others," Osythes continued now in a cold, remote tone. "You will be advised when to produce him and where."

With no further word, the Shaman turned to re-climb the stairs. Melkolf watched him go. The sulkiness was akin to hate in his expression. He turned and gave a vicious jerk to the cord about Ramsay's wrists.

"Come on, you!"

There were a couple of tricks Ramsay thought of trying. But the fact that the scientist was very careful to continue to hold the glass weapon on him was an excellent argument against any reckless gesture. He thought he could believe Melkolf's boasts about the efficiency of that arm. Perhaps the scientist would like his prisoner to try something so he could use it and then claim self-defense.

Melkolf rounded back of a tall installation to another open doorway giving on a very short hall. Here, two iron-barred cells faced each other. The scientist threw open the door of the one on the left, waved Ramsay in. When he had slammed and locked the door, he gave a sharp snap of his fingers.

To Ramsay's astonishment, the loops about his wrists loosed themselves, fell to the floor, and then the cord wriggled like a living creature out between the bars. Melkolf stooped and caught up the length, which now hung in his hold as limp as any length of ordinary thin rope. He wound it into a few neat loops and went away, with it swinging from his fingers.

Ramsay was left to explore his new quarters. Against one wall, there was a shelf that had some coarse coverings tangled upon it. He supposed this served as a bed. And there was a stool and an evil-smelling bucket. As accommodations, these were bleak enough, and he could see little hope of gaining any better in the immediate future.

However, as he settled on the stool, which was so low that he had to sprawl his legs across the floor or perch with his knees nearly up to his chin, Ramsay had enough to occupy his thoughts. He had been near complete extinction. He realized that now, with a sudden onset of mild panic.

That panic he had fought to control when facing Melkolf. Only, he was still alive, and that was what counted. Also, there was indeed a sharp division of opinion now over his fate. So far, Osythes had shown himself strong enough to overrule the scientist.

That exchange between the two—Ramsay began to consider every word of it he could recall. They had used the machine earlier, and it had worked as they wished. No untimely return of the safely dead then. So, as Osythes had pointed out, why had it not worked the same way with him?

Ramsay had to force himself to accept Melkolf's flat statement that Kaskar had been buried as Ramsay Kimble, that there was no return. However, at the moment, he was more than a little surprised at his reaction; he did not particularly care. Was it because the longer he was Kaskar's tenant, the more he became identified with this world? So that the thought of no possible return failed to be a great shock?

Very well. Suppose he had to stay here. Then what sort of future could he expect? Osythes had hinted that he would be of interest to the Enlightened Ones. Not that

that sounded too good. Ramsay had no intention of playing the part of some experimental animal while they studied him to see what made him tick, or rather *why* he made Kaskar tick. Ramsay smiled very grimly at that.

Melkolf wanted him dead, to expunge the mistake of his own experiment. Undoubtedly, his revival had sent Melkolf's stock on a sharp downward plunge, as far as the scientist's standing among his associates was concerned.

There was Ochall. How would he like another Kaskar all ready to hand? That talk of the High Chancellor's strange power over the real Prince—how much of that was the truth? Was Kaskar just a weak character under the sway of a man everyone believed was a very strong and malignant personality? Or had Ochall perhaps used drugs, hypnotism, what-have-you, to bring the heir of Ulad under his thumb, unable to operate without Ochall's express permission?

And Ochall had to have Kaskar as a front or he would go under. That was a point to remember.

Thecla—those in the conspiracy to get rid of Kaskar were aware now that she had been the one to help him in his first escape. But her own impression, that she was invulnerable to their counterattack—how true was that? Suppose she married Berthal as they all agreed she must. How much power would that give those of Ulad over her? Ramsay had no way of assessing the customs of this world enough to be able to answer for or against any future danger to the Duchess.

Adise—the mention of that name had plainly disconcerted Osythes. Yet Thecla had had the advice of that person, and the answer had been that he, Ramsay, had some part to play in Olyroun's future. That was why the Duchess had consented to his return.

His own record certainly was not one of glowing success. Though he had located the lab and found the machine, he was now in the hands of one set of the enemy. No matter how Thecla might feel toward Berthal, the old Empress, and her companions in intrigue, Ramsay did not trust them in the least.

All he had won by throwing that name at Osythes was a respite, to face up to his own stupidity. Certainly, he had gained no advantage that he was aware of at present. Thecla would know, or guess, where he was when he did not show up again. Did she have influence enough to demand his freedom?

Somehow, that thought made Ramsay uncomfortable. Ever since he had fallen into this web, it had been Thecla who had rescued him from one difficulty and then the next. It was about time he did something on his own— something more constructive than walking straight into the first trap they had set for him.

He was angry now. He got to his feet and went over to inspect the door of his cage. Though he thrust his arms through the bars as far as he could and groped about outside to try to locate the lock, his fingers encountered nothing but smooth metal. There was not even a keyhole, and he had not the least idea how Melkolf had locked it.

He squatted down to note how the bars were set into the stone of the flooring, and he could see there was no possible way to break out. Of course, if a jailer showed up, he might play one of the games the invincible hero of spy stories always pulled: gasp that he was dying, and when they opened up to make sure, simply batter his way out. But Ramsay had a grim premonition that if anyone did come, Melkolf would be standing by with his trusty glass squirter. And he had already decided he was not going to gamble a second body on being right or wrong in any showdown with the master of this den.

That left him the unproductive answer of simply sitting and waiting for something to happen. He had never been patient at the best of times, and at present, he was even less in favor of allowing the enemy nine-tenths of the advantages. However, there seemed to be nothing else he could do.

If he could manage a little constructive dreaming now—The sudden thought surprised him a little with wry amusement. Then he began to consider it with less amusement and more purpose. Sitting down again on that uncomfortable stool, Ramsay began methodically to recall all he had heard Greg tell about dream telepathy experiments. There were two dreamers and the control. Ramsay had never paid much attention to the apparatus part of the experiment and had absolutely refused to volunteer as one of the subjects. The control waited until the hookup suggested, by way of a brainwave reading, that the sleeper was receptive (they called that REM—rapid eye movements—because that was the physical signal that dreaming had begun). Once the dreamer was ready for action, the control pulled a picture from a stack waiting, one he selected at random. Then he concentrated on that, and the dreamer, in more than a random number of cases, picked up suggestions of the contents of the picture.

But there was nothing for Ramsay to work with here

on that level. Still, his mind played with the idea of dreams. Osythes had dreamed apparently from one alternate world to another to draw him, or else reached through to control Ramsay's dreaming. Could that very act have set up some rapport between them, so that now Ramsay, in turn, could reach the Shaman? He doubted very much that would work. Surely not to the point that he could bring Osythes here, make him open the door.

Melkolf—no. Ramsay did not believe that the scientist could be reached. Greg said it would not work against a closed mind. And Ramsay guessed that Melkolf's mind would be tightly closed, that the scientist believed it was his own ingenious machine that had had the major part in producing Kaskar's demise.

Osythes, however, was a dreamer. The point remained, when did the Shaman sleep—?

Ramsay's head dropped into his hands. He might just as well believe that he could get up now and walk through those bars as that he could accomplish anything by dreaming it.

❈ ❈ EIGHT ❈ ❈

RAMSAY THREW the unsavory coverings from the shelf bed to the floor before he stretched out on the hard plank, which he thought was not too unlike the bier on which he had first awakened into this world. He closed his eyes, not to dream but to concentrate on the Shaman, both as he had seen Osythes in his dreams and later in person during Thecla's welcome to Lom.

The Shaman's black-and-white robe was mentally visible. However, Ramsay discovered it was far more difficult to build a face feature by feature. Yes, the hair was white and somewhat longer over the brow, looking thicker, as if fluffed up and out by some wind. Below that the forehead, then brows—also white and thick.

When Ramsay tried to recall the eyes beneath those brows, he nearly met defeat. Dark, a little sunken back into the skull—yes. Still, there was a factor missing, a certain expression which Ramsay could not now define. Or was it *lack* of expression? There remained something masklike about the face of his vision—no true life behind it.

He had never tried such a feat of concentration before, not such an intense one. This struggle absorbed him even more than when he had tried earlier to recall the dreams that had led him here. One after another, those dream scenes again crowded in, overlapping, covering his attempted single vision of Osythes. Now those dreams spun a cover for the Shaman. Yet Ramsay persevered.

Then, for one moment, Ramsay singled out the face he wanted, no longer a lifeless mask. Those deep-set eyes were regarding him with a hint of astonishment. That contact lasted hardly more than a breath before it was broken. Again, he "saw" only a black-and-white figure misting away, into nothing. Ramsay's head, his whole body ached. Muscles must have tensed so much as mind while he had fought for what he had no reason to believe might succeed. Should he try again? Black and white—black—and—

Black became gray and scarlet. Someone else—he sensed another presence—yet one, he was certain, who was as yet unaware of him. He cowered mentally away, as a small animal might flatten against the ground seeking to escape the attention of an enemy. That this other personality *was* the enemy—more so even than Osythes—Ramsay believed. But he could assign no name—Ochall? What had they said concerning the High Chancellor gave some credence to that. Greatly daring, Ramsay tried to summon up a face. There was nothing— except that he *knew* there was another there; to meddle further was folly.

Ramsay opened his eyes. Almost he expected that

person to be leaning over him, willing to—to what? Ramsay did not know, but a sense of compulsion lingered. He sat up, looked around the cell. No, he was entirely alone. Nor did he catch any sound from the direction of the lab where Melkolf and the guard had discovered him.

If Melkolf was right—and at the moment Ramsay had no reason to doubt that the other believed exactly what he had said—there was no return to the past. He waited for his own reaction to that, perhaps even the rise of panic at being lost from all he knew.

Still—that did not follow. Ramsay looked down at the brown hands resting on his knees. Not his hands. But— they were! He did not feel any different in Kaskar's body than he had in his own. When he looked in the mirror, his features were those of Ramsay Kimble, though his skin might be several shades darker, his scar gone, his hair differently cut. Still, he had seen Ramsay Kimble there as he had all his life.

If there had was any trace of the original Kaskar personality left—well, he had not detected it. Therefore, he was *not* changed, only the world about him. It was like, he thought deliberately, taking a job in a foreign country— Mexico, perhaps, or one of the South American states. There, he would have to learn language, customs, which were alien to those of his own land as were the ones of Olyroun, Tolcarne, or Ulad.

There was no one back home to really care if he dropped out of sight. Second cousins— He had been a loner since his parents died in a car accident when he was seventeen. After that, he had been too busy fighting for an education and a living to make any lasting contacts. Greg was perhaps the best friend he had had, although Greg was so wrapped up in the Project that he really cared for little else.

So—he had been free, if one could call it that, to accept a job overseas. This was a little farther than overseas, and much more of an alteration in his life. However, if he could accept it as such, he could push any panic far enough away for it to fade into nothingness.

In fact, though he realized it only now, Ramsay had, in the past days at Kilsyth, begun to adapt. If he accepted the fact that there was no return, then where did he go from that?

Right into the middle of a nasty mess, from everything he had learned. To Melkolf and his aides, the pseudo Kaskar was a danger because he could reveal exactly how they had rid themselves of the real Prince. To Ochall, Ramsay would suggest a possible new game with another pawn—

But he was himself! He was not Kaskar. And it was *his* future they would try to twist and turn—or perhaps, erase entirely. Therefore—now he was fighting for himself.

And—

Ramsay started to his feet, facing the cell door. Someone was coming, not that he had heard any scrape of boot across the floor, but he was certain of movement within the lab, headed in his direction. Melkolf again, this time ready to finish him off? Ramsay drew a deep breath. No matter what exotic weapons the other was going to produce, Ramsay would not easily be killed.

Still, no sound his ears could catch, just the sure belief that there was someone there, coming for him.

He stooped and caught up the stool, swinging it by one of its legs. How effective a shield that might make, Ramsay had no idea, but it was the only thing he could use. Perhaps he would even be lucky and throw it straight enough to knock Melkolf's tube out of his hands. Always supposing the other did not just stand beyond the bars and ray (if that's what that weapon did) without coming into reach.

A figure stepped into the opening of the short hall where the cells were. Black and white—Only one man Ramsay knew within this pile wore such a robe. However, he did not put down the stool.

Osythes walked at a slow pace, but from the very moment he came into view, the Shaman tried to catch and hold Ramsay's gaze. There was danger in that! Just as he had sensed the noiseless approach of this Enlightened One, so now some instinct told him not to allow Osythes to meet him eye to eye. Ramsay dropped his own gaze to the other's chin, his wrinkled throat.

The Shaman reached the locked door of the cell.

"It is time that we speak, stranger." His voice sounded rusty, as if he did not use it much.

"Perhaps so," Ramsay returned. "What would you say to me? Since I am your prisoner—I am a captive listener."

"Not my prisoner—" Osythes extended a hand from the folds of a long sleeve, pressed his five fingertips against the door plate. The gate swung open. "Come forth, stranger—"

Ramsay hesitated. What if he did just that and his action was deemed an escape attempt so they could cut him down easily without question?

"I bear no arms." Osythes sounded weary now. "Nor do I intend you any betrayal."

Ramsay remembered something Thecla had said. "Word-bond for that?" he asked.

"Word-bond," the Enlightened One replied promptly.

Now that was unbreakable, according to Grishilda's comment. Ramsay dropped the stool with a clatter, moved out into the narrow passage.

"Come!" Osythes had already turned away, headed back to the lab. Ramsay stalked warily after him. The Shaman had given his word-bond, but that might not hold for the other conspirators in the Get-Rid-of-Kaskar intrigue.

They were not going toward those stairs down which Ramsay had come, rather toward the opposite end of the crowded room. As they passed one bench, Ramsay saw, lying there, the Feudman's hood. He paused to snatch it up: that disguise might be needed again, especially in Lom, where his present face was a liability.

Here was a second stairway, steeper, narrower. Osythes took the climb slowly, as if such effort taxed his frail body. Ramsay loitered impatiently a few steps behind. He constantly glanced back, expecting to hear or see pursuit at their heels.

The flight went straight up. A thin patch of light at the top suggested an open portal, and perhaps they were expected. Osythes, breathing heavily, reached the opening, Ramsay just behind.

Here was another richly appointed chamber. However, Ramsay was given little time to survey his surroundings, for Osythes had advanced to stand by the side of a tall chair from which extended a canopy of carved and gilded wood overshadowing its occupant.

She seemed very small in that thronelike seat, yet such was her aura of presence that she was not in the least dwarfed or belittled by it. Instead, the throne provided the perfect setting for her.

A fur cloak was drawn about her shoulders, although, to Ramsay, the room felt warm. And all but her face was concealed by a scarf of golden tissue held in place by a begemmed circlet. Her hands, as thin as bird claws, rested quietly in her lap. On her right thumb was a seal ring such as Thecla wore, a band so heavy and thick it overpowered the flesh and bone the metal encircled. And she wore other rings, too, all richly jeweled.

Her small feet, covered by soft boots, were planted firmly together on a footstool. All added to make her stance one of complete authority. That this was the old Empress, Ramsay had no doubt. And he studied her face curiously. What was she like, this woman who had rid herself of a grandson in the name of duty to her country?

Age had sharpened her features. If she had ever possessed any beauty, it was now withered away. Only she did not need beauty. She would draw all eyes in any company wherein she chose to move. Ramsay was impressed as he had never been before in his life. But he determined not to show that. As far as he was concerned, at this moment, she represented the enemy.

They were alone. A quick glance about the room told him that just Osythes and Quendrida were united in full power. What had Thecla said—these two found him a menace, but they would not agree to his killing. That left the other three: Berthal, the new heir; Urswic, the Councillor; and Melkolf. Where were those now? Did the absence of the junior three mean that there had been a split in the party? If so—how could that be put to Ramsay's own advantage?

At this moment, he was well aware of the very searching stare the Empress had turned on him. He met her gaze calmly, with none of that instinctive withdrawal that had warned him against Osythes. The silence in the chamber grew, but Ramsay determined to let one of the others break it first.

"What manner of man are you?" It was the Empress who spoke. She asked her question sharply, as if to gain some quick, perhaps too revealing, retort from him.

"I am a very ordinary man—" Ramsay hesitated, and then gave her the term of respect he had heard was used when speaking directly to one of the last reigning queens of his own world—"Madam."

She raised her hand to sketch an impatient gesture.

"In some manner," she retorted, "you have importance. Or you would not be here."

"You mean, ma'am"—Ramsay schooled to such indifference as he could summon—"I would be more use to you were I dead?"

Beneath her hook of nose, her mouth quivered. It was Osythes who replied to that challenge.

"You are bold—" There was rebuke in his tone.

"What else have you left me?" Ramsay was amazed that he could find these words; stilted they might be, but only such were appropriate in this company. "I am told that I am a dead man. In two different worlds, it would seem. Therefore, as a dead man, who can deny me plain speaking?"

To Ramsay's surprise, the Empress suddenly gave a cackle of laughter.

"That was indeed aptly expressed, stranger. You have a quick tongue and a mind"—she hesitated—"a mind that differs from those we know. Now what must we do with you?"

"What shall *I* do?" he corrected her. "The choice is mine now, ma'am."

Again, the Empress was silent, studying him. Then she asked, as if she might be inquiring politely, not really caring, concerning the intentions of any mere acquaintance: "What is in your mind to do, boy?"

Ramsay shrugged. "As yet, I have not been given any chance to choose, ma'am. Melkolf has told me there is no return to my own world. If I can believe him, then it is here I must make a place for myself."

She shook her coroneted head slowly. "Not here, not in Lom, not in Ulad, while you wear *that* face."

"And who presented me with it, ma'am?" Ramsay challenged again.

"We had no choice." Any momentary lightness vanished from her voice. Her tone was again that of cold authority. "You must know the situation—Kaskar's rule would have produced disasters our country could not endure."

"So—now you must accept me." Ramsay refused to be intimidated.

"I have said—we cannot." Again, authority in her voice.

"Your answer, then, is Melkolf's—kill?" he demanded.

Her ringed hands moved; the thin fingers tightened about the edge of the fur cloak, making the jewels in her rings catch and reflect light as rainbow sparkles. Osythes moved a step forward from beside the throne chair, as might someone guarding his companion. A faint shade of indignation crossed his face, breaking that masklike serenity he had worn since he had released Ramsay from the cell.

"You make too free!" Now the sharpness was in the Shaman's voice, but the Empress interrupted him.

"Who has a better right to question us so, Reverend One? No, stranger, we will not kill. But there is another—perhaps others—who will not be so forbearing, because they fear. When men fear, then they act, wisely or rashly, but still they act. If you would live—I say this again with all truth, if you will live—then not in Lom, in Ulad, even on this side of the ocean. You have taken the guise of one out of Tolcarne—very well—live by it!"

"And why should I be governed by any desire of yours, ma'am?" Ramsay did not ask that with insolence, but hoped that these two would get his meaning, that he was no man of theirs to be commanded.

"Such an *answer* is not my desire," the Empress replied. "It is only good reasoning. I can restrain Melkolf; my orders will be obeyed in that direction, as long as my son, the present Emperor—though failing fast—still lives. When he dies, I have still a place in Lom, but I cannot command such power. I can only suggest then, not order.

"In the meantime, you have been told of Ochall—of what he desires. One of his creatures, those Eyes and Ears that serve about this court, need only glimpse you unmasked and he will speedily hear of it. And I promise you, if Ochall comes to hunt you down, not death, but death-in-life will then be your portion.

"Do not believe that Kaskar was always a weakling, an easy tool in the hands of a stronger will. Once, he was as you stand now, a youth proud in his strength, quick of wit, able as to mind. This I do not declare because he was blood of my blood, flesh of my flesh, heir to my House— no, this I say because it was true.

"What evil means Ochall used to make Kaskar his we have not discovered. It may even be that he perverted some of the Old Knowledge, that which we believed only the Enlightened Ones retained, to achieve the fashioning of the Kaskar he would have. And, having done this once, can it not be that he will be able to do so again? Do you wish to be only a shadow of what you now, are, stranger?"

She was not trying to frighten him, Ramsay guessed that. This Quendrida who ruled in Ulad meant exactly what she said. Drugs—hypnotism—it must be such as these she hinted at. And he could also imagine what might happen *if* Ochall could lay hands on him. Suppose they were entirely right, that he had no future in this land? A quick retreat at present began to sound like the best move he could make. Still, it did not follow that he could not, at some future time, return. If they won their battle with Ochall—But it was the immediate present that mattered most, not the future.

"Can I accept," he asked of them both, "that Melkolf did speak the truth—that I have no return to my own place?"

The Empress left the replying to Osythes.

"It is true. I have sent the dream probe once more

into your world. It met with nothing. There, the man you were has passed the Final Gate, along with him who was Kaskar. May the abiding pace of all time gather about him now!" The Shaman made a small gesture, tracing some symbol in the air. For a moment, the Empress inclined her head.

"All right. Then if I go out of Ulad—say, to Tolcarne? How may that be arranged?"

"It is arranged. We needed only your consent," the Shaman replied. "Though the merchants trading overseas are in these times very few in number, there is one venturer whose ship lies now at anchor in the west harbor. He is willing to take a passenger. Clothing, weapons, credit with this merchant, all will be waiting for you on board. You will leave within the hour—"

"You make such a decision with speed," commented Ramsay wryly.

"It must be done so," Osythes answered. "For the sooner you are out of Lom, ocean-borne, the less either you or we have to fear. Ochall may have already heard rumors of your existence. There is no reason to believe he has not. And we do not understate your danger if he searches with all his resources."

Ramsay shrugged. "It seems I have no alternative."

"That you have not!" the Empress affirmed. "That you have been caught up in this matter we must deplore, but the reason for it was of such importance—we cannot deny that, if faced again with the same choices, we would make the same decision. One man weighs very little against the safety of a whole land."

Ramsay looked to Osythes. "I am told that is also the

belief of the Enlightened Ones, why they will advise but do no more. Yet it seems that here you have done more—"

"On my head and heart that action will lie. Which is none of your concern, stranger! But since you have said yes—then we only waste time with our chatter here. You must be on your way at once!"

"I would see the Lady Thecla first."

The Empress leaned forward a little in her thronelike chair, her old eyes turned searchingly upon him once more.

"Why so? Such a meeting has no reason. She knows well all we have just said to you and agreed to what we would offer. The child has done very well in every way. Now, she will do even better, joining peacefully our two lands, for the greater safety and progress of both. Berthal is not, as Pyran, my dying son—a great ruler. But he is one who will listen to good counsel, and he hates Ochall bitterly. We need not fear that that son of evil will much longer send his shadow out across our land!" Her voice deepened, was filled with emotion as she continued. "No—you go now—Osythes will accompany you to the gate. Beyond, there will be one to play your guide to the ship. And—wear that mask—put it on now! Would you allow a dead man to walk so all can see?" She pointed to the cap-mask swinging in his hand.

He could demand again to see Thecla, but he thought it useless. Anyway, the Empress had made it very clear that the girl knew all they had planned for him. Still, as Ramsay adjusted the hood and mask, fastening firmly the throat latch, it was with a sense of disappointment. Of course, he, as a person, would not matter to Thecla. She had been working from the first not to save Ramsay Kimble, but to salvage the plans of the two now fronting him, agreeing that the good of any nation came before that of one man, though she had refused to leave him prey to either Ochall or the hotheads on this side of the intrigue. For that much, he must thank her. She would now marry Berthal. Ochall would lose his power. And history would continue along the path this old woman, this man, saw fit to set it.

The Empress gave Ramsay no formal farewell, nor did he offer her any. She had leaned her head back against her chair, her face now much in the shadow of the canopy, but not so much that he could not see her closed eyes. Perhaps, she had already dismissed him from her mind now that the problem he had presented was neatly solved.

But Quendrida of Ulad could not foresee *all* the future, much as he had heard talk of the Enlightened Ones' foretelling. Perhaps she would have a surprise or two. Ramsay was already beginning to wonder if he was not the one to deliver such a surprise. He had made up his mind while in the cell below that he was no man's puppet. Nor did he intend to be any woman's. His own man, that was what he was going to be—even if he had to plan and fight for it.

They traversed corridors, descended stairs, came out at last in a courtyard like the one which Grishilda had led him to on his first escape from Lom Palace. Again, one of the flyers waited and, by its steps, a man wearing the uniform of the guard. He saluted Osythes and then Ramsay, waiting for the latter to climb into the vehicle before he himself entered.

The flyer soared aloft in such a leap as had startled Ramsay on his first ride, but now they were sky borne for a much shorter time. They set down on a square of pavement that was lapped by the water of what must be the sea. A wharf ran on out, and berthed alone it were ships, though they had no sign of spars or sails, only a stubby post in the center. The guardsman waited for Ramsay to join him.

"Not far—" He gestured down the wharf. "It is the—" He had been facing Ramsay. Now his gaze centered over Ramsay's shoulder. There was startled surprise in his eyes; his mouth dropped open.

Ramsay acted half on instinct, dropping to the ground, rolling. A man with a drawn "sword of state" in one hand plunged past. The attacker was slightly off balance, mainly because he meant that sword to have gone well into Ramsay's back.

That his treacherous attack had failed in the first blow did not appear to defeat him. The stranger whirled, to leap again. As he did so, he shouted: "Feud vengeance!"

Ramsay did not try to regain his feet. Instead, he rolled onto his back and waited, seemingly an easy prey. This fellow also wore a mask, only it was bright yellow. Through its slits, his eyes glistened avidly as he leaped again. Ramsay's back muscles tightened as he kicked out smoothly, felt his boots thud punishingly against the other's body.

❅ ❅ **NINE** ❅ ❅

THE ATTACKER, unprepared for such a countermove, sprawled backward. With another roll, an upward push, Ramsay regained his feet. Falling, the other had lost his sword. Ramsay planted one booted foot on the bared blade. As the man lunged at him for the third time, Ramsay brought the edge of his hand into precise alignment, not to kill, but to stun. For the last time, Yellow Mask wilted, face down on the pavement of the wharf, now to remain there. Ramsay, breathing hard, stooped, picked up the sword, wheeled with it bare and ready in his hand.

He discovered they had gathered a circle of spectators. However, if Lom had a police force of any kind, no such officer was present. Nor had any of the watchers moved to interfere. Among them, Ramsay did not see the palace guard who had been supposed to see him safely to the waiting ship.

"A clever toss, that—" remarked one man, moving out a step or two from the rest.

He was lean, tall, his dark hair almost completely covered by a crested cap, not unlike the one Ramsay now wore, except that it lacked a face mask. His vest-coat was as short as that of a servingman, but he wore a wide belt that supported both a short sword of ceremony and a bolstered weapon of some kind.

Also, there was no badge on his breast. Rather, a diagonal stripe of violet slashed dramatically across the uniform gray of the rest of his clothing.

As he addressed Ramsay, he raised one hand in a casual salute, as if in passing courtesy only.

"Dedan, out of Rental," he introduced himself. "Free Captain."

"Arluth of Tolcarne," Ramsay replied. He was thinking furiously. The prompt disappearance of the palace guard from the scene led him to only one conclusion. He had been set up for murder! Someone had taken neat advantage of Ramsay's cover as Feudman to do this. And he believed he need not have to search very far for the one, or ones, who had arranged the attack. All the Empress and Osythes had told him that been meant to lead him tamely here, to his death. Perhaps the plan reached further back than their interview; perhaps even Thecla, in arranging such a disguise, had had this eventual end in mind.

His anger shimmered within him. They had played games with him. Very well—he owed them nothing from this moment on. He was his own man. And now, there would not be any retreat to Tolcarne. Ramsay, at this moment, doubted very much that any ship bound there was really docked at Lom.

The Free Captain dropped on one knee beside the flaccid body of Ramsay's attacker, rolled the man over on his back to strip off the yellow mask. He gave a low whistle and glanced up, appraisingly, at Ramsay.

"Someone wishes you very dead, stranger. Do you know him?" He jerked a beringed thumb at the inert fighter.

"No."

"This is Odinal, a hired killer. And his pay comes high. Those whom you feud with must be willing to empty their pockets." He brushed his hands together as he rose. He might have been wishing to rid himself of any lingering trace of the touch of the mask.

"I would suggest," Dedan continued, "that you now cease to be the center of attention." His fleeting glance right to left indicated the gathering crowd. "It may well be that Odinal had a shoulder man to back him."

At that moment Ramsay felt lost. If what this fellow said was true, he might expect another attack. And, having surveyed Ramsay in action, any prudent back-up man would do his killing from a distance. He could see no one who looked suspicious among the crowd, but this life of constant peril was totally new to him, and confusing.

Dedan's hand fell lightly upon his arm. "I believe prudence indicates a swift withdrawal. Retreat is often the right arm of valor, or so we are told."

Ramsay nearly jerked away from that light touch. Why should he trust this Free Captain (whatever *that* meant!) any more than any other in the crowd? But the man was right! Ramsay had to get out of sight, hide until he could make some coherent plan.

"We are but a matter of strides from the Cask and Bowl—" Dedan waved down a street leading to the wharf. "Their fare is rough enough, but passable for a dock tavern. Shall we go?"

"Why—" Ramsay began.

"Why do I take a hand in this matter?" Dedan finished for him. "On two counts, stranger. First, I have a constitutional dislike of seeing an unaware man stabbed in the back. Secondly, I am very much interested in the strange ways you use your hands and feet. In my own profession, every new defense adds to one's capability, and eventually to one's worth as a hired fighting man. No." He shook his head as if he read Ramsay's sudden thought. "I am not of Odinal's cult brothers. I am a soldier for hire, not an assassin against one private enemy."

No one moved to dispute their going. And Ramsay went, mainly because at the moment he could not think of anything else to do. The betrayal had been so sudden, had so completely altered the scene for him, that he was nearly at as big a loss of understanding as he had been on his first awakening as Kaskar.

Dedan waved him through the door of the tavern, where a strong mixture of odors suggested stale and ancient meals, and not much use of water and soap thereafter. The Free Captain continued across the large room where there were benches and tables, massive, much stained and rubbed smooth at the edges, as if generations had eaten and drunk there. There was a buzz of conversation, for the tavern had patrons in plenty. However, Dedan skirted even vacant benches, proceeding into an inner room where there was a measure of quiet, though the smells were stronger.

He kicked a stool out from under a small table, waved Ramsay to another opposite him. A girl, her upper tunic slit so extravagantly that one could see well up the plump swell of her thigh, her hair caught tight to her head by a tarnished gilt ribbon, pattered in.

"Isa, my beauty, two cups of the White, and whatever you have now stewing on the right-hand stove."

She giggled and nodded, scuttling out as if Dedan were not one to be kept waiting.

"I will not ask who could have set Odinal on you." Dedan eyed Ramsay. "Tolcarne you have claimed for a homeland, and you wear a Feudman's hood. But it is not like the Houses of the West to reach overseas to pull an enemy down. And if you are a proclaimed Feudman, you should have been secure. Now, I wonder, whose boot toes have you bruised *here!*"

The Free Captain spoke lightly. Whether he expected a quick answer or not, he gave no sign. Ramsay placed the sword he had taken from Odinal on the top of the table between them. Now Dedan leaned forward a little to study the weapon.

"Good workmanship, and a double threat, too."

"Double threat?" Ramsay was surprised into asking.

"Yes. Behold!" The Free Captain touched the hilt, pressing his thumb firmly on one of the ornamental bead bosses. From the point of the blade oozed two large drops of a liquid.

"I would advise you not to touch that," Dedan warned. "It is not meant to nourish a man; quite the opposite. This is a sword out of Zagova, where they have some very peculiar customs. I am a little surprised at

Odinal under the circumstances. Even a hired sword does not usually choose such tricks."

Ramsay stared at those dark drops. He did not doubt in the least that Dedan was perfectly truthful. Perhaps the yellow-masked assassin need only have scratched his opponent. At the thought of what might have happened, Ramsay's hand clenched on the edge of the table.

"Just so. You were far more fortunate than you guessed, stranger, when you escaped that. However, it is how you escaped that interests me most. I could judge your actions well enough to believe that you have trained in a new form of fighting."

Though he did not make a question out of that, Ramsay nodded.

The girl Isa returned, balancing a tray on which were cups and bowls. Suddenly, Ramsay was very hungry. She was about to set the tray on the table when she sighted the sword, those ominous dark drops.

She cried out, jerking away so sharply that the liquid in the cups slopped over. Dedan threw out an arm to steady her.

"Isa, my beautiful one, do you now find one of those foul rags Bavar keeps to wipe down those outside tables of his. I promise then all shall be well. Put your tray here—"

She did as he bade, then was gone and back again so quickly, a grimy rag flapping from her hand, that Ramsay could only believe unusual fear had driven her. However, she would not come near the table. Instead, she tossed the rag to Dedan. Carefully, the Free Captain mopped up the spilled liquid. Then, holding the cloth folded together, he went to the fireplace, tossed the wad into the charred ends of wood lying there. Going down on one knee, he brought a small box from an inner pocket of his tunic, spun a wheel on its side with his thumb. The resulting spark fell on the material, which flared angrily, giving off a puff of evil-smelling smoke.

Isa voiced a deep sigh of relief. Still, she did not return to gather up the tray or serve them. It appeared she believed that the sooner she was out of the room the better.

Ramsay ate steadily; nor did his companion break the silence that filled the room now. While he ate, Ramsay's mind was busy. He wanted to know more about this Dedan who had appeared so fortuitously on the wharf and had knowledge of unusual weapons. However, as a man of this world, how much would Dedan presume Ramsay already knew? And if Ramsay dared ask any questions at all, would he not then reveal that he was more than a simple stranger? He had a very complicated problem.

Dedan finished what was in his bowl. Now he nursed his cup between both hands, watching Ramsay across its brim. There was a lazy, engaging quirk on his lips that was not quite a smile but implied something amusing in this situation, though Ramsay gained no indication that such amusement was aimed at him.

"I have an offer for you, Arluth—" For the first time the Free Captain used Ramsay's Tolcarnean alias. "If you teach me that trick with the feet, I'll give you safe passage out of Lom and guarantee you won't have to face another Odinal, or the same one recovered. You have hurt his professional prestige badly by that trick of yours. He will be prepared now to make your disposal a personal matter, you understand. I am not a merchant to bargain; my offer is a simple one. Teach me that trick, and leave Lom as one of my Free Company. We are due to sail up the coast tonight, land at Yasnaby, then proceed inland along the border there. If Odinal tries to follow, he will be as noticeable as a rashawk in the open-sky, always provided he can find the means to travel. In addition, if you are oath-bound to the Company, your quarrel becomes our quarrel. And the world knows well that the Free Companies protect their own. What think you of my offer? I do not believe that you shall have a better one, at least not here in Lom."

Ramsay, remembering the sudden and doubtless well-rehearsed disappearance of the guardsman, could readily accept that.

"Your Company—for whom does it fight now?" He made a guess that these might be among those rootless mercenaries whom Ochall was gathering. That being so, he had no intention of leaping from a fire set by the Empress and Osythes into another stirred up by the apparently universally detested Chancellor.

"Not for Ochall. Is that your problem, Arluth?" Dedan studied him shrewdly. "Be that so, you have a right to look over your shoulder night and day. No, we have been hired by the Thantant of Dreghorn. He holds the Western Marches for Olyroun, and they have been invaded twice by the Lynarkian pirates. Those raiders grow bolder. This time they managed to sack Razolg and hold it for a full week, standing off a siege by the largest force Thantant could put against them. Olyrounians will fight attackers, but they are not trained to the field. Thus, we are to join them. The pay is good, and there are bonuses added for each skirmish that puts those of Lynark underground or back to sea, licking wounds. Now, what say you—your knowledge for a safe passage out of Lom?"

Ramsay emptied his cup. As he set it down on the table, he said slowly: "I am no soldier. I do not even know how to handle such a weapon as this." He touched the hilt of the short sword. He knew such frankness betrayed him, for how could a Feudman be so ignorant? But Ramsay saw no other way. He did not believe he could bluff a trained fighting man. Now he continued, raising a finger to touch his mask.

"Neither am I a Feudman from Tolcarne. Though, as you have seen, there are those who want me dead. I believe now that this very disguise they wished upon me was to provide an easier target for Odinal, or one like him. I cannot tell you who—or what I am. But Lom—Ulad— means death—"

For a long moment, Dedan regarded him. Then, the Free Captain said: "Truth may be a harsh lady to her liege men, Arluth, but when a man is frank, he deserves the same openness in answer. Do you flee some crime?"

"If you count the fact that I exist at all as a crime, yes. For no other reason am I a menace to others."

"Ochall?"

"Among others, yes," Ramsay returned. "I have inadvertently spoiled a plan in which he had a prominent interest."

Now the Free Captain showed once more a faint quirk of smile. "That would fit well with what I have heard of that very unworthy Chancellor. So you are no soldier? Well, there is no lacking the means of making you one. And your own skill—that I wish to learn in turn. Hunted man or Feudman—what matters it? To me, the cases are more than a little equal. I owe no liege service to any within Ulad. Have you reason to believe that Olyroun would also close doors to you?"

Could Ramsay be sure that Thecla was not one of the prime movers in this intrigue? He longed to believe that she had been unaware of this last small refinement of plan someone had set in action to wipe him permanently from the playing board. But, Ramsay decided, he was going to take this chance.

"I do not think so," he guessed. "Though if certain powers in Ulad pushed—"

Dedan raised his eyebrows. "Now you interest me even more, Arluth, who is *not* of Tolcarne. But will they seek you among a Free Company?"

"Perhaps not."

"Well enough. Now—take off that mask. We shall make good use of the window yonder." He indicated the grimy pane, cross-latched with strips of metal. Then he counted some small coins on the table top. "It is better not to risk passing through the outer room again. Who knows who may sit there snuffling into his cup?"

Ramsay hesitated only a moment before he tugged off the masking hood. Dedan was already at the window, using his strength to force up a latch which plainly had been long set in place. A moment later, they slipped, one after the other, over the sill into a noisome side alley.

The hour was past sundown, and there were enough

shadows to furnish some kind of cover. Dedan's shoulder brushed against Ramsay's.

"To the wharf. Our coaster sails with the night tide."

Ramsay was very conscious of his unmasked face. The warnings, beginning with Thecla, that his features might mark him down to any spy, had deeply set in his mind. Still, he was not, he thought, even glanced at by the few men they passed. However, he gave a sigh of relief when he boarded the ship and passed down into the hold quarters of Dedan's company.

Three days later, in midmorning, Ramsay grinned as he lightheartedly surveyed, with mock criticism, Dedan, who sprawled on the deck.

"You merely use a man's own action and strength against him," Ramsay repeated for about the tenth time within the hour.

Dedan gritted his teeth. "Well enough, when you do it! However, my turn will come. Your hand is not as sure on sword hilt as it is against my aching neck!"

Ramsay had a half-dozen pupils out of the company of thirty, which was Dedan's command. The rest shied off from this new method of fighting, being content to watch, and jeer at those taking ungainly tumbles across the planking. Dedan was also right in his statement, for Ramsay remained certainly far from mastering the sword. He could use to better effect the odd handgun that was the other close-combat weapon of the company.

That impelled darts of glass, nasty when they broke upon impact, slivering to enlarge the wound. He saw nothing akin to the glass tube with which Melkolf had threatened him. There were also larger, long-barreled weapons, meant to fire globes, which burst in the air, loosing upon the heads of the enemy a burning liquid. Though these arms were faintly akin to a rifle, the military of this world appeared to have nothing that shot a solid bullet.

In addition to personal arms, Dedan showed Ramsay several field weapons mounted on planes, which, properly controlled, floated a foot or so above the surface of the ground. Weighing far less than their bulk suggested, these could be towed into place, and, once aimed, they broadcast, fanning wide in a way damaging to enemies, waves of vibration which tormented all not equipped with ear plugs.

The mixture of weapons—the relatively primitive sword with the strange and much more sophisticated "rifles" and "vibrators"—puzzled Ramsay. He learned that side arms, rifles, and floating vibrators were very costly. Dedan's company hire price went two-thirds into buying and maintaining these—while replacements could be found only at a metal market in the far north where another nation had rediscovered, and then copied, certain weapons from the Older Days.

These northern arms merchants were jealous of their monopoly, and the weapons they produced possessed built-in-destruct mechanisms. Thus anyone striving to decode their construction did not survive his curiosity. Or, if he did, he was not in such a state to enjoy life greatly thereafter. So far, no one had managed to circumvent this particular safeguard on a profitable trade monopoly.

One had to be sparing of ammunition, using it only when it would be to the overwhelming advantage for either attack or defense. Dedan considered the cases of ammunition his main treasure. In an attack, the mercenaries relied first on the swords. Thus, all of the men Ramsay watched in practice were, he admitted, deadly foemen with what was in his own world an archaic weapon.

Without the use of sails or other visible aids, the coaster headed steadily north. At intervals, the vessel seemed close to complete submergence. Ramsay speculated as to whether that stub of pillar in the midst of the ship was not the source of the mysterious energy that kept them going. Another vestige of the earlier and vanished civilization?

Ramsay had to be careful about questions. To display too much ignorance would be dangerous. He listened as men talked, attempted from scraps and pieces to build up for himself a more concrete idea of this world.

Descriptions of certain portions of the land, especially to the northeast bordering on Tolcarne, suggested that an atomic disaster had occurred during the ancient conflict. These man-made deserts were deadly, though some strange mutant races were reported to be living along the sea coast even within the fringe of that avoided area. Similar deserts existed to the east and had taken a large portion of the continent which now held Ulad, Olyroun, and two other nations. The people now living in these "clean" sections had a recorded history of having moved up slowly from the south.

Their ancestors had been wandering tribal barbarians when they had re-peopled the land. However, contact with the Enlightened Ones had brought about a radical change in their nomadic lives. They had settled and started to build anew, but their legacy of tribal custom led them to develop as feudal states often at war with one another.

Within three generations, Ulad had united some twenty of such small antagonistic kingdoms, duchies, and lordships, and now ambitiously proclaimed itself an empire. To the north, Olyroun remained free. Along the coast, still farther north, buffers between the culturally advancing south and the awesome merchants who dealt in bits and pieces of forgotten technical lord, were the islands of Lynark, which were the present seat of a loose confederation of dedicated pirates. Nearby, on the mainland, was Zagova, whose people were adept workers in metal and allied with the merchants of arms.

Mentally, Ramsay tried to draw a rough map of this world; he had yet to *see* one. He knew that what he learned in this way was far from accurate. The one thing that all his informants agreed upon was that the Enlightened Ones had certain gifts or powers that no ordinary man could counter with any known weapon or tool. The Shaman-born might originally have been of another race; speculation on this subject seemed divided. However, it was now well known that they did draw recruits, both men and women, from all the "civilized" nations.

Simply a wish to be an Enlightened One had no force. One had to possess qualities of mind which were recognized by those already gathered into that fellowship of power. It was necessary, after being selected, that the untested recruit retire for a number of years to one of the Groves, which were scattered headquarters. Rumor said that the lifetime of one of the Fellowship far outlasted that of ordinary mortals. The Shaman brood was held in awe, and also, perhaps, a measure of dislike, mainly because of their policy of selecting some goal of their own, thus refusing help at times, even if the cause was good.

Advisers entered courts as Chief Shamans (as Osythes was in Lom), but they could only advise as to certain actions. Oftentimes, they remained stubbornly dumb, refusing any words at all. They even had been known to desert a ruler at a time of extremity, simply because the course they foresaw as paramount demanded that this man or woman fall from power, a decision issuing from impending action.

"They are unchancy," Dedan stated frankly. "He who seeks out a Foreseer does so at his peril. I believe they can weave such a man into serving them, seldom to his own good."

"Foreseeing—" Ramsay said musingly. "Have you ever seen this done for another?" He wanted to ask *how* it was done, but knew that he must approach the question obliquely.

Dedan frowned. He did not reply at once. Instead, he shot a glance sidewise at Ramsay.

"Once," he replied shortly, "and no good came of it. It was—" He hesitated, again eyeing Ramsay. The Free Captain might have been trying to make up his mind whether the other could be trusted with confidence. "It was in the matter of the assault on Vidin. I was Second then—Tasum commanded the company. He, poor fool, thought that perhaps he could gain a high seat—the Rule of the Outer Reef Land. So he sought a Seeress and pressed me to go with him. Though I did not give assent to any reading, mind you. No ill luck from that would I have touch me.

"She threw Twenties and drew. I can see them yet, all lying out on the handboard of her table. There they were—Hopes, Fears, Fates, Dreams. Tasum got the King of Fate. He thought it meant victory. Only, he died the next day screaming, with Hot Rain flooding over him. No, I have no wish to see that again!"

Ramsay was no clearer in his mind after an explanation. He sensed that Dedan had no wish to continue his story either. And he was hoping furiously to find some way of learning more, when the signal was given from above the deck that they were nearing their chosen harbor.

Here was no wharf or easy landing. They had to lower their equipment and baggage into small boats, then be rowed through surf and lashing spray toward a rocky spit of land which projected into the tameless waves.

All of them were well soaked by the time they assembled far enough above the water to escape the dash of foam. Ramsay was not blind to the tension among them. There was more unease here than just a rough disembarkation would cause.

Ramsay had shouldered his own backpack and made sure his side arms, sword, and all were fast in place. Dedan climbed to the highest point of the rock, his head turned toward the shore, his eyes shielded from wind and spray by cupped hands. Ramsay thought that the Free Captain was seeking something he expected to see but which was not there.

The boats were all on their way back to the ship. Thus the wild rocky coast, the constant beating of the water, gave an impression of loneliness, which increased the unrest of those among the rocks.

Dedan signaled three scouts who fanned out as best they could, moving inland across the rocks. But the Free Captain held the rest of the company where they were until those he had dispatched reached the distant beach and climbed to the highest dunes there. Finally they turned to wave all clear.

Ramsay wondered what danger the Free Company expected. There had been no hint on shipboard of this lonely landing. He knew they were to meet, shortly after disembarking, men sent by the Thantant. Perhaps it was because that force was not already camped in sight that Dedan had turned so cautious.

However, the Free Captain now ordered them on, and Ramsay picked the easiest road he could discover across and among the spray-wet, weed-bedecked rocks.

TEN

THE ROCKY RIDGE slowly gave way to shifting dunes. Then they saw, flowing toward them across the ground, a mist—or a fog? Though this ground-based cloud appeared to move more swiftly than any normal fog, Ramsay thought.

Dedan's alarm whistle raised a shrill, ear-piercing call, echoing over the beach. The company closed in tighter formation. Now they began to take on the appearance of a beleaguered host. Still, Ramsay could see nothing ahead but the gathering of that thick yellowish mist. Again, more furiously, Dedan blew. Ramsay realized that, already, the scouts had vanished, curtained off by the fog. A glance back over his shoulder to the sea confirmed the fact that the ship was rapidly dwindling toward the horizon. Retreat in that direction was impossible.

"To the ridge—" Dedan's arm waved them right.

That tumble of stone that had formed a very rough wharf for their landing was here rooted in a rise of rock, pitted and crannied, but, even so, providing a more solid surface than the sand through which they had started to plough.

To that ridge they made their way at the best speed they could manage, the fog rolling inexorably behind them, rising not from the sea but, oddly enough, from an inner point of land. Ramsay was scrambling up the first of the stones when he heard, even through the now continuous pipe of Dedan's whistle, a scream of such agony that he clutched convulsively at the rock in instant reaction. Out of that mist had that cry come. He could believe it a death shriek. Friend? Or still unseen foe?

They fought their way higher among the water-worn rocks. Here was no spray to lash at them, but the footing was so treacherous, because of the many hollows and crannies in the stone themselves, that they had to give strict heed to their going. At last, they reached the crest, men fitting into hollows, dodging behind any rise of rock, dropping field packs, unslinging weapons. Those in charge of the two vibrations machines dragged off protecting coverings, swung fan-shaped antennae back and forth in search of the foe.

Ramsay squatted beside Dedan. None of the scouts had yet returned. Now the dirty yellow of the fog, washed around the foot of the ridge on which they were perched, was rising higher and higher.

He looked to the Free Captain. "What is it?"

Dedan shrugged impatiently. "Your guess will equal mine. I have not seen the likes of it before. But to my mind, the fog is not natural."

"Pirate magic!" A man behind them spat. "Some trickery of Northerners. Perhaps the sea devils bought such with their loot from Razolg."

"A gas—something noxious in the air?" Ramsay felt his throat tighten, his breathing grow faster, shallower, even as he asked.

Dedan shook his head. "With the sea wind rising, they could not control such an attack well enough."

"They might have masks to breathe through, to purify," Ramsay pointed out from the knowledge of his own time and space.

The Free Captain looked unconvinced. "I think this is to provide attack cover." He turned to the man who had suggested pirate magic. "Give me the message bird, Rahman."

From his shoulder, the other slipped a thong supporting a small cage in which sat, silent, yet watching them with its black beads of eyes, a gray-winged bird, slightly smaller in size than the pigeons Ramsay knew.

To Ramsay's surprise, Dedan made no move to fasten any message clip to either slender red leg. Instead, he lifted the bird, now lying calmly content between his palms, to eye level. Staring straight at the winged messenger, Dedan repeated slowly: "Besieged—Yasnaby—fog—foe unknown—"

The bird's long, pointed bill opened, then closed with a sharp click. From its throat there croaked a somewhat garbled but still understandable imitation of his speech: "Beesiege—Yassby—fog—foe—unnnknownn—"

"Right!" Dedan tossed the bird upward. Aloft, it spread wing, to circle the rocks of their natural fortress twice heading inland, flying well above the curtain of the fog at a swift rate of speed.

"Let that speaker reach the frontier post—" Dedan did not continue.

Rahman laughed. "The Marchers will then come thudding, perhaps in time to bury us, Captain. It is a long ride from the nearest post, though they may have a flyer or two." Maybe hope made him add that.

Dedan whistled imperatively. All heads turned in his direction. By now, the first wisps of fog had already curled between those men in lower positions on the ridge.

"Stay set," their Captain ordered. "Let them come to you no matter what ruse they may employ to shake us loose. With the stones of our walls, we shall not prove the easy prey they expect—"

His answer was a low growl of assent spreading from hollow to hollow. Already, some of the company farther away were half hidden from sight. Mist, damp and cold, puffed into Ramsay's face. At least his worst fear was not realized. However, this fog had been engendered, it was not a gas—

"Captain—"

A rattling sound rose from below. Someone was climbing toward them. Ramsay's hand tensed on the butt of his hand weapon. However, the man who climbed was no enemy, rather one of the missing scouts.

He fought gaspingly for breath, as if he had out-raced death. Then, as he spilled forward beside Dedan and Ramsay, he mouthed rough sounds before he could find meaningful words.

"Pirates—out there—" He gestured wildly at the

mist as he drew himself up to his knees. "They were waiting for us."

"How many?" Dedan wanted to know.

"I saw only two. They arose out of the very sand to cut down Hoel. You must have heard his death scream. Ury? Ryales?" He repeated the names of his two other comrades not accounted for.

"Have not reported in," Dedan returned.

"Then—count them as dead." The man spoke dully. "I could hear men moving through the dunes everywhere. It was only because I was closest to this ridge that I made it."

"Pirates?" It was not as if Dedan protested the report of the scout—rather that he was astonished at some other factor Ramsay did not understand. "You saw nothing of the beginning rise of this fog?"

The scout shook his head. His chest was still rising and falling swiftly as might that of a hunted runner. "Only that it spread first from a point north and inland. There, the mist arose into the sky as might the smoke of a fire growing ever stronger and thicker. I was on the crest of a dune when first I sighted it. But I swear by the Four Fangs of Itol, it is not of nature."

"So we had guessed. You saw no trace of any of the Thantant's force?"

"This only." The scout opened his clenched hand, let fall a small object which hit the rock with a metallic clang. By now, the ominous mist crawled up, to settle about them, so thickly that even Dedan and the scout, close as they were to Ramsay now, were enwreathed nearly to the point of invisibility.

There was just enough vision left for Ramsay to see Dedan pick up what the scout had dropped.

"A belt badge of the March forces. Such might have been dropped and lost any time."

"Uneaten by salt wind and with blood on the edge, Captain?"

Dedan held the badge closer to his eyes. He might not have been studying what he held but sniffing at it.

"You are right, that clot is fresh. Perhaps this explains the ambush awaiting us." If pirate scouts had witnessed the coming of the Marchers and wiped out those sent to meet the Company, there was little hope they could entertain for any help within perhaps hours—or days.

The yellow of the fog already lapped about the base of the ridge, rising about pockets where part of the Company had gone to ground. Dedan gave a quick glance right, then left, before he wheeled to face the crew of the vibrators that had been brought into position on the very crest of the ridge. His Second, standing by the vibrators, nodded. Dedan raised his whistle and once more blew a thin, shrill blast. Insert ear plugs—that was the order for his own small force. The Free Captain was going to bring into action his most potent weapons at once.

Ramsay fumbled for the plugs issued him, got them into his ears. The rest of the orders would come now in dumb show. He watched the vibrators lower their wide amplifiers to the farthest notch, so that the effect of their unseen assault would strike as close to the now-hidden dunes as possible. The Second himself stepped from one machine to the other to make certain of their aim. At his nod, Dedan brought down his hand in a sweeping motion of command.

What happened then Ramsay was never able to find any explanation for. Out of the fog, came a spear of light rising high, darting in. There followed a vast concussion that sent him sprawling, brought him up with punishing force against rocks, driving the breath momentarily from his lungs. But he lay in such a position as to see the site where the vibrators had been.

Had been! For only twisted masses of red-hot, smoking metal remained where, moments before, the two trim, highly prized weapons had been positioned for use.

Ramsay clawed at his ears, freeing them from the plugs. Now he could hear. Screams—shouts filled the air. Out of what had been an inferno of explosion crawled a single seared shape, inching painfully across the ground. It was plain that these pirates had come with an effective answer to Dedan's most cherished arms.

Somehow, Ramsay got to his feet, unable as yet to take in the magnitude of that quick stroke from below. The heat still radiating from the wreckage of the vibrators made him cringe away. But a small yammering cry from the thing which crawled brought him to his feet, sent him wavering into that blasting heat almost against his will.

Much of the clothing had been charred from the body. Ramsay had no time to be gentle. He stooped and hooked fingers under the armpits of the wounded man, heaved him up and away from that fierce furnace. Back— he must get back into some kind of shelter. At the moment, confused as he was, Ramsay guessed that the worst of the battle had just begun. Wedging the man he had rescued into a hollow behind him, Ramsay drew his needle weapon and crouched, waiting for the enemy to loom close enough in the fog to provide a target.

A glance around was enough to make plain the disaster. There had been eight men near the vibrators when those blew. Crews of two each serving those weapons, Dedan, Rahman, himself, and the scout. Ramsay saw at once those of the crews could be written off. And there was another blackened bundle where fire fanned sideways over the rock.

Half missing—out of that first count. He hesitated to leave the hollow in search of men already dead. Was the mist at last beginning to clear? Ramsay thought those evil billows more ragged—showing holes—downslope.

Through that now tattered cover came a wave of fire— but not such as had ruined the vibrators. No, this soared in banners upward from the hidden sand. Ramsay had never seen flamethrowers of his own world in action, but what he sighted now along the ridge sickened him. He fought the bile rising in his throat and mouth. These attackers were not trying to capture, to accept any surrender. They were simply killing as they came, and those of the Company had no shield against this new and fearsome weapon.

Ramsay squatted beside the man who was now moving feebly, moaning. He knew it would be only a matter of time before the pirates reached the crest of the ridge. Then, he and this other, in turn, would be roasted before they could even strike back. To wait for a useless and horrible death made no sense.

Half dazed, he tried to see any other survivors. As the mist cleared further, Ramsay bent over the one man he had found. Dedan lay there, his scorched clothing also stained with blood. Around the officer's neck still hung the command whistle.

If the others had sense enough to take out their ear plugs—But had they after the vibrators blew? Ramsay could only hope that a few had done so. He snatched off the chain, brought the tube to his lips, though he knew none of the coded calls. Perhaps just this familiar sound would lead any survivors to fight their way in his direction. Ramsay blew lustily. The discordant note he made must have carried through the inferno raging up the walls of the ridge.

No use waiting any longer in this exposed position. He had no idea if he might outpace the flamers with Dedan as a burden. But he could try. He lifted the Captain and began to move in and out, retreating toward the land end of this crest of jumbled rock.

As a figure loomed out of the mist, Ramsay, steadying his needle gun, ready to fire, just in time became aware of the other's crested hood. One of the Company. The man stumbled slowly along, and behind him wavered three others. Ramsay raised his arms, beckoned.

A moment later, Dedan was being carried between two of them, Ramsay and the others playing rear guard. No one else came out of that hell below. Under their feet, the ridge arose as they advanced. There was better cover, larger blocks of reddish stone that could stand between them and the flames. Also, the fog was fast dissipating, so they could better choose their path ahead.

The man by Ramsay was Rahman. One arm hung limp, and there was the scarlet print of a burn on his cheek. He muttered as he came, his eyes fixed, as if he did not really see Ramsay, instinct only keeping him moving toward an improbable safety.

Those ahead, supporting Dedan, halted. Ramsay impatiently waved them on. In reply, one shook his head determinedly. Ramsay drew nearer to Rahman, touched his shoulder. The man winced, showing a drawn face with empty eyes. He just stood there, staring, when Ramsay signaled him to cover. Finally, the mercenary had to be pushed into a hollow so Ramsay could join those ahead. The third man in their pitiful rear guard stepped with more alertness behind the same rock that sheltered Rahman.

"What is the matter?"

"They've got someone stationed upslope there. He just took a look down to see the fun," one of the men answered bitterly. "If he can get at us, we'll be fried like all the rest!"

Ramsay followed the pointing finger of his informant. Yes! He caught sight of a sleeved arm. The enemy must be very confident that they had little to fear from any of their victims who might possibly try to escape in this direction.

One man with a flamer? Or a whole guard here? Ramsay rubbed the back of his hand across his eyes. He was no real soldier. That seemingly easy victory over the assassin had been a fluke. Then, he had had no time to think out any move; he had merely reacted, and fast, to an attack. This was different. His mind had already closed to what lay behind. To think about that did no good. However, there was in him a stubborn determination to escape with this handful of men, to live as long as he could in order to make someone pay for the ghastly death of men who had welcomed him as a comrade.

"Have you sighted more than one?" he demanded, his own eyes searching for any hint of a possible second sniper.

"No, but he does have one of those flamers—I saw the mouth of it when he hitched it up."

"If there is only one, and they might believe one was enough to keep us bottled up here—" Ramsay was thinking aloud. "All right. You stay right where you are. There is only one way to handle this if he has a flamer."

None of them still carried the rifles that shot the exploding bullets. Ramsay had lost his own when the explosion hit. However, if he could move up close enough to get at that sentry—

He stripped off his overtunic and belt, nothing left to catch on any rocks. Clad in the tight-fitting gray undergarment, he hoped to match the mottled surface hue of the ridge. Ramsay moved out, flitting to the left and up the ridge.

From one outcrop to another, he raced as fast as he could, his palms sweating, his mouth dry, expecting any moment to be swept with flesh-crisping flame. So far, he had escaped notice. Now—over the highest point of the ridge and down. If he had judged his distance rightly, he must, at this point, be behind the sentry. Perhaps overconfidence in this disastrous effect of the new weapons would make the enemy less alert.

Ramsay was almost certain there was only one man. At least, though he stopped his advance several times and studied the landscape carefully, he could pick up no sight of another. And that one opponent was now revealed fully to him.

Crouching between two rocks, Ramsay drew off his boots. He must take no chance of making any sound. Moving as lightly forward as his bruised and aching body would allow, he leaped.

Ramsay's hand chopped so expertly at his throat that the sentry did not even cry out. He dropped, a dead man; perhaps he was not even aware that any attack had come. Ramsay caught the flamer, then arose, cautiously, to his full height, so that those in hiding out there would see and know the way was clear.

Ramsay remained where he was, alert for any sign of movement, ready to cover his comrades' advance with the flamer should a challenge arise. He could hear a ragged shouting, still see the flames wasting the lower ridge. There, however, some of the fog clung, enough to make him heartily glad, for it hid what must be the horrors there.

"The Captain—he can't go on much longer," panted the same man who had pointed out the sentry to Ramsay as they drew level with his guard post. "Nor us either—"

"Do any of you know this country?" Ramsay asked.

His only answers were shaken heads.

"Arluth—" Rahman, his eyes no longer blank, but his face twisted with pain, wedged the hand of his limp arm in to the front of his belt. "If the Marchers got out a message, they'll come riding right in—to that!" He indicated the battlefield behind without looking directly. None of them had, and Ramsay believed that the sight of it sickened them beyond endurance, hardened mercenaries though they were.

"Is there any kind of road inland, one the Marchers will take? I know you said this is country you are not familiar with, but do you know anything about it at all?" He appealed to them. Dedan lay at his feet, eyes closed, moaning a little now and then.

Again, shaken heads answered him. They could not go on much farther; that was the truth. Not one of them lacked burns or other wounds. Rahman was not the only one kept on his feet by sheer willpower. Also, sooner or later, someone was going to come hunting the sentry left here. And when he did, the chase would be up.

A sudden thought came to Ramsay as he glanced down at the body. A broken neck among these rocks might seem an accident. However, to stage such a scene would mean abandoning the weapon. He surveyed the ground about them. It could be set up—and success might be their only chance. Catching the body under the arms, he dragged the dead man a little to the left. Then he took the flamer, to drop it a pace or two farther on, as if it had fallen so from the enemy's hands.

"What are you doing that for?" Rahman lurched closer.

"He has a broken neck. There's no wound on him." Ramsay nodded at his victim. "Suppose he fell when he came up here? See, he is wearing clumsy boots, not footwear made for climbing around rocks."

"But the flamer," protested one of the other men. "With that, we'd have a better chance to fight ourselves."

"Without it, we may well have a better one," Ramsay pointed out. "If that was missing, its loss would be a sure sign that someone escaped from back there."

He could see by their change of expression that they understood what he aimed to do. And he wondered if they would agree. After all, he had no official command among them. The Second was dead. He had been standing within touching distance of the vibrators when they were blasted. Any one of these men might challenge his assumption of leadership at the moment.

However, Rahman had a tight grin. "You think fast, Arluth. I'd say this gives us a shadow of a chance. We are lucky." He looked about. "You can't leave any prints on such ground, at least none that sort can read. But we'd better watch as we go. And the sooner we do, that the better."

As they started on, Ramsay lingered to give a last searching survey to his carefully arranged "accident." He found himself rubbing his hands up and down the tunic one of the men had brought along, as if he must wipe from his flesh the feel of that death blow. Resolutely, he pushed that out of memory. He had struck to save his own life, and the lives of those stumbling ahead of him. He had never slain a man before. But somehow, this killing held no meaning for him—not after the flaming death among the rocks.

Their small party had to move very slowly. And they took turns, except for Rahman, who could not use his left arm, in carrying Dedan. However, they were now well above the dangerous level of the beach, crossing a cliff top. Ahead, a strip of green seemed to offer promise. Ramsay thought of water when he saw that, and moved his stick-dry tongue about in a mouth that seemed filled with salt.

All this shifting about might well kill Dedan, but they had no choice. It was necessary to get as far as they might from the scene of the massacre before any search for possible survivors began.

With much time and effort, they got Dedan down the steep side of another rocky drop and then pulled into a green pocket where trees provided cover. Rahman fell rather than lowered himself to the ground. His face was a greenish shade under the dark hue of his skin. But the others took first-aid kits from their belts, while Ramsay struggled on under the trees seeking water, until he discovered a small spring-fed pool.

At the sight, he flung himself forward, buried his whole face in the water. The raw burns on his face stung as he gulped several mouthfuls. Then he rinsed out his belt canteen, refilled it to the brim, and lurched back to their small and beaten company.

That they had lived through the massacre seemed now something hardly to be believed. He had a curious feeling that, having done just that, they were in some way immune to further disaster. Though, he reminded himself of that fatal carelessness of the enemy sentry, they dared not relax any vigilance.

ELEVEN

RAHMAN'S ARM was broken. Ramsay set the bone as best he could between splints whittled from one of the saplings that gave them cover in this pocket. But Dedan's burns were too serious for him to treat. It was Melvas who went hunting through the grass until he found a flesh-leafed plant which he jerked triumphantly out of the soil. After washing the leaves in the pool, he crushed them into a thick mass between two strips of bandage from the field kits.

This was, he stated, a native remedy for burns known to his own province. At least it would reduce the inflammation and pain. They spread-eagled Dedan on his stomach, and, with infinite care, Ramsay and Arjun worked to strip off the charred remains of the officer's tunic and undergarment. Ramsay had to fight rising nausea. Surely, Dedan could not be still alive! Yet he was, and moaned feebly as they worked.

When the burns were as bare as they could lay them,

Melvas, the mass in the bandage between both his hands, squatted to squeeze carefully from what he held in a thin green jelly, spreading that as evenly as he could over the tortured flesh. The shoulders and backs of the upper arms were the worst, but in the end, Melvas had them covered with the stuff, which dried quickly, leaving a glazed surface.

Dedan's moans ceased. At first, Ramsay feared that the young officer had died under their clumsy treatment. But he was still breathing slowly, as if now under the influence of some strong narcotic. Melvas studied the Captain's face, raised an eyelid to see the eye.

"He sleeps," the soldier announced. "Now, for the rest of you—"

They all had burns, but none as bad as those Dedan had suffered. Ramsay found that the stuff Melvas applied to his own burns brought a release from pain which he would have not thought possible.

Having tended their hurts, they sat back, Dedan lying at their feet, and glanced at each other. At last, their attention centered on Ramsay. And, for the first time, except when he had grunted under their treatment, the last man spoke.

"I served in Renguld under Nidud—before I joined with this company. Your face, stranger, suggests to me an odd thought."

"My face?" Ramsay repeated. Perhaps it was some action of the herb on his burns, but he felt slow of wit, drugged with fatigue.

"Your face. There is one—was one—who is like enough to you to look back from any mirror," the soldier continued.

With effort, Ramsay recalled the man's name: Sydow. He had been a Leader of Ten, but not one who had shown interest in the unarmed combat lessons. An older man, he judged, and more conservative.

"That other is reported dead—and is now buried," Sydow continued. "Then who are you who wears his face? Prince Kaskar—"

They watched him now, as hounds might center upon a fox unfortunate enough to have approached their kennel.

"I am not Kaskar." Ramsay made his voice as emphatic as he could. "However, there are those who would set me in Kaskar's place," he improvised. "That is why I wore a Feudman's mask and left Lom—"

"Ochall would pay much for you—" Rahman commented. "To have a Kaskar, whether or not he was the real one—The High Chancellor wants nothing more in this life at present."

"I begin to wonder"—Melvas now took up in question—"whether it was your presence among us that brought an end to our company."

Their concentrated stares grew hard, menacing. Ramsay wondered if they would turn upon him now to relieve their own misery. A suggestion such as Melvas made could set them at his throat!

"There are Eyes and Ears all over Lom," Arjun added. "You need only to have been seen in our company for a message to be sent to Lynark. Yes, it is possible, very possible!"

Ramsay did not like the expressions that were beginning to show on their drawn faces. At the moment, they sought a scapegoat on whom to unload the bitterness of their defeat, all that fury blazing in them as they thought of the ridge and those left there. He could understand that, but he had no mind to be such a sacrifice.

"Your Captain"—he spoke again with such force as he could summon—"told me that any wanted man, once he took troop oath, was one of you. I am not Kaskar, and if I am one who had to flee Lom because I wear a face like unto his, is that any fault of mine? Save your wrath for those who caught us with their fog and fire. Ask yourselves"—his mind began now to awake from the daze of that sudden accusation—"did pirates ever have flamethrowers or this obedient fog before? Are you sure they *were* pirates?"

Sydow blinked. There was a murmur from Rahman.

"The scout—he reported—pirates."

"Or perhaps men dressed as pirates," Ramsay supplied promptly. "In the tales I have heard of battles with Lynark raiders, no man has mentioned fog or flame—"

Sydow nodded. "That is the truth. Unless their chiefs have made some new deal with the Merchants of Norn, they would not have such weapons. I have never heard tell of these before. So—" Again his gaze narrowed as he stared straight at Ramsay. "If they were not pirates, then who are they?"

"I do not know. But think you—I met with your Captain only a short time before sailing. Could any message concerning me have brought this enemy into the field, so well equipped, in as short a time as the length of our voyage, with the additional information as to just where we would land?"

Ramsay was taking a chance now; he did not know what methods of quick communication this world might have. Sydow stirred, there was a reluctance in his expression, as if he had been made to face a fact he did not care to acknowledge.

"Such weapons," he answered slowly, "must have been brought secretly from Norn. Had they been used before by any force, the news of it would have reached the Council in Ulad. These must be of the banned—only those risking outlawry would handle them. While to transport such in secret—" He shook his head. "No, I cannot say, Arluth, that they were turned on us because of you, when I consider the matter."

Ramsay noticed that he was no longer "stranger," that Sydow now used the name by which he passed, a step toward closer understanding.

"Why would anyone wish to keep you from your engagement with the Thantant?" Ramsay persisted.

"Now that is a good question." Rahman shifted his shoulders where they rested against a boulder, as if his arm pained him. "Our commitment with the Thantant was simple enough. We all voted on it before signing. We are—were—to reinforce the sea beach patrol against raiders. It is—was—an ordinary enough engagement. The Thantant needed experienced men to patrol; his are used only for seasonal field service. They are not professionals, but are called up for six months or a year, and then returned to their homes and their work. It is ever so in Olyroun. The only real enemy they ever have to face is the pirates. But those have been growing bolder and stronger of late. Instead of one or two ships slipping in to strike and be away with what loot they can garner by a surprise attack, they have appeared twice in sizable fleets—"

"Yes," Sydow interrupted. "And *that* is unlike those of Lynark. Their commanders seldom serve together except in a very loose confederacy. They are too independent to yield much authority to any one man. I wonder—"

"Wonder what?" Ramsay prompted as Sydow did not continue.

"Wonder whether Ochall has not stirred the pot in that direction. It is common knowledge that he must have the mines of Olyroun in order to exchange the ores for the products out of Norn which he wants. There is the prospect of marriage between the Duchess and the Heir, true enough. But Ochall would rather have Olyroun under his thumb entirely, not through the agency of any woman, especially one whom it is well known he mistrusts. Suppose he put into practice arming those of Lynark and urging on them such raids as they would be only too willing to try, with the proper weapons, thus draining the forces of Olyroun. Then, in the end, he need have no fear of any rising, should he proceed against that land—"

Melvas gave a short, approving bark of half laughter. "Well argued, comrade. You have put forth thus a good reason for preventing any reinforcements to reach Thantant. But"—he arose suddenly—"we forget now that those whom we have sworn aid-bond may come rising in answer to our message, and go down in turn before that hellfire!"

"So what do you propose to do?" Sydow asked gruffly. "We know nothing of the way inland, we have not a second message bird. And night is coming—"

Melvas dropped a hand on the other's shoulder, gripped it tight.

"Remember the Isle of Kerge and what we did there?"

Rahman arose also, turned his head slowly, surveying those heights down which they had recently come.

"Were it between Company and Company," he said, "it might be done. But these halftime soldiers of Olyroun, what do they know of such matters? They would see a fire, that is all—"

"You forget they have already been warned of an attack," Melvas pushed the matter. "Also I do not speak of just any fire. I would have one laid out in the Fate symbol."

"The Fate symbol—" Rahman repeated. "Yes—a powerful warning. But do you think that those who have mauled us nearly to extinction will not be expecting some such move?" He shook his head.

"Not altogether." Melvas's eyes were fiercely alight. "We are on the opposite side of the sea cliff, remember. If we are able to find up there a spot whence the light can only be seen in this direction—then we are able to hope. Also there is a trick a man can use— Give me, each of you, what you can tear from your tunics and I will show you!"

Using their swords to hack at the stout cloth, they tore free strips, which Melvas began tying together until he had a clumsy knotted rope. Under a late-afternoon sun already dipping to the west, he strode back and forth among the trees and bushes of their hiding place until he found a stand of thick canes, brown and shiny, with leaves growing at sparse intervals from the knots along the surfaces. These he hacked through with his sword and cut them into pieces about the length of his forearm.

When he returned with his load, Sydom looked surprised. "Gasserwood—I had forgotten!"

Melvas laughed. "I thought I saw it earlier. Yes, here we have that which will help." He dropped cross-legged on the ground and began to tie the pieces of cane together to form a crude latticework.

Meanwhile, they ate sparingly of the rations they carried in their belt pouches. Dedan still slept heavily. At least he no longer moaned with every breath. His own burns, Ramsay realized, did not hurt enough to make him conscious of them. Whatever remedy Melvas had applied appeared to have an element of magic in it as far as the ease of pain was concerned.

Melvas had produced a firm lattice. Now, into that, he began to weave the cloth strip they had earlier knotted together, not to fill all the spaces of the cane work, but rather in a circle first and then two lines which crossed that, dividing it into quarters. When he had finished, he faced the frame around for their approval.

Now with the sun gone, twilight was well upon them. But Melvas did not hurry. He opened a small flask taken from an inner pocket of his much shortened tunic. From that, he dribbled, using extreme care, a dark liquid, spreading it back and forth across the cloth he had woven so carefully into place. When the last drop had been used, he rubbed fingertips gently along the lines he had soaked with the liquid.

"For once"—Arjun spoke up—"I am willing to admit that your taste in seasonings is worth much, comrade. I never thought I would see the day, or evening, when I might say that—having had to endure watching you spread that slime over your ration bread for years!"

Ramsay sniffed a rather sickening fishly smell spreading from Melvas's work. The latter laughed.

"Comrade, I am from Pyraprad. There we eat sea's fodder like men. The Oil of Shark is a fighting man's seasoning, as I have so often told you.

"Now—" He stood up, holding the frame of oiled cloth a little away from him. "Here we have Fate, and we had better get it in place before night is utterly upon us."

Ramsay pulled off his boots, as he had done before when he made the attack on the sentry. He got to his feet to join Melvas.

"Where do we plant it?" he asked.

The last thing he wanted to do was reclimb that slope down which they had had such a hard time making their way earlier. He moved stiffly, all the bruises he had taken when the vibrators had blown giving him notice of their existence. However, he was, he was sure, in better shape, in spite of them, than any of the squad except Melvas.

For a moment, it appeared that Melvas and Sydow might refuse his aid, then the latter said, "You did prove you know your way around rocks, Arluth, when you cleared the path for us back there. But if you would go, it must be now, before the dark comes."

They angled farther back, not down the slope whence they had earlier come, but along the edge of the cliff that enclosed this pocket of a valley, until they were as far west as they might go. Here the cliffs pinched together again to present a wall.

Luckily, the twilight lingered and that wall was a rough one with holes easily found for hands and feet. Melvas had slung the lattice on his back, and, though the frame was unwieldy, it was light enough not to cause him undue strain as he climbed.

They reached the top of the wall and went on, farther north, for Melvas was firm that any road from the March fortress must lie in that direction. At last, as the twilight was deepening so that they could no longer move safely across this broken terrain, he chose a site to wedge the lattice into place with stones, facing it toward the heart of Olyroun.

Both Melvas and Ramsay made very sure, as they piled loose rocks about the frame, that no chance wind could topple it. In fact the cliff wall at this place, rounded out a little over it—not hiding it from the ground, but providing something of a sheltering roof.

"Will they understand?" Ramsay asked. He did not mention the more important point—would any inland see it at all?

"That symbol? No one can mistake it for aught but a warning. They might believe that the enemy set it, of course. But then they would deploy scouts and take all precautions." Melvas was busy with his wheel lighter. He spun it vigorously so the spark fell on the oiled cloth.

As Ramsay and he drew away, that line of fire ran quickly along the dampened strips until the pattern was aflame. It could certainly be seen, Ramsay believed, for some distance.

"We go." Melvas jerked at his arm. "If any scouts of those sea devils sight it, they will come hunting. And this is no land to travel hastily in the dark," as they both speedily discovered, moving from one hold to the next by feel now rather than sight.

The circle of rags still flared out above them. Perhaps the oil Melvas had used was not so easily consumed, instead protected the material for a longer burning. Yet Ramsay realized that the other's warning was the truth. Their whole party would be better away from the small sanctuary they had discovered.

When they half tumbled down the last of the climb, landing in what was now a pocket of darkness, a low voice hailed them.

"Come on—we're moving west—"

"The Captain—" Ramsay was sure Dedan could not have recovered to the point that he was on his feet, no matter what miracle Melvas's herbs wrought.

"They've started on, carrying him," Rahman half-whispered. "We made a litter after you left, lashed him in. Only way we could hope to move him now—"

The other end of the valley, where a stream ran from the pool until it disappeared underground, took a curve to the left. Luckily, there was not a second wall beyond, rather a wider range of land covered mainly with scrub, but this caught at their already tattered clothing and raked their hands and arms viciously.

Their blundering ahead could not be made without sound, and Ramsay feared that, here, they were nearly helpless. To keep going minute after minute was all they dared hope to accomplish. Then, just when he felt if he stumbled once more over some exposed root he could not rise, but would lie waiting for some doom, they were again in the clear.

Here was a sweep of bush grass little more than ankle high, through which they swished. They were far too visible in this open.

Ramsay stopped short, brought both hands to his head, swayed back and forth. His mouth opened to cry out, closed again without giving utterance to that protest.

This sensation was unlike Osythes's dreams, yet instinct told him there was an underlying kinship to those in it. He only knew that he was—"summoned" was the only word he could find to describe that feeling. And in such a way that he had no hope of defying the power that claimed him.

Nor was he alone in his reaction. All of them staggered a little to the right, began to trudge forward as if they obeyed the jerk of a leash held in some strange and alien hand. None spoke, they only moved, the Captain borne between Sydow and Arjun, Rahman, Melvas, and Ramsay behind—six survivors, perhaps now fatally entrapped.

Ramsay had never experienced anything to equal this compulsion before. Even the aches and pains of his tired body appeared suddenly to belong to someone else. It was necessary only to obey, to reach a goal ahead. Though what the goal might be—?

Ramsay, locked in a struggle between his innermost self and that compulsion, became dimly aware of a light. Their cliff-top signal? By rights, they would have had their backs to that. Some dwelling in this debatable land? Even a campfire of the enemy, astute enough to move this far inland in order to cut off the escape of any who survived the ridge attack?

The beam was too steady to be fire, he thought confusedly. More like a steady beacon, such as were familiar in his own world. Toward it his party marched as single-mindedly as if they were on some ordained maneuver. They all made a quick right-angle turn that brought them onto a road of sorts. Not paved, but smooth enough underfoot to suggest that it was well traveled. Perhaps they had found their way to the frontier post— but why then this—*drawing?*

The light grew no stronger as they approached it—it remained very much the same. Yet Ramsay was sure that its source was not retreating in the same measure as they were advancing. That beacon was fixed, and someone there reeled them in, as easily as if they were hooked fish on a line too strong to fight.

Now the light touched on stones—erect, slender— Some half-buried memory moved in Ramsay's mind. Yes, that red rock pillar he had seen near the hunting lodge, the one Grishilda had described as part of a very ancient, shunned ruin. Were they indeed approaching the lodge? But even in the dark, he could not see the forest, which should have been wide enough across the horizon to make itself clear now.

Also, there were more than one of those pillars—six, to be exact, three flanking the source of light on either side, while their party was drawn away from the smooth surface of the road, which had curved again as if to avoid any close touch with those very ancient monoliths. Now Ramsay picked out a figure moving deliberately into the path of the light, one which threw a shadow like a long warning finger pointing in their direction.

Those left of the company were very close, close enough to see the light, a rod slender enough for Ramsay to span with his two hands, planted in the earth. The one awaiting them by it wore a black-and-white robe. Osythes? But the face was now turned half to the light, and these features were not of the Shaman who advised the old Empress. This was a younger man, though he had the same detached look about him. A second figure glided forward to join him, and this, in spite of the identical black-and-white and cut of her robe, was a woman, slender, delicate of feature. Impassive, the two stood waiting for the six fugitives to come to them.

As the men advanced into the light, Ramsay felt a tingling throughout his body. His nostrils expanded to take in a queer, unidentifiable odor. Sydow and Arjun put down the litter holding their commander almost at the feet of those who awaited them. Then, panting, they half collapsed, to sit beside it. Ramsay felt his strength ebbing also. He managed to push forward another step or two and then subsided, his hands braced against the ground on either side of him, fighting to keep both his mind control and what little strength remained in him.

The woman stooped above Dedan, who was lying face down, his back covered with the hardened crust formed from the herb. A hand came out of hiding in her voluminous sleeve as she touched the First Captain's cheek lightly. She spoke to her companion, but she did not use that language Ramsay had fought to learn. Then she turned to face the rest of them. From face to face she glanced, lingering on each set of features for the space of a breath of two as she studied them in turn.

It was her companion who spoke, and now in a language Ramsay could understand.

"Whom do you follow, beaten men?"

Ramsay watched the others stiffen, and knew a swift jab of anger at what he thought might be contempt coloring that question.

Sydow replied. "We are of the Company of Dedan. He, our First Captain, lies before you, Enlightened Ones."

"Mercenaries," the man returned.

It was Ramsay who flashed a swift, hot reply. "Men who give their lives to keep their oaths—and this time were betrayed." He did not know that for a fact, but he had no qualms against throwing the charge into the calm, expressionless face. "Men who were coming to serve this land and were—were—finished before they could raise hand in their own defense."

"Ah." The Enlightened One now looked directly at him and him alone. "Of you there has been knowledge sent us—You are the Knave of Dreams—"

"The what?" Ramsay was mystified.

"The Knave of Dreams, he who enters to disturb a pattern of foretelling, the one changing and changeable factor that cannot be controlled and whose advent completely alters all. You have already held two names, now you are granted this one—which is truer than the rest. That you and your comrades have won free so far means that there is still a use for all of you. It remains to understand what that use can be—"

"We are men!" Ramsay fought an insidious lethargy which threatened him—the him who was a man, who was Ramsay. "We are not used, we move of our free will—"

"No man moves of free will, he is pushed here, drawn

there, by events from his past, needs of the future, perhaps even the will of a stronger man or woman. No one is free of the chances life itself lays heavily upon him from the moment of his birth. But this is not the time to speak of freedom, of choice, of belief or unbelief. It is apparent that the game is not complete, or you would not be here. Therefore, we agree that you shall be under the protection of the Grove until such a time as we know what is meant for you."

The Shaman raised his hand with a quirk of the wrist, tossing back the full sleeve. In the light, his hand appeared to possess an extra radiance of its own. The lifted forefinger pointed directly to Ramsay's head.

Ramsay felt himself slumping forward. A few moments of panic and fear were swallowed by soft, welcoming darkness.

❊ ❊ **TWELVE** ❊ ❊

DID HE SLEEP and dream? Or had he come to this place unknowing and just now was beginning to see, hear, understand? So much had happened to Ramsay in so short a time that he wondered if he dared ever again depend upon the evidence presented by his own senses. He only knew that here and now, he was seated by a narrow table that glowed with a wan light, as if it were no real board, rather a slab that was in itself a lamp.

Yet the wan radiance so given forth did not spread far. Ramsay could see only what lay upon the length, two hands which moved deftly over that. Very slender were those hands, bare of the massive rings that were the common fashion of the people in this world. Their delicate grace made him believe that they must belong to a woman. Yet when Ramsay tried to see beyond, to make out even a shadowy outline of her who might be seated opposite him, nothing but a wall of dark faced him.

Thus, fascinated against his will, he watched the

hands at work. Against his will, because, deep within him, an ancient warning awoke hints of enslavement of his senses in a way he had not ever believed possible. Ramsay was only sure at that moment that, even if he drew upon all his forces and attempted to stand, to move away from the table, leave behind those hands with their quick, purposeful movements, he would not be able to do so. Whether he would or not, he must sit and watch.

His own hands lay clasped together powerlessly in his lap. He could not loose a single finger from that enforced intertwining. Fear was his immediate reaction to this complete helplessness. Then anger followed, and, with the swell of that, his will strengthened, hardened, as metal worked by the smith's knowledge and skill takes on a keener cutting edge, a greater power for use.

Still, in spite of the anger that strove to arm him, Ramsay discovered that he must watch the hands. The fingers had deftly dealt out slips of what might be some light metal, for, as each was placed firmly into position, it produced from the board a small ringing sound. On the slip's length there then blazed a symbol that might have been the direct result of meeting with the table surface.

The symbols were complicated. Now, as Ramsay continued to watch, he discovered he could pick out a meaning from some of the lesser ones used to border each slip. How *did* he know that those curling tendrils—which were not unlike those full-bellied clouds one might see in an old Chinese drawing of his own time and world—stood for Dream? And that the small heart from the center cleft of which sprang a five-petaled flower was Hope? A jagged lightning strip that took on a dusty, threatening purplish color upon meeting the board—that was Fear. Last of all came a small figure completely hidden in robe and cowl—pointing a too long-fingered hand to either right or left—that was Fate. These identifying borders were only the least of the pictures on the strips. For each had also a larger central design, very intricate. Those flashed boldly alive as they were put down, only to blur again, so that he could not distinguish them with any accuracy.

That there was a purpose—a pattern—the hands before him sought. Of that, Ramsay was sure. He did not understand the method of the dealing. Some strips were allowed to lie in place for a moment. Then the fingers, expressing impatience in the very abruptness of their movement, would sweep them into discard, to deal again. At last, only five cards remained in place between Ramsay and this unknown who played the game, if game it really was. For the first time since Ramsay had come to consciousness of where he was, the hands were quiet, fingertips resting below that line of cards.

Though they were at rest, there was a subtle emanation of impatience about them. In a moment, the index finger of the right hand tapped the board beneath the middle card.

"Did I not say it—" The voice was low, a whisper that echoed eerily through the dark. "Always the Knave—the Knave of Dreams! That Knave who comes to destroy all proper patterns and realign the Fates—" Now the finger tapped emphatically under that card farthest to Ramsay's right, where the cowled figure forming the border wavered, appeared to grow stronger, even threatening, as Ramsay's eyes followed that pointer of flesh and bone, centered on the card.

"Fate—Fear—" The finger pointed again. Now it passed the center card, indicated the first to the left, which also showed the lightning flash that threatened. "But then the Queen!—The Queen who rules the House of Hope. Dream, Fate, Fear—and at the end of Fear—Hope. Knave are you yourself bound to, and your way is the dark one which dreamers own. You have dreamed, you are dreaming—you shall dream! Fate and Fear linked together are a mighty enemy to face, Dreamer. But this is the truth of foretelling—you must rely upon your dreams before you depend upon the strength of arm, your quickness of wit. Dream—and ask—and then face Fate and Fear—and—" The hand hovered over that last card of Heart and Flower and a glaze of design his eyes saw only as a radiant blur. "No, there is no telling, even for me, of the end of this. For even the Grove must bow to a dreamer. Too often he dreams true!"

The hand swept in a flowing motion across the board. Light vanished. For an instant, Ramsay had a sensation of loneliness, as if he had been abandoned in some place of utter darkness.

Then—did he dream to the order of the owner of the hands? Or to his own whim?

He only knew that just as the dreams woven by Osythes to tie him to Kaskar had had this same vivid life to them, what he looked upon as if through a window must have a real existence somewhere.

A man dominated the scene. He had none of the calm and measured authority of the Shaman, none of the unquestioned inherited rulership of the old Empress. No, he radiated a kind of raw power. He was, Ramsay thought, of a little more than middle age, but passing years had not dimmed either the bull physical strength of his barrel-chested body nor the determination and will that were expressed by every curve of his heavy-jawed face, every turn of his eyes and lips. He was seated in a chair that aped in general the canopied one that had made a throne for the old Empress. But, whereas her mere presence within its shadow had turned it into a seat of state, this usurpation was unnatural, carried a shadow of menace. His left elbow rested upon the arm of that chair, his jowly chin was set firmly in the upraised palm of that hand, as he glared in Ramsay's direction with such concentration that, for a moment, the Dreamer could believe that he was now visible to the other.

Yet there was no sign of any astonishment on that broad and lowering countenance. In a second, Ramsay guessed the stranger's glare was a cover for the fact that the other was intent upon his own thoughts. That they were disturbing could be readily believed.

In the stranger's right hand was grasped a ragged bit of cloth, the color of which seemed familiar. That was like the hood Ramsay himself had worn when playing his role of Feudman, that pretended disguise that had nearly been a key to his death—for him—a second time.

Ochall! Ramsay's mind produced a name for the enemy he had never seen but of whom he had heard so much. So this was the High Chancellor who aspired to rule the empire. Ochall might have lost his main piece in the game, yet there was nothing about this brooding man to suggest that he saw defeat now for all his plans. No, much to the contrary, his expression was one that suggested a search, hunted a new way. And his fierce grip upon that rag of cloth meant that perhaps he believed he had begun to understand the inner meaning of a problem.

The Empress and the Shaman—Ramsay had believed in their offer—and as a result nearly lost his life. As he watched Ochall, now he began to wonder what sort of reception he might expect from the Chancellor were he to provide him with a second and perhaps more durable Kaskar.

What had they said of this man—those who were his enemies? That he had mastered and perhaps even hypnotized a weakling prince into a puppet. However, all that Ramsay had been told about Ochall had come from those who had good reason to be his bitter enemies. And it had not been through Ochall that he himself had been paired with Kaskar—killed—to be reanimated in a world where those representing law and order once again wanted him safely dead.

Ramsay could not say that he was in any way attracted to the man brooding in his dream. Ochall should be a nasty enemy—but perhaps an open one, apart from the uses of intrigue such as had led Ramsay out of Lom Palace to a waiting assassin. Somewhere in his own mind, a plan as nebulous as one of the clouds marking dream cards began to take on more weight and substance.

Ramsay's sight of Ochall vanished as completely as if a window had been clapped shut between them. Just as he had awakened from such ordeals in his own world, Ramsay found himself, sweating and shaking, sitting up on a narrow bed in the cold gray of a predawn. He gasped, then his heart settled into a more regular beat. This reaction appeared merely physical. He experienced no residue of any fear or unease at this time. Perhaps because he had been led to accept in a new twist of logic that what he experienced was normal, at least for the new Ramsay who had been Kaskar.

Kaskar—what if he were to *be* Kaskar again?

The plan that had been born at the far back of his mind as he watched the brooding Ochall was growing stronger, bringing in more details. The last thing that the Empress and the Shaman would want was Kaskar's return. They had set him up for death while masked, had warned him over and over against the folly of showing his face in Lom, even in Ulad. One of the company had known him, or thought the resemblance to the dead Heir very close indeed.

If—just suppose—if the people—not the intriguers of the Palace, the nobles who made up either the party of the Empress or that of Ochall, but the common people of the Empire—were presented with a true heir who had escaped both the control of the High Chancellor and the domination of the Empress, what would they do? Suppose a *third* party could so rise to challenge both? If he only knew more about Kaskar himself!

Though he might wear the Prince's body, no fraction of the other's identity remained to give Ramsay a single clue as to what had been done or undone. He only was quite sure that he was now entangled in a game played by others, and he resented that bitterly indeed.

The Enlightened Ones—what had been the reason for that dream of vision of the foreteller? Or had that actually occurred? Fate and Fear—those symbols to flank the Knave of Dreams. And the strange mistress of prevision had made very sure Ramsay understood that he was the Knave, that variable which could overthrow the regular patterns by which they wove their own designs of the future. But beyond had stood Hope—and as a Queen—which meant a sign of greater power.

"You must rely upon your dreams before you depend upon your strength of arm, your quickness of wit—"

Very well. He had dreamed of Ochall, and to him had come a meaning from that dream. He would—

Ramsay tensed. There was a curdling of shadow within shadow in the far corner of the small chamber in which he lay. He was not alone. And—such had been his experiences in this world—he was very glad that he now had a wall to his back through which nothing—or no one—could come upon him unawares. Carefully, he arose to face that form that had a misty outline, and he spoke first.

"What do you want?" There was truculence in his demand.

The other did not reply, only moved into the best light the small chamber had to offer, a gray shaft from a single window on Ramsay's left. A hand—and that hand he thought he knew—appeared to sweep aside a drooping veil. Here stood the woman who had come earlier to meet their broken band. When? Hours—days—earlier?

Her features were regular but lacked expression. Ramsay might be fronting a statue given the power of movement. Even her eyelids were half-closed, as if to conceal any betraying gleam of life within.

Yet her hands stroked her veil, smoothing that length across the shoulder of her dark robe sleekly, as if she absentmindedly caressed some pet animal, not woven fabric. Ramsay was very sure of those hands. Those long fingers had dealt out the strips of Fate, Fear, Dream—

"Yes." The single word did not trouble the lips between which it issued. "I am Adise, the Foreteller."

Adise? He had heard that name—Adise! This was that Enlightened One upon whose advice Thecla relied. Ramsay had no reason now to believe that Thecla was any real friend of his—

"You are the Knave—your path is of your own choosing," she continued. Never did those heavy-lidded eyes open to meet his probing gaze squarely. There was a kind of indifference in the way she stood, stroking her veil, which he would not allow to irk him.

"I have been told that the Enlightened Ones sometimes give advice which the unwary would do well not to follow, that their foretellings can mean either victory or defeat and are not to be depended upon." He did not know why she had come, what message she was attempting to convey.

The light within the chamber was growing steadily clearer. Somehow, the window rays centered upon those ever-moving stroking hands. Ramsay resolutely looked away, centered his attention upon her statue-calm face.

"We only foretell what *may* be." She accented that "may" as she spoke. "From any action, no matter how trifling, there spreads a circle of consequences. Each may alter again a variable future. Then there are those without the pattern—for such there can be no measuring of choice. Such as you, who are not seed or root of this World."

"Why do you come?" He was impatient with her failure to be plain. "Do you instruct—or warn?"

"Neither. If you have dreamed, then you already know what is to be done." Her tone was as remote as the sense of her words.

"Very well." Ramsay tried shock tactics. "Can you at least give me direction? Where do I find High Chancellor Ochall?"

If he expected to strike some vital spark from her with that sharp demand, he was disappointed.

"Three days ago," she replied, her serenity unruffled, "he was reported at Vidin—that Vidin which owes ancient allegiance only to the Heir of Ulad."

Ramsay digested that information and did not in the least doubt that Adise was speaking the truth. But if Ochall was at this Vidin—what was he trying to do? Did he still believe that Kaskar might live, or only hope that he could lay Kaskar's death upon his own enemies and so draw to him those who owed the dead Heir traditional allegiance?

"And where lies Vidin?" Even as he asked that, Ramsay knew that he had made up his own mind. He must seek out Ochall, know the man as he really was and not as rumor and his enemies reported him to be.

"A morning's flight southward. There is a flyer waiting to your order."

They appeared eager enough to get rid of him, Ramsay thought. He wondered if his being this "variable," which they so insisted upon, was in some manner an upsetting factor in their own private concerns. Or were they urging him into this action for purposes such as they had been accused of in the past—to bring about some change in the chain of events to favor their own far-reaching plans?

Adise raised her eyelids completely for the first time. Her eyes were odd; they seemed to have, in place of the pupils normal to mankind, small dots of flame. Only for an instant did he perceive that, if he did at all; then she was like any woman again.

"Do not doubt your place in the great game." For the first time a trace of emotion troubled her level, monotonous voice. "No one controls the Knave of Dreams—Remember that, for your own protection—*no one!*" The accent she put upon the repetition of those last two words might have been a warning.

It appeared clear that the Enlightened Ones wanted him away. Ramsay smiled. There was a certain satisfaction in being a nuisance to the All-Powerful, which, at the moment, he was inclined to relish. However, he was also willing to opt for any aid he could wring out of the aloof Foretellers, Shamans, and Masters of Dreaming Extraordinary.

"Those of the Company," he asked. "How is it with them?"

He owed his life to Dedan. Even in his preoccupation with his own affairs, he remembered that.

"They mend. The Thantant has been warned." Was there again a faint irritation in Adise's answer? She could be urging him to immediate action. And that impression became a certainty as she added, using the prosaic words of any ordinary housewife: "Food, clothing, all you need," she made a small gesture with one of her ever-moving hands, "shall be brought."

Without adding anything to that, she turned away,

back into a corner which was no longer a cave of shadows, disappearing behind a curtain she swept aside for her passing.

As if her exit had been a signal, a man wearing a shorter version of the black-and-white Shaman's garb entered, carrying a tray of covered dishes which he put upon the table. He did not speak—perhaps a servitor of the Enlightened Ones, he was under some vow of silence—but his eloquent gestures brought Ramsay to a bath, to fresh clothing, to a meal of fruit, sweet bread formed as small, puffy rolls, and a tart drink which was cool on the tongue and pleasingly warm in the throat.

The belt he had worn as a member of the Company had been laid with the new dress of gray over black underclothing. But that gray was not drab. The tunic bore on the breast that Eagle emblem that had been widely in evidence in Lom Palace. Also, there were scrolls and lacings of silver thread to suggest rank.

After Ramsay had buckled on the belt with its ceremonial sword-knife, plus the other, more potent weapon Dedan had supplied to him, the silent servitor ushered him along several passages and then through a grove of trees. These grew in so maze-like a planting that Ramsay believed that, without the other's guidance, he would have been completely lost while still not more than perhaps six feet away from the building itself, so ensconced by growth as to seem a mere lump of greenery.

That this concealment was meant, Ramsay guessed. But against whom or what had it been intended? By all the accounts he had heard, the Enlightened Ones had no active enemies. Yet they chose hideaways of this type.

As they twisted and turned to follow a way which was no vestige of a path as far as Ramsay could recognize, he saw that here and there among the trees were standing stones of the type associated with the half-fabled fallen civilization, which had left such a mixed heritage to the present time. Had this site, in those unnumbered years past, marked some ancient temple or sacred place?

The standing stones became thicker, drew closer together, until they formed a wall on either hand. Now Ramsay's guide led the way between those barriers, to come out from the shadow of both stone and tree into a cloudy open. Here stood one of the flyers, and his guide waved Ramsay toward it.

For a moment, he hesitated. Was he truly making this choice in freedom? And if so—what might he have chosen? Follow the dream—to Ochall— Then what? The future depended mainly on what he found in Ochall himself. At least he would not be betrayed again by trusting in any word or promise.

His hand shifted along the belt until his fingers touched the grip of the hand arm. There was something reassuring in it, though his first taste of soldiering had been short and disastrous. Yet to have it fit now into his grasp gave a last urge forward, and he climbed into the flyer.

There was no sign of the pilot because of the closed-off cockpit. Ramsay must assume that he had already been given orders as to where to deposit his passenger. As soon as Ramsay was buckled into his seat, the craft arose in one of those unsettling leaps, and they were circling well above the ground.

Or he supposed they were, for there were no windows in this cabin. Thus, Ramsay had nothing to occupy his interest except his own thoughts, which, he began to realize ruefully, were not so well sorted as to prove very useful.

He retraced in detail all that had happened to him since he had awakened on the bier of the dead Prince, to be given temporary safety by Thecla. Now, weighing one memory against another, he could not be sure that she had meant to save him, after all. That her allegiance was to the Empress Quendrida he had never doubted, though he gave her credit for joining in Quendrida's scheming for the sake of Olyroun.

He found he could now give mind-room to one excuse after another as far as the young duchess was concerned. Even her ultimate betrayal of himself could well be because she believed that was necessary for her duty.

In his own world, during these past years, duty, service, self-abnegation for the sake of an ideal, had all been sneered at by many of his peers. Not to "get involved" was the goal of their own twists and turns of action and thought. Now, he was involved in as wild a piece of action as any dream could raise. Yet, he stood alone with only his own personal desires, no ideals or "duty" to back him.

Ramsay shifted on the padded seat of the flyer. Loneliness. He had always been a loner. Why should he suddenly now feel the burden of it? With the Company— once more Ramsay's hand sought the weapon at his belt, the symbol of the only really carefree time, or so now it seemed—that he had known since he came here. His choice—*why* had he decided to go to Vidin—to confront Ochall?

It would have been better, easier, far more natural for him to throw away the past, to keep his oath with the Company, become one of them. Yet, in turn, his mind shuddered away from the slaughter along the ridge. Anger roused at that memory.

If he discovered that Ochall was indeed at the back of that massacre— Was it not now his "duty" to discover just what game the High Chancellor was attempting to play in the border countries? He could not believe that even the death of his chief pawn could stop Ochall from seeking power.

Well, the choice had been his, and he had made it. He was not going to slink out like some beggar. He was Kaskar—perhaps not Ochall's puppet prince—but, nevertheless, Kaskar now returned to his own holding as the ship settled down.

As firmly as if Dedan and the whole of a resuscitated Company played bodyguard behind him, Ramsay descended the ladder and stood looking about him.

He was on a rooftop, some private landing place situated on a building of impressive size and height. Beyond, he could see the rise of several towers; perhaps this was even within the heart of a city. But he was given little time to survey his surroundings. Moving swiftly toward him across the landing space came a squad of men.

This was it—his first trial in his role of Kaskar. Ramsay hoped that he showed no hint of uncertainty as he took only a stride or two forward and then stood, waiting for them to come to him, guessing that might be so by custom.

Though the men wore the crested hoods common to

the Company, their faces were bare. Now Ramsay could clearly see the play of expression across the features of the officer in command. Utter and complete surprise!

The advance faltered. Not only their leader had been struck by astonishment, there were others as open-mouthed, wide-eyed as he among that guard.

Ramsay raised his hand in the half salute of superior to inferior. The officer snapped out of his daze. He barked a command Ramsay could not understand. The others moved into line, their weapons pointed barrels to the sky, plainly offering Ramsay the official welcome due Kaskar, the Prince of Vidin.

THIRTEEN

THERE WAS SO MUCH that could go wrong in this masquerade, as Ramsay well knew. His presence here committed him, and with his first order to the Vidinian guards, he sealed the commitment.

"His Worthiness, the High Chancellor—?"

"Will be summoned at once, Your Presence." A turn of the officer's head sent one of his command from the stiff line, trotting across the landing platform.

Behind him, Ramsay heard the beat of the flyer's motor. He turned his head a fraction, just in time to see that craft leap into the sky, his last chance of withdrawal gone.

"Your Presence"—the officer moved a step or two closer—"may I express for all of Vidin recognition of the honor you pay us in coming to this, your own city, for the proclamation. That rumor spoke false and you are not dead—that is a matter for thanksgiving—"

Yes, thought Ramsay—just how *had* he escaped death?

He hoped that the rumors of intrigue and counterintrigue at court would be his cover for any vagueness on that score.

"When one has enemies," he began, "subterfuges are necessary. In Vidin, among my liege men, I need not fear that I go without shield for my back."

The officer's sword of ceremony whipped from its sheath.

"Your Presence commands—Vidin answers! By blood right and liege right has this always been so!"

"As well I know," Ramsay acknowledged the formal words of the other. "You are—?"

"I am First of the Inner Guard, Your Presence, Matrus of the House of Lycus. It is now your will, Your Presence, to proceed to your Chamber of State? Since the High Chancellor arrived among us, we have been prepared. For we did not accept the dark tales out of Lom."

So much, Ramsay thought, for that surrogate body Melkolf had produced to be buried with state among Kaskar's forefathers. He supposed that Ochall's suspicions had carefully fostered this unbelief in the one principality within Ulad that would be most fertile soil for the growth of a possible rebellion.

"That you did not believe," he returned aloud, "is heartening. To most of Ulad, Kaskar lies now entombed. There may be reason, for the present, that he not arise again too soon nor lustily—" Ramsay smiled, an expression which he had but seldom used since he entered into the dream world—so seldom in fact that the very stretch of lips came now with difficulty.

An honor guard formed—at least Ramsay trusted that

their movements signaled an honor guard and not a possible prisoner's escort, for his suspicions were not completely allayed by the response of the First Officer Matrus, who could be—probably was—Ochall's man. So surrounded, he reached a lift which descended from the rooftop landing strip, passed several floors, and came to a stop. More guards snapped to attention, and Ramsay was conscious, as he stepped out briskly, of a ripple of surprise that spread outward as those in sight caught a glimpse of Kaskar's features.

Though all he had heard of Kaskar in the past had not led Ramsay to believe his double (would he term the Imperial Prince his "alter ego?") had any great merit, it appeared that in Vidin, at least, his rule and importance were undiminished. The guard, the servants they now passed, were too well disciplined to break the silence of the corridors. Still, Ramsay sensed the spread of excitement. He never turned his head to see, but he was sure that the tramp of the boots of their party was fast doubling in sound, as if he now led a procession that grew larger with every passing moment.

More saluting guards. One hurried to throw open a door. Ramsay passed into a long room, one wall broken by a series of wide windows, each of which was bordered about its embrasure with red and gold. Opposite these, mirrors, with heavily gilded and carved frames, were set into the wall. The floor, on which the boots of those who entered rang so sharply, was of marble, the ceiling and as much of the walls as could be seen between individual windows and mirrors were of a burnished red lacquer interset with enameled plaques.

Silver candlesticks standing as tall as Ramsay's head formed two columns between which he was ushered. Flanking both mirrors and windows there were as many wall brackets made in the form of queer heads wreathed in flowers and ferns, all gilded, each bearing figures which glinted with enamel or gemstones.

The mirrors reflected and re-reflected all this magnificence, until it seemed that this was not just one chamber, but a series of fabulous halls echoing on into infinity.

At the edge of a two-step dais, the column of candlesticks ended. And on the dais was a chair almost as wide as a small sofa. This lacked the canopy of presence which Ramsay had seen in the palace at Lom. But it was equally impressive with its gold back and arms, cushioned crimson seat. As First Officer Matrus drew to one side, Ramsay gathered that this state throne was now his proper place.

He trod purposefully up the steps, seated himself on the chair, with, he hoped, the appearance of ease of one who was in the right place at the proper time. For the first time, he could see now that he had indeed gathered more followers along his route from the landing stage.

Guardsmen stood at impassive, statue-still attention flanking the candlesticks. The others, wearing heavily embroidered overtunics, could only be civilian officials of this miniature court, or the nobility of Vidin.

Ramsay hoped desperately that court etiquette might be such that he would not be required to single out for special attention any former acquaintance of Kaskar's. To play this role when so ill-prepared was dangerous, yet it was all that was left him.

"The High Chancellor!" From the now distant doorway

(the hall somehow appeared not only to have been widened by the use of the mirrors but also to have lengthened, as Ramsay looked back down the way he had come) that voice carried well.

A man, wearing a servant's shorter tunic, but that so emblazoned with stitchery as to emphasize his importance in this Household, stood forward. His right hand curled about a staff of silver. This he raised solemnly, thudding it down with a metallic beat against the floor three times.

Having so gained the full attention of the assembly, he took a step aside, giving way to the man Ramsay sought. This was the Ochall of his dream, except now that the raw aura of power held, power desired, power sought, was not so apparent. Were the dreams able to heighten emotions so that the inner motives of those who moved within them could be read better?

Ochall had plenty of presence still, but he was not the overwhelming, dominating character either rumor or dream had made him. There was even a trace of deference in his manner as he faced Ramsay.

This was not the confrontation Ramsay had hoped for. If he could only have met Ochall immediately after landing, been able to read the first reaction of the High Chancellor to Kaskar's dramatic second return from the dead, that would have given him some small clue as to Ochall's position. But by this time, the High Chancelor had had good time to assume any role he wished.

Now he advanced down the lane of the candlesticks, his longer overtunic nearly touching the floor. There was no sword of ceremony at his belt, rather around his bull neck lay a long, elaborately wrought collar of gold and gems. From that, resting against his burly chest, dangled an outsize golden key, probably his badge of office.

The slight hum that had hung in the chamber when Ramsay had taken the throne died away. There was not even the whisper of fabric against fabric as some of that company changed position slightly, not the scrape of a boot, not even the sound of breathing. The arrival of Ochall might have suspended all life in the court; those gathered there would not exist again until he chose.

Ramsay suspected this effect was deliberately produced by Ochall, that it fed his sense of power. But if he expected that it would also bring to heel a new puppet princeling— no! Ramsay's instinctive reaction was to prepare to fight the other's overpowering personality.

"I give you greeting, High Chancellor." He attempted to make his voice bland, though to his own ears it sounded odd. However, he must take the initiative in this meeting. "That you have so faithfully awaited me in this, my own court, I take as indicative of your ever-loyal service to the. Crown—"

He did not know where he found the pompous words. Perhaps the very air of this room could produce such a change in one's speech. Only the most rigid of formal phrases seemed appropriate to echo through such surroundings. What he wanted most of all was some small hint from Ochall as to what the High Chancellor was thinking. Yet Ramsay knew that Ochall would never reveal anything that was not coldly calculated and aimed directly toward his own advantage. If Ochall had been astounded at Ramsay's arrival, no one would ever know it.

Ochall bowed his bull's head in slight inclination.

"His Presence knows that Vidin is his liege state. Where else would his friends gather in a time when strange matters happen in Ulad and there is much to make those of the deepest loyalty uneasy? That Your Presence would be safe has been our constant prayer. That Your Presence now sits in our sight, unchanged, unharmed,"—Ochall's hand arose to his breast, touched the glitter of the key—"is our reward for trusting Providence during all the hours, days, of dark story and threat, now happily past."

Ramsay saw that, under Ochall's touch, the large key was moving slightly, back and forth. His attention was thus being drawn from the High Chancellor's jowled countenance to the key—its movements—slight as those were.

Back and forth—back—and—

Ramsay blinked, jerked his eyes up and away. Was his suspicion correct? Was the High Chancellor's play with that badge of office more than just an absentminded mannerism? What had they said of Ochall?—that he had held Kaskar in some spell. Hypnotism? Perhaps the Heir had been carefully conditioned to react to just such a supposedly innocent personal fidgeting as the movement of the key. That his own attention had been so quickly riveted by a gesture was a warning, Ramsay firmly believed.

"Your concern for the welfare of the crown," Ramsay returned, wondering if Ochall would read into that a double meaning, "has always been recognized. Those of the Imperial line are aware of the depth of your loyalty, that high sense of duty which always is an example to all."

Once more, Ochall's head inclined that inch or so of acknowledgment. But, Ramsay made sure with a single glance, he no longer fingered the key. If he had attempted to test the suggestibility of this revived Kaskar, the experiment had been a failure.

Ramsay believed that of all this miniature, attentive court, the High Chancellor might probably be the only one with courage enough to ask questions, those pertinent questions concerning the immediate past of an Imperial Prince who had been publicly buried with every pomp of ceremony, yet now dropped from the sky into his own domain very much alive. However, that Ochall would ask such questions openly Ramsay very much doubted. And this was his own chance to get widely circulated the very sketchy explanation he had worried together during his flight to Vidin.

"These are days of stress." He smiled at Ochall. "Sometimes it is difficult to tell friend from foe. That there are those who would willingly see me laid to rest with the elders of my House is a fact all within hearing must know. It is because of you, High Chancellor, that such a fate has not overtaken me. Your plan worked well—"

He was watching with the concentration of a hunter Ochall's impassive, heavy face. At this moment, Ramsay knew of no other way to achieve even a modicum of understanding with the High Chancellor than to provoke a response from him. Surely, the man, praised publicly for the salvation of his puppet prince, would seek to know what had happened. How it was that Kaskar lived, breathed, and declared these facts to be of Ochall's doing.

"I serve—" Ochall returned with no change of feature Ramsay could read. "That I am able so to serve is my pride, Your Presence."

"Your pride," Ramsay continued, "but Ulad's gain. Now, my lords." He looked away from Ochall. There was no prying open the High Chancellor's shell by such efforts. He would have to devise a much more vigorous attack. "My lords, my faith in your liege oaths, in those of Vidin, have sustained me through much these past days. Within these walls, I find that which will regain my inheritance in truth. For a man's strength is not solely of his own hand upon any weapon, or his own wit, but rather in the faith which others hold in him. Now—" Ramsay leaned forward a fraction on the wide seat of the throne. "There may come a day when our mutual faith shall be put to hard testing—for I shall keep no secrets from you in the name of needed security and possible safety. You may hear that Kaskar is indeed dead and buried. In fact, doubtless some of you were in attendance in Lom when this occurred."

Ramsay allowed his glance to sweep from face to face along the lines of the nobles. That he had their full attention there was no denying. There *were* troubled frowns, as well as startled surprise and the soberness of those who awaited enlightenment, to be seen there.

"Look upon me!" He stood up, moved one step downward from the throne. The glitter of the mirrors, the brightness of the sunlight from the windows, fully revealed him in a light that could conceal nothing. He held his head high, challenging silently by his very attitude any who might now dare to raise a cry of "imposter."

"They wished me dead, they employed certain stratagems to achieve that wish. But they failed. I have been hunted from Lom—secretly—lest the fact that I lived be known. Because I could not name friend from pretend-friend-secret-enemy I knew not where to turn.

"Until—" Now he undertook to advance his strongest attack. "I came by chance to the Enlightened Ones—"

For the first time, there was a faint, a very faint, change in Ochall's set of lips. However, those about the Chancellor were more open in showing their astonishment. There was a faint murmur, indrawn breaths.

"There was a foretelling given me," Ramsay continued deliberately. "And so I came to Vidin."

The murmur of those listening grew stronger; Ochall had his countenance once more under control, but open excitement spread through the rest of the company.

"Your Presence." An older man, one wearing a gemmed collar of state only a little less elaborate than that which encircled Ochall's neck, moved out a little from his fellows. "This foretelling—" He hesitated. Ramsay believed he could guess what lay behind that momentary check. The notoriously undefendable advice of the Enlightened Ones must be mistrusted by any who were prudent.

Ramsay nodded. "Yes—the foretelling. As is well known, the Reverend Enlightened Ones are far more intent upon a future that may run so far ahead out of our present years that the results of actions taken now will not be to the advantage of any living. So we must shift and choose, and hope that we have chosen aright. Believe it that I would and will walk warily and not pledge any liege man of mine to a dubious course. I am young in statecraft, but in this chamber stand men who can speak their minds from experience, and those shall be harkened to. Have we not at hand the High Chancellor himself? Any future plans we shall discuss in council. I have only this to say to you, that it is by the aid of the Enlightened Ones alone that I have come to Vidin. In that measure, at least, I think they have done me only good.

"Now my lords and liege men, I give you leave to withdraw until such a time as we must take council and—"

He was so eager to get Ochall alone that his impatience at this playing Prince in high ceremony grew. How *did* one dismiss a court, get some privacy—? He was sure that reference to the Enlightened Ones had given Ochall a jolt, and he needed to push any small advantage before the High Chancellor was again assured enough to lift his barrier.

Apparently, Ramsay had hit upon the right formula, for there was a ripple of bowing toward him; men were backing away from the line of candlesticks. All was proceeding smoothly—

Then came an eddy by the door. Men were pushed to one side or the other, last being he with the silver staff, who was thrust impatiently and protestingly from where he had tried to bar the way to a man wearing a military hood. Hands tried to grasp the newcomer's shoulders. He shrugged these off, strode forward, while the court froze in position, quickly sensing that this interruption to the formalities was important.

The officer tramped to the foot of the dais. Judging by

his badges of rank, one would say he was the First of some regiment, and he was fairly young. His dark features were a mask of excitement, and he was breathing fast, as if he had indeed raced to be where he now stood.

Raising his hand, he gave the salute to a commander, which Ramsay had wit enough to acknowledge. Then the man spoke.

"Supreme Mightiness! Our great Emperor Pyran has departed through the Final Gate. Trumpets have sounded his farewell from the towers of Lom. Now they call the summons to the Heir-of-Blood. Supreme Mightiness, may your rule be long of day and unshadowed!"

So the dying Emperor was at last dead! But certainly, they were not proclaiming Kaskar in Lom!

Ramsay schooled himself as he noted Ochall had taken two steps forward, almost as if he would grasp the messenger, drag him aside for some private word. There was no time left now for any bargaining. The Empress's party would have Berthal standing ready, perhaps near to crowning at this very minute. Ramsay's own small chance for any safety in this world had lessened—halved, been made a third, even a fourth, by the messenger's report.

"I think they do not hail Prince Kaskar—" For the first time Ochall took the initiative.

The officer showed his teeth in a grimace.

"No, Your Dignity. They have brought forth Prince Berthal and stood him high upon the Place of Flags. However, as yet he has not taken oath."

Now there was a rising mutter, exclamations from the court. Again Ochall asked a question that had already risen in Ramsay's mind.

"Yet, Jasum, you have come to Vidin, to see one proclaimed dead. What knowledge existed in Lom to bring you here?"

"There was word from the Enlightened Ones, Your Dignity. One came by night to my chamber with this news: that our Prince had truly not been dead, but hidden away, and that he had won to Vidin. Thus, knowing that he must be told—Supreme Mightiness!" Now Jasum addressed himself directly to Ramsay. "They will swear allegiance to this usurper. Already, they plan his enthronement in the Hall of Light, his quick wedding thereafter to the Duchess of Olyroun. Let him be sworn and wed, and there shall be many who would otherwise raise standards in the name of Kaskar who then will be persuaded not to make trouble lest such split Ulad!"

Ochall caressed his jaw with his wide-palmed hand.

"An astute observation, Jasum. I wonder now why this message was brought only by your voice, why the wire talkers of Vidin have not carried it. Unless, of course, those in Lom would do just as you have said before any loyal Vidinian has had time to object. Supreme Mightiness"—now he spoke to Ramsay—"let word now be sent throughout Vidin and the trumpets sounded at once—thus assuring that the usurper shall not be seated upon the throne with no voice raised against him. With protest raised, this becomes a matter of public knowledge, of confrontation with those who have named Berthal—maybe even of a Last Challenge!"

Ramsay had no idea what Ochall might mean by the letter, but Ochall spoke the words with such emphasis that Ramsay guessed it was some extreme of serious opposition.

"Let us take council as you have urged, Supreme Mightiness—first let it be known to the Lords of Thousands—yes, and even the Lords of Hundreds—that they must gather to show true allegiance."

"So be it," Ramsay agreed readily, though he had a feeling he had lost all control of the situation and that authority had slid smoothly into Ochall's grasp, exactly as the High Chancellor had always intended it should at this long-awaited·hour. So it was with a small warning chill inside that Ramsay again dismissed the court, watched the nobles of Vidin drain from the chamber until only he and Ochall remained there,

Much as Ramsay had earlier wished for this personal private meeting, he willingly would have foregone it at this particular moment. Yet, he felt he must wait for Ochall to take the lead, in that way perhaps learning what would move the High Chancellor.

"Time—" Ochall's fingers had ceased to caress his chin; instead with thumb and forefinger, he plucked at the thickness of his lower lip. "What time may we have? Did the foretelling of the Enlightened Ones in turn enlighten you, my lord, to any answer on the subject? Time we must buy somehow—" The last sentence was uttered as if he were thinking aloud.

However, Ramsay had a shrewd idea that the High Chancellor never so forgot himself as to utter *any* words of which he was not entirely conscious, both of the subject and of the person to whom any random-seeming remarks might be made.

"I was told," Ramsay answered deliberately with part of the truth, "that my own person was of significance in events to come, also that any choices I would make would in turn lead to changes in the foreseen future to an extent the Enlightened Ones were not yet able to assess."

"Kaskar—" Ochall eyed him from head to foot and back again with a detached measurement. "Life—or rather death—has been your portion in ways unknown to us who are but mortal men. First you die and lie in your last sleep in the Hall of Lords Gone Before.

"Then it is discovered, with the coming of the day, that four guards, plainly bemused, their recollections tampered with, corner an empty bier. Kaskar has risen say the ignorant. There is talk of a miracle, such as those of the very ancient of days were supposed to effect. Yet if Kaskar has arisen and walks his land, none has seen him.

"Once more a body is discovered, this time in such a state that only the clothing, certain well-known peculiarities of size and being, can identify it as the strangely lost prince. For it would seem that Kaskar perhaps *did* rise from the dead, perhaps mindlessly, and wandered from his royal bed, to crash from a convenient window. Perhaps his brush with death made him believe the tales of legends, that those of exemplary character, when they pass the Final Gate, are no longer bound by the limitations of this world but can ascend by their own desire into the skies about. Believing this, our half-dead prince strove mightily to prove legend fact, but merely learned that he had not yet discarded his mortal body.

"Thus we have a body which is buried with pomp and much outward grief, much inward satisfaction. Ochall," he smiled grimly, "has been outwitted, outplayed. So cleverly done, and if any have suspicions they are keen-witted enough to keep them shut tightly behind their teeth, not stupidly voicing them aloud. Yet in this hour Kaskar the lost, the—as you might say—'oft-buried' stands here in his very loyal holding of Vidin about to lead a loyal march against a usurper."

He shot a glance at Ramsay. "You speak of the Enlightened Ones. I will not doubt one word of what you have said of your relationship with them. Their games are well known to be devious, beyond the unraveling of those who have not their peculiar gifts. They say you are Kaskar. Thus it is for us to accept a second miracle. Only, perhaps even the Enlightened Ones are not above the side effects of miracles. That we shall in time come to see.

"Time"—he came back to his first statement—"is what we must have. No man can push wind, water, a flyer, a ship, a rail runner, faster than it is designed to go. I have not been idle, Supreme Mightiness. Given time, I can prove Ochall is not a piece to be easily swept from any playing board. Even that of the Enlightened Ones."

✵ ✵ FOURTEEN ✵ ✵

"BUT IT NOW SEEMS," Ramsay pointed out, "that such time may not be granted us, High Chancellor. You state my appearance in Vidin is a miracle. Well enough, but the news of that miracle must spread beyond Vidin if we do not wish to find Berthal enthroned lawfully." He was probing now. That something lay behind Ochall's preoccupation with time was very apparent. "How much time must *your* plan be given to bear the fruit desired?"

For a long moment, the High Chancellor did not answer. Once more, he kneaded at his lower lip with thumb and forefinger.

"It would seem that, momentarily, you have the favor of the Enlightened Ones. Or, if not their favor, their desire to cast a very large stone into the pool of Ulad, disturbing affairs—working now for you. As to time—perhaps five days—"

Once more, he played with that glittering key, and Ramsay averted his eyes. Then Ochall spoke again.

"Who are you?" He asked his question bluntly, as if such simplicity might well invite full truth in return.

Ramsay found a second smile less difficult than the first. "Kaskar, come out of great danger to claim his rights again."

Ochall uttered a strange sound. Though there was little that was jovial in it, it might have been a bark of laughter.

"Well answered, Supreme Mightiness. Kaskar you have claimed to be, Kaskar you shall be. But I wonder if you realize that you have put out your hand perhaps too willingly to grasp at a very unsteady crown. If you have fallen for the trickery of the Enlightened Ones, a man could find himself ready to pity you—"

"A warning, High Chancellor?" queried Ramsay. "I take it kindly of you to show concern. I only know that there are those in Lom with whom I have certain scores to settle. If claiming my rights will bring me closer to that settlement, then I shall outshout any of your trumpets of the tower. Be assured of that. And what"—he struck back for truth, if truth could ever be gained from such as Ochall—"will your needful five days bring?"

"Weapons, out of the North," the High Chancellor returned as frankly as Ramsay had asked. "There are certain new ones, as yet unused in any large combat, but well proven, as my own Ears and Eyes report. The merchants of Norn promised their efficiency, and all that they said is true—"

"Tested in action?" Ramsay schooled himself to what he hoped was only a small show of interest. What action? That in which the Company had been ruthlessly done to death? Had that only been a show, put on to impress such a buyer as Ochall of the worth of his projected purchase?

"Tested in action," agreed Ochall. "Proven. I know not what new secrets those of Norn have now chanced upon, but such arms have not been seen upon these shores since perhaps the last days of the Great Era."

"And those last-used arms," Ramsay pointed out, "are reputed to have left this world half dead. Even to rule in Ulad an ambitious man would be a fool to lay hands on such as those!"

"Oh, these are not the Ultimate Forbidden. No, these are still but as pebbles flung from a boy's sling in comparison with them. To use these would not break the Everlasting Covenant of the People Alive. In fact, they are merely superior modifications of two already known." However, Ochall went into no details.

"And where were those new weapons demonstrated— upon whom?" Ramsay pressed.

Ochall shrugged. "In a small skirmish of no importance, between pirates and a relatively inefficient mercenary company which had been hired by the Thantant of the Marches in Olyroun. It is to our interest, of course, that those of Olyroun be kept occupied by nuisance raids for the present. That the duchy should continue free is not to be supported. But to move outwardly against it, no."

The High Chancellor was watching Ramsay with a measuring stare as he spoke.

"With the Duchess Thecla united to Ulad in marriage," Ramsay returned, "such matters in the future can be quietly and carefully arranged without any need for outright invasion."

"Just so. Still, it is well that Olyroun be kept occupied with internal difficulties until that auspicious date. Any encouragement on the part of such as the Thantant, his hiring of mercenaries and the like, must be prevented. To try the weapons so thus accomplished two needful results. I do not think that the Thantant will find another Free Company to accept his offered employment, and the pirates of Lynark are invited to make themselves successfully busy—"

"The pirates!" Ramsay repeated. "Those were so armed? Is there not danger in that?" Inwardly, he marveled at the calm he was able to maintain. The realization that that hell along the ridge had been in the nature of a planned experiment awoke a rage which perhaps earlier in time he could never have kept under the control he now exerted. To discuss the death of those men who had accepted him as a comrade as the end product of a demonstration—! He seethed and fought his own emotions. The Empress and the Shaman—they could condemn one man to exile, and then to an assassin's sword under the pious cloaking of that conscience they labeled "duty." While Ochall could accept the horrible death of nearly a full company of men because it gave him another lever for his ambition—

"You plan to march then on Lom," Ramsay said, as evenly as he could, "with such weapons in hand, given your five days?"

He had been so overwrought behind the facade he fought to maintain that he had not been this time as careful of his choice of words.

"I, Supreme Mightiness?" Ochall shook his head. "My power rests only as a shadow of that you lawfully wield. Nor do I give any commands, except in your name—"

Ramsay did not need to close his eyes. There seemed to him now to be a weaving veil of illusion between him and Ochall. He did not see clearly this stocky man who was an embodiment of power, rather than a yellow fog torn through with flames in which men twisted and died screaming. This was no dream vision, yet the sight was as deeply engraved on his mind at that moment as any of those Osythes had turned upon him to begin this nightmare.

Work with or through Ochall? He had been supremely foolish in believing he might do that. In this world, he had no touch with any man except Dedan. And the First Captain lay far away—his wounds keeping him from any immediate summoning. An awful loneliness shook Ramsay during that second or two of true realization.

He was not aware that he wavered as he stood, that he reached behind him for support and laid hand upon the arm of the massive throne. Then, that mind-wrenching memory thinned as he saw Ochall's eyes, avid, greedy, fixed on him. What knowledge the High Chancellor had gained from those few seconds of loss of control Ramsay dared not speculate upon. But surely the High Chancellor believed that he dealt with another weakling prince, and Ramsay knew that, whatever move he made from this moment forth, he could not follow, even outwardly, any suggestion from Ochall.

To send that fog, those flames into Lom—that was unthinkable! Could the Enlightened Ones have known what Ochall planned? If so—then they were rightly the treacherous menace many thought them. He owed nothing to the Empress and her party. To go to Lom was to invite another attack from some hidden assassin. Still—where else might he now move? Even if he were somehow to disappear from Vidin as quickly and strangely as he had come, his very appearance here, his recognition of Ochall before the court, would give the High Chancellor the power to act in his name. No one would question any order given him in his supposed master's behalf.

"Five days—" Ramsay seized upon the first excuse he could summon. "Five days' wait may be too long. Let Berthal be proclaimed, then there will be, as has been pointed out, those who hesitate to support my dear cousin, but who would close ranks against me should there arise a hint of war between two factions in Ulad."

"Your answer then—?" Ochall asked.

"That you, High Chancellor, and I, and such dignitaries from Vidin as can best back us in a righteous cause, go to Lom. Not in threat, but as we should to support a claim that no man can question."

He wondered if Ochall would dare refuse. However, the High Chancellor seemed prepared for such a challenge.

"You go directly into a nest of enemies, Supreme Mightiness. Yet, too, courage is rightfully the virtue of any emperor, and with a guard of liege men, they cannot come at you secretly. Just as they dare not question openly the one who is so plainly Kaskar. When would you go?"

"Now, as soon as it may be readied." Ramsay did not doubt that Ochall had his own loyal followers, who would carry out to the letter any orders their master left. But he himself would gain some time to—to what—warn? He did not know. The only small satisfaction he had was that

Ochall would be with him, and that half vision of the High Chancellor advancing upon an undefended and helpless city behind a cloud of fog and flame would not now come to pass.

The flyer that took them from Kaskar's holding was far larger and more luxurious (being divided into several cabins of varying degrees of appointment) than Ramsay had heretofore seen. He noted before he boarded that there had been some hasty painting of insignia on the side, a reproduction of that fierce bird which he had seen on the hall paneling in the palace. It would appear that his liege men were determined that he make his entrance properly, with the bearings of a rightful ruler in full display.

"The Place of Proclaiming?" Ochall had not seated himself too near the well-padded and gilded seat Ramsay had chosen as properly being his. He had to lean forward now from his more lowly position in order to ask that.

And Ramsay, in relief at the solving of one of his problems, nodded. To enter the Palace of Lom without his presence being known to the city at large had worried him. This "Place of Proclaiming" sounded open enough to satisfy the most demanding of publicity seekers.

Having agreed with Ochall, he was apparently to be left to his own thoughts, for the High Chancellor settled back with a wriggle of his broad shoulders, closed his eyes, and gave every appearance of desiring a discreet withdrawal from any further conversation. Ramsay closed his own eyes. What had they told him—those unfathomable Enlightened Ones? To dream? But there was no way he knew of summoning dreams at will.

Instead, he recalled in detail again those cards and the

fluttering hand of Adise as she dealt and fingered the final ones that foretold his fate. Fate—yes, and Fear—Dreams—with only the promise of Hope at the end of it all.

Events were moving too fast, and he knew far too little. This was like being pitched blindfolded into some battle where everyone else he blundered against had both sight and purpose. Ramsay had had just one purpose—to save the skin of one Ramsay Kimble. Now he had moved by emotion to try to save a city—perhaps a nation. His mouth twisted bitterly. What allowed him to yield to the anger Ochall's matter-of-fact explanation had evoked?

Though he knew little of air distances from one city to another, he was a little startled at the short duration of their flight. Perhaps Ochall had given orders that their craft be pushed to the utmost. For Ramsay was still trying to marshal his chaotic thoughts into order when the signal flashed as the flyer spiraled downward.

The richly paneled walls of the cabin had no windows. Ramsay sat tense and stiff. They could be alighting in the midst of enemies waiting to ring them in. Ochall seemed to read his mind then; perhaps Ramsay's own posture gave him away. For the High Chancellor said: "Though it would seem that the talk-wires could not carry a message into Vidin"—his tone was sardonic—"our own clearance call has been openly broadcast, Supreme Mightiness. Be very sure that Lom knows *who* arrives—openly, with only his suite about him—coming as a rightful lord and no invader."

That that was any great condolence at the moment, Ramsay doubted. But he had chosen to play this role, and he would not allow the High Chancellor to see him flinching from it.

"Rightfully done," was his comment.

"We set down," Ochall continued, "in the Four Square of Heros. There is no landing stage, but our forecast will have cleared the necessary space. Then you have only to mount to the Place of the Sovereign Flags and show yourself—"

Ramsay thought he caught a flicker of a glance in his direction. Did the High Chancellor hint that so showing himself might well make him a target, providing some action that would totally settle once and for all who would be Emperor in Ulad?

The flyer touched earth, the vibration of the flight ended. Ramsay unbuckled his safety belt with hands he was glad to see did remain steady. After all, he had been through a similar experience before, when he had emerged from that other flyer on the roof in Vidin.

He arose as those of his following filed through to the narrow exit. The guard, now under command of Jasum, was first. The guardsman snapped to attention on the pavement below, forming an aisle through which Ramsay could walk.

Deliberately, he descended. They had indeed set down well within Lom. Buildings arose about them as thickly as those trees that embowered the Grove dwelling of the Enlightened Ones. The natural rusty red or dull gray stone walls were veiled and draped with brightly colored banners and swatches of cloth. Streamers, ribbonlike in their length and light weight, stirred in breezes that swirled them outward through the air.

Immediately before him was a pyramid of the red stone he had come to associate with the remains of that legendary Great World which had been. This structure was truncated, so that its top was like a triangular platform. About its rim were six sturdy poles from which billowed, in that same movement of air, five flags. The sixth pole was bare. Leading up to this was a flight of steps, hollowed and worn, as if the Place of Flags had stood there for more centuries than perhaps Lom itself had had existence. Among these other bannered buildings, this did have a curious barren look.

Deliberately, Ramsay set foot on the hollow curve of the first step. Though he looked neither to left nor right, possessed by his own sense of what Kaskar, Emperor of Ulad, must do at that moment, Ramsay was aware that Lom's streets were not deserted. There was a multitude gathering closer. None of those who had come with him from Vidin were following. Perhaps only his Supreme Mightiness (what cumbersome titles they chose) dared make this climb.

From below the sound of voices grew from a gabble into nearly a roar. Ramsay climbed on. He planted each foot precisely and unhurriedly, refusing to allow himself to look right or left. That gathering below might be getting ready to mob him. A bead of sweat loosened from the line of his black hair on the forehead, trickled slowly down his cheek. He kept his face impassive and climbed.

Now he reached the top. To his right, before he turned, was the pole of a yellow banner, one centered with a geometrically lined criss-cross of a violently vivid green. To his left was the pole that bore no banner at all.

As deliberately as he had climbed, Ramsay now turned, to gaze over that city Kaskar had meant to rule.

His head was bare except for a silver circlet tight across his forehead. There was no hood, no mask, to hide him now. And he stood, his feet a little apart, one hand resting lightly on the hilt of his sword of ceremony, looking out and down.

What he saw was a massing of faces, all turned in his direction. Even the windows of the neighboring buildings were packed with people crowding each other to look upon him. The effect was like a blow, yet he knew he must stand impassively under it.

They were shouting now, and from the din of sound rolling about the four-cornered Place of Heroes, seeming to echo from the buildings, he could pick out his borrowed name:

"Kaskar, Kaskar!"

It took him a second or two to realize that there was no threat in that recognition. Amazement, yes. Even if Kaskar had been so disliked by the court and those of his own blood, this city seemed not to have shared those sentiments. When he raised his hand in acknowledgment, it appeared that his liege men were not limited to Vidin— for there was a roar of cheering that must have reached even to the walls of the somewhat distant palace.

Someone else now moved up the worn steps. Ramsay saw a man wearing a brilliant short tunic, fashioned so the fierce bird of Ulad's crest hovered over the upper half of his body. He carried a horn of such length that he needed to balance it over his shoulder carefully as he made the ascent. Behind him, a second similarly attired and burdened trumpeter emerged through the thin line of guardsmen to climb in turn.

Ramsay stepped back a little when those two reached the summit of the pyramid. They bowed to him, then swung around, resting the bell mouths of their trumpets against the ancient stone, putting the mouthpieces to their lips.

Above the roar of the crowd sounded deep grumbling notes. They might have issued from clouds as thunder, except that there were no clouds; Ramsay stood in full light of a brilliant sun. Three times those notes were repeated. The cheering faded away, a silence fell. Still all the faces were raised to Ramsay. They were waiting, and he did not know for what! His hand twitched with a touch of panic—this was all part of an old ceremony. Courts and kings were enveloped, made secure in part, by the uses of ceremony. But he did not know what to do now—

To his vast relief, and in that moment he forgot his distrust of the High Chancellor, Ochall had climbed behind the trumpeters, though he did not join Ramsay at the summit of the pyramid. Instead, he swung about, not too easy a maneuver on that narrow, worn step, to speak.

"Hear you, all liege men! In this, the Square of Heroes, on the summit of the Place of Flags, which point lies in the very heart of Ulad, is now proclaimed our lord paramount and reigning—under whose rule shall we be as fruitful land well watered, warmed by a sun of glory. By the right of the House of Jostern, bearing the true blood of that same Jostern of old, comes now Kaskar—his birthright unquestioned. Pyran who was his passed through the Final Gate—may all the Watchers, the Comforters"—Ochall bowed his head and paused for an instant, his gesture of conventional reverence echoed by all in that throng—"bear him forth quickly to eternal life, joy, and blessing. In life, he acknowledged Kaskar, Prince of Vidin, as his true heir of body and line. Therefore, now this same Kaskar stands before you, as Supreme Mightiness, Guardian of Ulad, Watcher and Comforter this side of the Gate, for all his people. The Emperor is gone, the Emperor has come again!"

Four times the thunder of the trumpets sounded in nearly deafening blasts. Then the cheering broke out anew.

A shiver ran up Ramsay's back. He had heretofore looked upon this as a dangerous piece of playacting. But this—it was real! Far too real! He was not Kaskar; he wanted to run and run from those cheers. What new net was he caught in now? He swallowed. The cheers were lessening—They must expect something from him.

Almost against his will his hand went up. In answer to that nearly involuntary gesture, quiet fell even as it had before the proclamation made by Ochall.

He *had* to say something—But nothing in his past had prepared him for such a moment. The real Kaskar would have been carefully trained for this hour, so any fumbling on his part might now be remarked upon. Once more, the weight of his masquerade pressed upon him. Liege men—the term had a definite meaning in this world—it was a bond of honor. If he accepted their offering, then he must give something in return to keep the balance. He had begun all this thinking only of himself, his safety, of a private struggle against those who had used him. If he accepted what these now offered him—then he was tied. Already, he had gone too far, there was no going back unless he denied he was what his appearance labeled him. And that he could not do.

"Liege man also is your Emperor." Ramsay tried not to fumble for words as he searched to express emotions he had not had time enough to label or even fully understand. "Liege to Ulad. No more than that can any of the House of Jostern swear. For the safety of Ulad and those within its borders is the first duty of him who is proclaimed."

A short speech, perhaps an awkward one. But at that moment, Ramsay meant it as he had never meant anything before in his life. There was a moment of silence. Ramsay began to wonder if that abrupt speech had been the wrong thing, after all. Then the cheering began—

But also noted a flurry in the mass of crowd below. A party of guardsmen pushed forward, urging a path through the throng. Men and women were giving way to the determination of that group. And within the ring of guardsmen, Ramsay thought he saw the elaborate clothing of courtiers. At last, the Palace must be on the move. Though Ramsay could not believe that the intriguers would attempt any counterstroke in this open and very public place.

At the foot of the stair, his men from Vidin closed ranks a little. But Ramsay sensed some uneasiness in their stance. The purposeful approach of the other party began to make itself more strongly felt. Already the crowd drew farther apart, letting them through. When they reached a point where they faced the guard from Vidin, they drew up in a similar line, as if prepared to go into combat. Ramsay took a step forward, knowing that by all possible means he must prevent such a confrontation. Then, almost instantly, he realized there was no need for intervention, at least not on the level of the opposing guardsmen.

From their group the civilians whom they had escorted across the square now advanced. Berthal—and Osythes. The Prince wore scarlet and gold, bright enough to issue challenge by color alone, while the Shaman was almost a shadow of ill omen in his black-and-white, which, next to Berthal's ostentatious magnificence, was more black than white.

The Shaman's old face was as impassive as ever, but Berthal's was flushed to a degree that nearly matched the scarlet of his trappings. Though Osythes put out a hand as if to dissuade him from any imprudent move, the Prince avoided the Shaman with a twist of the shoulder, and sprang for the steps that led to the Place of Flags.

The noise of the crowd had faded to a murmur. It was plain that they expected drama to come and were not to be denied any of the action they could witness between the rivals to the Throne of Ulad.

Ramsay remained where he was. Berthal was the embodiment of rage. They might even meet in physical combat, certainly an edifying sight for Lom. Ramsay was sure he could handle the irate Prince without any interference from the guard. But he hardly wanted to be so publicly entangled in an undignified scuffle.

Berthal fairly leaped up those age-worn steps. Osythes, in spite of his years and the hindering long skirts of his robe, was only a little behind the Prince. Berthal, his eyes blazing, his mouth a crooked grimace of hate, had barely reached Ramsay's level when the Shaman joined them.

"Imposter!" Berthal was breathing so heavily that he gasped rather than shouted his accusation as perhaps he wished to do. "You thing of dreams! Think you to rule here? I say no! And with my body shall I make it so!"

He whirled out his sword of ceremony. Ramsay made no move to draw his own weapon. With narrow eyes, he watched the Prince, now foaming spittle at the corner of his lips. If Berthal was wild enough to rush him at that moment, the Prince would have to take the consequences.

But that knife was not pointed toward Ramsay's body. Berthal had grasped the point instead of the haft of his weapon and flipped it through the air. Not at Ramsay, but rather so that the blade crashed to the stone of the pavement and slithered across, until it lay, point foremost, at Ramsay's feet.

❈ ❈ FIFTEEN ❈ ❈

THE SOUND NOW—not the cheering of moments earlier—rather a sighing that might be produced by the indrawn breath of hundreds. This was surely some kind of formal challenge, but Ramsay, again caught in the net of his own defeating ignorance, was at a loss. Yet, if he hesitated, the Shaman did not.

His robes swirling about him, Osythes pushed between the two, planted his booted foot directly on the sword blade.

"No." A single word to erect a barrier, but it did. Berthal's color heightened, if that was possible; his hands twitched. To Ramsay's eyes, the Prince was fast losing self-control. He looked as if he were about to elbow past Osythes in order to leap directly for Ramsay's throat.

"It is my right!" choked out Berthal.

Osythes nodded. "Your right, by the code set by Jostern at the birth of your House. But this is not the time or the place." His hand closed about the Prince's right wrist and, though his thin fingers did not look to have such strength, Ramsay saw that Berthal could not break that hold.

However, it was to Ramsay that the Shaman now looked as if Berthal were no longer of consequence.

"You have returned." Osythes stated the obvious. "For what gain, dreamer?"

So simple was his question that Ramsay suspected some hidden guile. Yet it appeared that the Shaman actually wanted that answer.

"Perhaps," Ramsay answered, "because I am not yet ready to be a dead Kaskar as it was your will that I should be. There is that in all of us, Enlightened One, that will always struggle against death."

There was a faint frown, a very shadow of expression on the Shaman's face. His eyes probed Ramsay, who made himself face that searching gaze squarely. He sensed that he presented a problem the Shaman found baffling. And, in that bafflement, Ramsay himself discovered a small strength which made him add: "*Your* Heir has challenged me. Why not let us then settle this matter here and now— openly before what seems to be most of Lom—? I have had my fill of masked assassins ready to cut me down without warning. And I do not think that my sudden death from any cause will aid you now, not after this public affirmation of my right—"

"Your right!" cried Berthal, his voice scaling upward in his anger. "You have no rights at all—you barbarian out of—"

Perhaps Osythes then applied some punishing pressure to the wrist which he still held, for Berthal's protest ended in a grunt of pain. He shot a fierce look at the Shaman, but he was quiet.

Osythes was once more impassive. "Kaskar has been proclaimed, it would seem," he remarked tonelessly, though Ramsay had no faith in such sudden and complete surrender. "It is fitting that His Supreme Mightiness now appear before his court, having already been hailed by his people."

Enter the palace? Yet that, too, would be expected of him, and Ramsay believed he had no choice. He had already delivered a warning, one he knew would be enforced by those of Vidin, maybe also by at least some of these who had cheered him in Lom. Let him die for any cause now and there would be too many questions asked. If he must fight Berthal he would, and he had an idea that custom would decree that to be a very open struggle with plenty of official witnesses.

"His Supreme Mightiness"—Ramsay took a small pleasure in using the grandiloquent title—"agrees."

He glanced at Ochall, who had taken no part in this small flurry of rivals for the throne. In fact, Ramsay decided, the High Chancellor's attitude was one of strict neutrality. But Ramsay was not about to leave Ochall loose to give any orders, not if he could help it.

"His Dignity, our very worthy Chancellor, will accompany us," he stated firmly.

So it came about that a meeting, which had begun as a duel, ended—perhaps to the disappointment of many of the spectators—in a uniting of parties. By signal, and with much labor on the part of the combined guards to clear sufficient space, the flyer from Vidin once more set down and Ramsay, followed by Ochall and, at a slightly increased distance, by the Shaman who still had his hand on Berthal (now wearing a sulky, much-baffled look) embarked. Moments later, they settled on a roof landing, and the Palace of Lom welcomed them with a turnout of the guard.

As Ramsay acknowledged their salutes, Osythes saw fit to abandon his guardianship of Berthal to join the newly proclaimed Emperor. This time he addressed him shortly, without any of the honorifics one might expect.

"Her Splendor Enthroned would speak with you," he stated.

Ramsay smiled. "It is indeed gracious of her," he returned. "But perhaps it is even more gracious of Kaskar—"

For the first time, he saw what could only be anger flash momentarily in the Shaman's eyes.

"You have a free tongue!" he snapped.

To that observation Ramsay nodded. "But still I live. Very well, the same trap cannot work twice."

"I do not know what you mean—" Osythe's replied.

Ramsay laughed openly. "I did not think you would, Enlightened One. By what I have heard, you folk deal in obscurities upon obscurities. All I would have you understand now is that I shall march to no foretelling of yours."

Now he turned his head and spoke to Ochall. "I am summoned to my grandmother, High Chancellor. Her Splendor Enthroned must not be kept waiting. Whatever matters are of import, those we shall discuss later."

Ochall bowed. Berthal might have made some comment; he had opened his mouth. However, a quelling glance from the Shaman kept him mute. Berthal marched on their very heels as they entered a lift that carried them downward into the Palace that had so many secrets.

Where was Melkolf, Ramsay wondered as he tramped along the last corridor, the one with the secret door that led to the lab. Was Melkolf again at work, perhaps trying once more to match a redundant Kaskar to another victim on a third world plane? At least Ramsay had not had any dream to raise his suspicions. But he was certain now that, if he could put any power into an order, it would be given to destroy the machine squatting evilly below.

Neither Berthal nor the Shaman had said a word since they had left the landing stage. Perhaps their thoughts of revenge, needful action, defense, were as active as Ramsay's own. Berthal was the charge-at-all-obstacles-unheeding-of-the-cost type, so he could be countered that much more easily. But Ramsay was wary of Osythes, not knowing how far or how effective were the powers of these of the Groves. They appeared to be able to use minds in action as capably as the Company used its physical strength and experience in warfare. Therefore—they were to be most feared.

The doors of the Empress's apartment opened at their arrival. Ramsay, summoning up his old anger for a defense, went boldly through. There she sat, cloaked, crowned, small—deadly—in her canopied chair. Beside her, in another seat lacking that shadow-producing overhang, was—Thecla.

Ramsay shot a single glance at the girl. He had, through those days since that attack on the wharfside, kept—or tried to keep—her face out of his mind. She had been a part of the plan that would have left him dead and long since forgotten.

He supposed she would claim, if he ever accused her, that it was part of her "duty." That she owed Olyroun any life, including her own, if it was demanded of her. The odd sensation he had felt when Lom acknowledged his rule— yes, that made him understand, a little. She had been bred to the belief that a true ruler was a servant of the land, its defender to the death. She would accept any sacrifice the good of Olyroun would demand, and no one would ever know what private thoughts and desires she had set aside. Yes, he could understand, but this was not the Thecla he had held in foolish memory.

He bowed, deeply to the withered old woman in the chair of state, less lowly to the Duchess. Thecla's face was pale, her features set. Ramsay caught a glimpse of her hands, not lying gracefully in her lap, but with the fingers tightly laced together, as if to keep some control on herself.

"Your Splendor Enthroned." He spoke to the Empress.

She wasted no time. "We had a bargain, stranger."

"*You* had a bargain," he corrected her bluntly. "The one offered me in that hour was not the same!"

Thecla's hands flew apart. "What is it that you would say?" she demanded.

Ramsay turned his head deliberately, looked her full in the eyes. Amazing that she could produce that expression of strained surprise. He had always heard that royal personages never could be themselves, that their life of being on constant show must make actors of them from birth, but still her question surprised him.

"Let us have no secrets, at least none concerning the

past," Ramsay returned. "My Lady Duchess, you carefully provided the disguise of your kinsman, the Feudman. I warrant that you returned me so to Lom—though your first rescue of me now seems a little strange—or were you then acting on impulse that you later reconsidered? Back in Lom, I was able, of course, to discover the futility of trying to counter the act that had brought me here.

"Then"—he once more addressed the Empress—"we have the very timely intervention of the Reverend One." Ramsay nodded to Osythes. "Oddly enough, considering the need, he did *not* allow Melkolf to dispose of me. I wonder why the second and more complicated manner of erasing me was tried. There must have been a reason, but I don't suppose any of you are going to favor me with an explanation of it.

"At any rate, you were very frank with me—about the danger it meant to show this face"—Ramsay touched his own chin—"in Lom lest the High Chancellor be alerted and some strange and terrible doom be visited upon an innocent stranger unfairly drawn into your palace intrigues. Therefore, I was sent to a carefully arranged meeting with one who, I was later informed, was the highest-priced and most efficient assassin in Ulad.

"It was your misfortune that I, too, have some skills, which are not of your world and so escaped that tidy plot. That I did survive involved me in some other factors—"

"This is what you believe, you truly believe?" It was not the Empress who asked that, but Thecla. Her hands were no longer clenched; the fingers moved on the surface of her rich tunic. Seeing them so for a second, Ramsay was whirled back in time to watch other fingers, perhaps more slender, but no better shaped, flicking down upon a board those five strips with their potent symbols.

"This is what I believe," he replied with firmness.

Her hands stilled, she only watched him dumbly.

He discovered he could not look at her again. After all, in this company, she was perhaps the least of his enemies. That withered doll propped up in the chair of state might be the foremost, unless Osythes held that position.

There was a sound from the Shaman, but the Empress raised her hand in a quelling gesture.

"Let be, Reverend One. We have no time for the unraveling of old tangles. There is the present one facing us. So you have gone to Ochall, and you are Emperor in Lom—and in name—" Her eyes burned fiercely in her face. "And how are you the better for such a choice?"

Ramsay shrugged. "Perhaps I am not—but I am alive—"

"He who yields to Ochall has no life that will matter!" She attacked in force.

"Have I yielded then?" Ramsay returned.

He was aware that those three—for he didn't count Berthal, who stood, still sulking, near the wall—had centered probing gazes upon him. And he stared as steadily back. Did they not have the clarity of sight to understand that when they tried to manipulate events in the future they were only slightly removed in truth from the High Chancellor who had manipulated a man?

"If you are not yet his tool," said the Empress at last, "you cannot escape." But the tone of her voice was troubled. Her eyes shifted from Ramsay to Osythes, as if asking some unvoiced question.

"I have been told," Ramsay said deliberately seeking to strike some involuntary reaction from the three, "that in this game I stand as the Knave of Dreams."

The sound of sucked-in breath—Thecla's hands were now pressed against her mouth; above their masking her eyes were wide and frightened. But it was Osythes who spoke:

"And who did this telling?"

"One Adise," Ramsay replied shortly, and then elaborated, wishing to see the effect of his words upon them. "Fear and Fate, Fear and the Queen of Hope. Does that mean anything to you, Enlightened One?"

Osythes nodded slowly. However, when he spoke, it was to the Empress rather than in answer to Ramsay's question.

"Your Splendor Enthroned, *there* lies the answer! There—"

She interrupted him. "I do not understand your secrets, Reverend One. All I know is that in this hour this—this Kaskar who is not Kaskar rules Ulad. And at his right hand stands the dark one who will pull us all down! Well, we meddled with fate, and this is our reward. But while I live"—now her words were directed to Ramsay fiercely—"I shall fight for all my lord wrought here! And I promise you, I am no mean enemy!"

With lifted chin, and those eyes as bright and menacing as some bird of prey's, she offered him battle, showing far more dignity and purpose than Berthal's dramatics with the sword of ceremony.

"You do not know Ochall." Ramsay knew at this moment, enemy or no, he could not allow her to remain ignorant of what the High Chancellor planned. "He has already dealt with the Merchants of Norn, and what he has gained thereby—listen and believe." In bald, terse words he outlined the Battle of the Ridge, sparing them no detail that might clarify the horror that could be turned against Lom itself.

"In Yasnaby—" Thecla cried out. Now her hands covered the whole of her face, and she was shuddering as if he had produced, before their very sight, not just spoken the words but the whole scene of that massacre. "In Olyroun!"

"Monstrous!" The Empress's shoulders sagged a trifle. It would seem that more years had gathered in those few moments to weigh her down. "And yet you company with this man! Why do you then reveal his works? Do you mean to use fear as a weapon intended to cow us into a quick surrender?"

"I say only what I have seen—felt—" Absently, Ramsay raised his hand to his cheek where the searing fire had left no scar but memory. "If it was my intention to invade Lom, I would have given Ochall his five days—"

"What do you want of us?" Thecla cried now.

"What I have always wanted—my own place."

"But we—Melkolf cannot give you that!" Thecla was flushed; her back stiffened, and she faced him as she might a threat she must not openly acknowledge.

"Yes," agreed Ramsay. "Therefore—we are left with a problem. I am Kaskar now and cannot return. And who is Kaskar?"

"You play with words!" The Empress showed open anger. "The girl is right—what do you want of us?"

"I do not know—yet," Ramsay returned. "But I warn you—I play no more of your games. Nor"—he hesitated for a second to give emphasis to the rest—"will I play Ochall's. That he has power beyond my reckoning—that you had better believe. That he intends to hold Ulad, one way or another—that also you are aware of—"

"You accompanied him here—" began the Empress.

"I brought him because here he can be watched. Had I left him in Vidin—would you have the fog and flame come upon you?"

For the first time, Osythes broke into their exchange. "Knave of Dreams—" he repeated slowly. "And what have you dreamed?"

"Nothing—yet."

"Adise—" Thecla hesitated over the name and then continued with more confidence. "She is the Great Reader—"

"Take no comfort from that!" snapped the Empress. She gave the Shaman a hostile glance. "I begin to think, Reverend One, that Ulad's cause did not attract a true supporter in you. Rather, we have all been blind yet once again and have been manipulated, even as Kaskar was ruled by Ochall, into this situation because of some decision of the Enlightened Ones, which will do us no good at all! Blind! Blind!" She raised one hand to cover her eyes. "Old and blind and worthless! And so Ulad falls because I have failed."

"No!" Thecla moved to catch the Empress's other hand. "Do not think so!" She glanced up at Osythes. "Reverend One, tell her that is not true. You—all of you— could not be so cruel!"

"Ulad shall not fall." The Shaman said those four words deliberately, as if they did not form an assertion, but a promise.

"Another foreseeing?" Berthal came away from the wall, his lips bent in a sneer. "Well enough—let this—this outlander answer me blade to blade and I shall make sure of that!" His hatred was hot in his boast.

"A foreseeing"—Osythes again spoke in that measured way—"can only indicate probable events, which may be changed by the choices of those concerned. All of you are aware of that. But—" He paused as if to think his way thorough some web of mind. "There is a pattern—and it is far-reaching. Ulad is a necessary part of that pattern— the first stable government seen in this land since the Great Disaster. Thus, Ulad is the foundation upon which we must build anew. No, Ulad, because of our actions, in spite of our actions, will not fall. Yet that does not resolve our separate fates—"

The Empress had been watching him, her one hand clasped in Thecla's, the other now lying limply on her knee as if her outburst of moments earlier had exhausted even her indomitable strength and will.

"Be Ulad safe," she said now in a low voice, "and I care not that fate rises in my path."

"I care!" Berthal came a step closer to Ramsay, "True blood will rule here! Ulad is the House of Jostern! We made this land in the past, we shall maintain it now! And you"—he fairly spat at Ramsay—"are none of us. Live as Emperor and you will speedily die—"

Ramsay suddenly laughed. "For yet another time, Prince?"

But Berthal nodded as if that had been an accepted truth. "Yes."

"Enough!" The Empress's old authority was once more vibrant in her voice. "We do not bait each other here and now. Rather do we seek to come to some accord. You have made yourself Emperor," she said to Ramsay. "Do you hold to that?"

"Would you accept me so?" countered Ramsay wonderingly.

"I will accept everything—all—that preserves this land. You say that Ochall is not your master. If this proves true—then—"

"No!" Berthal's denial cut across her words. "He is not the Heir, he is nothing—a man who should rightfully be dead! Let *him* wed with Thecla, sit upon the throne? You are old! You are mad!"

Thecla was on her feet between the Empress and Berthal, who again had the appearance of one maddened to the point of losing all control, even as he had been at the Place of Flags.

"Be silent!" Like the Empress's voice earlier, hers now held the whiplash of unquestioned authority. "Her Splendor Enthroned remains the Head of the House of Jostern—"

"I need not your liege words, my dear," the Empress said. "And I am not shaken in my wits. Ulad must come first. We do not plunge this land into war with man against son, brother against brother, over any question of heirdom. If Kaskar proves that he is not Ochall's creature—"

Ramsay was the one who interrupted now. "Your Splendor Enthroned"—he gave her her title—"I am no man's—no woman's creature. What I decide shall be of my own free will. Since I was unwilling and unwitting player in your game for power, I now reserve my own decision."

He bowed to her, to Thecla, ignoring both the Shaman and Berthal, who made as if to step between him and the door of the chamber and then thought better of it, meeting Ramsay's gaze. Then, leaving them to think about his declaration of independence, Ramsay purposefully left the room.

Where Kaskar's apartment might be within this pile, Ramsay had no idea. But he was not subjected to the humiliation of trying to find out, for in the corridor beyond awaited Jasum and two of the Vidin guardsmen. Almost, Ramsay thought, as if they expected to be called upon to protect the person of their sworn lord. And with their escort, he reached a richly furnished chamber not unlike that in which he and Thecla had sat to exchange stumbling words the first night of his life here.

He dismissed his liege men with courtesy, wanting to be alone. Where was Ochall in this pile, and what might the High Chancellor be doing? If he, Ramsay, only had someone at his back whom he could wholly trust! The half promise of the Empress to support Kaskar—how much could he depend upon that? Very little. He should know that from his former betrayal. And to be Emperor—he had never intended that!

There was a tray on a table, bearing a stoppered, thin-necked bottle of cut crystal, a waiting matching goblet, and with these a plate of cakes. Ramsay sank into one of the piles of cushions, which here took the place of chairs, and began to eat ravenously, suddenly conscious of the fact that it had been a long time since he had last dined. He would rather have had a more substantial meal, but his own need to think in private kept him from summoning a servant.

Having wolfed the cakes, he sipped the liquid with more caution, wanting no unexpected potency to cloud his mind at this moment. Outside, the dusk cloaked the windows. A single lamp burned on a far table. And the radiance from it was very limited, so that he was well hidden in the swiftly gathering shadows.

There was an ache beginning above his eyes. He was tired—so tired—to try to sort out any impressions of this day was now a wearying task. That he had begun this wild venture at all—why?

Dreams—

No dream could be any wilder than this.

Ramsay longed with all his might to awaken, to know that this was merely a prolonged adventure born out of his own imagination. Dream—they had told him that—the Enlightened Ones.

Suppose he could dream himself awake in the right world? For all the proof they had shown him—perhaps that was as false as other things they had said and done.

No! He could not allow himself to be disarmed. Ramsay sat up straighter, glanced sharply about the chamber. He had that small subtle hint to alert him. Ochall—was the High Chancellor bending on him now some unbelievable power of will to lead him into this particular path of thought? He had to cope with the reality, not allow himself to drift into the dream again.

And in the Palace of Lom he had no one to trust. In all this world he had—

A face formed vividly in Ramsay's mind—Dedan! The mercenary had no company now. If he had survived his terrible injuries he would be left without resources. Dedan—

The thought of the First Captain was like a tonic. Ramsay nodded, though there was no one there to witness the gesture which approved his idea. Dedan would be sent for, through the Enlightened Ones—that need was as sharply clear as if Ramsay could see it all laid out in print before him. Dedan was also Ramsay's witness against Ochall—therefore this must be done in secret. And who was better able to handle secrets than Osythes?

He would—

Again Ramsay tensed. He had not heard that door open behind him. But hunter's instinct, sharpened by circumstances, told him he was not alone any longer. In the shadows, he shifted about to see who had come so silently and perhaps—for good reason—secretly.

✾ ✾ SIXTEEN ✾ ✾

VEILED, hidden, she advanced. But he knew her. This was the guise she had worn beside the bier of a dead prince, a newly risen man.

Ramsay arose.

"What do you want?" His voice was even more brusque than he intended. She had presented him with two faces in the past—her concern, the reason for which he had never understood, then the false concern when she had set upon him that near-fatal disguise of Feudman.

Thecla stood just within the farther reach of the lamp rays as she lifted her long veil.

"Why did you say such things—that you were marked for death by our will?" she asked simply.

He wondered that she would try to keep up a pretense of innocence—or ignorance.

"Because that was the truth."

Thecla came farther into the light, her intent gaze upon his face.

"I see that you believe it," she acknowledged. "But how can you? The Empress, Osythes, they do not deal so—"

"They did before," he reminded her deliberately. "What of Kaskar—and me—were we not intended to die together under the influence of Melkolf's machine? What did my life weigh then against their needs? And does it weigh even less now when I stand in Lom to refute, by my presence, all their plans?"

Under the warm brown of her skin there arose a flush. "They—they did not know you then. You were an abstraction—something far removed—not real—"

"So then, when by some slip I became real," Ramsay retorted, "I was even more a menace. Is this not so? I have learned something, my Lady Duchess, your strength is duty, and to that you are prepared to sacrifice all. Is that not the truth?"

"It is the truth," she agreed tonelessly.

"Therefore, as duty bid, you found a plausible story and those other two improved upon it. An anonymous Feudman slain on the wharfside by a known assassin for hire. Such an occurrence as would bring about little official investigation—and I am well removed."

"*No!*" Her protest was quick, hot. Now there was anger in her tone. "That was not the way of it! I—I demean myself to come to you, to beg you to listen." Her chin lifted. She drew about her not the physical folds of her veil, rather the inborn authority that was bred in her.

"It is only because—" She hesitated and then continued, all her pride displayed by her straight back, her flashing eyes. "It is because I will not have such a slur put upon Olyroun, for I am Olyroun—if you can understand that—I am here. The attack on the wharf was *not* of our planning—"

"Then whose?" Ramsay prompted when again she paused.

It would appear that she was loath to answer. He saw her hands twisting, wringing the edge of her veil.

"I am not sure, and I will accuse no one unjustly," Thecla said slowly. "But this I will swear by any Power you wish, the Empress, and Osythes, and I—we did not unite to send you to your death. I knew not that you had gone until later. And this is the truth which you can discover for yourself. That guardsman who was to see you safe on board the ship—he did not return to the palace. Her Splendor's Eyes and Ears have been busy—but even they could not find him."

"This, too, you will lay on Ochall?" Ramsay was more than half convinced that whatever intrigue had been aimed at him had not included Thecla. Perhaps because he wanted to believe that, he decided in a flash of insight.

What was this girl to him? He could not have honestly answered. With her burden of rulership, she was unlike any of her sex he had known. Still, in spite of that burden and difference, he realized now that he had been drawn to her from those hours when she had sheltered him in her chamber, been so efficient in arranging his escape.

"Ochall?" Thecla repeated the High Chancellor's name with an accent of surprise. "No, he would not want Kaskar dead."

"He knows Kaskar is dead," Ramsay informed her. "Though he accepts the fiction that I am Kaskar." Of that he was now as certain as if the High Chancellor had had told him so.

Thecla nodded. "He doubtless plans to make you his Kaskar. Your life is more precious to him now than any treasure—"

"So," Ramsay persisted, "we are now left with a mystery. If it was not the Empress who arranged my final disappearance, and Ochall could want nothing less, who remains?"

She was silent, there was a shadow of obstinacy about her lips. Ramsay thought that she would not give him more. Yet he must—somehow he believed that Thecla was in earnest—learn what she suspected.

Who would benefit by the death of Kaskar the second— and who had even been aware that there was a Kaskar the second? Thecla, Grishilda, the Empress, Osythes—and Melkolf!

The scientist had been ready to kill him out of hand when he discovered the lab. Somehow, Ramsay could not associate Melkolf with the devious attack on the wharf. But Melkolf could have been a link—with whom?

There was only one other—Berthal! Yet Ramsay would have thought after that exhibition of reckless temper the Prince had shown in his challenge, that Berthal, too, would not have been party to a complicated plot. He would have been far more likely to have made an open attack under some rule of the nobility—even as today he had delivered that challenge that Osythes had interrupted before most of Lom.

However—a last suggestion struck Ramsay—the Enlightened Ones? But he had a strong impression that, though they might stand aside and let death strike down a man if they thought that necessary, they would not actively arrange for a murder.

Watching Thecla closely, Ramsay made his choice and spoke two names aloud, hoping that the girl would reveal whether his guess was right or wrong:

"Berthal—and Melkolf?"

By an ebbing of her color he had his answer. "Berthal," he continued, "wants Ulad. Melkolf—perhaps he resents the failure of his experiment so much that he must erase the result—"

"I did not say so!" Her answer was too prompt. "Only—watch yourself—Kaskar." For the first time, she used that name. "This much I know—the Empress has ordered that the exchanger be dismantled. Melkolf—he is gone and no one can find him. With him he took things even Osythes has not been able to understand. He knew—knows—more of the Old Knowledge than we suspected."

They only needed that added to the rest, thought Ramsay grimly—Melkolf resentful and hidden, and, with him, and untold, unmeasured amount of what might be as fearsome knowledge as anything the Merchants of Norn brought into their dread market. His mind made a sinister leap, and he felt a cold shiver run through him. Melkolf would have only one market for his product—Ochall! In Berthal's present state of mind, that Prince might also be added to a dark company, willing to make peace with the enemy for Ulad.

Not only had Ramsay's thoughts marshaled those surmises into good order, but he had an odd sensation that this was what had happened. He believed this fact, though he could not state why.

If the Empress, as she had already proposed, supported Kaskar—Ramsay—rather than cause any dissension—yes, he could conceive of Berthal's being driven by hatred and a sense of injustice to the strongest aid he could find— Ochall. If only Ramsay himself had those he could depend upon—

Ramsay realized that he was striding up and down. Thecla was watching him. As his eyes met hers she spoke.

"You have the foretelling of Adise. Did the Enlightened Ones give you no other word?"

Dedan— Dream— He shook his head. Why had he begun to believe in impossibilities? Perhaps because he was caught in something beyond all the logic of his own world.

"They told you nothing?" Thecla must have taken that shake of his head as answer to that question.

"Something," he answered absently. Then he turned and regarded her narrowly. Would Thecla help? To allow himself to dream—here—unguarded? There was a danger in that which he sensed as one might suddenly sniff an evil stench.

"I must," he told her, "dream—and dreaming—"

He saw her hands close tightly on her veil. "You must not be disturbed," she stated firmly, as if she knew exactly what he proposed. "Dream—I shall wait."

She moved to the door, and now, with her own hands, she shot home the bolt to lock them in. Ramsay had a last weighing of his trust in her. He had to believe—after all, their purpose was now nearly united.

Stretching himself on a divan, he closed his eyes.

Dream—this was not what he had done before, a bringing to the surface of memory-old dreams to wring them of impressions and facts he needed. This was an attempt to reach out, to form a dream born of his own need and desire. And he did not know how to do it.

Dedan—in his mind he held a picture of the Free Captain. Not as he had seen him last in the litter, but as the mercenary had been at their first meeting, assured, vibrant with life and ambition. Dedan—he centered on that creation of his mind—Dedan!

He concentrated on creating Dedan. Was he dreaming—or merely exercising his imagination? He dared let no doubt trouble his thoughts—Dedan! The very intensity of his struggle to maintain that mind image, reach out to the personality it signified, was such an effort as no physical action had ever seemed to be. Dedan—

Ramsay—was—elsewhere! Not in any chamber such as he had had in the Grove of the Enlightened Ones. No, this was a state of being that was divorced from all he had known. He entered it with a sharp, breaking sensation, as if he had bodily leaped through some fragile screen to reach it.

There was—nothingness—

Then, up through the nothingness, as a plant might grow from the ground, arose—Dedan! First he seemed as Ramsay had striven to picture him. Yet there was about him a lack of response. His eyes were closed, he was more a puppet—a statue.

Was Dedan—*dead*?

Ramsay's concentration faltered. He saw that figure begin to sink again. No—Dedan!

His urgency of thought was like a shout to hail the personality he sought. There was a slow lifting of those eyelids in a face wiped free of all emotion, a face not of earth. The eyes were alive, if the face that framed them was not.

Dedan—to me! To me, at Lom!

Ramsay hurled that thought feverishly, afraid that any moment he would lose this contact, if contact it was. Now he saw the pale lips of the Free Captain open, move in words he could not hear. Feverishly he fought for the other's answer. But there came only the movement of lips. Then—

The nothingness changed abruptly. It formed a swirl of alien veiling, cloud, he was not sure, and Ramsay knew that in that cloud others moved, listened, were startled by his invasion. From those others he shrank. His will shriveled; he wanted only escape lest he see what would come out of nothingness.

His desire for escape was as sharp now as his need to reach Dedan had been. He gasped, fought, broke free. And was awake.

There was still only the low lamplight warring against the dark. But he had awakened once to an overpowering scent of flowers, so now there was also a fragrance, more delicate and elusive. Then he was conscious that hands gripped his, as if they had drawn him back—or anchored him—to safety.

The hands were Thecla's. She sat on cushions by his side, watching him. There was a measure of relief in her eyes when she saw that he knew her.

"You have dreamed." The girl stated that as fact, not as a question.

Ramsay croaked an answer from a mouth still dried with the fear of those last moments in the nothingness. "I—I do not know. This was different." Yet there would be proof—if Dedan came to him, then he would have his proof that he could exert a measure of control over this strange new faculty—whether it was "dreaming" or something else.

"Who is Dedan?" Thecla asked.

Ramsay levered himself up on one elbow to face her more squarely.

"How did you know—?"

"You called upon that name," she returned quickly before his question was half voiced.

So he had called aloud! But in his dream—vision—he had only thought. Real—unreal—Again he shook his head, trying to throw off the dazed feeling that closed about him.

"He is—was—a Free Captain of the mercenaries, one who will have good reason to hate Ochall when he learns the truth..If I can reach him—"

He was talking too much. Why let Thecla, anyone within Lom, know that he felt the need for someone he believed he could implicitly trust?

"Any enemy of Ochall's," Thecla returned—she had risen from her cushions; about her once more she had drawn her cloak of pride and dignity, "should be useful at this moment. I hope that he comes to your calling—"

Somehow, she had moved farther from him than one could measure. Now she was draping her veil once more about her head and shoulders in a way that made Ramsay sense that a barrier had risen between them. He had not consciously voiced his doubts. Perhaps she had guessed in some fashion—that a mercenary First Captain had his full trust over all others in Lom.

Before Ramsay could sort out his tangle of thoughts and surmises, blurt out thanks, Thecla had released the latch, was gone. He pulled himself up from the couch. Waveringly, feeling nearly as weak and unsteady as he had when the Enlightened Ones had drawn him and the others to the grove, he gained his feet. He staggered across the room to set that latch firm once more. Thecla had come upon him earlier without warning; who else might be prowling the corridors of the Palace, eager to have a private meeting with Kaskar?

His head ached with a steady throb that made him queasy. And he had to steer a way with caution back to the divan, afraid at any moment that he might go down again. Melkolf—Berthal—Ochall— The names followed him on and on into troubled sleep.

Ramsay woke with a sense of disorientation. There was a pounding—voices— He moved sluggishly, stiff, his body aching. The noise continued, he turned his head. Daylight swept through windows, though its brightness was filtered by drawn curtains. There was a door, latched—and the noise came from beyond that.

He could make no sense of that gabble of sound, but the urgency of those beyond his door he was now able to feel. Getting up jerkily, he was relieved to discover that the sickness he could dimly remember no longer plagued him. He was able to walk firmly to the door, lift the barring latch.

For a moment or two, he half believed that he was

under attack, for three of those outside had been backed against that door. Jasum, in the uniform of Vidin, was the centermost of the trio, while opposing him were two differently clad. At the sight of Ramsay, the two drew back, saluted, relieving him of the suspicion that a palace revolution might be in progress.

"What is this?" He raised his own voice. Jasum turned smartly, about to salute.

"Your Supreme Mightiness, these men say they have news of importance—that they must speak with you. But it is not fitting that those not of Ulad intrude upon the Emperor unannounced and without stating their reason for their coming—not even if they are of Olyroun."

"Olyroun? Admit them—alone!" Ramsay added when he saw signs that Jasum was preparing to play not only court usher but bodyguard.

"As the Throne speaks—so shall it be!" the officer returned, but when he stood aside there was an uneasy shadow on his face. And he closed the door behind the Olyroun guardsmen with what Ramsay thought was reluctant slowness. Was Jasum perhaps Ochall's man? Again that feeling that he could truly trust no one plagued Ramsay.

Once the door was closed, he turned to the two standing at strict attention.

"This so important message—?"

"Supreme Mightiness, it is our lady! She cannot be found—and there are—"

Ramsay stiffened. "Cannot be found? What say her ladies—the Lady Grishilda?"

"Supreme Mightiness, the Lady Grishilda sleeps and

none can wake her. The Reverend Osythes has been summoned and—"

"Let us go!" Ramsay wasted no more time. One of the guardsmen leaped to open the door, nearly sending Jasum flying with the force of his push, so close had the Vidinian been to the portal.

"Attend me," snapped Ramsay as he strode by, keeping pace with the Olyrounians who had sought him out. If this was some further intrigue, then he would resolve it here and now! No longer was he going to accept secret upon secret. Yet he had a growing premonition that this was no act planned by Thecla. To arouse the palace and cause an open search was not her way.

"When was this discovered?"

"Our lady had audience with Her Splendor Enthroned. When she did not come and sent no message—then Her Splendor Enthroned inquired. The door of our lady's inner chamber was fast locked. There was no answer to any summons. Then Fentwer"—the speaker pointed to the other guard—"swung from the balcony of the outer presence chamber. He found the Lady Grishilda lying upon the floor deep asleep. Our lady's bed was empty. There was no sign of what had happened to her, but neither is there any other way out, except the door where we stood guard—and the balcony. We cannot believe our lady would have gone that way—"

No way out, thought Ramsay as his pace increased to a half trot. Yet Thecla had come to him, and he did not believe that anyone, except perhaps Grishilda, was aware of that visit. He dismissed the thought that Thecla would have been a party to any drugging or other interference with her own senior lady-in-waiting. They were too much in each other's confidence.

Which meant that Thecla might not have returned to her own chamber after she left him—And someone, for some reason, had made sure Grishilda would not be able to testify to facts. At least not for a while.

His memory reached back to his first awakening. Thecla had in some manner then either hypnotized or dazed the guardsmen by the bier. She was reputed to have some of the natural gift of the Enlightened Ones. But Grishilda—could the lady-in-waiting have deliberately submitted to such for some reason to benefit her young mistress?

No, again his knowledge, though that was small, of the bond between Thecla and the older woman denied that possibility. Osythes? He also possessed those "powers" so vaguely defined, and held in awe by most. For what reason?

Ochall? Kaskar's enslavement was attributed to some abnormal control. Ochall wanted Olyroun—needed its ores—Where was Ochall at this moment?

They crossed from one corridor to another, turned into a third. Halfway down there was a door Ramsay recognized. Thecla had once more been given the same chambers in which she had concealed him. There were guards about, some in the tunics of Olyroun, others wearing the eagle-like badge of the palace. They drew to either side as Ramsay came into their sight. Then he was through the outer presence chamber and into Thecla's bedroom.

On a divan to one side lay Grishilda and over her stood the Shaman. As Ramsay entered he glanced up.

"Well?"

Osythes shook his head. "I do not understand, Supreme Mightiness. The Lady Grishilda is in the Deep Sleep which it is believed only an adept can provoke. It cannot be broken, she will so slumber until some hour, already determined upon and imprinted upon her mind, arrives. And that we cannot know—"

His concern appeared honest. But the Enlightened Ones were masters and mistresses of subtleties. However, Ramsay could perceive no gain for Osythes here.

Did the Shaman have the power to read thoughts? For now Osythes regarded Ramsay intently and said with a compelling note in his voice: "Supreme Mightiness, this is no doing of the Grove Fellowship. It is rather a trick, perhaps played to induce such belief—to sever confidence and sow discord between those who should be allies, weakening defenses—"

Logical, good sense. Still Ramsay had his reservations. The old reputation of the Enlightened Ones, that they would turn against an ally to further some project of their own, might make any word Osythes was willing to swear suspect.

Ramsay could see only one action possible now. He wheeled on the men who had followed him, Olyroun and Vidinian palace guard alike.

"I want," he said grimly, "such a search of this palace as not even a fly on the wall will be unseen! I want each and every person questioned—and any who has seen—or heard—anything out of the ordinary is to be brought directly to me, here in the Duchess's presence chamber. You will begin at once!"

There was an advantage in standing in Kaskar's boots

at that moment, and he would make full use of it. The guard saluted, scattered. When they were gone, Ramsay spoke once more to the Shaman.

"Ochall, Melkolf, Berthal?" The names that had haunted him into slumber came readily enough. But men could not be arrested on suspicion alone, nor could Thecla be found by merely listing possible enemies.

He had been bold in so naming two of Osythes's own party. However, the Shaman showed no surprise.

"We must have more than just suspicions—" Now that they were alone, he omitted, one part of Ramsay's mind noted, the wordy title.

"I am told Melkolf has not only disappeared, but that he took with him knowledge unknown to others. Berthal wants to rule. And Ochall wants not only Ulad but also Olyroun. If they took Thecla to bargain—or to wed Berthal—"

"That cannot be done—the wedding, I mean—while there is another Emperor in Ulad," Osythes replied. "Such a union could not hold—for she was betrothed in the name of the Emperor. But that they might hope to conclude a bargain—yes. And it is true that we do not know the complete sum of what Melkolf learned and can put to use. The Merchants of Norn deal in the antiques of war. Others seek to salvage different knowledge. Where Melkolf has sought—it was thought that he was well overseen—but—" Osythes shook his head. "In all lie error. And, in this case, error has in turn become danger. There are those now set on Melkolf's trail—but we know only this: that he learned more than was good for the state of Ulad—or perhaps of this world. He is being sought diligently—"

"Time may run out," Ramsay interrupted. "Ochall wanted five days—already those have shrunk to four. How many days may Melkolf need to produce something worse than a flamethrower or a blinding fog?"

He slammed his fist against the frame of the door with bruising force. Thecla—he had let her go into the night—let her go believing—he was sure—that he had no trust in her. Now she was gone where no one could find her. The palace might be busy as a well-stirred ant hill, but that anything concrete might come from all their endeavors at searching—that he doubted.

❈ ❈ SEVENTEEN ❈ ❈

"—THE WORTHY PRINCE sent his own body servant to our station, Supreme Mightiness. He bore the seal ring of Prince Berthal and said that this was a matter of grave import, ordering that we have ready a distant flyer completely fueled. We had no reason to believe that there was any wrong intended."

The man standing to attention before Ramsay was obviously nervous. He was one of the attendants of the landing areas where were parked the private flyers of the Family and the highest officials of the palace.

"And when did the Prince arrive?" Ramsay's headache had returned full force. Pain ringed in his eyes as he sipped from a glass Osythes had slid before him. Ramsay barely knew what he did, intent only on sifting all the scraps the intensive search of the palace was providing.

"We do not know, Supreme Mightiness. It was in the Prince's message that the flyer be readied for instant use, and left unattended."

"The pilot?"

"The Prince is often his own pilot, Supreme Mightiness."

"And no one saw who came to the ship? That I find very hard to believe." Ramsay kept his own voice level, his impatience under what control he could muster. "There are guards on duty, are there not?"

The man swallowed visibly. "Always, Supreme Mightiness. But—but the Prince Berthal has often been angered by too close a watch. He had before ordered that the guards were not to be on hand when he sent a private message. He—he said something once about not giving the Eyes and Ears a chance to meddle—" The man was half stammering now. "Supreme Mightiness, believe me, I only repeat what the Prince said in anger when he found guards by his flyer some months ago."

"So this flyer is now gone you know not where, bearing you know not whom—" Ramsay summoned up the gist of what the other had told him.

"Supreme Mightiness, we are under command. It is for us to do as we are bid," the man returned.

Ramsay sighed. He was right, of course. Yet there was something—a feeling—perhaps because this answer was too much of a direct defeat. Was that why it was so hard to accept? Berthal's seal ring and a message to be obeyed. A takeoff witnessed right enough, but no knowledge of who had winged into the night.

"You may go," he told the landing attendant. But before the man had thankfully disappeared, Ramsay appealed to the one who had come with this witness. "There is no way of tracing the flyer's course?"

"None, Supreme Mightiness. The director had not been set. But this is not unknown. Those about private errands sometimes neglect that ruling."

"Especially," Ramsay said, allowing some of his rising anger to color his words, "if they are of sufficient rank, is that not so?"

The other made no answer, which was an answer in itself. Ramsay rubbed his forehead. There was sun bright in the room. He could not have told the hour, but it seemed more like days since he had come to find Thecla gone.

In the bedchamber, Grishilda still slumbered, always under the eyes of the Empress's own trusted maid, who would report the first sign of waking. For the rest—what did they have?

A handful of bits that he could not fit together. A flyer that had taken off—the fact that Ochall was certainly not to be found anywhere within this palace—a report from a guard on the second level of the tower that he had challenged something and from that time could not remember what happened until discovered by his commanding officer standing at his post in a state bordering on sleep.

Ochall—Berthal—Melkolf—none to be found. Slowly, Ramsay raised the glass he suddenly realized he was holding, drank the rest of its contents. The stuff was bitter enough to give him a slight shock. Was the Shaman drugging him now—?

"What—?" He looked to Osythes, who in turn was watching him intently.

"A cordial only, Supreme Mightiness. And food is

being brought. You cannot drive yourself past the point where your mind still rules your body. If the body falters—then what may you do?"

Ramsay leaned back in his chair. There were no more possible witnesses waiting to be interviewed. He fought the wave of fatigue that was a part of the ache in his head, the frustration of his useless efforts.

Perhaps Osythes's remedy was already beginning to work. The throb over his eyes was certainly less strong. And he was suddenly conscious of hunger. As he rested his head against the back of the chair, he asked: "What do you make of this coil, Enlightened One?"

"What do you?" Osythes countered.

Ramsay frowned. He had fought to piece together bits, rule out wild surmise for more definite evidence. Yet now all he had was a hunch, and that was so strong that he could not shrug it aside.

"It would seem," he said slowly, "that they escaped—that they can now be anywhere in Ulad—or out of it. With a world to search, where do we start?"

Osythes said nothing in answer as Ramsay paused. Did his silence mean agreement with what seemed to be facts, or did he also have some premonition that that was all too easy, too direct? Ochall might wield a club, but it was not his nature to proceed too directly to his goal. Ramsay could not be certain of his own deductions—he might be guessing wildly because he wanted to believe in his hunch—he did not dare to think that what he had stated was the truth—that there was no hope of pursuit now.

What had they managed to discover about Ochall in their hours of patient and impatient questioning? That there was absolutely no witness to any communication between the High Chancellor and Berthal. Which did not mean, of course, that such had not taken place.

The High Chancellor had gone at once to the chamber always allotted him when he stayed at Lom on matters of state. He had dismissed even his body servant—who had been the most severely interrogated of all those questioned today—with the comment that he had urgent need to study certain reports which the new Emperor would soon be calling for. The guard swore that he had never come forth from that chamber.

Which report meant nothing, Ramsay knew, with his own experiences of guards under what might be termed control. However, when summoned to attend the conference concerning the disappearance of the Duchess, his apartment had been entirely empty.

Melkolf, the third of their trio, was perhaps in his own way as dangerous as Ochall. His disappearance had come first, several days ago. And there was plenty of evidence of a strong tie between him and Berthal.

Ramsay was shaken out of his thoughts by the arrival of a tray of food. He ate quickly but cleaned each plate. Either the food or the cordial had given him new vigor. With that inner renewal, his confidence rose once more.

"What did Melkolf take—instruments, machines— records—?" he asked as he pushed away the last dish.

"None of the machines," Osythes replied. "But the location beamer of the exchanger was gone. And we discovered indication of records hastily combed—including two empty hiding places—neither large."

"The exchanger?"

"Her Splendor Enthroned ordered that destroyed. I myself saw that it was done."

"Could it be rebuilt?" persisted Ramsay.

"Such a task would require great resources—time—"

"But it could be done?"

"With Melkolf's knowledge, yes." Agreement came reluctantly.

"Could Melkolf then operate it as before?"

"No! Not alone," Osythes was quick and emphatic with his answer. "The machine makes the actual exchange, but it cannot be used to locate the proper personality pattern."

"No, that you do with your dreaming," Ramsay returned flatly. "So even if Melkolf reproduced his exchanger, he could not activate it without the aid of those extra powers your fellowship exploits. *Would* they aid him?"

"No!" Osythes leaned a little forward.

"You are very sure—"

"It is decreed so. We want no more variables to upset our patterns for the future."

"One thing I have accomplished at least, merely by being," commented Ramsay. "Then why did Melkolf see fit to take with him the most important part of the exchanger?" He stood up. "I think I want to see the lab."

His hunch pointed him into action as might the keen nose of a hound picking up a faint but traceable scent. He could not put aside a strong feeling that the departure of the flyer was only a screen—a ruse—that what he sought now was not so far beyond their reach.

"Supreme Mightiness—"

Ramsay, for a moment, found it difficult to answer to

that title. Half engrossed in his speculations, he blinked at the guard waiting in the doorway.

"Yes—?"

"One has come, he says he was summoned. He was dropped from a flyer of the Enlightened Ones—"

So much had happened since the night before that Ramsay took a second to remember. Dedan—could it be—?

"Admit him!"

The guard stepped aside for the man in the plain mercenary uniform. He was pale and had lost some of his assured air of command. His face appeared aged by several years, and had undergone another subtle change; yet this grim-countenanced man was indeed the First of the Company.

Ramsay moved forward quickly. "You came!" Until this moment, he had not been sure that his meeting in the place of nothingness would bear any results.

Dedan gave a shadow of his old shrug, but there was none of the old warmth. "I have come, Supreme Mightiness. Why—"

So now, there existed a barrier between them. Dedan's eyes might not be shut as they had been when Ramsay fronted him in the dream, but his face was closed, perhaps his mind also. He was as stiff as the guardsman who admitted him.

"Leave us!" Ramsay ordered the guard. Only when the door closed did he speak again, though the sharp change in the only man he thought he could claim as friend daunted him.

"Dedan, I speak now as Arluth. Do you want

vengeance on the man who sent the flamers to wipe us out?" Was that the promise that could strike through the shell of the First Captain now?

Dedan's blankness of expression vanished in an instant. "You know him?" His demand was harsh, but he was alive, as if only the thought of vengeance could reach through some cloud horror had laid upon him.

"I know who and why. Listen—" Ramsay swiftly outlined what he had learned from Ochall—of how the Company had been used in the callous, horrible experiment to test the new weapons out of Norn.

Dedan's mask tightened again, only his eyes burned in his gaunt, worn face. When Ramsay had finished he said briefly: "In this matter command me—and I shall follow!"

"Then do so now," Ramsay returned. "For we seek a private place in which other strange things were once stored. There perhaps we can find the beginning of a trail that will lead to Ochall—"

Osythes was already at the door. "You have something in your mind," he said to Ramsay. "You do not believe that we must seek the flyer."

"A feeling only." Ramsay could not defend that feeling, but it was so strong in him now that he felt driven to find some proof.

"A feeling may be more valuable in the end than any fact," the Shaman replied. "And you are the Knave, trust in your feelings, in your dreams."

Once more, Ramsay found himself in that well-hidden room which he had not been given a chance before to explore fully, the others crowding in his wake. But now, the chamber was in a state of utter chaos. Apparently, the Empress's orders had been carried out with great thoroughness and also muscle. For the machines he remembered standing in square rows had been literally smashed, as if sledgehammers had been used with force and fury.

The floor was littered with shards of equipment, broken glass, twisted metal, so that one had to pick a careful way, yet still crunched bits under boot heel. Whoever had been at work here had made very sure that nothing was salvageable.

Osythes took over the lead, gathering up skirts of his robe in one hand as if fearing contact with the wreckage. He ushered them past the flattened, disemboweled exchanger, from whose wrecked casing trailed coils of fused and tangled wire, to the far side of the chamber where there were a number of small cupboards.

The doors of each had been sprung, and now either lay free of their hinges on the floor or swung open to show masses of blackened stuff within, from which arose chemical stenches.

"This," reported the Shaman, "was not done at the Empress's orders. These records were destroyed before our men went to work here. And"—he came to the end of that row of cupboards to show a rent in the wall itself, behind which they could see two bare shelves— shelves—"this part was entirely secret—we never knew of it at all."

Ramsay's mind since the meal, the disappearance of his headache, was clearer. He now felt as alert as if he had had a good night's rest with no worries to trouble him. "Then you do not really know what Melkolf looted before he went. Where did he—did you—get the knowledge to set up this place in the beginning?"

For the first time, Osythes wore an uneasy expression. "Not all the knowledge of the Great Era was lost. There were those who were farseeing and established caches which might and did enable them and their civilization to survive. We have found some of them. Now I believe that Melkolf has also discovered in the records we showed him some hint to others which he plundered in secret. His ability to handle our notes, which are often vague, was too sure, too ready—"

"Who *is* Melkolf?" Ramsay asked.

Osythes seemed unhappy in his answer, which he gave slowly and with obvious reluctance. "He is from the Grove in Marretz. Not all who seek the Way of Enlightenment are fitted by temperament to our training. Yet they may have a brilliance in one thing or another that makes them of potential worth in the outer world. Thus, if they cannot take the full vows, still they are encouraged to develop such talents and work with the Fellowship in other ways. Melkolf's talent was"—he swept his hand about to indicate the well-wrecked chamber—"centered in experiment with ancient equipment. He showed a genius for being able to read the cryptic notes we have discovered. But he had not the spirit to make him acceptable in the Inner Circles.

"Thus, he left Marretz and wandered for a while. It is during that time perhaps, that he did discover some secret cache of knowledge. He was in Yury and there met with Prince Berthal, who was hunting. It was Berthal who brought him to Lom, and what he had to offer then—" Osythes shook his head. "Her Splendor Enthroned was impressed, she summoned me in turn. It had been ordained that Ulad be protected—" Again he hesitated.

"It is the sworn duty of my Fellowship to raise mankind again to what our species once was. In Ulad there has been a beginning of lawful and peaceful government. To preserve that we were willing to advise. Also—the research into ancient knowledge—to that we are pledged."

"Did Melkolf or the Fellowship suggest the exchanger?" demanded Ramsay. He was more than a little surprised at this explanation. He had never expected Osythes to speak so freely.

"The principle of the exchanger," Osythes answered, "was known to us. Melkolf was able to build from the study of those principles. Also—" He faced Ramsay now squarely. "We had a foreseeing—we had to learn concerning the power of dreams. When it was proved that dream and exchanger together could work—that was knowledge we needed—"

"Lord Emperor," Dedan interrupted abruptly, as if impatience to be in action whipped him sorely, "who is this Melkolf of whom you speak? Was it he who gave the order that ended the Company?"

"No. But he is a part of all that lies behind that order," Ramsay returned. He was standing still, his eyes on the stinking mess of destroyed records.

There was something—idea—hunch—? Just as he had been convinced, against concrete evidence, that Melkolf and Berthal had not fled Lom in that flyer, so now this new sense of something of importance here grew in him.

He walked to the first of the cupboards. Picking up a broken metal rod from the debris on the floor, he stirred the sodden mass of the stuff within, awaking only a stronger odor, enough to make him cough, but discovering nothing, except that which had been systematically destroyed. It was like the old, old game of childhood when one hunted for a hidden object directed by the cries of "hot" or "cold." Except that those cries did not come now from his two companions, but were generated within his own mind.

That this section of the lab was the most important— of that Ramsay was sure. Yet, as he sought to find a clue his instinct told him was there, sweeping out the destroyed records to the littered floor, pulling the remains apart with his rod, he came no closer. It was not until he reached those hidden shelves that his inner monitor assured him that he had come near "hot." But there was nothing here, not even debris.

The hidden section was a narrow panel rising from the floor for about four feet, containing two entirely bare shelves. Ramsay thumped those—perhaps a secret within a secret—? But he could tell nothing by the noise that he had heard.

He turned again to Osythes. "What lies beyond this wall?"

The Shaman shook his head. "Nothing. This place was known of old—a treasure room and secret prison which dates back to the days of Gulfer, when Lom was the main city of the old Kingdom of Ulad."

But that hunch within Ramsay was not satisfied. Somewhere here still lay the clue that would lead them to Melkolf. And he believed that with Melkolf, there would also be the Prince, Ochall, and—Thecla.

Once more, he thumped the interior of the hiding place. He could see that the backing was stone, solid, with the air of having been set for ages in those blocks. He might put men to tearing down the wall and finding nothing, but the feeling was strong here, that at this one point was the beginning of the trail.

"I want"—he made up his mind—"this wall stripped! If there is anyone who knows the ways of this building, get him here!"

Dedan had gone to examine the space. "Lord Emperor—" Having armed himself also from the wreckage on the floor, he was prodding industriously into the cavity as Ramsay had earlier done. "This is stone that has no crevice. If you seek a hidden way—only such flamers as slew the Company might be able to cut a path for you—"

"Cut a path—" Ramsay repeated slowly. "We cannot waste time in cutting a path—we must know the direction!"

"And only you can find that, Supreme Mightiness!" Ramsay gazed at the Shaman.

"Yes," Osythes nodded, "only you. And already you know the way that you must go."

Ramsay hurled his prodder from him. "I give no man such power to meddle with my life again!" he said grimly.

"You need no man, Knave. The power is yours if you will have it so."

The place of nothingness again? But his attempt *had* brought Dedan to him. Could that world again—

Now he spoke to the First Officer. "You know what we seek. Now I tell you plainly, Dedan. In this palace I can trust no man, except perhaps yourself. For your need now is as mine—to find a murderer, not of one but many. This

Enlightened One says that perhaps it can be done—not with fire or any tool or weapon one holds in hand. If I so essay this search, will you be my shield man, seeing that none approaches me?"

"Lord Emperor, if the trail you seek brings down that murderer, then I am your liege man—for so much!"

Ramsay nodded, reassured by what he knew to be a promise as strictly given as a blood-oath, even though the man who offered it was this Dedan he hardly knew.

"Well enough. All right, Shaman. I shall take the dream road. Yet, from you also, must I have a promise—on what you hold sacred enough to blind you. I will have no aid from you—or any of your ilk. This I do alone, and free, or not at all!"

"So can it be done," Osythes returned. "You are the variable. We could not if we would—control or direct the future for you."

Though his suspicion of the Shaman and his kind ran deep, yet at that moment Ramsay thought Osythes's assurance was as empathic and to be accepted as Dedan's had been.

"Then let us to it—" He turned away from that plundered cupboard that still was in his mind a door of sorts, though he did not know the trick of it.

Back they went to that chamber where Ramsay had waited for the reports of the searchers. He saw that the sun was almost gone now—night advanced quickly on Lom. And night, somehow, seemed better for the task he set himself.

Osythes gave certain orders which brought more food, drink. Ramsay waved Dedan to join him while the

Shaman himself would sip only from a brew served him in a small, curiously fashioned flask.

"We eat for strength," Ramsay said. "You, Dedan must watch the night—or as much of the night as is needed. For I am to sleep—and—dream—"

"Dream?"

"Dream true. Believe me, Dedan, in dreams do lie truths. This I have proved."

The Free Captain eyed him thoughtfully. For a fleeting moment, Dedan seemed shaken out of his obsession. "You wear the face of Kaskar, the Emperor, you seem to rule here in Lom. And now you speak of things that are said concerning the Enlightened Ones. What manner of man are you?"

Ramsay laughed. Perhaps the Dedan he had known was not yet dead. That meeting of their eyes assured him even more than the other's words. "The tale is a long one, comrade, and not easily credited. But I am neither Kaskar nor an Enlightened One—I am myself—and perhaps only a true dreamer. This I must discover. I lay upon you, Osythes"—he spoke secondly to the Shaman—"to make clear to this promised liege man of mine that what I attempt may come true."

Osythes put aside the small glass from which he had been sipping his cordial.

"There are many truths," he said. "And there are secrets that are better not disclosed—"

"Except to those who have the right to hear them," countered Ramsay. Within him, confidence was growing. He was about to turn to his own this trick of the Enlightened Ones—no wonder the Shaman was reluctant.

"Dedan"—Ramsay did not wait for Osythes to reply to that thrust—"this is the way of what I would do. I must sleep—a sleep so deep that perhaps I shall not be easily awakened from it. And while I sleep, so shall I also dream—and learn how thus to open that door I know lies below. Your part is to stand guard that none wake me before my time."

"This you believe you can do?" the Free Captain replied in a wondering tone. "Well, if it leads as you say, then I am willing—"

Ramsay went to the divan, stretched out upon it. There was a faint spicy scent which seemed to come from the pillow under his head. Thecla—as he had concentrated on Dedan to summon the mercenary, now he would fasten on the Duchess. He closed his eyes and began to form Thecla, not as he had seen her last slipping from his door, that barrier rising between them, but Thecla as he had known her at the lodge among the trees, free, sometimes laughing at some mistake he made in speech. Not a Duchess locked in the tight formality of a court, but a girl who had somehow found a place in his memory—his mind—which no one else could or would fill. Thecla—thus she was—would always be—

❈ ❈EIGHTEEN❈ ❈

RAMSAY WAS FLOATING—not as if he were enclosed in a flyer, but rather as if he were free to wing the air; the art men had so long envied the birds that they had sought for generations to equal it. At first about him was the nothingness—the absence of all. Then, out of that nothingness, arose a shadow, taking on solid substance as he winged toward it. Only this was not Thecla as he had expected.

A wall—block upon thick block.

Ramsay hung suspended in the space of nothingness, facing that barrier. No door, not even a promising crevice or crack. In him surged his will, strong as rage—he was not to be easily defeated.

There was a way through, he determined upon that. A way through—

Just as he would have used his hands in the world he had left behind to test and examine each of those ghostly gray blocks, so now he drove his will, a spearhand of force against each block in turn. Through!

As his will touched, here and there awoke small points of light—not on each of the stones, but rather on two that were set one above the other. Those points of light looked as if they had sprung from the imprint of fingers—five above, five below.

When the last flashed into life, the stones began to turn, slowly, with great reluctance—but they turned. He had found his door and now he sped through it, again a thing of the air. Nor was there nothingness beyond.

Rather, here was another lab, which was near twin to that which had been destroyed. It was not quite the same, being smaller, far less crowded with apparatus. In the very middle of that chamber stood once more an exchanger, undamaged. Only from the top was missing the selector.

Movement centered Ramsay's attention elsewhere. He distinguished four figures. But they had not the concrete, vivid representation of those he had sighted in other dreams. Rather they were veiled in a way that made each one blur as he tried to see it clearly. Ramsay fought with all his will to clear his sight, to know—

There was a flickering of light, swinging back and forth like a pendant supported somehow in the air. Ramsay flinched. Remembered—Just so had Ochall swung the key of his office. There was danger in that swinging pinpoint of light.

He tried to avoid watching it, tried to reach beyond to the dim figures. Two were in constant movement, but he could not make out what they were doing. Always as he tried to concentrate, that flicker arose. He began to feel drained, confused, for a second or two the force of his will lessened.

Thecla!

Was she one of those ghostly blurs?

Even as he wondered, he saw her—far to one side, her face clearing under his gaze. It was a face such as Dedan had turned upon him in the place of nothingness—a face without life. Nor did she open her eyes in answer to his dream demand.

The flickering had stopped. He was somehow warned by that. They must know of his invasion, they *wanted* him to be sure that they held a hostage. He had only realized that when there was imprinted over Thecla's face, even more clearly, something else—a black object—

It was the selector missing from the exchanger!

A threat—a promise? Either or both, Ramsay knew. Search out this hidden den, try to free the prisoner, and she would be gone—rift away to the death they had tried to give to Kaskar!

He who planned this—who was protected by that flicker of swinging light—Ramsay continued to watch what he had been allowed to envision as if shocked by the implication so easily induced by that other. To open himself to attack—was that what the other sought, to provoke Ramsay into trying to reach the source of the threat?

There was a feeling of vast confidence, so strong it might have streamed visibly from behind the flicker. The mind, the will, hidden beyond, believed his position impregnable. He alone would state terms, all others must surrender.

Let him believe so!

Ramsay relaxed his will, withdrew— And sensed the high roll of triumph, following him as a hound might be dispatched to snap at the heels of a beggar, hurrying the hopeless on his way. Once more he hung in nothingness, the wall closed before him.

Something he had learned, but not enough. To force the issue now when he was too ignorant—no. He relaxed his will again—and awoke.

Dedan's face, then Osythes. He was back. But he did not try to rise.

"I know where—" he said slowly.

"Yes, but that may avail us little," the Shaman answered him. "There has come a message. Grishilda roused moments ago, nearly out of her senses with fear. If we do not surrender to their demands, the Duchess—"

"Will be sent to her death," Ramsay interrupted. "Then they will begin on the rest of us, no doubt. There is a second exchanger—behind the wall. They are still in the heart of Lom, and one of them has knowledge that may equal yours. Ochall, I think."

Osythes muttered, but his words were not plain enough to hear. Dedan merely watched Ramsay's face, his eyes narrowed.

"Which is the murderer?" he demanded, intent upon his own dark hunting.

"Ochall. But he is not the one we can easily take." Ramsay lay still. "Shaman"—he put into his voice now the crack of a demand from equal to equal—"what forms a defense against a dream search which appears as a flickering light? You have the resources of the Enlightened Ones, and surely you know enough to find explanations. Let me warn you—in your dream searching you have unloosed what perhaps cannot be controlled, a weapon worse than any out of Norn, put into the hands of one ruthless enough to use it at will."

Osythes seemed to shrink in upon himself. He had always been an old man to Ramsay; now he was a withered remnant of the one he had been only hours earlier. His lips parted as if he would answer, then shut again; his fingers plucked feverishly at the folds of his robe.

"These—" His voice came as a ghostly whisper, grew only a little stronger as he continued. "These are forbidden things—you are not of the Grove. I cannot reveal to you, an UnEnlightened—"

"Then prepare to have your own weapons turned against you," Ramsay returned. "Do you think that Ochall will spare any of us now? He apparently has some power of his own, he has the secret of the exchanger. Be ready to dream yourself into death, Shaman. For you he may now consider the most important of his resident enemies."

"I have not the authority," Osythes made answer. "I must consult with—"

"And while you are consulting," Ramsay pointed out, "Ochall may be on the move. Your secret is no longer any secret to him!"

Dedan got to his feet. "You say, Lord Emperor, that this burner of men is behind the wall? Then it is simple enough, we tear down that wall—"

"I wish it *were* so simple." Ramsay turned his head wearily. Again he was drained of energy. "The fact is we do not know what defense stands beyond. Would you send more men to face flames?"

Dedan grimaced. His fist struck into the open palm of his other hand.

"Then what *will* you do, Lord Emperor?"

"Bargain—" Osythes began.

"No!" Ramsay returned. "Ochall would use the time to concentrate his own position. He will yield nothing in any bargain, merely play with us to his pleasure. You know him, Shaman—can you say that I am not now speaking the truth?"

Osythes was silent. Then, as if the words were dragged from him one by one through some torture, he spoke.

"I will be breaking oaths that are beyond your understanding if I do as you wish. There are great matters to which men are nothing—"

"You have said," Ramsay broke in, "that the safety of Ulad is a part of the plans of your Fellowship. Very well, where will that safety be if Ochall achieves his purposes?"

The stricken look Osythes had worn earlier was going; the Shaman sat straighter in his chair, his head erect, will and a gathering determination about him.

"You are the Knave," he said. "And as the Knave, you have such power as no one, not even one who is outside the disciplines and restraints of the Grove, can in the end defeat. But what you draw upon can be lessened by lack of confidence in yourself. To battle, you must commit all that is you, body, mind, spirit. And this is also true, that in such a struggle you may lose mind, body—spirit I do not know, for though we can measure two of the possessions of men, the third is beyond our understanding.

"If you are willing to risk all that you are, then you can drag Ochall down. But there is no promise that you will not also fall. This I say because once more yours is a choice no one else may make for you."

Ramsay's gaze lifted from the earnest face of the Shaman. He lay now with his eyes on the ceiling overhead. To commit himself utterly—never in his life had he made such a choice. There was a finality to this that threatened a part of him now rising to active rebellion. Though he could not understand to the full Osythes's warning, there was that in it which chilled his tired body.

When he had been proclaimed Emperor, he had touched upon a choice, but that was only a pallid shadow when compared to this. He knew that there would be no return—

Still, he had, in a manner, already gone well down this road.

"*You* will tell me now"—he did not look to the Shaman as he said that, but continued to stare upward— "what I must do."

"You must confront Ochall both as a dreamer and one who wakes," Osythes replied. "You must hold on both planes against all his powers, believing in yourself strongly enough to defeat him. How this may be done no other can tell you."

Ramsay pulled himself up. His weariness was a weight, and now he made another demand of the Shaman.

"I must have strength—"

Osythes nodded. "First"—he spoke to Dedan—"unite with me!"

He held out his hand, and Dedan, looking puzzled, clasped it. Then Osythes leaned toward Ramsay and, with the fingers of the other hand, he touched the younger man's forehead.

Ramsay felt that flow, first slowly, then feeding into

him—energy that spread downward through his body, banishing that burdensome languor that was a part of waking from the dreaming.

Rising as the Shaman broke contact, he knew that he was ready, as ready as he would ever be.

"To the lab." He drew a deep breath. "Let those guards you can trust the most," he added to Osythes, "come. And comrade"—Ramsay turned to Dedan—"you are at my back, armed. I will not deny that we may meet death beyond that wall, for I could not see their weapons, and they may have worse than we met, even at Yasnaby."

Dedan showed his teeth in the grin of a wolf. "Comrade." For that first time he used the warmer address as if the promise of action were indeed afire. "You need not waste words in such advice. I am ready." He reached behind him and plucked a needler from beneath the pile of cushions where he had been sitting.

Once more, they descended to the hidden chamber that had been Melkolf's domain. Ramsay led, with Dedan at his shoulder, Osythes behind, and following the Shaman, those of the latter's choice from the guardsmen. Ramsay went directly to the secret cupboard.

"Rip out the shelves," he ordered. One of the guards moved instantly, using strips of metal to pry and pound out the wooden lengths, clearing the ancient stone behind.

Ramsay closed his eyes, bringing to mind the picture from the dream. There—there—

His hands were outstretched, fingers crooked. Just so must he finger the well-concealed lock.

Beyond—Thecla's dead-alive face before his eyes—

that black threat of the box blotting it out. Ramsay fought
away that vision. He dared have no doubts now, nor allow
any fear for himself or another to deflect what force of will
he could summon.

There were no visible spots on the blocks he chose,
but when his fingers were on the stone he felt out a double
set of depressions. Pressure— It was as if now his flesh
were sinking into the rough rock, being swallowed—
Pressure—

Along with the strength of his arm, Ramsay exerted
his will, for it seemed to him that the resistance of the
stone was amplified by another, more subtle thing. As if
Ochall and the others were reinforcing the holding of that
physical barrier with their own force of projected power.

Slowly, even as it had in the dream, the blocks slipped
back, showing light beyond. Ramsay spoke. "Be ready—!"
He delivered a last vigorous thrust and jerked aside, out of
the path of any weapon that might be set to cover that
doorway.

The flash of fire, or projectile he had expected, did
not follow. With caution, after a long moment of waiting,
he slid back to the opening, stooping to peer into the hole.

Beyond—no, not the nothingness of his dream—but
a haze that did not quite have that turgid look of the yellow
fog that had rolled across the dunes at Yasnaby but was as
hard for the eye to penetrate.

Ramsay pushed his way through that opening, into the
haze. Though he could not now depend upon his eyes, he
had another guide. Some unknown sense that was allied to
the dream told him those he sought were here.

On the other side of the opening he stood, his hands

consciously half raised to ward off attack, his head turning slowly from right to left. Then he caught that flicker of light, seeming less strong than it had been in his dream, but, he guessed, nonetheless deadly to his purpose because of that.

Behind that glinting of light was the enemy, believing himself safe. For it was something in the flickering that was both shield for defense and weapon poised for attack. And it was the light which Ramsay must face in its unknown strength, beating down the defense, warding off the attack.

He took one step and then another into the swirl of the mist. If any followed him now, he was not aware of it. All his senses, both the five of his physical body, and the new one of his mind, were centered only on what was before him.

Out of the mist loomed a solid shape. He thought it the corner of the exchanger. But he heard no sound. If they did shelter here, they were using a cat's trick of freezing, waiting for its prey to approach within striking distance.

The flicker—it was playing with his mind, weakening his will. But there was only one way he could reach the one behind it—and that was to force him out of ambush into the open. That mist, it swirled— Did or did not the forms stride through it? He glanced from the light to the solid edge of the exchanger, riveted on that for the space of a breath to steady himself. Then, once more, he looked steadily at the swing-dip-swing that reached not only into his eyes but his mind, weaving a web to entangle his will.

Behind that light—reach behind that light!

The man—not his weapon—reach the man!

He knew what was to be done, but to accomplish that—

Ramsay fought to see beyond the flicker, to reduce it to something that mattered no more than perhaps the glass of a window. He must break the pattern of the flicker, yet let him concentrate on the seeing and he saw only that. With sudden inspiration, he closed his eyes. See the dream—he ordered his mind—SEE!

Spin—swing—dip—He was dizzy, fear rising in him. SEE!

Into that one thought he poured his strength.

Behind the flicker—yes! There was now a form, dim, hardly to be parted from the swirls of the mist. But it was there!

Then—

"You die!"

No cry that rang in his ears, but rather a blast that clawed at his mind.

"Look—and die!"

Ramsay held against the blast. "OUT!" he countered. "Out to face me. I am the Knave—" From somewhere flooded those commands. "I am the one outside the pattern. Out to face ME!"

"You die!" That was like a scream torturing his mind with its lash of red fury.

"I live! Out—" And into that command Ramsay poured for an instant every trace of his own will, of the strength that was Ramsay's life and identity.

The flicker was still spinning, more and more furiously. But behind it—behind it now a face. Only not the face he had reached for. So that the very identity of his enemy nearly shocked him into making a fatal slip.

"You die!"

"I live!" Ramsay rallied before the other could take advantage of that half-breath length of shock. "Out!"

The flicker spun now as a confiscating cloud, but it could not hide that face again, no matter how hard it tried. There was a spouting of maddened, fiery particles, like an explosion.

"No-o-o-o—!" The scream that came to his mind was not now that of fury, but rather fear, fear which accompanies fate.

"Yes!" Ramsay held. The fiery particles shot out at him. He opened his yes. There they were, as visible to his sight as they were in his dream state. A mad whirl of sparks to envelop him. But he looked beyond and held that gaze level.

The fire enveloped Ramsay; there was a scorching heat around him. This was not real; to that belief he held firmly. And he who tried so to trick that attacker was—

Aloud, Ramsay spoke a name.

The fiery particles were snuffed out, the mist tore raggedly. He faced the enemy clearly for the first time. In the other's hand—

Ramsay leaped. He was past the exchanger as his hand shot out and down. The edge of his straight, firm-held fingers met a wrist with an audible crack.

There was cry of pain and the selector fell to the floor. Then the other was clawing for his throat, yammering like an animal, the very wildness of the attack driving Ramsay back until his shoulders were pinned against the exchanger. He dropped to the floor, confusing the other, heard a shout which he knew was a warning though he could not distinguish the words.

The crackle of a needler warned him to remain where he was. But only inches beyond his hand lay the box which brought the exchanger to life. Ramsay grasped at it. Above him someone cried out. Ramsay threw himself to the right, the selector tight in his grip.

Once more, the needler cracked as Ramsay fought to his knees. Another bore down on him, gas gun ready. He had only time to strike forward with the box. It met flesh, wringing a grunt from his new attacker. But muzzle of the side arm had been deflected. Mist shot to the roof, not directly into Ramsay's face.

He drove his fist into a belly where muscles stiffened to meet the blow, took a jolt in return against his cheekbone, one that had enough force to send him reeling back. His boot heel caught and he crashed down, falling prone over a body on the floor.

Then Ochall gave a strangled whoop, his hands rising to his chest, and went to his knees, to fold up, his head against Ramsay's boots.

"Enough!" Ramsay only half heard that voice. His head was still spinning a little from that one good blow the High Chancellor had landed.

He was struggling to get once more to his feet when he heard a scream. Not this time in his mind, but ringing in his ears. And he wavered around to see—clearly, for the mist was now gone—Berthal backed against the wall, in his arms Thecla, not now any blank-eyed, mindless captive, but a raging, struggling fury, fighting against the Prince's grasp so that he could not hold her and bring his weapon to bear on Ramsay. Even as Ramsay faced him he stopped that attempt. The barrel of his side arm pointed into the girl's face.

"Move—" he panted. "Give us a free road out, or by all the Blood of Jostern in me, I will fire!"

Ramsay froze. He glanced toward the door. Osythes was there, Dedan also, with that needler that had taken out the greatest of their enemies. Then he looked back to Berthal—there was madness in the Prince's eyes. He was on the edge of killing from fear alone.

In that instant, Ramsay used the only weapon left to him. For the second time in this hidden room, he summoned the full force of his will and sent an arrow straight into another's mind.

Berthal's mouth jerked, he shook his head. But his arms fell limply. Thecla broke from his grasp with a force of her own that almost sent her sprawling. She half fell forward and Ramsay caught her, steadied her gently.

"Take him!" he ordered, and guardsmen moved to Berthal's side.

As they led the Prince away, Ramsay looked to the Shaman.

"We were wrong. Ochall must have been *his* man, not the other way around—"

It was still hard for him to believe that one with the High Chancellor's supreme confidence in himself, possessing that aura of raw power, could have been second to anyone—no matter what strange knowledge that other might use.

"Not wholly." Osythes had knelt by the crumpled body beside the exchanger, had shifted it so that Melkolf's face was turned uppermost. "I believe that they were rather partners. We judged Ochall to be the complete master because of his outward nature. However, I do not think that, even had they won, he would have easily ruled in Ulad. Not with all Melkolf knew." Gently, the Shaman touched the forehead of the dead man. "So much this youth knew, yet not enough. He wanted everything, in the end even what little he had was reft from him, and he was left naked to a storm of his own raising."

Ramsay felt Thecla shiver. "You do not know what they planned—" Her voice was ragged. "They would have sent you—us—all who opposed them to other level deaths. He"—she glanced at Melkolf and then quickly away again—"boasted that he could do it now without a dreamer. He said—that dreaming had no force compared to that of the machines he could master—"

"And so he died," Osythes answered, "because he disdained self-mastery and trusted most the work of his hands, rather than that which lay within himself. That was the Great Sin of the Ancient Ones, and one that we are very prone to—valuing the visible always above the unmeasurable."

"Lord Emperor—" Dedan brushed aside the Shaman's words as if they had no meaning. "Here we had three men. Which of these gave the order for the Company's slaughter?"

"He—" Ramsay indicated Ochall. "Or so he told me."

The First Captain went to look down at the High Chancellor.

"It was my hand that ended him. I am content," he

said slowly, half as one waking from a nightmare. "Those of the Company will now rest well."

"There is one thing more, comrade," Ramsay said.

Dedan looked up. "What is that, Lord Emperor?"

Ramsay nodded toward the exchanger. "That—and any more such apparatus as may be found here. Will you see that it is left so no man can once more attempt to solve such secrets?"

"Well enough—"

Content, Ramsay turned to the door, supporting Thecla who shivered and stumbled as she walked. The girl did not speak until they were out in the wreckage of the outer lab.

"Melkolf and Ochall—" Her hand had a wondering note. "They—they are finished. And Berthal—what will be done with Berthal, Kaskar?"

He noticed the name she had given him.

"He will have justice—"

"From whose hand?" Once away from that hidden room she seemed to revive in strength. Her trembling had stopped, she walked more easily, but she made no attempt to draw out of Ramsay's hold.

"I suppose—from those who deal with justice in this world."

"He is of the House Royal—justice comes from you, Kaskar."

"I am not—" Ramsay began and then stopped. Thecla had turned her head, was watching him intently.

"What are you not?" she asked, when for a long moment he had stood in silence, unable to finish that statement.

"I do not know what I am not, but perhaps I know a little of what I am," he said slowly. "Once I was one man— it seems I have become another."

Ramsay Kimble was dead. He was dead in body in his own time and world; here, he had died slowly in another way.

"You are Kaskar who shall rule in Ulad," she said softly.

"Am I? Or am I a dreamer who has gone too far into his dreams to return?"

"If the dream is Ulad," she replied confidently, "then you have dreamed true. Are we so poor a dream that you would seek waking from it?"

She raised her hand and drew her fingertips along his cheek.

"Tell me, Kaskar—Knave of Dreams—are we so poor a dream?" she pleaded.

His arm tightened about her. "Never so—!" he said with the same firmness with which he had faced Melkolf.

Thecla laughed softly.

"Then dream on, Kaskar, and never wake!"

"So be it!" His lips met hers, and the last of Ramsay Kimble died forever.

Epic Urban Adventure by a New Star of Fantasy

DRAW ONE IN THE DARK

by Sarah A. Hoyt

Every one of us has a beast inside. But for Kyrie Smith, the beast is no metaphor. Thrust into an ever-changing world of shifters, where shape-shifting dragons, giant cats and other beasts wage a secret war behind humanity's back, Kyrie tries to control her inner animal and remain human as best she can....

"Analytically, it's a tour de force: logical, built from assumptions, with no contradictions, which is astonishing given the subject matter. It's also gripping enough that I finished it in one day."
—Jerry Pournelle

1-4165-2092-9 • $25.00